In A Second

KATE CANTERBARY

copyright

copyright

For quiet girls.

And for the em dash—each one lovingly placed by a wholly human author.

about in a second

The last time Audrey Saunders saw Jude Bellessi, he begged her to ditch her wedding and run off with him. She said no. In her defense, she was already in the dress.

Years later—divorced and done with relationships—Audrey runs right into the one man she never managed to forget.

Except Jude isn't the rebellious bad boy she remembers.
Now Jude's an aerospace engineer, a fiercely protective single dad…and, apparently, her fiancé. At least that's the story he spun for his sick mother.

When Jude asks her to play along for the summer, Audrey knows better. She really does. But unfinished business is a powerful thing —and so is the pull of the boy who once held her whole heart.

Besides, how much damage can one summer vacation with the biggest mistake of her life really do? Answer: epic.

Catastrophe looks a lot like a mother-in-law in turbo wedding-planner mode, a preschooler who doesn't miss a beat, and a suspiciously high number of hotel rooms with just one bed.

So why does lying about forever feel like the first honest thing she's done in years?

Content notes: divorce (main character), history of emotional abuse and abandonment by a previous romantic partner (main character, off-page), depression, death of a previous romantic partner (off-page), chronic illness (main character: food intolerance, irritable bowel, inflammation), history of pregnancy loss, serious illness (parent: breast cancer in remission/NEAD, no on-page recurrence, very limited on-page discussion of treatment), toxic/narcissistic family system, discussion of custody agreements, experiences with selective mutism (secondary character).

Additionally: This is a second-chance romance where, during their years apart, both characters had relationships with other people.

chapter one

Audrey

Twelve years ago

Today's vocabulary word: steady

"Could I possibly get a sip of water?"

Or something harder?

The wedding planner's lead assistant peered up at me from her knees, both brows cocked like I'd asked for a whole blueberry pie. "I don't think that's a good idea." She motioned to the lace overskirt she was busy straightening. The toe of my shoe had caught on the hem and if we didn't have a schedule to keep, I'd be taken out back and lashed for it. "Not after what happened here."

My cheeks flamed. I hadn't expected to be chastised quite so much on my wedding day. More to the point, I hadn't expected it to be my wedding day. I'd figured it just wouldn't occur. That he'd find someone more interesting and call it off.

A naïve assumption, obviously. That seemed to happen to me a lot—life happening to me while I didn't know any better. More now that I didn't care about much of anything. Myself least of all.

But standing here in the back of a church, bouquet in hand and seconds ticking by until I walked down the aisle, it felt as though only a small portion of myself was actually here. The rest was... Well, it'd been a long time since I'd been anywhere. Soon enough, I wouldn't exist at all.

There were a few people who'd probably prefer it that way.

"Gina." The assistant snapped to attention at the sharp whisper of her name as my sister stalked down the hall. "We need you to deal with a strap that won't stay up."

Gina gave the overskirt one last touch before pushing to her feet. She hurried away while my younger sister stared at me with that same old disgusted lip curl of hers. Too bad that always made her look like she had a snaggletooth *and* a mustache coming in.

I met her stare. "Do you need something, Cassidy?"

She eyed me up and down, her nose scrunching into an unfortunate piggy shape. She was a beautiful girl. But when she wanted to be ugly, she really was.

She pressed her lips together into that hard, practiced smile of hers. As if rock candy was a nineteen-year-old woman. "I just hope you're so very happy with Christopher."

Other people would think she meant those words. "You should go," I said, tipping my chin up, toward the room where the other bridesmaids were waiting for their cue. "They probably need you."

She gave me and my dress another lip-curling scoff and turned away, her heels hammering against the hardwood floor as she went. I wanted to work out some of my nervous energy and let my fingertips travel over the lace covering my dress, but I'd already had my hand slapped for that once today.

I felt the energy shift before I heard him, before I saw him. Like the sudden stillness before an explosion.

When I turned, I wasn't surprised to find him standing there in dark jeans and a butter-soft leather jacket. It'd been four years since seeing him last, but some archaic part of me had known he'd be here today. It was good that we were doing this now. The suspense would've killed me if he'd kept me waiting all day.

"Audrey." My name was little more than a sigh. A plea, maybe.

I glanced up and down the hall. There'd be hell to pay if anyone found him in this church. "Jude, what are you doing here?"

There were no fewer than forty-five different ways for him to answer this, but he chose none of the ones I wanted to hear. Instead, he raked his gaze over me, rough and irritable, asking, "Why are you doing this?"

A breath whooshed out of me as I stumbled back a step. "Please be quiet," I said.

He pushed a hand through his dark hair. His impatience sucked the air out of the hallway. "We don't have a lot of time, princess, so I need to hear you say you actually want this."

Light poured in through tall stained-glass windows, bathing the floors in streaks of gold and red. He was in the perfect spot for the light streaming through the yellow glass to cast a halo around him. Very fallen angel of him. It was hard to speak, not that I trusted myself to say anything. I'd make it worse, I knew that. It was already pretty bad.

"Say it, Audrey," he said, his voice rising as he slashed a hand toward the nave. "Tell me you want to marry this guy, that you love him and want to spend your life with him, and I won't stand up in the middle of the ceremony and fucking object."

"No, you can't do that," I said, taking a panicked step toward him.

He looked at me with wild eyes. "Convince me this is your choice and I'll believe you. I'll go. I'll give you what you want and leave you alone for good."

Everything inside me reached out to him, my fingertips craving the worn leather of his motorcycle jacket, the familiarity of him. The safety. But all I could say was, "You can't be here."

"Don't do this, Audrey," he begged. "I'll get you out of here. I'll protect you from" —he shot a disgusted glare at the nave doors as if he could see my father waiting on the other side to walk me down the aisle— "all of it. Whatever it is, I can help you. Just come with me now. *Please.*"

I stared at the floor. The glow of the stained glass soaked it in deep, vivid red. It made me think about the old stories of altars and virgin sacrifices. Wasn't that why I was here? To be sacrificed? My parents wouldn't find any humor in that. I wasn't sure I did either.

Still, it was nowhere near the darkest thought I'd had today. "If you've ever loved me at all, you'd leave and stay away."

I was proud of myself for keeping my voice steady. For not bursting into tears. For not gathering up my skirts and running away, no matter the devastating cost. For standing here with a hole in my chest and my still-beating heart in hand.

"I can't believe you're saying this," he whispered.

"Then don't," I said. "But you have to leave. Now."

I held his gaze as he shook his head at me, more disappointed than ever, and watched him storm through the front doors without a backward glance. The impact of it was subtle, a fatal wound I wouldn't notice until the adrenaline wore off and there was nothing left to be done about it.

I was still fixated on those doors when my father appeared beside me. He made a wet, congested sound but I didn't acknowledge him. I couldn't. Not after sending Jude away like that. If he didn't hate me yet, he would now.

"Let's get on with it," my father said.

He gave the old, heavy doors a pointed stare as if he could see straight through them. A motorcycle engine revved on the street outside. I knew that sound the same as I knew my own heartbeat.

My father made another thick, rattling noise in his throat. "You wouldn't be forgetting our agreement now, would you?"

Tears filled my eyes as I shook my head. As if I could forget.

I dropped my gaze to the floor as the wedding planner fixed my flowers, my dress, my posture. Thought about the stained glass blood as I willed away my tears.

Virgin sacrifice seemed a lot more straightforward than marrying a man I'd never love after sending away the one man I'd never stop loving.

chapter two

Audrey

Today's vocabulary word: cede

ONE THING THAT WAS TRUE ABOUT ME WAS THAT I HAD A NEAR-perfect track record of making the wrong decision when it mattered the most. I was not a cool head in a crisis...or even medium-stress situations. My critical thinking took a swan dive into shallow waters and my fight-or-flight instincts actively wanted evolution to come and pick me off.

When it came down to it, when my path diverged in the wood, I could be counted on to take the trail that would fuck up my life. Every time.

Chairing the planning committee for my high school's eighteen-year reunion wasn't close to the worst of my decisions but it was the worst *right now*. I'd lived through a lot of low moments in my thirty-five years but there was something uniquely painful in putting on a party for a bunch of people who didn't remember my name and only wanted to know where my ex was tonight.

It pinched in all the wrong places to be reminded, half a lifetime later, that I was no one without *him*. Yet on the other side of that coin, I was here only because I knew he wouldn't be.

Jude would sooner fill his pockets with stones and walk into the sea than set foot on the campus of Aldyn Thorpe Academy again. This world of old brick and creeping ivy was mine to keep, along with the self-important scaffolding built around it. He wouldn't enter this Thunderdome of generational wealth tonight because he'd given up this place, this city, the same way I'd given him up. Land won in a war that'd killed me to fight.

Except— No.

Except yes, he *was* here and watching me from the other side of the tent.

I had a thousand apologies, a thousand explanations that never would've mattered to him anyway—but in the span of time it took to register that he was here and staring at me after more than a decade of silence, those words abandoned me.

Just as quickly, the oppressive weight of the last words we'd shared, the ones that echoed in the dark of sleepless nights and the cold, lonely lows of being lost to everything, everyone, filled their place.

Why are you doing this?

I remembered gasping, the question landing with all the impact he'd intended. I thought about that gasp a lot. About how childish I must've looked to him. All dressed up—and for what?

He didn't know it but I threw myself on a grenade when I told him to leave that day. I still searched for some of the pieces of me lost in the blast, still felt my way around the tender, broken spots that never seemed to scab over. And he'd never understand why I did it.

I always knew our paths would cross again, one way or another, but I never thought it would be here. Not with him dressed in a crisp dark suit that looked as natural as the beat-to-hell jeans and vintage t-shirts once had. Not with me frozen in place while all the monologues I'd rehearsed emptied out of my mind. Not in this lavish tent, chandeliers glittering overhead while our old audience looked on.

I'd prepared myself for many things tonight, but this was not one of them. Painful conversations? Two separate people had pointed at my name tag, frowned, and told me they'd always thought my name was Emily or Sarah or *maybe something stuffy like Constance*. Graceless moments? Someone spilled a glass of wine down my dress and I apologized to them for it. Latching onto the familial connections? I'd already smile-shrugged my way through five requests for my father to "take care of" legal matters ranging from a *Low-key DUI* to *We're hoping the Securities and Exchange Commission doesn't get involved.*

I'd also steeled myself against the onslaught of questions I knew I'd get about Jude. It was a damn good thing, because everyone wanted to know why he wasn't here, what he was doing now, why we weren't together—and how it ended. An entire lifetime had passed since high school and they were dying to know what happened and how it all fell apart.

There was a hungry glee woven into those questions, like they'd been waiting to pick my broken little heart from my chest, and any other organs damaged in the breakup, and simmer them into a stew. Because I'd never deserved him. Never good enough, not even close. That was what they thought. What they said when they didn't know I was listening.

As if it wasn't enough to have everyone talking about him, he decided this wasn't a party without his full participation and had to show up looking like a storm cloud in a bespoke suit. And since that still wasn't enough for him, he had to watch me with a gaze that stripped a layer from my skin with each passing minute.

I had no clue what would happen between us tonight. Whether we'd talk for the first time in years or he'd leave me to squirm under his watchful gaze all night without saying a word to me. He probably thought I deserved that type of torture. Probably thought I'd earned myself an uncomfortable evening of him treading on my territory like a heavy-handed reminder that I was the one who'd made this mess. Part of me agreed with him.

The other side of me wanted answers. Wanted to know why he was here when I knew for a fact he hadn't even opened his invite, let alone clicked the RSVP link.

And as Jude stepped away from his group and started across the tent toward me, I had a good idea which side would win.

chapter three

Audrey

Today's vocabulary word: ascend

IT SHOULDN'T HAVE SURPRISED ME WHEN JUDE RAKED AN IMPATIENT glare from my shoes up to the hair I wore loose around my shoulders, and the first words from him in years landed like a kill shot.

"Your mother must be pleased."

The unfortunate truth was that my mother *was* pleased. She was the one who'd cornered me into this gig and she'd added to my servitude by setting me up on a lunch date for tomorrow. This made my response of "Don't get carried away with the assumptions," all the more brittle.

Jude's answering laugh was a dry, rueful sound that sliced into my skin like a paper cut. "I'll see what I can do, Saunders."

Another true thing about me was that I was a thoroughbred good girl. Good daughter, good student, good dancer, good friend, good person. I was kind and thoughtful and generous. Quiet and attentive, as all the best people-pleasing doormats were. I wasn't snappy or sarcastic, and I never argued or sparred with anyone.

Unless Jude Bellessi was around.

It was like a switch flipped inside me when he was within shouting range and I transformed into a blowtorch of a woman. Gone was the constant itch to put everyone at ease, even at the cost of my own comfort. Not only did I invite myself to confrontations with him, I started them.

It was like stepping into someone else's skin—and I'd never made peace with the fact that it fit so much better than my own.

Jude went on studying me, his gaze catching on the damp spot from my earlier run-in with the wine. Introducing red wine to a navy dress was no tragedy but the slight shake of his head made it seem like a moral failing.

He could stare all he wanted. Pin me like a rare yet ultimately unimpressive butterfly. I could take it. I'd endured far worse than some unpleasant moments and hard glaring. And honestly, I wanted this. I wanted him to take all the hurt I'd handed him and throw it right back at me.

For once, I wanted to feel something real, even if it was awful.

Just as long as we maintained a polite distance from each other, because that blowtorch situation of mine? There was no controlling it when we were close. I burned through all my safety nets and guardrails, and my mind kicked and skipped, never stopping to analyze every thought or rehearse every word.

I folded my arms over my chest and spent a full minute fighting to keep my emotions from using my face like a billboard as I waited for... I didn't know. An explanation of whatever it was that'd brought him here tonight. He responded to my obvious struggle with a tolerant smile that was the equivalent of a pat on the head.

I didn't know what it was called when you knew you owed someone a minimum of seventeen specific apologies and probably needed to throw yourself off the side of a mountain but also wanted to violently remind them how little you enjoyed being patronized. Whatever that was called, it was my current state of being.

Sincerely apologetic but also not so sincere that I couldn't scratch his beautiful face off.

Through the veil of my bloodlust, I couldn't help but notice the years had treated him well. As if time would have the audacity to give him anything else. He'd never had an awkward stage, which was criminally unfair since my entire life was a series of overlapping awkward stages. But that wasn't Jude. He'd started high school with a full, almost-black beard and the kind of biceps that would've had him under suspicion of steroid use if he'd bothered with sports. He passed for twenty-something by the time he was sixteen, no fake IDs needed, and now—now he looked the same as always but *better*.

He was built like an old Gothic cathedral. Ridiculously tall, broad beyond reason, and too damn pretty for his own good.

He'd settled into himself in the years that'd passed. His dark hair was still thick, a rogue wave running through the strands and snatching back any hint of pretty boy perfection. He was sun-kissed as always and his espresso eyes gleamed in the soft chandelier light. Time and distance had done nothing to dim the ever-present buzz of restless energy that tightened his jaw and kept his fingers drumming against his thick thigh.

The suit was a very nice touch. Quality tailoring. Expensive, but not obviously so. No tie, though it didn't matter. He would've gotten away with strolling in here wearing jeans and a leather jacket, his motorcycle helmet tucked under his arm.

Since I wasn't equipped to win this staring contest and I'd evaporate into the night if I didn't fidget with something, I turned to the catering table to busy myself with consolidating trays of blueberry feta crostini. I hated feta but it hadn't crossed my mind to ask the caterer to switch it out. I hadn't planned this party to suit my tastes. It was funny how I was still the last person I took into account.

That was when I noticed the quiet around us. Save for the

band's bluesy rendition of a popular Beyoncé song, the tent was almost silent.

Everyone was looking at us. Staring, gaping, whispering as if this was the main stage and we were the evening's headlining act. I swallowed hard. "I should really—"

He held out his bear-paw hand. "Dance with me."

No no no no no.

When a few seconds passed and I was still blinking, he added, "Let them watch, Saunders. Give them the show they came to see."

Except they weren't watching *me.* They never watched me. It was always Jude. From the start, he'd had an upside-down relationship with this place and everyone in it. They loved him almost as much as he loathed them.

All the things that should've made him an outsider here had turned him into an unlikely hero. The way he insulted old-moneyed man-children and ignored them and refused to give a shit about any of the silly, posh things they adored? Nepo babies lived to be negged. When you had everything handed to you, working for the attention of a guy with true, effortless confidence was a dopamine hit unlike any other.

The pieced-together motorcycle he rode to school long before he could legally get a driver's license? Proof he was a champion in an arena built on white-collar crime.

His unpolished arrogance and the canyon-deep chip on his shoulder that cast no doubt as to whether he'd received a full scholarship *and* just begged them to pick a fight with him? No one was thirstier for a fight than rich boys who'd sooner hide in the trunk of someone's Audi to avoid actually throwing hands.

Even the teachers loved Jude. They'd never admitted he was one of their favorites since he had minimal concern for dress codes or arriving on time, and not a day went by without him poking holes straight through their course material. But he cruised to the top of every class, and whenever it seemed like he was becoming too much of a self-righteous jackass, he'd do something like fix a teacher's flat tire or tell that one criminally disruptive kid to shut the fuck up or get the hell out of the class.

And when Jude Bellessi chose me, the bookish girl with a severe ballerina bun and long, knobby limbs I hadn't grown into yet? Over everyone else? Well, it baffled them. I couldn't say it helped his ascension but I was enough of a blank slate that I didn't matter much in the end. That bloodless love of theirs was laced with just enough fear for the boy from the wrong side of Hartford to know better than to cross him when choices had been made.

It was so like him, really, to be invincible.

And so like me to be the opposite.

I eyed his hand for one crackling moment. There was no way for this to end well if we spent the next three minutes pressed together. But I'd imagined this so many times. Not *this* exactly but seeing him one more time. Talking to him. Maybe even getting the closure I'd craved.

And being that blowtorch without worrying about who I'd burn in the process.

We stood almost at eye level, with my heels adding a few inches to my five-ten frame. I tipped my chin up and slipped my hand into his. I forgot how to breathe. Turned myself inside out between blinks. Then I remembered his comment about putting on a show and I scoffed, asking, "Don't you think you're giving yourself a bit too much credit?"

"Not at all," he replied.

His gaze dropped to my hand and his expression tightened. He stroked his thumb over my knuckles several times. His brow creased and he drew in a breath that pulled his shoulders up like he was bracing himself.

He traced the spot where my wedding rings once sat. He closed his eyes for a second before he glanced away, toward the dance floor. As the band transitioned to a slower song, he settled his palm on the small of my back and this familiar comfort sent tears rushing to my eyes. I fought them off but I knew this was just the beginning of my emotional journey here tonight.

When we stopped at the center of the floor, he pulled me close to him and I had to flatten a hand on his solid chest to keep my footing. My heart stuttered against my ribs, hard enough that I was sure he felt it.

For a second, we just stood like that, wrapped in a moment waterlogged with history. I tried to tell myself that this was just a dance, just a long overdue chat between people who used to mean everything to each other.

But then his thumb traced a careful line down my spine and I forgot all of it. We swayed together, silent as I breathed him in and the years telescoped down to nothing.

Then he went and ruined the moment when he asked, "Where's your husband?"

I could almost hear my nervous system kick into hypervigilance at the mention of that man. "Not here," I said. "Not anymore."

"Good." Jude gave a sharp nod that told me he'd already known the answer to his question and just wanted to hear me say it. But then the corner of his lips quirked in a wry smile and he asked, "Divorced? Or did you finish it off the right way and leave him for dead?"

I rolled my eyes. "Does it matter?"

He cut a glance to the side and surveyed our classmates as we moved together. I expected a bland comment about the throwback music or the opulent decorations or anything, but he shook his head as if he was already bored with the topic, saying, "Not tonight, Saunders. But you'll tell me eventually."

"Yet another bold assumption."

"If you think that's bold, you need to pick your bar up off the floor."

I stole quick glances at him as I indexed the lines in his forehead and the creases at the corners of his eyes. There was a faint tan line on his temple, right where the arm of his sunglasses would sit. A few strands of silver shot through his dark hair now and the utter truth of it, the proof of life after all this time, punched hard into my belly.

I doubted he'd give me a straight answer but still I asked, "Why are you here?"

His brows knit together. "The better question is, why are *you*?"

I didn't want to admit that my only objective with running in this circus was buying myself some breathing room with my mother. I didn't want him to know that, in too many ways, I still fell in line when my parents demanded it.

"It's our class reunion. I *want* to be here," I said.

His gaze lingered on me, waiting for me to walk back the lie. The silence stretched taut until he finally broke it. "Let's get back to that husband of yours."

"I'd rather not," I fired back, voice steady even as my chest squeezed tight. "He's not mine. Not anymore."

Jude dipped his head, his brow nearly touching mine. "Isn't that nice for you."

I couldn't bear to be that close to him *and* maintain eye contact, so I shifted my attention away, over his shoulder. Clusters of our classmates filled in the spaces around the dance floor, though no one else joined in. Most stood with drinks in hand and their faces half turned to catch whispers.

His hand slid higher on my back, thumb drawing a slow, steady circle between my shoulder blades. "When did it end?"

I gave a brittle, not-quite laugh. "It doesn't matter and I have a strong suspicion you already know, so why don't you save us both some time and get to the point."

"I guess it's good to see you didn't let Christopher Wexler the fourth take your tongue and your teeth. A gentleman, after all."

I stepped back, nearly out of his hold. "Is this what you want?

To rile up your fanboys and remind me that your default mode is fuck gremlin? Then, bravo. Job adequately done."

Jude's eyes narrowed, his fingers flexed around my hand. Then he yanked me back into his arms and I resented the wave of recognition he set off inside me with that touch—and the heat that chased it. "You deserve credit for lasting as long as you did with him." There was an edge in his voice, something rough and a little unsteady. "Did you get it out of your system or is there another heir apparent teed up?"

I'd dreamed versions of this where we yelled at each other. Screamed it all out. And versions where we ran into each other's arms and stayed there a long, long time. I never dreamed up a verbal dagger fight or the overwhelming urge to take off my shoes and throw them at him.

"I'm single," I managed, mentally stepping around my mother's endless attempts at matchmaking. "And I like it that way. I like it very much."

He leaned in until his lips brushed over my ear. "I don't believe you."

"And isn't it funny how I don't care?" I gave him a stubborn shake of my head that succeeded only in bringing my cheek to his lips. *Oh, god.* That simple contact almost knocked me flat on my ass.

He drew back just enough for his gaze to search mine. "Except you do," he said flatly. "Don't forget, Saunders: no one knows you better than I do. I can tell when you're lying to me. Always have, always will."

I stumbled back a step, then another. Words caught somewhere in my chest, clunky and sharp like scrap metal, and I let my silence say what I couldn't—that he was right, and he knew it.

And then I sprinted out of the tent.

chapter four

Jude

Today's vocabulary word: initiate

I GAVE AUDREY A HEAD START BUT I DIDN'T LET HER OUT OF MY sight. I knew better than to make that mistake twice.

She cut a wide arc around the back of the tent and vanished into an academic building like she'd mapped an escape route in advance. Couldn't say it was a bad idea, considering the company.

I had no idea how she covered so much ground so quickly. I knew for a fact that she hated running (made her feel "gangly"), but she moved like a gazelle. Fast. Confident. Fully aware of the threats in this particular animal kingdom.

Those killer heels of hers clicked against the marble floors as she dashed down the hall. The lizard portion of my brain took some pleasure in this chase—and that was a big fucking problem. I didn't have time to care about her shoes or those long, long legs or the way her hair shone in the low light while she ran away from me.

Big. Fucking. Problem.

Unfortunately for me, this infuriating woman was only one of several big fucking problems on my list at the moment.

The interior smelled the same as it always did, like wood polish and stale coffee, and I resented my brain for holding on to that data point all this time. I could count the things I cared to remember about this place on four fingers, and three of them involved the blonde hellcat who made up most of the punctuation marks in my adult life.

She ducked around a corner, that corn silk hair trailing a split second behind her. I heard the sweep of a door and a harsh, bright light spilled into the hall.

I almost laughed when I realized where I was.

If she didn't want to be followed, she shouldn't have led me straight to the most secluded girls' washroom on the entire campus. It was smaller than most and had a hairpin entrance that gave the occupants ample notice before anyone came in. An ideal spot for ditching classes when going off-campus wasn't an option.

I strolled inside, calling out, "Fuck gremlin, huh? How long have you been waiting to use that one?"

Audrey heaved out a breath, her hands flat on either side of the sink and her eyes screwed shut. Her chest rose with quick, gulping breaths that had nothing to do with sprinting through the halls.

"I haven't been waiting," she snapped. "I don't have to store up my thoughts like acorns for the winter, you know."

"Never suggested you did." I slipped my hands into my pockets. Safer in there, for everyone. "Listen, we need to talk."

"Oh my god." She dropped her chin to her chest, sucked in a shuddering breath. "Can you please just give me like five minutes to—"

Laughter blasted in from the hall. Audrey's hazel eyes popped open and a choked squeak sounded from her throat. I met her gaze, her cheeks flushed and eyes shining with unshed tears.

Of all the blades to throw at me, her tears were the most deadly.

Any amount of resolve I'd walked in here with disintegrated by the second. I pointed at her as I closed the space between us, whispering, "Stop that."

"Right, because I'm the one intruding on your attempt at experiencing a moment in privacy," she whisper-snarled. "Let me make *you* more comfortable here in the girls' room."

I exhaled through my nose as the voices closed in, on the other side of the door now. "Just remember, I asked you nicely."

Her face twisted into a murderous glare. "You didn't ask—"

I hooked an arm around her waist and pulled her into the far stall, the one nobody ever used because it was the size of a small coffin. What it lacked in elbow room, it made up for as an unmatched hiding place. The partition walls extended to the floor and the overhead lighting barely reached this corner, leaving us concealed in the shadows. Even if we did have to stand with our legs braced on either side of the toilet and we were never more than an inch away from putting an eye out on the coat hook.

It also left us tangled together without so much as a breath between us. I was painfully aware of every knob of her spine, every gentle curve of her hips, every strand of her hair where it brushed my cheek. Of her body tucked against mine, no daylight between us, and the muscle memory that came with it.

"What the hell is wrong with you?" she seethed.

I could feel the anger humming through her body, the tension pulling her shoulders tight. It was wrong, and not at all my objective tonight, but I wanted more of that. More of anything she'd give me. All of it. I wanted to suck it off her fingers, wanted it to drip down my chin, wanted to wake up with it wrapped around my throat. And I fucking hated it. "If you don't settle down, you're going to make this much worse."

She shot a bony elbow into my side. "You're the one making this worse."

"All right, that's enough." I banded my free arm over her chest as the door creaked open and those voices poured inside. My lips at her ear, I breathed, "Stay still for a damn minute."

She aimed a side-eye glare over her shoulder that leveled me like an axe to the gut and followed it up by shifting her foot just enough to bring her heel down on my toes.

"*Fuck*," I gasped. Red, bleating pain radiated out from under that heel. My forehead fell to her shoulder. Barely resisted the urge to bite her. *Barely.* "You've made your point."

"Have I? Because—"

I closed my hand over her mouth. I felt it the second her anger switched from the entry-level shit we'd started with to straight-up, fire-wielding fury.

Again, not my objective, but fuck, it was fun. Almost enough to make me forget why I was here and what I needed from her, and how it would be great to leave with all of my toes. Almost enough to forget everything.

And those heels. Those were new and posed many threats.

"Either you settle the fuck down in here," I said, "or I open this door and give our friends something new to talk about."

I felt her weighing these options, her body rigid against mine. She sagged in resignation but wasn't interested in admitting I was right, and put some more heat into shattering my toes.

"…hasn't been the same since moving to the new firm," one of the voices said. "I can take off a month for vacation in the summer no problem but I'm a lazy bitch if I leave the office before nine every night. Like, there's no logic to it."

"No actual balance," another voice said. "Yeah, it's bullshit. They all say they're family-friendly but when it comes down to it, it's still an hours game."

"At least your dad is your managing partner," First said. "There's gotta be some advantage there."

"You'd think that," Second replied with a wry laugh. "But nope."

"Ugh, that's brutal."

A stall door closed, then another, and the conversation continued while they peed. A silent laugh puffed against my palm, and I caught the end of a grimace from Audrey. She probably knew these women, knew their families and their law firms. No one needed to remind me that this world belonged to her, not me.

"Okay, I'm literally going to die if I spend a whole child-free night bitching about practicing law." The water turned on, then off. "Can we please talk about Jude Bellessi's ass now?"

Audrey's forehead crinkled, her brows pitched up. No poker face on this girl.

"Jesus, he's aged like fine wine," First said with a groan. "And he still has all of his hair."

"My paralegal would call it pussy-eating hair," Second added. "It's always messy but in that freshly fucked way you only get from doing time on your knees."

One—or both?—of them let out a hungry groan. "I bet he's a beast. Like, I'd need a ketamine drip, seventy-two straight hours of sleep, and pelvic floor rehab to recover."

I smothered a laugh against her cheek. Audrey fired a glare at me that could've curdled milk.

"Oh my god, yes. The things I'd let that man do to me—" A grunt and then, "The limit does not exist."

Audrey's lips parted against my palm which sent a lot of incorrect messages to my body. Ones I really needed to shut down before things became...obvious. She let out an indignant little huff that I was quick to hoard right along with all her other unfiltered reactions. Later, I'd take them out and examine them until the edges frayed and I could no longer mine them for meaning. Later, when I wasn't fighting to put an inch of daylight between us just to keep her from knowing how much she still held over me.

"Be good," I breathed. That my lips brushed the shell of her ear and my cheek rested on her spun gold hair was purely coincidental.

Unimportant, really. Then she stabbed me with the other heel. I smiled, only because she couldn't see it.

"Side note, but your para sounds like my kind of people," First said.

"She's the best. If it came down to it, I'd sell both of my kidneys to pay her salary." After a beat, Second asked, "Can I be awful for a minute?"

"Please. You know I'm a vault. And part-time awful myself."

There was a sigh and then, "I've never understood what he sees in what's-her-name."

"Right? Like, yes, she's pretty but she has to *reach* to get anywhere near his league. It's like he's doing community service."

My head snapped up from Audrey's shoulder at the same time she leaned her forehead against the door and let her eyelids drop. I shifted my hand to cup her jaw. She wasn't going to say anything. She'd sooner give up her corporeal form and the rest of this mortal life than make her presence known to these women.

"Huge fucking reach," Second agreed. "And I'm sorry but the personality is not there. She's about as interesting as an antacid."

"No wonder she's divorced," First said. "Though I heard she came out of it with a nice settlement."

A cruel laugh followed. "He probably paid her to go away."

I didn't want to react to their words, to their cackles. Didn't want to tear this door off the hinges and tell these women where they could shove their opinions. Didn't want to rescue her. Hell, I didn't even want to be here tonight.

But I'd dug myself into a hole and now I couldn't leave without Audrey's help.

I must've telegraphed my desire to make them repeat those comments to my face because Audrey's elbow found its way between my ribs again and she whispered, "Don't."

It was then, probably a result of every muscle bracing for impact, that I fully registered all the places where her body had melted into mine. And I realized the true danger of holding her this way was that it made me think I wanted this. That I wanted her. All because my body recognized her in a way that never should have survived years apart, sending heat and memory straight into my bones. One wrong move and I wouldn't just lose my purpose for being here—I'd lose myself, plain and simple.

I'd known from the second I laid eyes on her that she'd grown and changed over the years but feeling it was a different thing altogether. She was still tall, still lean, but she seemed solid, as if she'd traded in her long, elegant ballerina strength for something more durable. Her hair wasn't the straight column of platinum silk I remembered. She had highlights and layers now, and maybe she'd smoothed it out for tonight but I couldn't find the near-permanent crimp from where she tied her hair into a tight bun every day.

I wouldn't admit to the number of times I let my cheek pass over those strands or the amount of slow, deep breaths I took to swallow down her scent tonight. She smelled the same as always— soft, warm, expensive—but there was something new in there, something I hadn't been able to pin down.

But the real change was the armor. She was tough, weathered in ways she'd never been before. I knew from the hard, slicing gaze and how her jaw ticked with the barely contained desire to verbally whip these old "friends" of ours that she'd come by her steel honestly.

It was about time. She'd needed it. As the women on the other side of the stall door made obvious, there was no surviving this cage match without growing some bulletproof hide.

Laughter followed them out into the hallway but we didn't move until long after the door swept shut and their voices faded into nothing. We stayed in that tiny stall, every inch of Audrey gathered in my arms. Like no time had passed at all.

But then the tension cracked open and she let out a low, self-conscious chuckle that cut as hard as one of her vicious elbows. "I really should've taken Jamie's advice and done this drunk. Or at least popped a gummy."

Shrugging out of my hold, she flipped open the latch and exited the stall. I trailed behind, watching as she leaned close to the mirror. A finger skimmed under her eyes, over her brows, into the corners of her mouth. She fussed with her hair, the stall door clanking behind me.

I didn't care—not *at all*—but I couldn't stop myself from asking, "Who's Jamie?"

Her reply was smooth, like she'd rehearsed it enough times that she believed the lie. "You're not entitled to that information." She met my eyes in the mirror, her gaze dropping to where I had my hands propped on my hips. "But she's one of my best friends."

There was no reason to examine the relief I felt at hearing *she* and *best friend*, so I barreled ahead. "We need to talk. Let's get out of here and—"

"No."

It took me a second to fully absorb her response. Funny how I still couldn't comprehend her rejections in real time. "Don't tell me you want to stay here. Not after—" I motioned to the door like I could summon those women. "Come on. We're leaving. I *know* you don't want to be here. I'll buy you a drink. Or three."

Audrey leaned back against the sink, her shoulders loose and her arms folded over her waist. The look in her eyes told me she didn't give a single fuck if I got my way and—and maybe I'd miscalculated. Maybe I'd read this all wrong.

"Thanks but I think the toilet stall abduction put me over the limit for tonight." She nodded to herself. "Yeah, you've made quite a splash with this whole surprise appearance of yours and *let's give them a show* and then stalking me halfway across the campus and barricading me in the bathroom while listening to the true confessions of law moms. Don't you think you've done enough?"

"Don't you think you owe me a real conversation? For once?"

Color flooded her cheeks and I knew I'd finally hit the one weak spot she'd never learned how to protect—guilt. No armor there.

"I'm not leaving until we talk," I went on.

"Then I hope you have a pleasant stay in Connecticut." She pushed away from the sink and moved toward the door. "I'm done with these games for tonight."

It took me a minute to recover from the satin slap of her words and say to her back, "Then you'll meet me tomorrow at ten. The usual place."

Her spine straightened and her chin lifted, and she didn't turn around or meet my eyes when she asked, "Why now?"

The truth was an option but not a good one. Not if I wanted her to show up tomorrow. Instead, I went with something on the inside of honest. "It's time. Don't you think?"

Audrey exhaled the whole world and I knew I had her.

"Ten o'clock." Her gaze still trained on the door, she held up one finger. "There will be no performance art, no kidnappings, no moving to second or third locations. Understood?"

"Sure, just as long as you understand I won't let you run away every time you don't like a question."

Her shoulders lifted. "And remind me what gives you the right to all my answers?"

My phone sounded in my back pocket and I knew my time was up. I wouldn't win this round, not in the way I wanted to. I was probably a fool—a desperate fool—for thinking I could. "I'll tell you tomorrow."

She scoffed as she shoved the door open. There was a pause when she stepped into the hall, a beat before I heard her heels hammering the marble floors, and I let myself believe she was waiting for me to follow. More likely, she was straightening her dress or cursing me in five different belief systems, but that stupid, stubborn part of me that didn't know how to let go had a different explanation.

I slumped against the wall and pulled out my phone.

Percy: call me

Jude: can you give me 5 minutes?

Percy: <thumbs-up emoji>

Since I didn't care to be accused of stalking again tonight, I took the long way through campus back to the parking lot. Music and voices filled the thick night air and my palms itched with the memory of her skin. I wanted to dunk myself in freezing water and wait for frostbite to take over. Give myself something new to feel.

When I reached the rental car, I pulled the door shut with more force than necessary and took a minute to breathe. This...hadn't gone as planned. But in truth, it never went as planned when Audrey was involved. All I knew was that woman fucked with my brain chemistry. I never wanted to see her again and I wanted her back more than anything else in the world, and that was a real fucking problem.

And I already had too many problems. No room in my life for another.

I grabbed my phone and opened a video call with my favorite problem. Percy answered in a dark room, the light of the screen reflecting off his glasses. An infantry of stuffed animals surrounded him.

"What's up, buddy?" I asked, trying like hell to chase the tension out of my tone. "Everything okay? You're up late."

"Grandma fell asleep in her chair again," he signed.

"Maybe she's just resting her eyes," I said while firing off a text to my attorney. "It's not easy keeping up with an almost-five-year-old. You're a high-energy kid."

He responded with a glare that my mother would call a taste of my own medicine. He climbed out of bed and crept down a short hallway, muffled television sounds increasing with each step. With a flip of the screen, I found my son's grandmother asleep in her recliner, a stainless steel tumbler in the crook of her arm, and a pair of reading glasses perched on top of her head and another pair sliding off her nose. A rage-bait cable news show blared in the background and a knee-high pile of newspapers teetered next to the recliner.

"She's been asleep since after dinner," he signed.

I pressed a fist to my mouth to keep from yelling, *Are you fucking kidding me, Brenda?*

At least he'd eaten this time.

"Okay, man, take me to the front door. Let's see about these locks."

We went on a journey locking the doors, checking that the kitchen appliances were off, and getting Percy's teeth brushed. I kept one eye on him between blowing up my attorney's phone about this custody agreement and searching for flights to Saginaw. I'd meet with Audrey in the morning and still have time to drop in on Brenda by the evening for a chat.

Percy returned to his bedroom and spent several silent minutes rearranging his stuffed friends until he was satisfied. When he climbed into bed, he settled his tablet against the wall and flipped the screen back to me, signing, "When can I come home?"

I felt those words like a hatchet to the chest. "I'll talk to Grandma. We'll make it better."

"I want to go home," he replied, his motions sharp. "Don't make me stay here."

Nothing hurt like watching tears roll down my son's round cheeks. Even Audrey couldn't hurt me like this and she'd ripped my heart in half—twice. "I will fix this. I promise," I said. "Have I ever broken my promises to you?"

His lips pressed into a pout as he shook his head.

"I'm not going to start now," I said. "Let me work on it. I'm going to make this better for you. In the meantime, it's far past your bedtime, sir. Hell, it's past *my* bedtime."

"You don't have a bedtime," he signed.

"Believe me, I do and you'll love your bedtime when you're my age." His watery laugh filled the rental car and everything in me ached. I just wanted to get my boy, take him home, and shield him from all the shit that kept turning his little world upside down. "You know you can call me anytime. Grandma knows it too. And you know you can go next door to Miss Maddie if you ever need help."

He nodded and clutched a stuffed wolf to his side.

"I love you," I said.

"I love you too, Dad," he signed.

"I'll stay on with you until you fall asleep. Do you want a story?"

He shook his head. "It's okay. You can go."

"If you think I have more interesting things to do than watch you try to fight falling asleep, you're wrong."

Another soft laugh, then a sniffle. "I'm sleepy."

"Then take off your glasses and put your head down. I'll be right here."

I started the car and pulled out of the lot. From what I could tell, the party under the tent was still going strong. If I knew that crew— and unfortunately, I did—they'd go hard until the booze ran out. And then order the underlings to fetch more.

Audrey wasn't in there. No one had to tell me how good she was at disappearing when the air grew thin. Good at slipping into the cracks when nobody else was looking. She'd live in those cracks if the choice was hers.

If I were smarter—or maybe just meaner—I'd have let her. Let her dissolve into the background until she was nothing more than a ghost of my past. There were times when I wanted that more than anything…and there were times when I fucked myself into situations I couldn't solve without her.

I leveled a glare at the tent one last time, the gulf between the resentment I had for this place and the energy I wanted to waste on it growing wider as my son's breathing evened out. I'd watch him until I reached my hotel near the airport. Longer, if I couldn't get the rumbling panic of being seven hundred miles away from my functionally unsupervised child out of my chest.

I swore under my breath as I turned onto the main road. I wouldn't get another second chance after tomorrow.

chapter five

Audrey

Today's vocabulary word: nostalgia

I WOKE UP TO A MESSAGE FROM MY MOTHER REMINDING ME (AGAIN) about my lunch date. Today's sacrifice was a guy who'd graduated from Aldyn Thorpe several years ahead of me and had made some kind of fortune on Wall Street. Our mothers knew each other from pickleball or mah-jongg or getting all their calories from the lime juice in their vodka sodas, and thought we'd *have fun* together.

Little-known secret but *have fun* translated to *socially and financially compatible for legally binding ventures such as marriage*.

For a minute I debated keeping the date. It would place a clear time limit on this meet-up with Jude and—this was my favorite part —it'd piss him off to know I hadn't carved out the entire day for him. And as a bonus, I wouldn't have to deal with my mother crashing out over me canceling the lunch.

But then I mentally slapped myself, chucked my phone across the bed, and let out a pathetic, whiny groan. I hated how I knew what I had to do but that my brain always invented a minimum of forty alternatives that would spare me some pinprick pain now in exchange for the pain of a broken blister on a pinkie toe for the rest of my life. I didn't always choose the blister but I never failed to give it serious consideration.

In today's game of mental hopscotch, the role of the blister was being played by Jude. As time had taught me, he'd own territory in my mind until we found some closure. Even if I walked away worse off than when I went in, it was time to let this wound scab over.

Except last night felt like a weird, winding detour and not the first step on a healing journey.

It felt complicated and messy, and nothing like the scripts I'd written in my mind. There were trap doors labeled *my ex-husband* and *my parents* and *my inability to do the right thing even when I try very hard* and *god, I've missed him* everywhere.

It scared me how easily that old familiarity rushed back in, the comfort of it. The way my entire existence wanted to melt into him.

I didn't think it would be like that. For as long as I could remember, the only emotions I'd been able to conjure when it came to Jude were regret and shame and grief. And now…well, the big three still lingered off to the side as they made room for intense curiosity. Who was he these days? Where did he live, what was his life like? Where had the world taken him?

These felt like dangerous questions to ask. Like I'd never recover from the answers. But I needed to know why he'd come looking for me—and why now?

I fished my phone out of the blankets and canceled the lunch date guy.

OUR USUAL PLACE WAS SEMANTIC CAFÉ, A SHADOWY, LOW-ceilinged coffeehouse-meets-community gathering spot carved into the attic above a garage between the state capitol and the Frog Hollow neighborhood of Hartford. They served Irish coffee frappés (which rhymed with *traps* in this part of the world) and hibiscus teas and the kind of artisanal peanut butter and jam sandwiches that made me nostalgic for a childhood I'd never experienced. Their muffins still visited me in my dreams.

The tabletops were game boards—chess, checkers, Monopoly, Scrabble, Pretty Pretty Princess—if they didn't have seventy years of local political stickers and pamphlets preserved under a slab of glass.

Climbing the old stairs behind the garage was like walking back in time. This place was so drenched in our history that it ran through my fingers and down my wrists. This had been our second home, one where the problems and pressures of the world outside could wait a minute.

I stopped on the landing and glanced at the city sprawled out around me. I thought about texting Jamie for some last-minute advice—or requesting an emergency call with my therapist—but in the end, I shook out the anxiety buzzing down my arms and pushed the door open.

It was always dark inside Semantic and it took a beat for my eyes to adjust. When they did, I found Jude seated at the far table under the dormer window. It was the best table in the house, my all-time favorite, because the window and the ventilation system above combined to create a kind of soundproof alcove. We could hear the music and everything going on in the café but no one could hear us unless they came right up to the table. This didn't seem like such a great feature now but we'd lived for it at seventeen.

I dredged up a smile and crossed the space toward Jude, keeping my eyes busy with long glances at the artwork on the walls and the menu board propped up next to the espresso machine he'd fixed more times than I could remember.

If he could take it apart, he could fix it.

I used to believe that included me.

I dropped into the empty seat across from him and all I could think was that he didn't fit in this alcove anymore. His legs bracketed the table, those tree trunks cocked wide. His body overwhelmed the space and swallowed the peeks of sunlight coming in through the window. It seemed like he could bear the weight of the roof on those shoulders alone.

It was jeans today, not surprising, though I wasn't prepared for the pale blue button-down. Washed, not dry-clean starched, with the cuffs rolled to his elbows and the collar open to the base of his throat. They'd been right last night, about the well-fucked hair. Couldn't unsee that.

"Hi," I said, hooking my bag over the back of the chair.

He made a pointed glance at his watch. "Only five minutes late." I watched his throat bob as he swallowed. "Impressive, considering I didn't think you'd show. Given your history."

I leaned in, dropping an elbow on the table and cupping my chin as I peered at him. Would it count as an apology if I delivered it while wrapping my hands around his throat? I wasn't sure.

Silence pulsed between us, a thick, living thing. It nearly filled the café and blew out the windows before I gathered up the words to say, "Tell me what you're doing these days."

He regarded me for a long second, the corner of his mouth kicking up like he didn't expect me to make the first move but he respected it. A grudging point in my favor. "Mostly performance art and low-key kidnappings. Nothing too remarkable. Just your basic bathroom abductions." When the only response I gave him was my unamused teacher stare, he added, "I work in aeronautics."

"Oh. Okay." I tipped my head to the side as I thought that one over.

I couldn't imagine him—or anyone—walking away from that mechanical engineering scholarship. It seemed I wasn't the only one whose plans had taken some unexpected turns. "How did that come about?"

He gave an unbothered shrug. "I realized jet engines were interesting too."

I tucked my hair over my ears as I tried to process this. The Jude I used to know was obsessed with cars and motorcycles. He taught himself how to rebuild a transmission in the garage downstairs. His motorcycle had been a labor of junkyard love. "That's what you do? You work on jet engines? Like, airplanes or...space shuttles?"

He folded his forearms on the table. A few wavy strands of hair fell over his forehead though he didn't bother pushing them away. It bothered me that I thought about pushing those strands away myself. "Let me make this easy for you since you're obviously struggling."

"Is that how we're going to do this? I could've sworn you said last night that you wanted to talk—and I thought we were doing that—but it seems like you just want to kick verbal rocks at me every few minutes."

"Don't worry about it, Saunders. I can do both." That patronizing tone soaked all the way through his words. "I work in jet propulsion. Specializing in thrust."

I wasn't positive but it seemed like he said that with his whole penis.

A server appeared beside the table, a loaded tray in hand, before I could unload something savage and blowtorch-y in response. "All right, all right. I've got an iced coffee, light and sweet, iced hibiscus tea shaken with blackberry puree, one toasted morning glory muffin, one *un*toasted sweet potato chai muffin, and a bowl of animal crackers. Is there anything else you fine folks might need this morning?"

"We're good," he said, the low rumble of his voice loosening a lock in the back of my mind. "Thanks."

I pressed my fingers to my lips. I could feel him watching me as I blinked at the mismatched dishes and old mason jars but I couldn't pull together words or even solid syllables, as though I'd traveled back in time.

The spell broke when Jude swirled a metal straw through his coffee, the ice clanking hard against the glass. He nodded at the goods between us, asking, "Do you want something else?"

"No. No, this is fine," I managed, though it sounded like I was in the bottom of a well. "Thank you—for remembering."

"Yeah." His gaze followed my hand as I reached for the tea. When I lifted it to my lips, he looked away. Cleared his throat. Then, "I started out working on fighter jets after grad school. Bounced between all the major aeronautics and defense contracting firms. Spent months, years even, on air force bases and naval air stations. Took some time off from that a few years back because I realized—among other things—I don't like being part of bombing the shit out of people. I played around with starting a doctoral program but then I remembered how much I hated all the bullshit hierarchy in grad school. There was a minute where I thought about going back to basics and looking after a fleet of planes and vehicles for a private security firm but circumstances changed and it turned out that wasn't the opportunity I thought it would be."

Jude stared at me as he took a deep pull from his coffee and I couldn't escape the sense that I was supposed to hear something he wasn't saying.

"I still work with the big aeronautics and defense firms but as an independent contractor. I have some breathing room in my schedule now, which is a big help, and I only take on the projects that interest me. These days, I work mostly on fixed-wing aircraft and helicopters developed for Coast Guard use."

"Oh, wow. That's—"

"Yeah, it's fascinating." He crossed his arms over his chest. "About that husband of yours."

"Ex-husband," I said automatically.

A harsh smile cut across his face. "You're damn right."

I didn't like talking about my ex. I went out of my way to avoid thinking about him. Being reminded that marrying him was the compromise that cost me everything made me want to burrow into the earth and live out my days in a dark hole. My ability to dig into those memories was shaky on the best of days but today all I could find were badly healed scars, tight and inflexible and splitting as they flexed over joints.

"I understand why you'd want to gloat," I started, "but believe me when I say I don't need anyone reminding me of my mistakes. I can do that all on my own."

"Is that what you think?" Jude eyed me, his brows low like he had to squint to see me properly.

"I don't know what else I should think." It hurt to speak, as if my throat was swollen shut from the memory of Jude pleading with me to run away from my wedding. Shame rolled inside me, all broken glass and boiling heat. All these bad decisions, all piled up around me. "It seems like you're just waiting to say *I told you so*."

He trailed a finger around the rim of his mason jar, his solemn gaze locked on me. "I'm not." He glanced away. "I didn't want to be right. About any of it." His eyes caught mine for a second and then they were gone again. "I'm sorry that I was."

I nodded and ripped the top off the chai muffin. "Okay."

Silence enveloped us for a minute and I could feel the dust settling. I didn't understand the ground we'd covered but I didn't feel like it was a trap when he asked, "You're in Boston now?"

"Yeah. I teach fourth and fifth grade and live a little ways outside the city."

"Only ballet? Or all kinds of dance?"

"No, no," I said, laughing. "I'm an elementary school teacher. Reading, writing, math, social studies. No dance."

His lips parted and I saw disappointment flash across his face. I couldn't put my finger on exactly why his reaction said more than any fine-tipped comment could. It left me feeling exposed, like he'd read the summary of my years since leaving him in that church and found it full of stale cheese and dead houseplants.

"What do you mean, *no dance*?" he asked.

"I haven't taught dance in—" I could tell the truth here and admit I'd stopped teaching after my parents informed me I'd be going to college in California and not Barnard in New York City as planned. That they'd dropped me into an emotional wasteland and I proceeded to spend a decade not caring whether I lived or died, let alone danced. Or I could do what I usually did and smooth down the sharp edges to keep everyone comfortable. "It's been awhile. I haven't had much time for it."

"You're going to have to do better than that, Saunders, because your entire life was ballet."

A shake of his head sent those unruly waves spilling down to his eyes, and I had to curl my hands into fists to keep from reaching out. He didn't want that from me. And nothing good would come of it anyway.

"I did live for ballet," I agreed. I'd lost a lot over the years but there wasn't much that hurt like losing dance. "And I loved teaching the little kids. But things changed. I changed."

He stared at me like he could reach across the table and wipe the lies off my face.

"I didn't go too far though," I said. "I worked at the San Diego Ballet after college. In development. Fundraising."

A whip-hard laugh cracked out of him. "How long did that last?"

"Long enough," I said, suddenly indignant up to my elbows.

"You're telling me your entire job was asking people for money, and you, the same person who allowed most teachers to get away with calling you *Aubrey* for the duration of your high school career, were successful at that? Apologies, but I have some questions."

"It wasn't like I was asking for money face-to-face," I argued. "There were galas for that. Silent auctions. Annual campaigns. And I can go on about dancers—their backstories, their talent, all of it—to anyone. They'd throw money at me just to get me to shut up."

He scooped up some animal crackers, tossed them in his mouth. "But you hated it."

"I loved the company. The shows were amazing. The directors were great."

"You *hated* it."

"I mean—" I held up my hands, hoping he'd let me off the hook. He went on crunching those crackers. "It wasn't the best job I've ever had. Okay? Happy now?"

"Delighted." The sharp arch of his brow said otherwise. "Elementary school, do you like that?"

"It's exhausting and infuriating and micromanaged to death but I can't even explain how much I love it." I reached for my mason jar, slicked my palms on the condensation. "My school loops in fourth and fifth grade so I'm with the same kids for two years. I wasn't sure about that part at first but now I wouldn't dream of anything else. I'm sending my kiddos off to sixth grade at the end of this week and I'm very ready for summer break but not at all ready to say good-bye to them."

"This is your last week of school?"

I nodded as I took a sip of my tea. "Yeah, wild week ahead. Field day, portfolio share day, art showcase day, stepping up ceremony."

His eyes brightened. "You do love it."

Another nod. "I do. I could write a hundred pages on the big and small problems gridlocking education right now, but every

September is a fresh start for everyone, and that's what I love the most."

"That's—" He held up a finger as a chime sounded. He pulled a phone from his pocket, saying, "Give me a minute to check on this."

I split the halved morning glory muffin in two and ate small, slow bites while he scowled down at his screen. I pretended I wasn't watching or trying to read upside down. At last, a quiet laugh huffed out of him and he glanced at me, his eyes warm.

"Everything okay?" I asked.

He shrugged in a way that said *yes* and *no* and *it's a pain but I'll deal with it later*. Then, "Percy needed me to know that the toaster waffles at his grandmother's house are inferior and he'd like a care package sent immediately."

"Percy?"

Jude unlocked his phone, revealing a photo of a small, dark-haired boy with espresso eyes hidden behind round glasses. Eyes just like the ones watching me from the other side of the table.

"My son," he said.

chapter six

Audrey

Today's vocabulary word: litigate

I COULDN'T DECIDE IF THIS WAS SIMPLE JEALOUSY OR THE KIND OF old, desperate longing that sat in your bones and refused to budge. It twisted somewhere deep in my belly, a feeling equal parts familiar and unwelcome. There was no reasoning with it or explaining it away. It made me restless, like I needed to get up and run to save myself from saying something I'd never be able to take back.

"He'll be five at the end of September and he's pissed off about that because he wants to go to kindergarten in the fall but the cutoff is September first."

I nodded. I hadn't stopped nodding since hearing Jude had a *son*. He was a *father*. To a human *child*. Which he had with a woman. Who was not me.

I knew I had no business having any reaction to this news. It wasn't about me, even if it did stab my side like a bra's busted underwire. I'd surrendered the right to react to any part of Jude's life a long time ago.

"He—Percy—he's visiting with your mom?" I asked. "Is she still in the Hartford area?"

Jude's features shifted to granite and the warmth in his eyes followed suit. "He's with Penny's mother," he said, the words carefully plucked from a thorny vine. "She lives in a small town on Saginaw Bay. In Michigan."

Penny. Her name was Penny and her family lived in Michigan and she was Jude's—well, she was Jude's. I worked hard at pulling a warm expression that hid the fact that I was still choking down a handful of glass.

"Oh. Okay," I said, my words coming out high like helium. "That's—that must be a fun spot in the summer. With the water and...everything."

He swept a glance from my still-bobbling head to the stranglehold I had on my tea. His brow arched up. "You can ask."

What a charming idea. As if I'd be able to say anything now that I wouldn't flog myself for later. And Jude knew this because another smile twitched at the corner of his mouth.

I focused on my tea, taking several long sips before fussing with a paper napkin and rearranging the plates on the table like the coward I was. Then, when the options were saying something or walking out of here now and straight into the Connecticut River, I met Jude's watchful gaze. "Tell me all about your family. I'd love to hear about them."

He reached for his coffee, saying, "It's a good look on you, Saunders."

"Excuse me?"

He brought the glass to his lips. "Jealousy," he said with a grin.

Leave it to Jude to wind me up and back me into a corner only to turn me around and prove it'd never been a corner to begin with. "I am not jealous."

It was an easy lie, if not a complicated one.

"Keep telling yourself that," he said. "You've always been good at outrunning your reality. No reason to stop now."

Okay, we're doing this.

"You wanted to talk so here I am, talking. If the only purpose of this meeting was to see how long I'd put up with your shitty comments, then"—I pointed to his watch—"note the time because I'm done. I hope you got everything you wanted from this visit."

As I reached for my bag, he leaned across the table and caught my wrist. "Spare me the dramatic exit, princess."

I stared down at his hand. No rings. Though I couldn't see him wearing one. He probably spent too much time elbow-deep in engines and machines. It didn't mean anything. "Do *not* call me that."

He eased back, his fingers skating over my palm as he went. Oh, *hell*. Why did I feel that touch on the back of my neck and deep behind my belly button? "The princess wants to hear about my family." Glancing away, he cleared his throat. "Where to start? Right, okay. I barely knew my son's mother, she's been dead for more than four years, and I have a clusterfuck of a custody agreement with his grandmother." He met my stunned gaze. "Still jealous?"

I wasn't sure how many times a gal's world was supposed to tilt in the regular course of business, but at this point I had to believe I was on the high side of normal. Or I was living inside a snow globe and no one had seen fit to mention it yet.

"Jude. My god. I'm so sorry for your loss—"

He held up a hand. "I spent one night with her. I don't get to grieve her."

"Of course you do."

He gave a stiff shake of his head, saying, "I met her in a hotel bar in Chicago. I was there for a meeting or something. She worked trade shows and industry conferences." His massive shoulders inched up toward his ears. "Almost a year later, a private investigator tracked me down for a DNA test."

"Wouldn't have guessed the business traveler bar scene was your vibe."

He laughed, and something in that raw, honest sound shredded the tension. "I swear to god it's not," he said, still laughing.

I heard it then. I heard the Jude I used to know. The one I'd loved.

"It was only the one time."

"Yeah, sure," I teased. "Take those odds to Vegas, my friend."

The levity lingered for a minute before he blew out a breath, saying, "It was a car accident. One of those unbelievable icy highway pile-ups. She died on impact and—" His voice hitched and I had to knot my fingers together to fight off all the instincts telling me to reach for him. He glanced away for a second before continuing. "Percy was in the car with her. He was…just about six months old. Broken leg. Traumatic brain injury. Lost some of his vision in the left eye. But he came out of it."

"Oh my god. Jude."

He shook his head like he had to sweep away the memories to speak. "They were driving home after I'd come in for the weekend. We'd agreed on monthly visits to start and then we'd shift to—" He shrugged like none of it mattered anymore. I guess it didn't.

"I'm so sorry." When he tried to wave me off again, I added, "It couldn't have been easy. Even if you didn't have a relationship with Penny, it all happened at once."

"Definitely not easy," he agreed, "but the kid pulled through after two months in the hospital. He doesn't speak, though the doctors can't decide whether that's a result of the TBI or a stress response."

"But he communicates with you," I said, pointing to his phone. "That's really impressive for his age."

"He got tired of the alternative communication apps and learned to read and write over the past year." A warm, adoring smile brightened his expression. "Between ASL and texting, he doesn't shut up."

Fatherhood looked good on Jude. It looked really damn good.

A hollow spot inside me pinged though I managed to say, "He's lucky to have you."

"That's what my mom says," he replied, a laugh in his words. "She also says I deserve all the headaches and sleepless nights he gives me too."

"How is Janet?" I asked. "Are you staying with her this weekend?"

I'd always loved Jude's mom. She gave the best hugs, the kind that squeezed all the broken pieces back together tight enough that it seemed like they might hold. I'd missed her after everything ended and my parents shipped me off to California for college. Though I doubted she shed many tears over that change of plans.

She'd argued hard for us to go off to college separately. We needed time to figure ourselves out, she'd said. We had our whole lives to be together. Though even when she disapproved, she'd left the decision in Jude's hands. My parents did not share that approach.

He pushed a hand through his hair and gave me a look that said *Just wait till you hear this*. "No, she moved out to Arizona last spring."

"Arizona? What prompted that?"

"Mostly the breast cancer, but she'd had enough of the New England winters too. Also, there was something about *better energy* though I still have some questions about that."

Slumping back in my seat, I absorbed the physical blow of those words.

"She beat it," he added quickly, taking in the open-mouth alarm written across my face. "For a minute it didn't look like she would, but she pulled through. It's been a full year of no evidence of active disease now."

"That—that's such a relief," I said. "But going forward, I'm going to need you to tell me everyone's all right before getting into these tragic stories. I'm bracing myself for what's to come."

"I'm tapped out on tragedy," he said. "Aside from the damage you did to my toes last night."

"You'll survive." I gave him a tart smile before tearing off a chunk of chai muffin. "I've been trying to develop a recipe for these muffins for…well, for years. Never get it quite right."

"You like baking." There was something odd embedded in that statement but I couldn't pry it out before he said, "I need you to do something for me."

Ah. Finally.

I'd known it was coming but a shiver still raced down my spine and I had to work at chewing the muffin I'd crammed in my mouth. I made a real effort at looking casual as I swallowed hard.

"Yeah, okay, let's get into it," I said, tipping my chin at him. "I've been dying to find out the real reason for this visit."

I expected an arched eyebrow glare, a broody stare that said nothing could prepare me, a scowl that sent me into a cold sweat. What I got was Jude ducking his head and blinking down at the table for a remarkably long minute.

Then he pinched his brow and ground out, "We need to be engaged. To be married."

I waited. There had to be more. A punch line, perhaps, or a chasm waiting to open under the café and spring me from this mortal slog. Anything would be better than leaving me to tread water while holding up that—that *announcement*. Because it had *not* been a question, not at all.

When I couldn't bear the weight any longer, I edged my chair closer to the table and tapped my fingertips on the surface. "I-I'm sorry but what did you just say?"

"I need you to be my fiancée." He met my eyes before quickly glancing away. "Just for a week."

"I'm sure *just for a week* makes it all make sense to you," I said, my hands turning into little birds and fluttering around me as I spoke, "but that doesn't clarify anything for me. One week is very specific. Why this time frame? What's happening in this week? Is it a specific week or are we just tossing darts at the board to see where we hit?"

What I really wanted to ask was *Are you just looking for the most painful ways to punish me?*

He rubbed a hand over the back of his neck. "Do me a favor and dial it down, okay? There's zero need to shriek."

Everything inside me cooled. "I can promise you I'm not *shrieking.* I might have a few things to make up for but if this is how you're going to treat me, you'll be waiting another decade." I held his eyes for a long moment. Longer than he'd expected, if that flicker of surprise could be believed. "We can talk about all the things that went wrong and I can apologize for each of them but I'm not here for your fake-engagement games."

"No games, Saunders. I need you to be my fiancée for a trip to Arizona to visit my mother. We'll go next week, if that works for you."

I tried to swallow this piece by piece but the more I chewed it over, the less it made any sense. "Why?"

"Because my mother was dying," he said, the words broken off and heavy. "She'd taken a turn and it didn't look like she'd pull through. I would've promised her anything if I thought it'd make her comfortable, if it would've brought her some peace." He reached for his coffee but didn't drink. He just held the glass, sliding his finger-tips through the condensation. "She wanted to know I'd be all right when she was gone. Not just with Percy but that I'd find…someone. It mattered to her, and the only thing that mattered to me was putting her at ease."

"I can see that," I said, all hesitance, "and I understand you wanting to make her comfortable." I still couldn't choke this down. "But I'm still not sure I understand how *I* figure into this yet."

He stared at the table, his gaze far away. I desperately wanted to put this into a comprehensible order, give him what he wanted—if I could, and I had some doubts about that—and then get the hell out of here. There wasn't a world where I could talk about being engaged to Jude, even as some kind of side quest, without feeling like my belly was filled with steel wool.

"I told her we'd reconnected and—" Jude waved a hand between us as if that explained anything. "Yeah. Well. She pulled through."

We. At least eighty-four different emotions flashed across my face and I was working too hard at continuing to cosplay as a regular, functional human rather than the howling hound inside me to hide any of them. "*We* reconnected? And somehow that translates to us getting *engaged*?" I leaned in, pressed my palms to the heat flaming my cheeks. "Jude, what? And why? Also, how? Just…how did that happen?"

"I didn't think she'd make it through the night," he went on. "She was in and out of it. Heavily medicated. Half the things she said made no sense, but then she'd be clear as day for a few minutes. She wanted me to get married, said it was important for Percy and…for me."

He shoved a hand through his hair and then let it fall to the back of his neck, gripping and kneading the muscles for a minute as he stared out at the café. The move highlighted the biceps straining under the fine, soft weave of his shirt. His arm was a solid mass I'd struggle to get both hands around.

Eventually, he dropped that hand to his leg, his broad palm flat on the denim while his fingers tapped out a hurried rhythm. "I told her what she needed to hear, that I'd picked out a ring and was waiting for her to make it through that last round of treatment to propose. I just wanted to give her something to hold on to. Something good, even if none of it was true."

"And now you're stuck with it." *Stuck with me.*

He shrugged. "More or less."

That was when I realized that between all of our rocks and hard places, we had a real problem on our hands.

I frowned at the dishes between us and started consolidating the half-eaten muffins and empty glasses. "Wouldn't it have been better to pick someone less"—I laughed to myself—"complicated to fulfill your mother's dying wish?"

Jude pinned me with a stare that told me precisely how little he wanted this complication in his life. "Yeah, it would've," he said, "but there's nothing I can do about it now."

I picked at the muffins, pressing the pad of my finger to the crumbs. "What exactly are you asking me to do?"

"Come to Arizona with me. Spend a few days with my mom. Let her throw us an engagement party," he said, ticking off the list on his fingers.

I shook my head but didn't tear my focus away from feeding myself tiny bits of muffin. Much easier than eye contact. "You want me to—what? Pretend we're together? That we're *engaged*? How would that even work?"

And why did you choose me?

"We both know you owe me one, Saunders. Help me make this happen."

I blinked up at him, half expecting to find a smirk on his face or some indication this was an elaborate joke constructed to fuck with the last of my frayed nerves. But no, there was nothing but cool, unwavering seriousness in his eyes—and a challenge we both knew I'd accept.

"What about your little boy? Won't it be massively confusing for him?"

Jude's lips firmed into a tight line. "Penny's mom has him for six weeks every summer. He won't know anything."

At least that wouldn't be an issue. There was no way I'd involve a kid in this sort of thing. It was bad enough that we were talking about taking our fraudulent engagement on tour.

"How does this end?" I asked, my throat suddenly tight. "Or have you failed to mention that we're actually faking it for the rest of your mother's life and there *will* be a wedding at some point?"

He cocked his head to the side as if he hadn't thought that far ahead. "We'll realize we want different things come September," he said, eyeing me with a bit more attention than necessary. "Or maybe you'll run off on me once again."

My entire adult personality was a carefully stacked tower of bad decisions, the foundation built on falling in line because my parents said so, and the mortar a mixture of grief and regret. I drifted off to sleep every night replaying my most painful moments and rehearsing new, less disastrous versions of them.

So I knew what it looked like when I was staring down a dark, thorny path that would inevitably drag me to hell and back. I also knew Jude Bellessi didn't want anything to do with me. If not for that deathbed promise and the miraculous events that followed, he never would've spoken to me again.

And I knew I'd do anything for him. Always. Even if it broke me in the end.

chapter seven

Jude

Today's vocabulary word: transition

I COULD ADMIT WHEN MISTAKES WERE MADE.

Returning to Hartford, showing up at that reunion, asking Audrey to help me out—I knew I was chasing trouble going in but the enormity of it didn't register until her first series of panicked texts came through.

> Audrey: I'm sorry but I still don't understand how your very observant mother is going to believe that we've reconnected to the point that we're ENGAGED.

> Audrey: When did this relationship occur? How did it happen? Are there stories to tell? Photos to share? Anything?

> Audrey: I don't even know where you live!

> Audrey: How are we supposed to get the story straight if we're pulling it out of thin air?

> Audrey: We'll screw up and she'll know!

I glared at my phone as I shuffled through the rental car line at Detroit Metro. I had a drive ahead of me to Brenda's place up in Saginaw and I'd planned on making the most of the time I had before seeing my boy. First, I was going to rant at my attorney about the custody agreement. It wouldn't solve anything other than adding an hour to my tab but there was no one else willing to listen while I complained about a grieving grandmother.

Then, I'd run some mental lock-picking drills on how I intended to fake loving bliss with Audrey next week. She was worried we wouldn't be able to pull it off. I was worried I wouldn't be able to stop.

She was the reason I'd wasted the entire flight from Hartford. I'd sat down with the intention of clearing out my email inbox and then returning to my research into private schools for Percy in the Alexandria area. But then I blinked and the wheels touched down, and I'd lost that time to replaying every minute I'd spent with Audrey, examining every inch of the woman she was now. Of how she felt against me. Of how difficult it'd been to watch her walk away.

> Jude: Don't worry about my mother. She's been too busy getting well to be observant these past 2 years

> Audrey: Right, about that: how does this make any sense? Your mother goes through CANCER treatment, almost DIES, and I don't check in on her even ONCE? She must think I'm a horrible, callous person

> Jude: You have a problem with people thinking that now? Wouldn't have guessed that about you

I knew better than to take a shot like that, but knowing better had always been my problem when it came to Audrey Saunders. Sense and self-preservation had never stood a chance when she was involved.

> Jude: I live in northern Virginia. Alexandria. Outside of DC.

> Audrey: ...okay?

> Jude: you said you didn't know where I lived. I'm telling you I live outside of DC.

I watched the screen for a minute, waiting for a response, but nothing came through. I probably deserved her silence. At least I had a reprieve from more questions I couldn't answer. Those questions were why I'd put this off for months and they were why there was no way we'd make it through a full week together without some fatal wounds. Not when those careful, studious glances of hers had felt like she was peeling back my skin and finding all the rotten and hollowed-out things inside me.

And that was my problem. I had all the years and miles and scars separating us from the past, and the most raw, fragile parts of me—the ones that fucking knew better—still ended up leading me back to her. It was wrong but that old, reckless streak of mine still believed there was no one safer to claim than the one person who could actually ruin me—and had done it twice.

For a long time, I'd nursed an unhinged little theory that I could put all the things that'd broken between us back together if she'd just let me get close enough to pick up the pieces. To show her that there was nothing we couldn't fix together. Another mistake, but that hadn't stopped me from circling the wreckage when I wanted to remind myself of the damage she could do to me.

And here I was, waiting in line for more.

As I saw it, my options were limited. I could break my mother's heart. I'd considered that more than once, and every time I'd tried to walk back this phantom love story, she'd make an offhand comment about how thrilled she was that I'd found Audrey again. How excited she was for us to get a fresh start. After "all that mess." How much she wanted to throw us forty different parties to celebrate. How she'd wanted this for me, and now Percy too, for so long.

Which meant no, I actually could *not* break my mother's heart.

That left me to forge ahead with Audrey and this half-cocked plan of mine. Sure, it would all come crashing down eventually, but my mother had spent the last two years fighting for her life. She'd earned some uncomplicated joy, even if it was built on a massive lie. I'd deal with the fallout later.

But god help me, I wasn't sure I'd survive a trip to Arizona with Audrey. The plan had made sense at first, but even texting with her now was like trying to outrun a serial killer by hiding in a basement. She was going to unravel my every defense and I wouldn't even try to stop her.

That was the real problem—not that she'd break me again, but that I'd let her.

———

"I DON'T KNOW WHAT YOU'RE WORRIED ABOUT. WE'RE GETTIN' ON just fine," Brenda drawled, a pointed stare hiding right behind her smile. "You really didn't have to come all the way up here to check on us."

"I had some down time between meetings," I lied. "Figured I'd swing by."

She packed a dozen different emotions into her quick response of, "Isn't that nice for you."

If there was one person who hated sharing custody of Percy more than I did, it was Brenda. Most of the time, I didn't blame her. For fuck's sake, I was the one-night stand and Penny hadn't gone looking for me until *after* Percy was born. She'd spent the entire pregnancy planning to raise him on her own—same as my mother raised me—and Brenda had been right there with her every step of the way.

Brenda didn't know me, and as far as she was concerned, my involvement here had been a gift granted to me by her daughter, which I'd damn well better remember.

The least I could do was let her resent me.

"It's good for him to be here," Brenda said. She didn't try to hide the defensiveness in her words. "It's good for him to be outside and play like the other kids. He shouldn't be cooped up inside all the time."

Was it possible for my jaw to permanently clench? Could it lock up and stay this way for the rest of my life? Felt like it. "He's not cooped up inside all the time."

"He needs to run around more and spend less time on that tablet," she went on. "All the experts say screen time is terrible for children."

"Unless those children are using the screens as assistive technology," I said, but Brenda wasn't listening to me.

She was as stubborn as they came. Set in her ways to no end. I didn't know how much of that was a coping mechanism, like she'd frozen in place when the worst happened and was still there. But it was as though she was on fire and couldn't bring herself to let me hose her off.

Percy wandered toward us from across the grassy yard, his feet bare, a bucket hat hiding most of his face and a worn hardcover book tucked under his arm. He walked straight into me, his little face mashed against my leg and his free hand curled around my belt.

"Hey, man," I said, rubbing his back. "I'm digging this hat. Good look for you."

He tipped his head back, his eyes wide and owlish behind his glasses. Passing me the book to free up his hands, he signed, "Are you taking me home?"

One thing that'd blindsided me in this parenting journey was the brutal pain of watching my child struggle and not being able to do anything about it. He loved Brenda and he generally liked visiting her but the transition here was always tough. Getting out of step with the preschool schedule, his regular therapies, and the routine we had at home didn't make this any easier.

I cut a glance at Brenda. She'd dropped into a rocking chair on the porch, her face pinched and her gaze fixed on Percy. But she only knew the bare basics of ASL. She'd tried to learn when we realized this was more than a speech delay but she never got the hang of it. And since he had communication tools on his tablet, it didn't seem like a major issue to her.

"I'm just dropping in for the night," I signed, "And I'll straighten things out with Grandma."

His shoulders sagged. "Nothing's ever straight with Grandma."

I had to swallow a laugh at that. He was a cranky geezer with a soul as old as dirt in the body of a four-year-old. "We'll figure this out," I signed. "And we'll get the good waffles too."

He tugged on my belt and I scooped him up. His arms went around my neck and his head settled on my shoulder, and I finally exhaled all the way.

"We went to the playground this morning," Brenda called. "Did Percy mention that? He made *two* new friends."

"That sounds fun," I said to him.

"All they did was run around and scream," he signed.

"They played a game for *an hour*," she added. "All three of them together."

He rolled his eyes. "The rules didn't make any sense and they forgot all about them after five minutes."

"That's what kids do," I said. "You know that. Because you're a kid."

"Then I don't like kids," he replied.

"I didn't like a lot of kids when I was younger," I said, low enough that Brenda wouldn't hear. "But then I realized I just hadn't met the right ones."

"I don't think I'm going to meet the right ones when Grandma follows me around saying 'This is Percy. Can he play with you?' I look like a dumb baby."

Despite his complaints, Percy could hold his own with other kids and they tended to be cool with him too. It was the adults who invented the problems. Either they wanted to structure the hell out of every minute or they felt the need to over-explain his communication differences. All of it backed him into a corner where people talked *at* him and not *to* him, and he became more of an object than a participant. Or—this one really fucked me up—they felt entitled to the details of his story.

It didn't make me popular in the playdates-and-birthday-party circles but I had a lot of experience educating other parents on how to treat my kid like a human being.

Brenda…was a different situation.

She wanted the best for Percy but she didn't trust most of the information I gave her. Accommodations, adaptive tech, unconventional systems—it all sounded like overcomplication to her. Her way had worked before when Penny was young, so in her mind, it was still the right way, even if it meant bypassing what Percy needed now.

I had to tread lightly with her. I had to respect the glass foundation our relationship had been built on and the weight of her grief resting upon it. She was a link to a history I'd never be able to fill in for him.

"Didn't you have a great time?" Brenda asked him. Without waiting for a response, she said to me, "Percy had a *great* time. We're gonna set up a playdate for next week."

Another eye roll from my son. "All they're going to do is run around and scream."

An hour spent running and screaming would probably solve a minimum of fifty percent of my problems. The freedoms of childhood were wasted on children.

Before I could convince Percy this wasn't the worst thing in the world, Brenda let out a long, noisy yawn. "It's been a day," she said through another yawn. "We're going to sleep well tonight, aren't we, Percy? And a good breeze too. Nice night to have all the windows open."

Percy glanced up at me, his eyes saying, *See what I'm dealing with here?*

If the past few days had been any indication, Brenda would be zonked out within the hour. I gave him a nod before saying, "The summer sunsets fool you into thinking it's earlier than it is."

"Sure do," Brenda said. "But my sweet Percy knows right when it's time for bed. Just like his mama."

Her words broke on a sob, and a moment later she bustled into the house, the screen door snapping behind her.

I sucked in a breath and slowly let it out. "Let's take a walk along the water," I said to Percy.

"Why does it make Grandma sad that I'm like my mom?"

I took his hand and led him down the slight hill of Brenda's yard to the shores of Saginaw Bay. The house was postage stamp small but the location couldn't be better. A gentle tide lapped against a narrow strip of sandy beach as night saturated the horizon.

"You don't make her sad," I said. "She's sad that your mom isn't here anymore. She misses your mom a whole lot."

"But I remind her of my mom and that hurts her feelings."

I wanted there to be a quick, clean explanation that would remove this burden from his young shoulders. But I knew there wasn't one because I'd searched for it many times before. "Grandma loves that she sees parts of your mom in you. It's special for her, even if it's hard."

He considered this for a moment, the bucket hat bobbing as he nodded. Then, "What if I do things that don't remind her of my mom anymore? Will that hurt her feelings too?"

"No, my dude, that won't happen. Grandma loves you exactly as you are. Seeing those pieces of your mom in you is a special gift."

"Like an extra chicken nugget in the bottom of the bag."

"Yes, precisely that."

"But I don't cry when I get an extra nugget. Nuggets make me happy."

"Sorry, man. It's not a perfect metaphor."

"What's a metaphor?"

I rubbed the back of my neck. There was no limit to this kid's questions. "Are there any cool rocks on this beach?"

Old souls loved a good rock.

"Yeah, so many, over here, let me show you, come on," he signed all at once.

chapter eight

Jude

Today's vocabulary word: pressure

> Audrey: I'm going to send some flowers to your mother on the day of the engagement party she's hosting but I wanted to check if she has any allergies or sensitivities first.

I STARED AT HER MESSAGE IN THE DARK, DRAFTING AND DELETING responses while Percy slept starfished in the twin bed beside mine. Half his stuffed friends were already on the floor.

As predicted, Brenda had passed out in her recliner before we returned from our rock hunt. She'd draped a quilt made of Penny's old t-shirts and pajamas over her legs and—not for the first time today—I felt like an asshole for wanting sole custody. I'd never prevent her from seeing Percy but we couldn't keep going like this. Not without some big changes.

I reread Audrey's messages even though I could hear every one of them in my head as if she'd spoken the words right into my ear.

That was a fucking problem.

> Jude: You don't need to send her anything

> Audrey: Why? Because we're operating under the assumption that I'm a coldhearted demon spawn who doesn't care about anyone but myself?

> Audrey: Or are you too busy being belligerent to answer a simple question? If that's the case, you're going to make it really obvious to your mother that this is a sham.

> Audrey: I'm trying to help you here but you're too busy being a shitfinch to notice.

I didn't know what a shitfinch was but there was no doubt in my mind I was being one. There was no good reason to give her such a hard time but seeing her and talking to her again unleashed something in me. I couldn't stop being an asshole.

Or a shitfinch.

Maybe I was just getting it out of my system. Burning off the worst of it before we were in front of my mother and we had to—*Fuck.* I couldn't think about what it meant to bring Audrey home and call her my fiancée. I couldn't put myself there yet. We'd make it happen when the time came. All I had to do was build some mental walls around it until then.

> Jude: Not sure when you leveled up your vocab but it's colorful

> Audrey: You're about as helpful as old yeast

I was shoehorned into a lumpy little bed with a roommate who snored like a buzzsaw and I had a very difficult conversation with Brenda waiting for me tomorrow morning, yet I couldn't wipe the smile off my face. There was no reason for this. Not a single fucking one.

> Jude: My mother's been asking if we've set a date. Feel free to invent one.

> Audrey: Yeah sure no problem, on it...since I'm inventing everything else

> Audrey: I take it I'll be doing all the talking too. There's no possible way for that to blow up in our faces

> Jude: take a breath pls

> Jude: you know my mother. She's a squirrel on a chill day.

> Audrey: right and squirrels never notice when they're being scammed

> Jude: it makes sense that we'd do the long-distance thing for a while with me traveling for work all the time and you being based in Boston. Go back to the basics. Don't sweat it. She just wants to see you and throw a party.

> Audrey: I really don't understand how you think it's that simple

> Jude: Maybe it's not but I think we'll figure it out when it's go time

> Audrey: Can you just tell me if she has any allergies?

> Jude: I don't think so but I meant it when I said you don't have to send anything

> Audrey: Sorry but I can't show up to a party being thrown in my honor without a gift for the hostess. The choices are to send flowers in advance or carve out a lobe of my liver and hand it to her at the door.

> Jude: Those good girl manners die hard

> Audrey: They die but they stick around and haunt the attic

I laughed and a heavy pressure built in my chest, right behind my breastbone. It was like indigestion but deeper—and worse. I really didn't have time for a heart attack.

> Jude: Did you get your flight info?

> Audrey: I did, thank you.

It annoyed me that I knew from that response she was holding something back. I wanted to wipe my memory of her quiet tells and quirks, and return to a time when I didn't think about her every minute of every day.

> Jude: You're good with it?

> Audrey: I'm worried about getting home in time for my friend's wedding.

> Jude: You arrive in Boston on Thursday night. Your friend's wedding isn't until a full week after that.

> Audrey: Right but we have a bunch of events before the wedding and I have the entire bachelorette bar crawl to plan. I can't get behind schedule.

> Jude: I think you'll be okay for the bar crawl

A few minutes passed without another message from Audrey. There was nothing else to say and I needed to get some sleep but the pressure in my chest only increased. I checked my work email just to have a new problem to bother myself with but there was nothing waiting for me. I skimmed the headlines—depressing—and glanced at the weather in Seattle, where I was due for meetings later this week. Then I tried to get comfortable, but in this bed that wasn't much of an option.

I resented myself for it but I went back to our text thread.

> Jude: My mother's always liked hydrangeas. The blue ones you'd see around Hartford in the summer.

> Jude: She's mentioned it's something she misses now that she's in the desert

I rubbed a hand to my sternum, hoping to ease the twinge there. Didn't help.

> Audrey: I appreciate that. Thank you.

> Jude: Yeah, no problem

> Audrey: I guess I'll see you in Phoenix this weekend then. Could you send me your itinerary so I know where to find you when I arrive? In case there are any delays with your flight?

Something snapped inside me, like an old rubber band stretched too far for too long. I went to my calendar though it didn't matter much what I found there because I'd already decided.

> Jude: Small change of plans actually. I'm flying out with you from Boston.

> Audrey: I thought you had to work on the west coast this week

> Jude: Only the first part of the week

It wasn't true. Then again, none of this was true.

> Audrey: Oh okay

Audrey: then I'll see you at the airport

But at least I could breathe without feeling like my chest was about to cave in now.

Jude: I'll pick you up

chapter nine

Audrey

Today's vocabulary word: pure

"I KNOW IT'S ONLY NINE THIRTY," JAMIE ROUSELLE SANG AS SHE swept into my classroom, "but I need you to feed me."

I dropped my phone, pushed up from my desk, and clasped my hands behind my back in the most suspicious manner possible. Honestly, it would've raised less notice if I'd dumped a bucket of live lobsters on the floor.

She pointed at me. "Okay, that was weird."

I shrugged and tried to look innocent. "I didn't bake last night but I have leftover molasses cookies."

I didn't bake every night. Sometimes, but not always. Not anymore. Not since washing the blood from the worst of the wounds left behind by my time married to my ex-husband. But there'd been an era when kneading dough until my arms gave out was the only remedy for the stress that'd taken up residence inside my body.

Looking back on it now, I couldn't believe I'd found the strength to put any of it into a blog. I'd been so…small in my marriage. So hollow. Because sharing thoughts and photos and detailed instructions onto the internet for others to consume required a level of confidence I'd left in my teens. That was probably why I'd started with a blog like it was the olden days of the internet. I didn't expect anyone would notice me there.

I started The Ballerina Bakes about a year before leaving Christopher. The first recipe I posted was a gluten-free pumpkin cranberry bread. The flavors because they reminded me of autumn in New England. The lack of gluten because life with my ex made my body shut down to the point that I couldn't digest much of anything.

I added videos of my baking process not long after but I stayed off camera. My hands made appearances but nothing else. I preferred it that way. I didn't have to be myself when I baked. I could be The Ballerina. I found that I liked her better.

These days, I posted a new recipe once a week, down from four or five when my mental health had been at its worst. I had them planned out and edited months in advance, which meant I baked molasses cookies in June for a holiday series that would publish in late November.

My friends—the ones who taste-tested all my recipes—didn't mind. One universal truth about teachers was that they were always hungry. Jamie in particular.

"I will take those molasses cookies," she said as she crossed the room, "and I'll sit right here and eat them while you tell me what the hell's going on with you."

I went to the closet behind my desk and grabbed the Pyrex container of cookies. "I think I did something bad," I said.

"I don't think you know how to do anything truly bad," the first-grade teacher replied. "But prove me wrong."

I met Jamie when I started teaching here, right after my divorce was finalized. She was about five years younger than me but that didn't get in the way of her taking me on like a mangy foster dog in need of serious socialization. She wormed her way into my life whether I wanted her there or not. Considering that all I'd wanted to do back then was walk through my days like a ghost and I'd perfected the art of disappearing into myself, it was a noteworthy accomplishment.

She taught me how to have fun again, how to laugh at life—and myself. She'd cornered me into eating lunch with the other elementary teachers and folded me into a group of friends that were now my favorite people in the world.

She'd taught me how to open up without worrying about anyone using those vulnerabilities against me, but I still had something to learn in that area. My friends knew about my divorce though I hadn't gotten around to sharing anything about Jude. Talking about a bad marriage to a pathologically narcissistic man was relatively simple when the alternative was admitting I hurt someone who'd deserved better. As far as Jamie and the others were concerned, the divorce and the blog were the cornerstones of my lore. I didn't hint toward others and no one went digging into that story any deeper.

But here I was now, days away from a whole summer vacation with the guy who'd wanted to stop my wedding, and I had some explaining to do.

Busy week for getting bitten in the ass by my own bad decisions.

"I can see you being benignly bad," Jamie mused, half-eaten cookie in hand. "Not offering to let someone cut in front of you at the grocery store when they only have a few items and you have your usual forty pounds of flour and all the butter on the shelves. Or cutting across three lanes of traffic to make an exit but not waving at the people who let you in."

"Why do all of your examples involve cutting?"

"Because cutting is a capital offense in first grade," she said, her mouth full. "So, what did you do? What's so bad that it looks like you've been waiting to sneeze for the past six hours?"

I glanced at my phone before turning it facedown. Nothing new there anyway. "I went to that reunion, like I told you about," I started, hedging and wobbling my way through, "and I ran into someone. Who I used to be close with. Very close, actually. We'd— well, there was a time when we'd made big plans together. For life after school. And beyond that. For our whole lives, really. But I ruined it all because my parents said— It doesn't matter what they said anymore."

"It probably matters a whole lot." I found her staring at me, eyes wide and cheeks crammed full with cookies. "What did they say?"

I grabbed a pen off my desk and let my thumb trace the edge of the cap. "My parents, they aren't like most people."

"Honeychild, my father didn't know I existed until I was thirteen and was deposited on his doorstep by social services. You will find no judgment from me."

I didn't know how to let myself believe that. I didn't know what it meant to exist without judgment stacked up on my shoulders. "They—well, when I was a kid, they gradually took up some new religious views. But it wasn't actually religious, which probably doesn't make any sense. I guess I'm trying to say there was no faith to it, no traditions or spirituality. Just…shame and intense vibes and obsessing over how everything looked. It didn't matter what it was, just how it looked."

Jamie murmured in agreement. "We're talking about the purity culture, the institutionalized gender roles, the unhinged hatred of anyone considered other? Generally shitty and morally corrupt from the inside out?"

"All of it," I said, relieved that I didn't have to elaborate.

"Then I take it they didn't approve of this young man in your life," she said.

"They didn't approve for so many reasons." I started ticking off on my fingers. "He grew up with a single mom who cleaned houses for a living. One of his jobs was working at my father's country club, repairing the golf carts and equipment. He went to my school on a full-ride scholarship. He rode a *motorcycle*, James. They didn't like him *at all*. No part of this was acceptable and they made it very, very clear that I had no say in the matter."

"But sweet little Audrey was defiant," Jamie drawled. "She kept secrets and did what she wanted, didn't she?"

I ran a thumb over my fingernails. "No one was paying much attention to me in high school. My sister was always being bullied or targeted by a teacher, or so she said, and my parents focused more on her. And we'd moved to a new house in a different neighborhood and my dad finished his second term as Connecticut attorney general—"

"Oh, so, your dad basically had the state police at his disposal? And the boy still deflowered you? Must be tough on him, carrying around those titanium balls. Requires a lot of core strength."

"I can't believe you said *deflowered* and—I won't repeat the other part. Oh my god. Someone is going to walk in here and we'll never be able to explain this."

"I'm just saying the boy knew the stakes were high and he chose to dive into your hedgerow anyway." She pressed her palms together in prayer, closed her eyes. "Bless us, Dolly, and the boy's big, shiny balls too."

I choked on a laugh. Leave it to Jamie to take an emotionally grueling situation and boil it down to its wackiest parts. "We're not talking about"—I dropped my voice to a whisper—"*balls* anymore."

"Fine, fine, fine," she said. "The parents must've caught up on your extracurriculars and they didn't like what they found."

"They threatened and issued ultimatums and they scared the hell out of me."

"Nouveau religious father who also has the police on speed dial? Yeah, I believe those threats packed a punch."

For a minute, I couldn't claw my way out of the memory of when my father called me into his office, locked the door, and informed me I'd be leaving home that day. Either I'd go with the bags that'd been packed for me with fresh, new, *modest* clothing and supplies, or I'd be leaving with all the things I owned—which was nothing. Not even the clothes on my back.

And it just kept getting worse after that. So much worse. The restrictions, the requirements. The punishment that'd last until they decided it was over.

I'd never figured out how to breathe inside that memory. There'd been a time when I wished it would just suffocate me already.

"I—I didn't really have any options," I said eventually. "Not any that felt real to me. I had to do what they wanted. And it was awful. They made me leave and wouldn't let me talk to him. Wouldn't let me explain. And they were so furious, so *disgusted* with me."

"Oh, baby girl."

I shook my head. The last thing I wanted was sympathy. "No, it's fine—"

"*Is* it fine though? And does it have to be?" A few tendrils of her long, dark hair slipped free from a claw clip. She batted the hair away, saying, "Just because you can't see the bruise anymore doesn't mean it won't hurt if you press on it."

I was quiet for a minute, thinking of all the bruises I ritualistically pressed. The ones I kept black and blue just to prove to myself they existed. They'd been real.

"I have several follow-up questions for you but two big ones before we go any further," Jamie said, wiggling two fingers. "First, how long do we have until your critters are back from their visit to the sixth grade? And second, do you have any more cookies or food items you'd share with me? I cleared out my snacks last Friday and most of my working memory too because I forgot that I graze all day long."

I glanced at the clock. "We probably have another half hour." The last days of school were completely lawless. Schedules? We didn't know her. "I have contraband almonds. Do you want those?"

"Audrey, love, I almost ordered delivery of a taco platter for twenty. The only reason I didn't is that they don't open for another two hours. So, yes, I'll take your almonds even if you throw them at me individually like I'm a sea lion while you tell me what happened with this old, iron-balled boyfriend of yours."

"He was there," I said as I emptied out the goods cached in my closet. "At the reunion. I didn't think he would be, but he was. We met for coffee the next day and we talked and—and he asked me to go on a trip with him out west to visit his mother and pretend to be his fiancée."

Jamie blinked a few times and then shrugged as if this wasn't unusual at all. "And you said yes."

"I did, because I've broken all my promises to him in the past and this is the one thing I can do. But now I think I've made a huge mistake," I said, the words running together. "More like a series of mistakes."

"Here's what I need you to do. Give me the minute-by-minute recap of this reunion. What was said, how it was said. Full dramatic reenactment." She rolled her hand as she chomped on the nuts. "Walk me through it and I'll decide if mistakes were made."

I continued organizing the closet as I went back to the tent on the tennis courts, with the wine down my dress and the blueberry feta crostini I hated. To the dance floor and the bathroom, and the next day at Semantic and the long drive back to Boston.

I didn't love voicing the tragic comedy vibes of this, especially with me playing the part of the tragedy, but I trusted Jamie enough to tell her the whole, horrible truth.

"Wait, wait, wait," she said. "Wait a minute. Just wait. You're telling me his mother is deathbed-dying and she commands him to get his single-dad shit in order with you and he says, 'Wedding bells ring in the morning.'"

I still wasn't sure I understood why he'd offer up such a thing, even on the verge of losing his mother. Maybe I didn't have enough experience with deathbeds. I could see him pacifying her with some vague promises but an engagement seemed like a hard stretch. "Basically, yeah."

"Oh my stars and garters," she murmured.

"But the joke's on him because she made a full recovery," I continued. "I mean, the 'healthy as a horse, jumping jacks up and down the hospital halls, picking up her life and moving to Sedona with her bestie' kind of recovery."

"That boy put himself in a world of hurt, didn't he? The holy spirits must've heard him rolling those dice and said, 'Bet.'" She cackled as she scooped up another handful of almonds. "What's his endgame? Is he going to need you to marry him and live happily ever after to stick this lie to the wall?"

"No. We'll go to Arizona and do that thing and then be done with each other. Sometime around the end of the summer, he'll tell his mother it ended."

Jamie brushed salt from her fingertips. "Yeah, I don't need a crystal ball to tell you that's not happening. I've been down this path before and I can promise you it never ends that way."

I stared at her as she snatched a stale box of cheese crackers off my desk. "Except that's exactly what will happen. We've agreed." It sounded like I was trying to double underline my words. "I'm helping him and finally getting some closure after all these years."

"Sure you are."

"What?" I peered at her. "What does that mean?"

"It means I'd really appreciate daily updates. Hourly, if you can manage," she replied. "It also means you should splurge on some new bras and undies for this trip. Cover those bases."

"We're not— I'm not—no. No. That's not what's happening here."

"Of course not," she drawled.

"He has no interest in me anymore," I said, and I could hear myself fraying. Could feel where he'd held me on the dance floor, in the bathroom. The way he'd stared at me across the café table, a picture of disinterest until it came time to launch this wild setup. "That's over. It's done. And he's not looking for anything. He's busy with his son and that's not where it's going with us."

"Yeah, you're probably right," she said, elbow-deep in the box of cheese crackers. "Fuck that guy."

I went to respond but stopped myself. Closed my mouth. Frowned at her. "You say that like it's a suggestion, not an insult. It was 'fuck that guy—question mark' and not 'fuck that guy—period, end of crude, declarative statement.'" I blinked a couple hundred times. "You meant it in a derogatory sense, right?"

"Go with your gut. You already know which one is right. But I hear condoms are north of ninety-five percent effective and no one's ever sad about packing extra lube."

"I'm posing as a fraudulent future daughter-in-law and stomping all over a nice woman's dying wish. Condoms are the last thing I'm going to need. We fly out in a few days and there's a greater than zero chance this is going to blow up in our faces," I said. "All I need to know is whether I'm making a huge mistake. Should I back out?"

She downed a handful of cheesy dust. "What's this boy's name? You haven't mentioned it yet."

"Jude," I replied. It was nice saying it out loud after going all those years only hearing it in my head.

"Heavens help us." Jamie set down the box, her mouth round and eyes wide. "I've never once seen that smile from you. You just turned into a bright, shining sunbeam." She reached for me, closing her cheesy-dust-free hand around my forearm and giving me a meaningful shake. "You still have feelings for him. Big feelings. *Serious* feelings."

"That's not it." I said this and I meant it…but I also knew seeing Jude made me feel like I was waking up from a long, dreamless sleep. He forced me to the edge of my limits and pushed me to say exactly what I was thinking, even when I took aim at him. There were no comfort zones when he was around, no boundaries to speak of, and something about that was outrageously freeing.

It also felt like he pushed me off a new cliff every five minutes —and wasn't that fitting for such an overgrown super-specimen of a man? With his commanding personality that'd never once been compared to an antacid, and his well-fucked hair.

I really had to stop thinking about that last one.

Jamie balled up the empty cracker bag and started ripping the box to shreds. "If it's not big feely feels, what is it?"

After a gaping pause where I overthought my entire inner world, I finally said, "We have a past but not a future."

She nodded. "What if things change? What if he says—"

"They won't."

"Hypothetically speaking," she said, "would you be open to a future?"

I crossed my arms, protecting the darkest of the bruises no one could see, and shook my head. "It's just for the summer. Then, it will be over."

chapter ten

Audrey

Today's vocabulary word: notions

I STARED INTO MY CLOSET, WAITING FOR IT TO SOLVE ALL MY problems, but it only invented more. I didn't have the wardrobe for a convincing fake engagement.

Not helping: my mother, yammering on about my flaws and failings while I tried to find the right look for conning my old boyfriend's sweet mother.

"I'm making a simple request, Audrey. I don't know what's so difficult about that."

My mother was absolutely livid that I'd ditched Brecken, the guy she'd so artfully orchestrated for me to meet after the Aldyn Thorpe reunion and who I'd bailed on to see Jude. Though it was worth noting that *livid* for my mother took the form of stiffly worded statements and the kind of long, frigid pauses that could freeze your fingertips off.

I could hear her pacing in the kitchen in their Hamptons cottage —which was not a cottage at all but a garish estate filled to the brim with horrible antique reproductions. Her designer slides clacked against the stone floors as she rattled off a list of all the ways I was selfish and impractical, forever rejecting the guidance my parents offered.

It amused me to no end—in *what the hell is my life* and *everyone here needs massive amounts of therapy* ways—that I continued to be the most disappointing black sheep in the family pasture. It didn't matter that I had a comfortable home and friends and a good career. That my digestive system wasn't trying to kill me and I didn't feel like a living ghost anymore. That I was content with the cozy life I'd cobbled together for myself. That, by all relevant standards, I was doing okay.

Normal parents would be thrilled. My parents…were not.

For reasons that only made sense in my parents' warped worldview, a thirty-five-year-old divorced daughter who wasn't closing in on a new husband was a plague on the house. Being single at my age just begged too many questions for their comfort. It would've been so much easier on them if I'd fall in line and marry another subhuman demon spawn who fed on souls and private equity buyouts.

They missed the days of my blind obedience more than anyone, but what they really missed was the fear. There'd been a time when they could truly scare me into compliance.

There wasn't much of that left in me anymore.

"It's not a good look," she went on. "Men like Brecken Wilhamsen do not wait around. Certainly not for divorcées."

She said *divorcées* like *sociopaths who couldn't be left alone with the family pet.* It was fitting as far as her faux-righteous bizarro world went.

After my father's tenure in the attorney general's office, he took over a think tank that concerned itself with aggressively rigid notions of family values and maintaining American traditions. The gig came with buckets of money and a long line of wealthy, powerful people tripping over themselves to curry favor or gain connections.

It also came with a ruthless yet skin-deep commitment to those wind sock values and traditions. Two-dimensional portraits of an idea of perfection.

"I'm not sure why my look is a problem since it's just a friendly lunch," I said. "It's not like I'm trying to make something happen with him."

"You might not be but I am!" she whisper-yelled.

I tuned out the rest of her tirade while I pulled items from my closet for Arizona. That breathless urgency about lunches and social obligations and the things people were saying about us just didn't matter to me anymore. I wasn't sure it'd ever truly mattered but I used to be able to play along well enough to escape my mother's notice.

This time, though, instead of delivering her greatest hits album — "Don't you understand I'm only trying to protect you?" and "Is it that hard to do this one thing for me while I'm still alive?" and "Can't you see how delightful Cassidy's life is with Holter? You could have the same thing if you tried a little harder" —she breezed right into announcing she'd already made plans for another visit with Brecken for next week. Right in the middle of my fake engagement.

"Wait just a second," I said. "I'm not available for that."

"I believe you are," she shot back. Translation: *You will make yourself available or you'll face the consequences.*

"No, I have plans with friends." Not strictly accurate but she'd have to torture the truth out of me. If ever there were two things that didn't go together, it was Jude and my parents. "Look, Mom, I don't want you sending me on pseudo-dates."

"I'll move it to the next day if you're suddenly so busy."

"I am unavailable," I said, overenunciating every word. "And more importantly, I don't want to be set up with these random guys."

My mother did not appreciate that. She huffed and sniffed and slammed a few cabinets—a real feat considering she had premium, quiet-close doors.

"You need to get serious about where your life is going," she said. "You've had your fun as a single girl. You've floated along with this experiment in independence for several years and that's more than enough. It's obvious to me that you won't do what's in your best interest, so, once again, I'll do it for you."

I held my boundaries quietly. "I don't think that's necessary."

"If you had any idea what was necessary, you would've stayed with Christopher!"

Okay, maybe this boundary would need to be a little louder. "With the man who emotionally abused me for six straight years? Staying with him wouldn't have helped anything."

"You say that like he locked you in a dungeon and threw away the key." She slammed another door as if I was the one minimizing her experiences. As far as she was concerned, my divorce *was* her trauma. It was something I'd done to her, to *the family*. "It's merely a lunch date, Audrey. Perhaps it will be a match, perhaps it won't. All I'm asking is for you to be polite and meet the gentleman. There's no need for you to go into one of your fits about it."

I rubbed my forehead. My *fits* were any response that wasn't in complete, unflinching compliance with my parents' directives. If I so much as sighed, she flagged it as hysteria. A flat "no" might as well be a riot in the streets. There were times when I wondered if she considered emotional repression our family's greatest asset.

Behind the shady money and property and questionable political connections, of course.

"I'll make the arrangements and send you the information," she continued, picking up where she'd left off.

I sank onto my bed, two of the dresses I had in mind for this fake-engagement party folded over my arm. I didn't say anything. I didn't know what I could say that she'd hear at this point. Silence was the only weapon worth a damn.

My parents armed themselves to the teeth with guilt and money. If ever one didn't work, the other always paved the way. These days, the money didn't matter to me. Threats of cutting me off held no water when I hadn't taken anything from them in years. The guilt, though, that one still hit hard. Especially when mixed with a lethal amount of shame. But even when I gave in to their demands now, I knew I wasn't beholden to them. I knew I could walk away at any time and return to the small, safe life I'd built for myself. I'd agonize and curl into myself but I knew how to leave.

I hadn't learned how to do that when I was eighteen and they ripped apart my entire world. I knew better now.

"And please wear something flattering," she continued. "I'll have a few pieces sent over if you can't find anything. No more of these dowdy teacher clothes, please. They're completely shapeless. You look like a corn cob."

But this silence wasn't surrender, not really. It was strategic: say little, let her talk herself out, and keep myself squarely out of reach. I couldn't dismantle every little bomb she threw my way so I'd wait until she was finished and cut the one wire that would end it all.

Or, end enough of it.

"Please understand me when I say you don't need to send information or clothes because I won't be meeting up with Brecken next week," I said, steeling my tone as if I was speaking to one of my most defiant students. "If you make a date for me, I need you to know I won't be there. I have to imagine it'll be very embarrassing for you."

"It's just a lunch, Audrey," she said with a gusty sigh. "Don't you see how good this could be for you?"

She went on but my thoughts were already drifting, groping for the mental checklist I'd been building: what to pack for Arizona, how to act around my old boyfriend-slash-new fake fiancé, everything we needed to hammer out before visiting Jude's mother.

Research told me that nights in the high desert could be cool, so I'd need a sweater or two. Jeans if I had space to spare. I didn't know how far I was supposed to lean into the bride aesthetic but I did have a couple white, summery dresses that were cute.

The clothes I could handle. It was the backstory that was a nightmare.

I knew only the broadest strokes of the stories he'd told his mother. I still didn't know who Jude needed me to be on this trip—the Audrey he'd loved once upon a time or the newer edition he barely met last weekend? I tried to mentally script out answers to questions I couldn't possibly anticipate yet I knew it wouldn't matter. For every scenario I could imagine, there'd be a dozen others lying in wait. I'd drive myself to distraction if I kept this up.

I'd absolutely keep this up.

"Mom, listen," I said, suddenly exhausted. "I have to go. As a reminder, I won't be joining Brecken for lunch or anything else next week. Understood?"

She slammed another cabinet. "I don't understand how I raised such an impertinent child."

I looked at the dresses on my arm. The ones I'd wear to play Jude's make-believe bride—and to be the fire-breather he allowed me to be. "Yeah. It's a mystery," I said.

chapter eleven

Jude

Today's vocabulary word: resigned

AUDREY BAKED SCONES.

She offered me one in the early morning cab to the airport, and when I didn't immediately respond, she rattled off a list of the ingredients and presented an overview of the merits of oat flour.

I didn't have a single reason to pass on a homemade scone but I did, and I was enough of a dick about it that she put the container away and stared out the window the rest of the ride.

Yeah, I was taking to this fiancée thing real well.

It didn't get much better at the airport. Our conversation consisted of *thanks* when I grabbed her bag out of the back of the car and then *there's the gate*. We kept our rolling luggage positioned between us like a demilitarized zone with snipers on the roof.

I figured it was really fucking early and travel was a hassle and I'd been a dick about the scones. That was all. None of this was a sign that I'd made a terrible mistake in putting her up to this and we'd live to regret everything.

But I needed her to stop being so goddamn polite. Stop thanking me for handing her a damn bin in the security line and waiting while she filled her water bottle and pointing out some empty seats near the gate. Stop shifting her body away from mine when she crossed her legs and stop quietly reading her book like we were strangers who happened to be stuck waiting at the same gate. I just wanted her to fucking stop it all.

I didn't want this cool, smoothed-down—*smothered*—version of her. I wanted the truth, the unpolished, imperfect honesty of hers that she liked to pretend didn't rumble right under the surface.

She could hack me to pieces with an axe and I'd prefer it. And I knew I couldn't take a whole week with her like this. I didn't trust myself to last the hour.

Since the one thing that always caught the attention of the little demon hiding behind the porcelain doll façade was picking a fight, I leaned forward, my elbows on my thighs. "Hey. Listen," I said, the words razor-sharp. "This isn't going to work if—"

"Announcement in the terminal," a robotic voice called. "Please be aware all flights are grounded until further notice due to air traffic control communication outages along the East Coast."

After a beat of silence, the terminal exploded into chaos. People rushing the gate agents, garbled announcements reiterating that we weren't going anywhere anytime soon, everyone talking at once.

Well, fuck.

Audrey closed her book, a finger holding her place, and turned to me. "It sounds like you're right." She glanced at the passengers swarming around the gate agents and the long lines of people who didn't have the stomach for this shit show and were exiting the terminal. "This *isn't* going to work."

I held up a hand. Usually, I liked it when she slapped me with my own words but all I felt now was panic. She could be as polite and porcelain as she wanted as long as we were airborne before the end of the day. "Let's give it a couple of hours."

She arched a pale brow. "Your fix-it abilities now include air traffic control systems?"

"Just give it some time. I'm sure this will all blow over and we'll be on our way soon enough. These things happen all the time."

They did not happen all the time and we both knew that.

With a resigned sigh, she said, "Okay. We'll give it a few hours."

chapter twelve

Jude

Today's vocabulary word: subtext

IT DIDN'T BLOW OVER.

The outage gridlocked everything everywhere for several hours. Gate desks were shut down and agents went into hiding while the stranded contemplated their options. More than half of all flights were canceled and all the others were substantially delayed. Commercial airplanes weren't my niche but I knew enough people in the industry to find out which regions were hardest hit and when fixes might be in place.

By some miracle, Boston came back online right around the time Audrey started giving me pointed stares between the loops she walked from one end of the terminal to the other.

I did everything I could to get us on a flight to Salt Lake City since the earliest availability for Phoenix wasn't for two days. It meant a long drive down to Sedona, but the only other options were Boise or Boulder. I had a lot of tricks up my sleeve but convincing Audrey to spend a minimum of thirteen hours in a car with me after this hellish start wasn't one of them. This would work. It had to work.

Except the flight to Salt Lake was delayed with an aircraft issue and we'd need to wait for another plane—which was also delayed.

When that announcement came through, Audrey crossed her arms over her chest and flicked a glance at me. Her teeth pressed into her bottom lip the way she did when she was deciding what to say. I could see her commitment to this experiment flagging. One more delay, one more setback, and she'd be on her way to that sweet little house outside the city in no time at all. She'd say something gentle like it wasn't meant to be. That the universe was sending us a sign by taking down a national air control network and then fucking up every available plane.

And maybe this was a sign. A huge, blinking sign reminding me that I was making irreversible mistakes. But the universe liked fucking with me. It was a good thing I'd learned how to fuck right back.

"It's time for lunch. We should find something to eat," I said, grabbing the handle of her bag and leading her toward the string of restaurants at the head of the terminal. "What are you in the mood for? We've got a brewery, burgers, seafood, and something with an artsy logo I can't read from here."

"Artsy logo, every time," she murmured. "But I can take my—"

She reached for the rolling case but I shifted it to my other hand. "I got it. Let's go."

We were seated at a quiet table deep in the restaurant, far from the terminal noise.

"It's nice to sit down and breathe," she said, spreading a napkin over her lap. "Without all that"—she waved a hand to the terminal, shuddering—"drama."

"If it matters, I travel at least once a month and this is the most drama I've seen in years."

"I could never do that," she said. "Too much stress."

I watched as she sipped her water and straightened the silver-ware before turning to the menu. Her expression shifted with each item she read. Eyes brightening, tiny smiles, little nods, quick shakes of her head. Studying her like this scratched an itch in me I didn't entirely understand. I had a hard time moving on from simply drinking her in.

"After a while, I started thinking of it as part of the commute," I said. "I hardly notice it anymore. And I have millions of frequent flier miles."

She spared me a glance before returning to the menu. "I would think it would be difficult to travel that much with a small child at home."

"It is," I agreed. "But being based in Virginia now means most of my travel is no more than a train ride away, and longer trips I'm usually able to hold for when Percy's with his grandmother. If all else fails, the nanny doesn't mind staying the night."

"The nanny," Audrey murmured. "Why didn't you hire her for this adventure? I have to imagine it would've been much simpler."

I stared at the spill of pale blonde hair over her shoulder. I still wasn't used to seeing it down but I liked it. It felt more like her than the ballerina bun ever had. "Wayne's been a lifesaver for us, but I don't think he'd go for that."

"Wayne," she repeated.

I'd take another hellish day of flight delays just to watch her gulp down the realization that Wayne wasn't some hot twenty-something au pair trying to slide into the mom spot but a retired firefighter in his fifties who handled my kid's attitude like no other and had a top secret pancake recipe that could open some doors in the world peace process.

"More importantly," I went on, "he's already off on a camping trip across the Canadian provinces with his partner, so he's not available."

"Well." She gave a short, high hum, a sound I recognized as the placeholder for everything she wanted to say but swallowed down instead. That single syllable was the cork on a pricey bottle of champagne one hard shake away from exploding. "It's good you have someone you can trust with Percy."

Before I could stop myself, a bitter laugh snapped out of me. "Wasn't always like that. I'll spare you the long-form account of our history with caretakers, but suffice it to say, not everyone is built to work with kids who have different needs."

Audrey started to respond but stopped herself when the server appeared. She ordered a rice bowl, holding half the ingredients listed on the menu, and I went with a burger. Airport restaurants could always be counted on to get a burger close enough to right.

"And a beer," I added. "Whatever's in season and on tap." To Audrey's arched brow, I held up my hands. "After the morning we've had?"

She considered this a moment before asking, "Do you have any hard cider?" The server rattled off five different options. "I'll try the Woodchuck. Thank you."

When we were alone again, Audrey ducked away from my attention and checked her phone. I did the same and found seventeen texts from my mother. It was clear she'd heard about the outage and mass cancellations, and was now thinking out loud as she rescheduled her dinner party plans for this evening. There were a few from Percy too, though they fell into the *General Complaints about Grandma's Food* category. I knew for a fact he had enough toaster waffles and chocolate hazelnut butter to survive a year with Brenda, so I wasn't going to stress over that one.

Our drinks arrived and Audrey pulled hers close, circling her hands around the glass as she stared at the tabletop. A moment passed before she said, "You're right about not everyone being built for kids who require something different from us. My student teaching supervisor was amazing like that. Everyone loved Mrs. Carroll. Everyone wanted to be in her class. Watching her in action was like—well, all I could think when I observed her was that I'd feel pretty happy about my teaching if I was half as good as her."

I sipped my beer and nodded. My only goal was to keep her talking and I'd probably fuck that up if I opened my mouth.

"The thing that made her really incredible was that she could adapt to any kid's needs in the moment. It didn't matter what the problem was because there was always a different way of reaching the endpoint." She glanced up at me. "It basically took all the things I'd learned in my elementary ed program about rigid performance goals and demonstration of mastery, and knocked it over." A shy smile pulled at the corner of her mouth. "And I liked that a lot."

"How'd you make your way into teaching?"

She leaned back against the booth, history rippling across her expression. "There came a point when I needed to make some changes," she said, her words measured.

When her marriage ended, she meant. I didn't push it because I knew she was one minor inconvenience away from telling me to have a nice life. But the subtext was clear and I was dying to suck the juice from every ounce of that story.

"I could've stayed at the ballet, but leaving San Diego was one of those changes I had to make. There was nothing left for me there —or anywhere in California," she added. "I wish I had a meaningful story about becoming inspired to shape young minds or make a difference. Most of my friends have stories like that. But I just read a book where the protagonist was an elementary school teacher and it struck me that it was something I could do. Maybe even do well." She laughed. "Looking back on it, I realize it wasn't a very accurate portrayal of teaching."

"But you're good at it."

She waved me off, a craggy little grin on her face. "Eh, it depends on the day—and the phase of the moon." At my confused *huh?* she added, "Kids are like baby werewolves. The full moons do a number on them. Trust me on this."

She finally took a sip of her cider, and I didn't know why I cared but I watched, waiting for her reaction. Didn't bother breathing for a minute. "All right?" I asked when she set the glass down.

"Mmm. Yeah." She nodded at the glass. "I'm not good at ordering. My friend Jamie is usually the one to mix the drinks and tell me what I'll like. I always forget."

"Is she the one getting married?"

"Oh, no," she said, laughing. "Jamie's never getting married. It's Emme's wedding coming up. Or, her second wedding. They eloped last spring and now they're having the big party." She smoothed her napkin a few times, her focus trained on her lap. "The wedding is being held at this beautiful tulip farm in Rhode Island. My friend Shay—she used to teach kindergarten down the hall from me—she and her husband own the farm. It's stunning. I love it there. Sometimes I think about moving there."

The food arrived and I stalled with my beer as Audrey picked at the bowl like she expected to find a severed finger in there. I couldn't tell if she didn't trust airport kitchens or had stopped trusting food in general at some point. It made zero sense but clearly mattered to her—and now it mattered to me too. More than it should've, perhaps, but I'd never been good at limiting myself when it came to Audrey.

She took one delicate bite, chewed thoughtfully, then relaxed against the booth as if she'd won this battle. That little flicker of relief in her expression stuck with me as I turned my attention to the burger waiting on my plate.

"Is Emme a teacher too?" I asked between bites.

She went for another sip of the cider and said, "Yeah, she teaches second grade. Jamie's in first. Grace used to teach third grade with us but she moved to a school with a better commute." She leaned in, her cheeks pink as a devious smile stretched across her face. The cider was a good call. "We tried *all year* to gather up the new kindergarten and third-grade people for lunch but Jamie says we're too much for them."

"Nothing about that surprises me."

"It should! Jamie might be a handful and Emme has some big opinions, but I bring baked goods at least three days a week. There's nothing overwhelming about someone handing out muffins and brookies."

I glanced at the thin gold chains that circled her neck, the baggy cardigan she wore over a t-shirt with fine navy stripes. All very simple, but when paired with that cornsilk hair, cheekbones like she'd been chiseled from raw stone, and big hazel eyes, she was the source of all light in the room. And she still didn't know it.

"Give yourself a little more credit," I said.

"For what?"

I pointed a french fry at her. "Have you met yourself? You're intimidating as fuck."

"That is a wild exaggeration," she said primly.

I grabbed my phone and toggled to the calendar app. "When is this wedding again? I need to meet these women. See what happens when you join forces and multiply your powers. That might explain all those small earthquakes on the Eastern Seaboard recently."

"You should know it's a very exclusive guest list."

"If there's one thing I'm good at, it's showing up where I don't belong."

Audrey met my gaze, her eyes bright and warm like she could spar with me all day. Like she finally remembered that we knew how to do this. I found myself leaning forward, hoarding every last piece of her I could get because I knew I'd need them when this ended and all I had left were the memories.

"Trust me, I know all about that," she said.

Pressure rose in my chest again. Probably inhaled that burger a little too fast. I dragged in a breath but it didn't help.

"Tell me about Jamie," I said. "What kind of trouble could a first-grade teacher be? Really, Saunders, I don't know how you expect me to buy that."

Audrey ducked her head as she laughed, her napkin pressed to her mouth. When she stopped, when she dropped the napkin to her lap, I found myself swallowed whole by a smile that was so full of love and adoration and devotion that I had to clear my throat and look away. It hurt to see that radiating out of her and know it'd never be for me.

The pressure compounded in my chest as Audrey told me about Jamie and Emme, Grace and Shay. She spoke in careful sidesteps where every reference to her cross-country move from San Diego and her teacher training program in Boston existed without mention of her ex, her divorce, or her family. There was a great, dark canyon between the day I walked away from her in that church and when she touched down in Boston years later. Cutting such wide margins around the past only made me hungrier for the details.

Tell me, honey. Tell me everything.

She didn't have to say it but it was obvious these women had stood by while she'd built this new version of herself brick by brick. My throat ached a bit when she talked about them plucking her out of her classroom and folding her into their group.

She wasn't one for collecting people in her life. She had to be collected, scooped up by the relentless ones who refused to let her drift on the sidelines.

There'd been a time when I was the one collecting her. I just didn't know if I could do it again.

chapter thirteen

Jude

Today's vocabulary word: altitude

It was almost four in the afternoon when the flight to Salt Lake finally boarded.

We'd talked through a few more rounds of drinks and then a plate of nachos built to Audrey's custom specifications, and I knew everything there was to know about her school, her friends, and their significant others.

Good people, if not a little chaotic where it came to love and relationships—though I wasn't sure I was free to throw those stones at the moment.

The flight was packed and everyone involved was already fried. Kids were crying. The plane smelled like old olives. The overhead bins were stuffed with things that belonged under the seat. The crew looked like they were ready to strangle complainers with an inflatable life vest.

None of it bothered me. Audrey was seated beside me, her book in her lap and her cheeks still rosy from the drinks and the stories, and we had the next five and a half hours ahead of us to talk about every little thing in her life. If I played this right, my mother might actually believe we were engaged.

I didn't let myself register the way her elbow brushed my arm when she shifted. I knew I'd feel the press of her hip against me if I let my legs spread even a few inches. Didn't think about it at all.

"Uh, excuse me. Hello. Hi there." We glanced over to find a man smiling at us from the aisle. "I'm traveling with my family today and we're thankful to be on our way but we're scattered all over the plane." He motioned to a pair of kids next to him who didn't look much older than Percy. A woman sat perched on the edge of the seat across from us, bouncing a toddler on her lap as she watched. "We were able to cobble together a few seats over here but I was wondering if one of y'all might be willing to trade with me so my wife isn't all on her own with these little monsters."

Before I could process the request, Audrey shot up and stepped into the aisle, saying, "Oh my goodness, of course. You can have mine and I'll move."

I stood but the only thing I could manage to get out was "But—"

Ignoring me, the guy pressed a hand to his chest and said to Audrey, "You don't know how much I appreciate this."

"No worries," she replied, pulling her carry-on out from underneath the seat. "I don't mind at all. It's been such a hectic day for everyone." She glanced at me as she stepped into the aisle. "I'll see you when we land."

I nodded, still reeling from the newest change of plans. "Yeah," I managed. "I'll wait outside the gate." She smiled, her arms wrapped around her bag and her finger still wedged between the pages of her book. For no good reason at all, I added, "Let me know if you need anything."

She gave a quiet laugh that seemed to say *What would I need you for?* and then, "I'm sure I'll be all right."

I watched her pick her way to her new seat and kept staring even when the only thing I could see was the golden crown of her head. I wasn't sure what I hoped to accomplish but I edged into the aisle. There was a chance I'd be able to barter myself into a seat closer to Audrey. It was possible. Maybe not realistic or even smart but still possible.

But maybe it was better to let her go. Give her space. Remind myself how to function around her—and how to shield myself from that gravity of hers. This journey hadn't even started and I was already drunk off her smiles.

A flight attendant stopped in front of me, her hands fisted on her hips. "Sir, I need you to take your seat right away."

"Yeah," I said with one last glance toward Audrey. She wasn't looking for me and that told me everything I needed to know. "Sorry for the disruption."

When I dropped into my seat, my new companion shoved his hand toward me, saying, "Clint. Thanks again for helping us out."

"Hey." I shook his hand but I didn't like it. I wanted to glare at him for the next five hours. I rubbed my forehead until new grooves formed in my skin instead.

The flight seemed ridiculously long. The hours stretched out every second into thin eternities just to fuck with me. The work I should've tackled sat unopened, my laptop screen going dark only for me to swipe the touchpad every few minutes and wake it up again. Engine test data, design analysis, even new models—things that usually caught my attention and swallowed me whole—blurred after a minute.

I told myself to stop thinking about her. There was no point in obsessing. I'd learned that the hard way—and then learned it a few more times.

But that didn't drive her out of my head. The whole damn plane seemed to vibrate with her presence. Every attempt to concentrate spiraled into an endless mental loop of her voice, her hair falling over her shoulder, her fingers tracing the edge of her glass.

By the time we hit cruising altitude, I'd already turned the same thought over a hundred different ways: I was in so much fucking trouble.

chapter fourteen

Audrey

Today's vocabulary word: halfway

BY THE TIME WE LANDED IN SALT LAKE CITY, I WAS HOT TRASH. Every muscle held a grudge after nearly six hours crammed between a knitter with stabby elbows and someone who'd claimed the armrest and at least twenty percent of the real estate around it, not to mention the very robust perfume situation behind me. Everything was wrinkled and slightly damp from the recycled air and clammy seat. Hot, hot trash.

The hard cider hadn't done me any favors either. My brain felt like it was the wrong size for my skull. My belly was annoyed with me even though I usually tolerated cider pretty well and hadn't eaten anything that should've caused a flare. *Should've* being the operative word here. There was nothing more whimsical than an irritable gut, forever selecting the worst times to reject foods that'd long been proven safe and causing all kinds of merry havoc.

I'd kept watch for an opening to grab my meds and a peppermint tea bag from my carry-on without agitating my seatmates, but it never came. The one time I attempted to inch the bag into reach with my feet, the armrest imperialist bumped my knee which sent me into the knitter, who *accidentally* jabbed me in the side with the butt of her needle. Her apology sounded a lot like a ruler slap to the wrist. No tea for me.

All I did was sit and read—and fend off land wars—but by the end of the flight, I was exhausted like I'd barely finished a wilderness survival race. I needed a hot shower, a soft bed with silky sheets, and forty-eight hours to reincarnate.

I would not be getting that shower. Or the bed. Or any sleep at all.

"What do you mean, we're driving to Sedona *tonight*?" I ask-shrieked as Jude led me toward the rental car center.

All I'd wanted when I'd stepped off the jetway and into the terminal was a moment alone in a non-aircraft bathroom, hot water for my tea, and some eye contact with the knitter to give her a solid teacher stare.

I'd already doled out justice to the armrest guy. So sad how he was standing too close to me in the aisle to notice when I shouldered my bag and nailed him in the junk with it.

But I had bigger problems on my hands now. Namely, my fake fiancé's insistence on keeping these good times going with eight hours of driving through the night.

"Hotels are going to be packed with all these canceled flights," he said over his shoulder. "No point wasting time when we could hit the road now."

"Oh, I don't know, how about getting some rest?" I asked. "We've been awake for almost twenty hours now. There's a point in sleeping."

He swept a quick glance over me. "I'm good." Reaching for my rolling bag, he added, "You can sleep. I'll drive."

I yanked the bag behind me. "I know you want to get there as soon as possible but I don't think driving on unfamiliar roads at midnight is the best idea."

"They're not unfamiliar to me."

Right, because Jude knew *all* the roads. As men always did.

He pried my fingers from the bag's handle. "Let's go."

"I'm getting some tea first," I said to his back.

Without glancing back at me, he motioned to the shuttered storefronts throughout the terminal. "We'll stop after we pick up the car."

I glared after him as he continued following signs for the rental car facility. At the black t-shirt that stretched taut across his shoulders and hugged his biceps in a way that would've been gratuitous if it'd been intentional. I didn't think it was. At the jeans he'd probably owned for at least a decade. At the easy, smug way he maneuvered our bags *with one hand.* I would've pulled off to the side twice by now to straighten out the wheels and cry while people shot annoyed looks at me.

"Let's go, Saunders," he called.

Despite the fact that I absolutely hated making a scene and drawing attention to myself in public places, I shouted back, "It's not like you're going to leave me here. I'm kind of important to this operation, in case you've forgotten."

He stopped then and shifted to face me, caring nothing for all the other weary travelers forced to stream around him. A few of them pinged glances between us but most were just as tired, wrinkled, and pouty as I was. They didn't care.

I stared at him for a minute, my chin tipped up and my arms crossed over my chest. I didn't know which point I was trying to prove with this but I was committed. Not backing down now. I'd live the rest of my days in this terminal if I had to.

But then he beckoned me, his gaze hard, his tone low as he said, "Come here."

And I went. Jude met me halfway, a scowl carved into his face.

He studied me with a slow sweep. When he finally met my eyes, he brushed a ratty strand of hair off my forehead and reached for the bag on my shoulder. "Give me this."

I pulled back. "I can handle it by my—"

He closed the distance between us, slipping his fingers under the strap. Against my shoulder. "And you should know I haven't forgotten a fucking thing."

He dropped a hand to my lower back and steered me forward, and I didn't say another word.

I didn't know what that said about me. Or Jude. Or any of this.

chapter fifteen

Audrey

Today's vocabulary word: appearances

IT SURPRISED ME NOT AT ALL THAT THIS MIDNIGHT ROAD TRIP WENT off the rails almost immediately.

The car Jude had reserved before we departed from Boston was no longer available and it was obvious he wasn't a fan of the alternative provided. Engine guys. A very particular lot. It was always something with them.

Road construction brought all traffic around the airport to a standstill. When we were finally free of that, we realized the entire city was closed for the night.

After getting my tea fix and foraging for a hodgepodge of goods at a truck stop an hour outside of Salt Lake, we were on the road again. I pressed my palms to the paper cup and inhaled the minty steam. Sometimes that was enough—or all I could manage. It was exactly what I needed tonight.

The tea settled my stomach and I was feeling better now that I had the air conditioner blowing and the seat warmers switched on.

They did not, in fact, cancel each other out. It helped that Jude stayed quiet, sipping his iced coffee and occasionally glaring at the navigation screen while we ate up miles of dark highway.

I'd always imagined that spending time with Jude again would mean immediately falling into deep, earnest conversations where we'd unearth every sad and broken truth we'd carried around all these years. We'd confess everything—but the more I thought about it, I wasn't sure I knew what *everything* was anymore. And I didn't know why my daydreams kept missing the mark.

All I knew was that this stilted new reality of ours would crack before the end of the week. If nothing else, I'd crack. Cracking under pressure was one of my specialties. And I guessed that would make it easier to call off this fake wedding.

Another hour or two into the drive, I sensed Jude looking at me. I was half asleep—the best I could manage in a car—with a truck stop hoodie draped over my legs like a blanket and my arms tucked inside my shirt. I blinked when he cleared his throat. My eyes felt sunburned and the taste of perfume stuck to the back of my throat.

"Do you have any more of those scones?"

I blinked a few more times before I realized he was wearing glasses. Simple, wire-rimmed frames that glinted in the passing light. I dug through my memories, pressing into the moments when I'd been too much of a whiny toddler to notice anything but my exhaustion and trying to find those glasses hiding in there all this time. I didn't come up with anything. It was just like Jude to spice up his standard uniform of denim and black with something so casually academic.

He'd always been a closeted nerd, after all.

My voice sounded like crushed ice when I said, "Yeah. I'll grab the scones."

But in my new fixation on those glasses, I forgot I'd swaddled myself. After a minute of wrestling my way out of this homemade straitjacket and remembering how to work my limbs, I dug the container from the bottom of my bag.

"Shit," he muttered.

I glanced up to find road crews and flashing lights ahead. Signs announced construction and detours to come. "Is that the way we're supposed to go?" I asked. Jude nodded, an impatient noise rattling in the back of his throat. "Is it going to take much longer?"

He tapped the navigation system and groaned when the map rerouted. "That's just wrong," he grumbled. Our arrival time flipped from nine in the morning to shortly before noon. "For fuck's sake. This has us going all the way down the 15 and cutting around Vegas."

"That seems like a big detour," I said as I popped open each side of the container. "Like, into a whole other state. And the states are big out here. We're not talking about cutting through Rhode Island to get to Connecticut."

"Yeah. We're *not* going that way. We'll take the old country highways and pick up Highway 89 past the construction."

I glanced at the narrow road ahead of us. "You're telling me *this* isn't the old country highway?" When his only response was a sharp side-eye, I decided to revisit the obvious. "You're sure you don't want to find somewhere to stop? Even for a few hours?"

He rubbed the bridge of his nose, pushing the glasses up to his forehead. There were greater matters at hand, but I had so many questions about these glasses. I couldn't wait for the moment when he glared at me over the rims. Because he would, and it'd scratch some kind of nostalgic itch I didn't know I had. I really needed Jamie to explain to me what was happening here.

She'd say something about uncovering my kinks and that it was about damn time I got around to it.

"My mother has planned this week down to the hour. We've already missed one dinner party and now we're going to miss the red rock Jeep tour she booked for tomorrow. Today. Whenever the fuck."

"I get that," I said carefully. "But it's really going to mess with the schedule if we veer off the road and die in a ditch."

He exhaled for an entire minute. "We're not dying in a ditch tonight. I've driven from the naval air station in northern Nevada to my mom's place. Twice. I know these roads, even in the dark, and the conditions are good."

"Okay, yes, I appreciate the optimism, but you should know I'm halfway through a couple of Netflix series that I hate. If I die before finding out how they end, I'm going to haunt you forever."

He laughed and rattled the ice in his coffee cup. "I wouldn't mind that. Might be nice to see you do the chasing for once."

I couldn't decide if that was a joke or a jab or something else altogether. I just knew it landed in a tender place that made my belly swoop. I held out the scones. "A few of them fell apart but those two on top are in good shape."

Jude took one that'd broken and ate it in two bites. He went for another piece, humming as he chewed. "These are incredible."

There was a note of admiration in his voice I hadn't expected. I hadn't let it bother me that he'd passed on the scones yesterday morning. Not everyone favored scones. Some didn't fully understand where they existed on the muffin-biscuit-bread spectrum.

But I'd wanted him to try them. A small, mostly pathetic part of me wanted him to be impressed. To take something I'd made from my own two hands and an alarmingly large collection of cookbooks, and appreciate it. I wanted him to see me do something right.

And when he did, nothing could force the smile off my face. My cheeks burned. My throat tightened. If I let myself, I'd cry. I had to look out the window to keep myself from flailing under his praise. Or throwing myself at him.

"How's Cassidy these days?" he asked.

I stifled a groan. That killed my silly grin. Most of the time, I didn't think about my younger sister at all—and I knew the sentiment swung both ways. She probably had her hands full with harassing baristas who weren't nice enough to her and blaming mental health disorders on sunscreen or something. "Married. Two kids. Lives in Palm Beach."

"Sounds like things are still going well between you two?" he asked with a chuckle.

Cassidy's claim to fame was being a two-faced agent of evil skilled enough to switch between backstabbing and playing the victim on a second's notice. I never understood how anyone took her seriously but that didn't make her any less vicious. She'd had a girls' volleyball coach more or less run out of the state by the time she was twelve. All because the coach made her run an extra lap after cutting corners the first time around.

My parents adored her. They'd gotten it right with her, or so they liked to say. It helped that she was the blank slate they wanted, if we didn't count the faked fragility. Sometimes I wondered if that was the true basis of their value system.

Either way, Cassidy delivered a stunning performance of the loving little sister role throughout my high school years while secretly gathering enough information to end my life as I knew it. She found out about my IUD, about the hours spent at Semantic when I'd claimed to be at the dance studio, and our plan to go to New York City together after graduation. Then, in the spirit of her profound "concern" for me, she made sure my parents knew too.

I'd go to my grave with my jaw clamped around that grudge.

"She married a guy named Holter and named her kids Holt and Cassen."

"Originality was never her strength." Pointing to the scones, he asked, "It's maple, pecan, and what else?"

"Oatmeal," I said.

"Do you make them in any other flavors?" Jude took the

container from me and nestled it on the center console. "Percy's obsessed with chocolate right now, which isn't good for anyone, but he'd go for this without the nuts. He has no use for nuts unless they're ground into a spreadable form."

"Um. Well." I fussed with the seat warmer settings. It was weird getting exactly what I wanted. It happened so rarely that I didn't know how to wrap my arms around it. "Seasonal flavors, usually, or whatever I have around the house."

He grabbed another broken bit, nodding to himself as he ate. "These are the best scones I've ever had, Saunders."

"And you've had many scones?"

He glanced over, a grin I'd never be able to forget stretched across his face. "Enough to know."

I smoothed out the hoodie and tucked my arms back inside my shirt, and I burrowed so deep that Jude wouldn't notice another smile I couldn't wipe off my face.

chapter sixteen

Audrey

Today's vocabulary word: provisions

AS THE NIGHT FADED INTO THE EARLY SHOOTS OF DAWN, WE PASSED through towns with names like Anderson Junction and Hurricane and Booze Crossing, each one feeling more remote than the last. In some, the population only numbered in the hundreds. I wondered aloud whether I'd like living in such a small community. I liked small towns like the one Shay lived in, but I didn't want to be isolated.

Jude listened but never offered his take.

We stopped for gas at one point. I headed straight for the restroom and offered all my gratitude to the patron saint of excellent sanitation practices. When I emerged with provisions, I found Jude with the car's hood popped, a little penlight snagged between his teeth as he examined something.

"Everything okay?" I asked, trying to keep the wariness out of my voice.

He pulled the penlight from his mouth, clicking it off. "Yeah, we're fine." He didn't sound too convinced. "Just a minor issue. Nothing to worry about."

I nodded, not reassured but willing to take his word for it. It wasn't like I had a better solution.

We weren't on the road an hour before Jude took an exit for Grandwood Valley. The sunrise was almost upon us with fingers of blinding light edging into the horizon and turning the incredible red rock formations into deep, radiant colors.

Jude steered the car toward another gas station—or a building that'd started as a gas station and had lived through several identity crises and construction projects. He parked in front of the station's garage bays and immediately popped the hood, his focus already zeroed in on the task at hand.

Jude didn't say anything about the car trouble and I didn't ask. I knew how he zoomed in on problems and how he had trouble zooming out until he had a solution.

I climbed out to stretch my legs. It was good to breathe clean mountain air, the sharp scents of pine and mesquite trees heavy on a breeze. Even with the last dregs of night still lingering to the west, it was hot here. The afternoon sun would be toasty.

I paced away when Jude pulled a tablet from his backpack. Whatever this was would take a minute.

Red dust edged the road where scrubby brush grew in spite of itself. I could see small structures spread out across the valley and climbing into the rocky foothills. Houses and stables, maybe. We'd passed signs announcing river rafting and rodeo events in the area.

People lived in this town and they traveled here to visit, though it seemed as though we were alone. The only sign of life came from the cars and trucks passing on the highway. Probably for the best since my hair felt like I hadn't washed all the soap out, I smelled like the back of an earlobe, and crumbs rained from my clothes with every step. I wasn't fit for meeting the locals.

When I made my way back to Jude, my cheeks already warm

from the heat, I found him with his arms folded over his chest and a murderous glare aimed under the hood.

"I'm guessing it's not a minor issue anymore," I said.

"We're going to be here awhile," he said.

IF THERE WAS ONE THING I KNEW TO BE TRUE, IT WAS THAT JUDE Bellessi could fix anything.

I learned today that this superpower didn't include corroded engine plugs.

Another thing I learned: cars had a ton of different computerized plugs and they couldn't be swapped in and out for each other like extension cords. Apparently, this part was unique to this car model, and though he tried, Jude couldn't make it work with any of the options available at the garage.

That left us stranded here in Grandwood Valley until the rental agency could send someone out with a new vehicle for us. They'd promised a replacement by noon and, the naïve children we were, Jude and I believed them.

We went down the road to a diner that sold meat from a walk-up window. We devoured an amazing breakfast and stared at the table with zombie eyes for an hour. Then we waited on a bench outside the gas station, boldly expecting that new car as promised.

The owner of the gas station, a man who swore up and down that his name really was Woody Grandwood, prodded us to explore the county fair. He promised to call if the replacement showed up—we should've noticed how he kept saying *if*—and said we'd find a good time there.

We didn't go to the fair. We waited on that bench as the sun climbed higher in the sky.

Noon came and went. Then one o'clock and two. Jude had several intense conversations with the agency, and every time, they insisted someone was on their way and was scheduled to arrive within thirty minutes. And then another thirty minutes. And another.

I plugged in my phone after forgetting about it last night and discovered dozens of missed calls, voicemails, and texts from my mother. She wanted to strategize for my get-together with Brecken Wilhamsen—which she'd decided would happen at a garden party in the Hamptons next month—and casually, *gently* invited me to join her for some shopping.

I took that as a sign my mother had something big invested in making it work with me and Brecken. She wasn't one for gentle invitations. She preferred to inform me of these things and then lash out with an inventory of my most significant flaws when I didn't immediately fall in line. Maybe it was the delirium setting in but I couldn't believe that I'd ever let that fly. Even to avoid confrontation and keep the peace, blindly submitting wasn't doing me any good.

I replied with a quick message reminding her that I was traveling and then tied up with Emme's wedding, and we'd figure this out afterward.

Woody Grandwood strolled out of the gas station office and tipped his chin up in greeting. "Give me a day and I'll get that part ordered up for you," he said, hooking his thumb toward the car.

"The replacement should be here any—" Jude glanced at his watch. It read five fifteen. "What the ever-loving fuck is wrong with this company? They were thirty minutes away three hours ago."

"They probably don't have enough cars to send one out here and another to bring the driver back," Woody said. "It's high season. They run out of cars all the time." He pulled a phone from the back pocket of his worn jeans. "I'll call over to the motel and tell 'em you're coming, and then order that part. Probably be here tomorrow, maybe the day after."

"The day after?" Jude repeated, the words low and brutal.

Woody shrugged. "We get deliveries when we get deliveries. All there is to it."

"We need to leave now," Jude said, pushing to his feet. "There has to be another option."

"Don't think there is." Woody glanced down the road, scratching his chin. "But now you can see about that fair."

chapter seventeen

Audrey

Today's vocabulary word: booked

I STOPPED LISTENING TO EVERYTHING AFTER *MOTEL*. I'D BEEN awake, more or less, for thirty-six hours. As long as there was a bed waiting for me the details didn't matter.

I barely noticed the fifteen-minute walk from the gas station to the motel or the intense desert air transforming me into a sun-dried tomato with every breath. My pants and shoes had turned brick red from the dusty road, but I couldn't bring myself to care. Everything would be better after a long, hard month of sleep.

I perched on my suitcase and stared at the surrounding mountains while Jude arranged for our rooms in this long, concrete block of a motel. I carried on a small debate with myself—would I shower first or sleep?—and didn't notice him talking to me until he dropped a hand on my shoulder and gave me a shake.

"Don't pass out on me now," he rumbled.

"Hardly," I replied, though I had some doubts about standing up again. My god, it was so embarrassing to be alive. "Are we all set?"

He glanced down the row of doors bordering a parking lot filled with pickup trucks. "There's only one room."

I stared up at him, my mind gummy. "What?"

He held up a single diamond-shaped plastic keychain. "One room. It's all they have. Everything's booked for the fair."

My butt fell asleep as I processed this, and I wobbled on the suitcase. Jude grabbed my elbow and he didn't let go when I tried to shake him off. I didn't try very hard. I didn't actually want him to go. "It's not like we have any other options."

That...was not going to work. I needed somewhere to exist without him. I needed to be able to breathe and not wait to see his reaction to it. And, my god, I needed my own bathroom. The plain truth was the girls who had janky guts *required* our own bathrooms. We needed a private space where we could take all the time in there necessary without concern for how it could impact anyone else.

"I'm sorry about this," he said. "I'll come up with a solution tomorrow."

"Not your fault," I mumbled. "Let's just go."

He gave a slow, tight nod and we started toward the far end of the motel, our rolling bags bumping along beside us. When we reached the door, I leaned against the wall and decided I'd wash up first. There was nothing worse than climbing into bed and feeling grimy.

Jude gathered the bags and motioned for me to enter the room. The damp smell hit me right away, which was comical since everything was so dry here. But where a second bed would've been, I found an empty bed frame and a large trash can positioned under a hole in the ceiling.

I hadn't moved more than a step inside the doorway and Jude stumbled into me, his arm settling around my waist as he said, "What the—"

I pointed to the trash can, surrounded by the ancient metal

frame. "I'm guessing this is why they had a room available on short notice when everything else was booked?"

"Fuck." The word fell out of him on a sigh as his hold on my waist shifted, his fingers flexing. "Just...fuck."

A loud *plink* sounded and I wrinkled my nose at the trash can. "I know I didn't ask any clarifying questions about this room but I guess I just figured it would have two beds and zero roof leaks. Was that wrong?"

That seemed to remind him that his hands were getting real comfortable on my body. He cleared his throat and stepped away all at once.

"No." He closed the door and stayed there, his hand flattened on the panel. "You can have the bed"—we both glanced at the queen bed draped in a slippery-looking coverlet—"and I'll take the floor."

"I know you think I'm some kind of stone-cold evil bitch, but I'm not letting you do that. At a minimum, there's bacteria and fungus down there. Probably some MRSA too." I waved a hand at the bed, hopefully dry and short on fungus. "We can be adults about this. At least for tonight. We'll make it work."

Jude stared at me for a long moment, his brows arched high like he couldn't believe what I was saying. *I* couldn't believe anything about the past day and a half. I had a sneaking suspicion that this was one big, messy dream and I was a minute away from waking up.

When that didn't happen, Jude said, "I need to make some calls. Let my mother know we won't be there tonight."

"Yeah. Okay. You do that," I said, realizing in pieces that we'd be sleeping together in this room. In this *bed. Together.* All *night.* After we took off our clothes and changed into pajamas and—my god, what if Jude didn't sleep in pajamas? What if he'd turned into one of those men who slept naked? He'd wear boxers for my benefit. But maybe he'd abandoned boxers in his earlier years and made the switch to boxer briefs or regular old briefy briefs—or some other style I didn't know about because having that much information about a man wasn't one of my top thousand priorities. I'd be sleeping beside him and that new underwear. Images raced through my mind of Jude as a paper doll, each version of him dressed only in different types of undies—and the glasses. Always the glasses.

And saying my scones were the best. That too.

I slapped a hand over my eyes as if that would make any of this go away. All I knew was I had to stop thinking about his underwear.

On second thought, the floor didn't look so bad.

He yanked my hand away from my face. "What are you doing?"

"Just...trying to remember if I know anyone in this part of the world who also has a helicopter handy or a driver on staff. Or, just a lot of sympathy." I didn't meet his eyes. Couldn't. "No one comes to mind."

I felt him staring at me. Studying me. Probably waiting for a non-ridiculous answer. "Are you hungry? Do you want me to get anything for you? There's not much around here, but I could swing back to the diner."

The diner food was incredible and I ate like it was my last meal, which meant it would seriously destroy my gut for the next ten to fifteen business days. "No, thanks. I'm going to take a shower and then get some sleep."

He nodded but lingered by the door. "I am sorry about this, Saunders."

I waved him off. "Eh, you enjoy seeing me suffer."

Jude gazed at me for a second but didn't disagree. Because it was true. Then, "I'll be back in an hour."

I watched as he closed the door behind him and then let my attention wander back to the bed.

"It won't be that bad," I said to the empty room. "I hope."

chapter eighteen

Jude

Today's vocabulary word: recognize

I DIDN'T HAVE A LOT OF EXPERIENCE IN SLEEPING WITH AUDREY Saunders.

We'd shared plenty of nights when her parents were out of town but they'd been the kind where sleep was the last priority. Back then, it was about gulping down those frenzied, forbidden moments. I'd been too caught up in the primal, screaming need of it all to slow down and appreciate the simple goodness of being close to her, of *sleeping* with her.

It wasn't simple anymore.

When I returned to the room last night, Audrey had a small cylinder plugged in beside the bed—a white noise machine or something like that—and a pillow cleaving her side from mine. She'd been asleep, or doing an excellent job of faking it, and I couldn't believe how thoroughly I'd fucked this up.

I really didn't know how I thought this plan would come together for me. For months, I'd told myself all I had to do was find a way to get Audrey on board and everything else would fall into place. I dodged the technical details wherever I could. I did everything in my power to avoid thinking about the reality of being with her again.

But the trouble with Audrey was that she changed me. It'd always been that way, right from the start. I hated it at first. Hated the way the back of my neck prickled and blood pumped harder in my veins and my chest seemed to open up, like I hadn't known what it meant to take a deep breath until she ignored the shit out of me in school. But also, I couldn't breathe at all when she was around. Couldn't think, couldn't function until I learned everything about her.

And when I knew her, she changed me a little more. She softened the pointless anger I'd clutched tight like a security blanket and smoothed my self-righteous rebellion into something useful. She allowed me all the contempt I wanted because she came armed with her own supply of it.

More than all of that, she gave me a sense of calm I'd never known before and never since. There were days when I didn't trust the memories to tell me the truth. How could I? The only other time I'd felt anything close to that calm was when I had a tooth pulled and the drugs hit me all at once.

But now, waking up in this nightmare of a motel room, I realized the memories barely did it justice.

We'd abandoned our mindful posts on the far edges of the bed and turned toward each other in the night, our heads bowed together on the pillow meant to separate us. There was a light, gentle scent to Audrey, different from what I'd remembered but I still recognized it as hers. I stared at the long braid draped over her shoulder and the way her lips pulled together in a pouting frown. She'd wrapped her hand around my forearm at some point, her fingers pressed to my pulse.

I'd been a fool, all those years ago, to think sex could ever be more important than waking up with her like this.

And I was still a fool because I thought I could pretend with this woman. That I wouldn't bend toward her every chance I got. That I wouldn't let her destroy me all over again.

I stared at her for another minute before prying myself from her grasp. We'd slept late and there were things to do. I had to check in with Woody to see about progress on the car, apologize to my mother another fifteen times, confirm that my son wasn't being left to wander the shores of Saginaw Bay on his own, and let my attorney bill me two hundred dollars for a five minute call.

The most important item on that list was getting out of the bed and into the shower while Audrey was still asleep. If she woke up to find us sharing a pillow, we'd be finished here. The fact we'd shared a bed was some kind of miracle, but if she realized she'd reached for me in the middle of the night, she'd shut right down. And I wouldn't blame her. It was fucking with my head too.

The shower was about as awful as I'd expected. Dark and oddly narrow, and the pipes made noises I didn't trust.

I'd been in there about ten minutes when the bathroom door banged open and Audrey said, "Jude, I need you." I blinked water from my eyes as she pulled back the curtain, a towel waiting in her grip. "Now. Please?"

Instinct took over as I turned off the water. "Anything, baby. What is it?"

She didn't glance away while I wrapped the towel around my waist and all the anatomy that sprang to life whenever she was around. That should've raised a red flag about what was to come, but saying she needed me overrode everything else.

She pointed to the door, her other hand looped around the tail of her braid. "There's a lizard on the curtains."

"Slow down, sweetheart, just—" As I brought a wet hand to her shoulder, I finally comprehended her words. "Did you say *lizard*?"

"Yes, a lizard and it's on the curtains in the room we slept in and I need you to get it. Now. Please."

"Shit."

"Yeah, basically."

I darted out of the bathroom, Audrey close behind me. The metal bed frame and leak-water barrel stood between us and the window. I stepped around the frame and focused on the heavy curtains. The fabric was gray, though I didn't think it'd started out that way. I could tell from here it was thick and textured.

"Up there," Audrey said from behind me, her fingertips barely pressed to the center of my back. "Near the rod. I heard something —like soft scratching—and then I saw the curtains move."

I spotted the creature then, and while it didn't help anything, I let out a snarled, "Holy fuck."

"Yeah, I know, don't remind me. I've already died several times," Audrey said.

It wasn't one of the little guys that sunbathed in my mom's backyard. It was probably a foot long and I was pretty sure it had horns. In this area, there was a solid chance it was poisonous too.

I didn't have a game plan here. I searched the room but the best I could come up with was ripping off this towel and catching the lizard in there, which was a terrible plan because it left me naked and holding a pissed-off, possibly poisonous reptile.

Then I caught sight of Audrey's scones. I pulled the lid off and dumped the remaining chunks and crumbs on the dresser. "When I tell you, open the door and get out of the way."

I stepped around the bed frame, the container and lid in hand, and kept an eye on the lizard as I went. When it seemed like I had the best angle possible, I took my shot. I felt the thunk of that big boy as he landed in the dish and then held the lid down like her life depended on it.

"Open," I yelled, striding toward the door.

She flung it wide and pressed herself to the wall. I jogged

across the parking lot, the pavement like a hot griddle on my bare feet. When I reached a cluster of cactus and scrub brush, I set my friend off on a new adventure.

The motherfucker definitely had horns.

On the way back, I chucked Audrey's container in the dumpster. I had a feeling she wouldn't be using it again.

As I approached the room, I saw her peeking around the edge of the door, her eyes wide. "Taken care of," I said.

She nodded, still clinging to the door as I stepped inside. She shut it behind me and we scanned the room as if we'd find more uninvited guests waiting for us. Nothing jumped out at us—thank god. I didn't think we'd survive that.

Audrey twined her legs together, the bottom of one foot layered over the top of the other. I knew this wasn't the time, but I followed that bare skin and devoured every inch of her silky pink pajamas. Tiny shorts and a shirt I could unbutton in five seconds flat. I could probably run my hand up the inside of her thigh and— No. *No.*

Fuuuuck. I fucking hated that she did this to me and I hated that I didn't want to live another day without her. And more than all of that, I hated that I invented this whole stupid situation. If I hadn't lied to my mother, I could've gone about my life without sleeping beside the woman who broke me—twice—and rescuing her from a small dragon. And I damn well would've been happy about it. Or something close enough to happy.

"I'm obviously never sleeping again," she said, fully immune to the nonsense running through my head.

"Valid," I replied. "Really fuckin' valid."

"Can we agree we're burning this place to the ground now?"

Best idea I'd heard in days. "One hundred percent. Hand me the lighter fluid."

She laughed but it sounded like a cringe. "How long do you think that thing was in here?"

"I really don't want to know," I said.

"Yeah, the more I explore that thought, the more I want to sit in a simmering pool of acid because what if the lizard was *on* me last night? What if it licked my ear or—"

"Stop." I held up a hand. "Don't do that to yourself. Or to me, because it could've licked either one of us."

She gave an irritable shrug that told me she didn't like it when I was right and glanced at the discarded bits of scone strewn across the dresser. "Thanks for getting rid of the container."

"I didn't think you wanted it back." I nodded as I picked up the wastebasket and cleaned up the debris. "Sorry about this."

She glanced at the towel around my waist and then quickly away. "Sorry about barging in on you." Pink rose in her cheeks. She rolled her lips together, still avoiding my eyes—and towel. She *had* noticed her effect on me, then. "I panicked and didn't think about what you were—well. I didn't think." She ran her foot up the back of her opposite leg and twisted a finger around the end of her braid. "I should probably let you get back in there."

I was suddenly very aware of how thin this towel was and how very much my body missed being close to her. "It's all good," I said. "I was just about at the 'contemplating life' stage anyway."

"Oh. Okay." She brushed the end of her braid over her lips and along her jaw. I heard myself swallow. "If you don't mind, I'm going to—" She pointed to the bathroom door.

"All yours." I closed my hand around the towel's knot. Couldn't believe it'd held up through all of that. "I'm going to touch base with Woody and see if he has any updates on the car and then make a few calls."

She swept a gaze around the room like she expected something to jump out and bite her. I didn't blame her for that but it occurred to me she might not want to be left alone. Before I could offer a change of plans, she said, "That's great, actually, because I was thinking about walking over to the fair."

"Yeah. Okay." I nodded as she went on teasing her hair over her lips. If she kept that up, this towel would start telling all my secrets. "I'll message you with any updates."

She grabbed a few smaller bags and ducked into the bathroom. The door snicked shut and then the lock popped into place, and I let out a long groan as I rubbed a hand down my face. "What the fuck just happened to me?"

chapter nineteen

Jude

Today's vocabulary word: detours

"WHAT DO YOU MEAN, THE ROAD IS *CLOSED*?"

"I mean what I said," Woody replied, his focus on writing out a receipt. "There's a monsoon rollin' in."

I pinched the bridge of my nose. I'd spent the entire day in this gas station, alternately reaming out the rental car agency for that fuckup, waiting for the part to arrive because I didn't trust Woody to not forget about it until the morning, and distracting myself with work.

I was also avoiding Audrey, though I preferred to think of it as giving her space. We'd be back in close quarters soon enough, and arriving at my mom's house as a happily engaged couple before bedtime. Assuming Woody was wrong about the road closure.

"Monsoon season doesn't start until next month," I said. "*Late* next month."

"That's how it usually goes," he said, stroking a hand over the beaded lariat tucked into his collar. "But it's stirring up early this year. Big one too. That's why they closed the passes."

I pointed to the endless blue sky on the other side of the windows. "Show me the storm, Woody."

"Oh, it's comin'. You can't see it, but it's comin'. The winds and dust storms tend to miss us up here but we'll get the rain, the floods. Thunder and lightning too."

I pulled up a map on my phone, zooming in on the area. Sure enough, the roads leading out of the mountains popped up with hazardous condition warnings and local access only restrictions, and the major highways around Flagstaff and then Sedona were already ruby red with flash flood warnings. Only an hour ago, it'd been smooth sailing all the way to my mother's house.

"Fuck." I dropped an elbow on the counter. We couldn't spend another night in this town. For so many reasons. "If we leave right now—"

"Then you'll get stuck in the worst of it and I don't think that pretty wife of yours wants to find out what a water rescue's all about."

I dug a knuckle into my temple and didn't bother correcting him about my *wife*. "Fuck."

"I know our little town isn't much but it's not that bad," Woody drawled.

I dragged my gaze up, taking in his deeply tanned skin and salt-and-pepper hair he kept tied back in a thin braid as I went. "The town's not my problem," I said. "The problem is that we needed to be in Sedona two days ago."

"You'll get there when you get there," he said. "We're havin' ourselves a rodeo tomorrow. You should come along."

I gathered up my laptop and notebooks, and shoved them all into my backpack. "Thanks for the tip," I said on my way out the door.

The car was up and running now but I didn't drive back to the motel yet. I sat there, staring at the mountains and the fine layer of dark purple clouds pressing in on the distant horizon. After a few minutes of letting my frustration boil over, I put in my earbuds and called my mother.

It rang for longer than I thought possible but then she picked up and I heard Gloria Estefan playing in the background for at least fifteen seconds before she said, "Hello?"

"Hey, Mom."

"Oh, Jude! I've been wondering where you were," she said. "Please tell me you'll be here before the storm. We've been out bringing in all our outdoor cushions because everyone says they'll blow away if we don't. Gary up the street says his got stuck in a tree last summer. Had to hire some kids to get 'em down."

"Gary up the street, huh?"

"He's a real character, that one," she said. "He likes to know what's going on in the neighborhood."

"I bet he does," I said. I wanted to meet this Gary from up the street. "About this storm. It doesn't look like we're going to make it there tonight."

"I don't think I believe this story about delays." She chuckled. "I think you're hiding out in the middle of nowhere and having fun in that motel."

Memories of sprinting across the parking lot with a lizard trapped in Tupperware flooded my mind. "Yeah, that's not really what's happening here, Mom."

"You know, you could've just told me that you wanted a few nights alone," she went on. "You think I don't understand what it's like? Being a young parent and wanting to get some *adult time*—"

"Let's just end that thought there," I said. "Believe me, no one wants to get to Sedona more than Audrey. We're just having a run of bad luck."

"Or it's very good luck," she said. "Road trips and middle-of-nowhere motels can be very romantic."

I pushed past the memory of Audrey's palm on my forearm while she slept. Of her turning toward me in the night. Of her brushing that braid over her lips. *My* lips. "We'll be there tomorrow," I said, the words crisp. "It's a five-hour drive but we'll hit the road early and be there by noon."

"What's the rush? Sleep in. Enjoy yourselves. I'll be happy to see you whenever you roll in."

I didn't know how we'd gone from a packed itinerary with events scheduled morning, noon, and night to *What's the rush?* but I wasn't going to call her on it. "I'll let you know when we're about an hour away."

"Give my love to that darling girl of yours. Tell her I have lots of plans for us," she said. I wouldn't be telling Audrey that unless I wanted her to ask fifty-four thousand times what it meant. "I'll see you tomorrow. And stay safe out there, kiddo. Gary says it only takes a few minutes for flash floods to wash you right outta town."

"Good ol' Gary," I said. "I'll talk to you tomorrow, Mom."

She made kissy sounds that I used to find annoying and now I just appreciated I still got to hear them. "Love you, kiddo."

"Love you too."

I headed toward the motel, and the minute I made the turn into the parking lot, I spotted Audrey sitting in a metal chair outside our door. She had a book in her lap and her hair gathered over one shoulder, big sunglasses blocking her eyes from view.

She paid me no attention when I pulled into the slot in front of her. I drank her in, allowing myself to study the long line of her legs and the slight downturn of her lips as she read. She'd grown and changed so much that there were moments when I barely recognized her, but this quiet woman lost in her book, this one I knew better than anyone else on earth.

And she was going to kill me when I broke the news about tonight. That, or she'd insist I deliver her to the closest airport and put an end to this adventure.

After this morning and the...reactions I'd had, it wasn't the worst idea.

I grabbed my backpack and climbed out of the car. I slammed the door behind me but the book kept her attention. I strolled into her space and tipped the book back to get a look at the cover. *Inkheart*, I read. "Must be good because you've been lost in those pages for a few minutes."

"I'm thinking of reading it with my class next year." She fidgeted with a skinny pink highlighter. "It's a little longer than I usually prefer but it's a great story."

I skimmed the back cover. "This might be Percy's vibe."

"What does he like to read?"

I rocked back on my heels because that was a loaded question. My kid had some wild preferences. "Many things, but especially stories with connections to mythology."

"Do you want any recommendations? Because I spend half of my fifth-grade years on world mythologies and modern retellings, and I've read *everything* out there."

"That'd be a big help. Thank you."

She blinked as if just now noticing the rental car at my back and shot to her feet. "It's fixed? We can go?"

"It's fixed," I started, "but there's another problem."

"No, there's not." She tossed the book and highlighter to the chair. "There are no problems because we've already had all the problems and we're done with problems. The only problem is that we're standing here talking and not getting the hell out of this town."

I slipped my hands into my pockets. "There's a storm coming in. A big monsoon. I guess some of the roads have a tendency to flash-flood and they shut them down as a precaution."

"We are not stranded here for another night," she said, the words frayed. "We can't stay here. I *won't.*"

"Believe me, I want another option as much as you do."

"I don't actually believe that," she cried, flinging her hands out at her sides.

"That's tough shit, princess, because it's the truth," I said.

"We should've waited for the rescheduled flight to Phoenix," she said, shaking her head as she paced away from me. "We're going to arrive at the exact same time, but instead of spending that time in my dry, lizard-free home, we're out here roughing it like settlers on the Oregon Trail who're going to die of dysentery."

"We're nowhere near the Oregon Trail."

She whirled around, her hands fisted at her hips. "Would you just shut the hell up? Because I get it. You want to punish me. You want me to suffer."

"That's not true. It's not true at all. You know it's killing me to be stuck here when we're missing everything my mom planned for us."

Her scoff could've cracked ice. "Right, because dragging me in front of your mother and making me put on the fiancée show isn't one more punishment. Because this entire week isn't full of opportunities for you to make a fool out of me and watch me squirm."

"That's not what I'm doing," I said through gritted teeth.

"Maybe you didn't plan the delays or the broken-down car," she said, pacing again. "But you can't tell me you didn't love shoving me into a damp, dingy motel room. It's almost better revenge than trapping me in this heinous lie of yours."

"Would you just calm the fuck down?"

She turned toward me, a murderous glare in her eyes. I'd swear I heard fangs descend. "Do you want me to calm the fuck down? Or have you just been waiting for me to throw a spoiled little rich girl tantrum? It'd give you all the permission you need to confirm every terrible thing you already think about me."

I closed the distance between us and leaned in, just enough to pick up the scent of her shampoo. "I've come by all my knowledge of you honestly. I don't need confirmation of anything. You've done enough of that on your own."

"You have no idea what you're talking about," she said, the words low and cold.

"Yeah? Then consider the possibility that neither do you."

I shouldered my backpack and, once again, walked away from Audrey Saunders with no clue where I was going or what I'd do when I got there.

chapter twenty

Jude

Today's vocabulary word: imperious

ONE OF THE MANY PROBLEMS WITH BEING STUCK IN A REMOTE TOWN in the high desert was that there was nowhere to go. Short of wandering into the mountains and feeding myself to the coyotes, the pickings were slim.

The diner was closed for the day along with the general store. I ended up parking myself at the laundromat—they had free wifi—and throwing myself into work for a couple of hours. The steady hum of the machines took the edge off some of the tension that'd gathered between my shoulders but I still wanted to march right up to Audrey and explain why she was so fucking wrong about everything.

And she was wrong. About all of it.

Once the sun melted behind the mountains and I heard the low rumbles of thunder off in the distance, I hiked back to the motel. Audrey wasn't there, though I didn't think she would be. She'd wait until the last possible moment to return, if for no other reason than to prove to me that she could.

She wasn't the only one who could prove a point.

I ditched my backpack and headed for the bar across the street. Or, I assumed the low-slung building was a bar. No name, no sign, just two dozen pickup trucks and the throb of music bleeding out the doors and into the evening air. I'd be able to burn a few hours in there.

The place was packed but it added up when I remembered what Woody had said about the county fair and tomorrow's rodeo. I found an empty spot at the end of the bar and ordered a beer.

I was halfway into a one-sided argument with myself when a laugh snagged my attention. It was like a fishhook right through my gray matter, pulling me against the currents of noise and bodies until my gaze landed on a smile so wide it was like I was staring straight into a floodlight.

There she was, her cheeks pink and her hair loose around her shoulders as her laughter cut through the country music.

And some fucking guy in a cowboy hat tucked her into his arms as they danced across the floor. She'd changed into jeans that fit her like a dream and a shirt that fluttered with every move. A few wisps of hair curled around her face from the heat. She'd been at it awhile.

All I could see were his hands. On her hips, her waist. Around her shoulders. His smile pressing against her cheek. But I realized my mistake too soon. The song was finished but Audrey wasn't. Another guy in a cowboy hat offered her his hand and she took it, laughing like the night belonged to her and not to the history between us.

The songs blurred together as Audrey moved from one partner to the next, each with big, shiny belt buckles and well-loved boots. The cowboys tipped their hats at her and she took their hands without a second thought. She kept dancing and laughing through each tune while I tried to remember the last time I saw her so completely happy. It was the only thing that kept me from bolting off this stool and flipping every table in this place.

"Those bull riders found themselves something fun to play with," the bartender drawled when he caught me staring. "Thinkin' about askin' for a dance?"

I rolled the beer bottle between my palms. It was warm now, mostly untouched. I watched her hair whip her face as her partner spun her away and then back until she was flattened against his chest. When she shifted out of his hold and into the next sequence of steps, her gaze tripped over mine. She went on smiling but raised a brow in challenge. She held my eyes for a second before picking up the dance but it was enough to remind me she still knew exactly how to gut me without saying a word. "Maybe."

He tipped his chin at the beer. "Another?"

I nodded, my gaze still locked on Audrey while I tossed down a few bills. She threw her head back and laughed at something the guy—the bull rider—said. She had one hand laced with his and the other between his shoulder blades, and the way she leaned into him, completely at ease, made my jaw clench so hard I gave myself a headache. I went on gripping the beer bottle, running my thumb over the raised marks along the neck while reminding myself to keep my ass on the barstool.

She was smiling and laughing and having fun, and the last thing she wanted was for me to interfere with that. Still, each time her smile flashed at someone else, it sparked in my chest like a dare. Like she was reminding me just how thoroughly she'd lived without me—and how little she cared that I was right here, watching. Waiting.

My muscles pulled taut with every next song, every wild spin, until even the barstool seemed to whisper *Get the hell up*. It shaved years from my life but I fought off the urge to stride across the room and steal her away for myself.

Until one of those bull riders draped an arm around her shoulders and steered her toward the door. I was off that stool and across the bar in a blink.

I rounded on them, saying, "Thought you'd save the last dance for me, Saunders."

The rider glanced between us and tugged her closer. "Do you know this guy?" he asked, his lips nearly brushing the shell of her ear.

Audrey nodded but made no move away from her new friend. If anything, her smile sharpened like she knew exactly how deep this knife was sinking and wasn't about to pull it free. She wanted me to watch, to stew in it, to *suffer*, and god help me—I was. And she knew it too.

I swallowed down all the words scraping the back of my throat —the warnings, the promises, the questions that'd burrowed into the back of my mind for too long. If I took one step closer, I knew I'd forget all the bullshit stories I'd told myself about what I wanted from her and why we were doing this.

"Is he bothering you?" the rider asked. When she didn't reply, he turned a hard-jawed glare in my direction. If I wasn't busy being furious at Audrey, I'd appreciate him squaring up on her behalf. "When a lady says she isn't interested, we don't hang around and make them uncomfortable. We move the fuck on."

"Heard." I held my hands up as I took a step toward Audrey. "But you should know that's my fiancée you've been dancing with and she won't be leaving here with you tonight."

"Oh my god. Would you stop it?" she snapped, shrugging away from the bull rider. "I wasn't going home with him, you fuck mollusk. We were getting some air." She waved a hand at her face, damp and rosy from dancing. Her shirt clung to the dip between her breasts. I had to wrench my gaze away before I let myself drown there. "Because it's hot in here and some of us aren't sitting in a corner and chewing on glass."

The rider glanced between us several times like he wasn't sure what to believe. To Audrey, he asked, "Is this a safe situation for you? I think some of the barrel racers have space in their trailers over at the campground. If you'd be more comfortable there tonight, I could ask around."

Audrey dropped a hand to the center of his chest. "You're such a sweetheart," she said. "And it's good of you to worry about me, but if there's one thing I know how to do these days, it's looking after myself. I'll be all right. Thank you for checking."

She anointed him with a loving smile and a lot of truly unhinged thoughts moved through my mind but the worst of them was *Mine*.

The sick truth was that I'd do anything to carve that instinct out of me. To free myself from her, once and for all. Because I'd never stopped loving her, not even when she walked down the aisle and gave herself to someone else. I didn't know how to stop loving her any more than I knew how to stop my heart from pumping blood. And there was a part of me that always wondered whether I even wanted to stop. Whether I liked tracing my fingers over the scars I couldn't see but still felt. Whether I wanted every thought to circle back to her in one way or another, simply because her fingerprints were on every inch of my life.

"If you're sure," the rider said to her, still raking me over with a glare.

"Thanks for the dance," she said.

He tipped his hat at her. "Thank *you*, ma'am. It was a lot of fun. You're a damn good dancer."

"It's nice of you to say so." Then she swung her gaze in my direction and I found unbound fury waiting for me. "Now, if you'll excuse me, I need to have a conversation—with my *fiancé*."

She turned on her heel and stormed away. I knew it was wrong to enjoy riling her up but I loved it when she was too pissed off at me to be anything but real. I loved all her reactions, even the ones I had to mine for the truth, but especially when she dropped the filters and hit me with her worst.

"This is none of my business but I don't think that girl's gonna marry you," the bull rider said.

"Probably not," I said, watching the door slam shut behind her. "Still worth a shot."

chapter twenty-one

Jude

Today's vocabulary word: strike

I FOLLOWED AUDREY OUTSIDE AS LIGHTNING STREAKED THROUGH the sky. The storm would be here within minutes. "You're going the wrong way," I yelled after her.

She stopped and turned in the other—also wrong—direction. "I'm going where I want to—away from you!"

A small chorus of laughter sounded nearby and I noticed a few groups of smokers gathered on the side of the building.

She must've decided she wanted to holler at me more than she wanted to be alone because she stomped up to me, her hands fisted at her sides. "What the hell was that, Jude? I mean, *what the hell*?" Before I could respond, she continued. "In case you've somehow lost your own plot, we're only engaged to keep your mother happy. I'm not your fiancée anywhere but immediately in front of your mother, and even that's due to end in short order. Everywhere else, we're just two people who used to mean everything to each other."

"What do we mean to each other now?"

She let her eyes close for a second as she ran a hand through her hair. "I don't know yet."

Raindrops began to spit around us. "Yes, you do."

"No, I don't, and yelling at me in front of a bunch of people isn't going to change that."

We stared at each other for a long, brittle moment where all I could see was her dancing with those cowboys and her head on my pillow and the way her lips moved when she told me her husband was finally out of the picture. Through it all, my mind rang with the same questions as always. The ones I didn't think I'd ever be able to ask because the answers had the power to end me.

I stared off at the bruise-dark clouds instead. When the silence pulled too tight, I asked, "Why did you agree to this?"

"Because you—" She shook her head, sighing as her shoulders sagged and she closed in on herself. "It doesn't matter. I'm here."

"Don't start lying to me now, princess."

"I'm here because you needed me. Because you asked for help. Happy? I wasn't able to make it right between us before but I could do this, and now you're being a complete shitpickle about it." Her eyes sparkled as she pushed past me. "Thanks so much for that."

I turned to follow her as a long roll of thunder filled the air. "Why couldn't you make it right?"

"I don't want to talk about that," she shouted over her shoulder, all huffs and rage.

"So you're just going to run away again?"

She stopped, her back to me as she straightened her shoulders and fisted her hands. "I'm not running away from anything. I'm going back to our room because you decided to piss a pointless circle around me in the bar and no one's going to want to dance with me now."

I should've apologized. I should've told her how much the past few days with her had fucked me up. Should've said she was amazing on that dance floor and I'd give anything to watch her a little longer. Should've shut my mouth and walked her to the room. But I found a small well of courage and loosed one of the questions that'd chased me since I was eighteen. "Why did you do it? Why did you go to California?"

A crack of lightning lit up the sky and I saw those words hit her like an open-handed slap. They hit me just as hard.

"Does it even matter?" she asked.

"All of it fucking matters, Audrey," I yelled. "We wouldn't be here if it didn't matter."

She turned around and the skies opened, hard, driving rain soaking us through within seconds. There was no avoiding it.

She pushed her wet hair off her face. "Why didn't you fight for me?"

"What?"

"I didn't run away. My parents canceled my enrollment in Barnard and put me on a plane to California and I didn't have—I couldn't do anything about it. You probably knew that too, because you have a way of knowing everything and then acting like I should explain it all to you. What I want to know is why you didn't fight for me," she said. "It was like you didn't even notice when I left."

I'd known some of that but I couldn't spend any time on the new information because she was missing a few key details. "Are you forgetting the—"

"I waited for you for three years but you didn't come after me," she yelled. "I *needed* you and you didn't fight. Not until it was too late."

"That's what you think?" I shook my head. I couldn't believe this.

"That's what I *know*," she shot back. "They sent me away and took everything I loved. I lost my whole world in one day and I was all alone for *years*. Everything we had was gone like it'd never existed. We were just...over, and it killed me. I barely got out of bed for months. I failed the whole first semester. It was all gone and I had nothing."

Her chin wobbled and I knew she was crying through the rain. My chest cracked open as she turned away. I reached for her arm. "We weren't over," I said, pulling her back. "Not then. Not now."

I cupped her chin and brought my rain-soaked lips to hers for the first time in too fucking long. We crashed together as the thunder roared, her fingers clinging to my chest and shoulders while I gripped the waist of her jeans. Over the downpour, the smokers cheered us on.

Distantly, I knew we couldn't stay out here. We had to take cover. Standing out in the open during a lightning storm was not smart.

"Come here," I said against her lips, and boosted her into my arms. Her long legs went around my waist and her arms circled my neck. I kissed her like there'd never be enough and strode toward the motel, the rain pounding at my back.

I made it across the road and into the parking lot before another burst of lightning pierced the skies. The thunder echoed like the roar of a jet engine off the mountains. We were soaked down to the bone.

None of that stopped me from pushing her up against the door and sinking into the embrace of her body. I ran a hand up the delicate line of her neck and held her steady, my thumb pulling on her bottom lip. "More," I said, claiming her mouth again.

"Jude," she whispered, her fingers in my hair. I almost died from that touch alone.

"I know," I said between kisses. "Fuck, I know."

Everything around us jolted as another peal of thunder broke free. "Inside," she said.

Her legs still around my waist and her lips on my neck, I fumbled for the key. When I finally freed it and opened the door, I carried her inside and perched her on the edge of the dresser. The hole in the ceiling had turned into a waterfall and the lights wouldn't turn on but none of that slowed me down.

We clawed at each other, pulling at clothes and hair and every inch of skin we could reach. There was no patience, no thought, no art to it because we knew this spell could break at any minute and everything would come crashing down.

I rocked into the cradle of her thighs, making no mistake about what she was doing to me and what I wanted to do to her. She groaned like I'd never heard before, her head lolling back and her heels digging into my ass. She ripped at my shirt, nearly strangling me in the process of freeing my arms and pulling it over my head.

"Easy there, princess," I said against her jaw. "You'd be sad if you killed me right now."

She tugged hard on my hair and dragged my bottom lip between her teeth. I was stunned I didn't come on the spot. Honestly stunned. "Not as much as you'd think."

"Feel better?" I emptied my pockets onto the dresser, throwing down my keys, wallet, and phone before she used any of them against me. "Now that you've stopped being so fucking polite?"

She raked her nails down my neck. It yanked a growl from deep in my chest. "There's nothing wrong with being polite." Her words were barely a purr as she broke my skin and twisted my soul around her fingers. "You should give it a try."

I scraped my teeth along her jaw. If she wanted to leave a mark, so would I. "You like me rude."

"Sometimes," she whispered, her hand dropping to my belt. *God fuck more yes.* "And sometimes you should shut the hell up and let me dance."

"Admit it." I kissed my way across her collarbone. "You wanted me to see you dancing with all those cowboys."

She blinked at me between hard, hungry kisses, her hands mapping my shoulders and raindrops still clinging to her lashes. "Why would I do that?"

I hooked my thumb inside her waistband, traced the warm skin at the small of her back. "To get me jealous."

I felt her laugh against my cheek. "And now that you are? What are you going to do about it?"

Her lips tilted in the same taunting curve she'd worn on the dance floor, the one that gutted me while cowboys spun her across the room. Only now, I wasn't watching from a distance—and that was worse, because after all this time I finally knew how it felt to get her back. It scared the hell out of me—and made me feral in wanting to prove she'd always been mine.

I grabbed her by the belt loops, yanking her all the way to the edge of the dresser. "I need to get you out of these wet clothes," I said, my hand flat over her zipper. My middle finger traced the seam running between her legs. Slow enough to catch my breath. Slow enough for her to change her mind. "Don't want you catching a chill."

A shiver moved through her shoulders. "Can't have that."

I thumbed the top button open and for a split second it wasn't dazed lust in her eyes but something older and far more delicate. Something like relief. Then it hit me too. Felt like I was a minute away from my chest bursting open or laughing until I couldn't breathe or holding her so tight that all the pieces of me she'd stolen slipped into place and I felt whole again.

I tipped her chin up and kissed her. A gasp squeaked out of her and I growled against her lips. If I wasn't climbing out of my skin to hold her and taste her and *keep* her, I would've spent the next ten hours doing everything in my power to tease that sound out of her once more.

"Arms up, baby," I said, gripping her shirt. "That's it. Good. Let me get you warm."

When I tossed it aside, I buzzed my hands down her sides, up her back, across her belly. Her lips parted in the most delicious way and her body was a fever dream of memories.

I leaned in to press a kiss between her breasts. Goose bumps broke out along her arms and chest as I traced my knuckles over the cups of her bra. Instinct told me to hurry the hell up, to just fucking *get there*, but something even older than instinct told me to go slow, to get it right. "You're different now."

"You too," she whispered, her hands scrabbling at my torso, my back. Gulping down everything she could reach.

"Looks good on you." I turned her around to face the dresser and mirror hanging above it. Dropping my attention to the spot where her neck and shoulder met, I kissed and nipped at her until she laughed, shrieked, squirmed in my arms. "I like it."

Though it was dark, I met her gaze in the mirror as I rocked my shaft against her ass. I brought a hand to the flat of her belly, countering the pressure from behind, and spread out my fingers until two slipped into her panties.

Her lips parted on a breath, and then, "You never answered my question."

I stared at her reflection as I tapped her clit. "Which one? You have me a little distracted with other matters here."

"What are you going to do about me making you jealous?" she asked, her hands fluttering at her sides like she didn't know where they belonged.

I solved that problem with a quick, hard pinch to her clit. It wasn't nice and wasn't meant to be, as her guttural cry confirmed. But it put a stop to the overthinking. "Let me show you," I said, grinding into her once more. "Don't move unless you want me to stop."

I placed her hands on the dresser in front of us. Pressed a palm between her shoulder blades until she bent at the waist, her cheek on the faux wood surface. My blood whomped through my veins at the sight, loud and reckless. Goddamn, I didn't even know where to start. I just knew I didn't want it to end.

With her jeans out of the way, I dropped to my knees. I wasn't interested in fucking around with panties, as fuck-hot as they were, and peeled those off next. Her breath caught when I widened her stance and she yelped when I traced my knuckles down the inside of her thigh. Those long, lean dancer's muscles trembled under my touch. *Perfect.*

My imagination went to a dangerous place and it dug in there. Filthy, desperate thoughts unspooled before me, each one a little wilder, a little more devastating. I could pick her up and carry her to that bed and worship her until the sun burned out. Defile her in every way I knew, come up with a few others I didn't. Show her that it wasn't over, had never been over. Prove that I could give her everything she needed. Promise her anything, everything. Fuck her until she forgot the names of everyone who'd come since me.

I ran my fingertips between her legs, barely a touch at all but still enough to have her slapping a hand against the dresser. A shudder moved through her as I stroked, and while my hands trembled, I grinned at the perfect heart shape of her ass. Too cute. I rubbed my cheek against her, letting her feel the scrape and bristle of my beard against that smooth skin.

"Jude," she cried out.

I nipped at her backside. Couldn't see the welt but I knew it was there. "You want me to stop?" A breath passed, then another. No response. "That's what I thought."

I rubbed my thumbs along her seam, spreading all the wet I found waiting for me. I leaned in, speared my tongue through the same path I'd just teased. She jerked against me and I heard a yelped "*Oh!*" between the rumbling thunder.

I knew if I even *thought* about that sound again, I'd lose it. I wanted to make this good for her but goddamn I was already hugging the edge. I wanted to play and explore and learn this gorgeous woman all over again. But I also wanted to devour her until she lost the ability to stand on her own—and that desire won out in the end. I gripped the back of her thigh hard, hard enough to dent her perfect skin. "What did I tell you about staying still?"

I didn't wait for a reply and went back to drowning myself between her thighs. Her scent surrounded me, rich and intoxicating. The feel of her against my tongue woke up one of the purest memories of her I had. One I'd buried so deep I'd almost forgotten. But I *knew* this. I'd always know it.

Her legs shook as I dragged my tongue around her clit, though when I shifted my hand to steady her, I realized I was shaking too. I ran those trembling fingers up her thigh, across the crease where her leg met the round of her ass, and over those plump, pretty lips. She breathed out a gorgeous moan as I pet her and I wanted—fuck, I wanted everything. I wanted to take her the fuck apart and make her watch while I did it and I wanted to let her crush me into shards too small to ever put back together—just fucking end me, once and for all.

I pushed a finger inside her, then another, and heard a choked "*Oh my god*" that had me grinning into her cunt. It was nice to know I could still do something right.

She rocked against me and we fell into a tentative rhythm, my fingers shuttling into her as I sucked and stroked her clit. I fucking loved it. Even if we went no further, I knew this would be enough for me. Tonight, this week, the rest of my fucking life. If I stopped and thought about this at all, my cock would burn a hole through my jeans and spill for entire minutes.

We didn't speak. My mouth was fully occupied and Audrey stayed quiet, offering little more than soft gasps and murmured hums. But I thought we needed it that way. We still couldn't find the right things to say to each other but this—*this* we could do.

I sank onto my heels and pulled Audrey with me, forcing her legs wider and tilting her hips to feed me that sweet, shining clit. I wanted her to get it, to use me, to go after the friction she needed.

With my free hand, I wrested my jeans open, gave myself a quick, quelling tug. Nothing short of obscene, the two of us.

A tremor moved up her legs and into her core, and I felt a gorgeous clench that drew my fingers deep into her cunt. She clawed at the dresser as I kept the pressure steady on her clit and my arousal turned into a sharp, concentrated thing. It would rip me open if I let it, and I would.

I'd never known how to save myself when it came to Audrey. Never cared to learn.

"Oh— Oh my— *Yes.*" That last word spilled out in a sigh and I was certain I'd never be able to get another woman off without hearing that sound in my head. Fuck, I'd never be able to get myself off without hearing it.

I felt the pounding of her pulse against my tongue and my hand was wet down to my wrist. I could've stayed here all night. Could've served her from my knees until we both collapsed.

Except, no. That wasn't what she needed now.

Skimming my fingers along the outsides of her thighs, I pushed to my feet. Everything inside me yanked tight like a hunger pang. Breaths heaved out of her as I dragged her up from the dresser and folded my arms around her. I pressed my lips to her neck as she shook against me.

It was good that we didn't say anything. It would be wrong, whatever I came up with. And she'd find the smallest possible string of words to destabilize my entire existence.

She reached back, blindly pawing at my jeans. When she got a handful, she fumbled them down far enough to make her point.

"I don't have a condom," I said, hating myself more in that moment than ever before.

"Doesn't matter," she panted.

I blinked at that. I could *not* have heard her correctly. "Say that again?"

"I can't get pregnant right now," she said. "And I haven't been with—"

"Fuck, princess, say less." I locked one arm around her waist, holding us steady as I gripped my cock. She was so fucking wet. And soft. Like nothing else in the world. Her head dropped back against my shoulder and her nails bit into my forearm. We groaned together at the unbelievable pressure.

I was barely inside her when the room filled with artificial light and my phone buzzed like a record scratch, Percy's photo flashing across the screen.

We stared at it as her fingers dug trenches in my forearm. I swallowed hard. My brain was buried an inch inside her and only the thinnest shred of my consciousness wanted to be someone's parent tonight. If he could just go to sleep without me this one time... "I'll talk to him later."

She sucked in a long breath that squeezed the almighty fuck out of my shaft. "Are you sure?"

The buzzing stopped but it started up again before I could promise that my son had the ability to wait thirty minutes. An hour if we wanted to be ambitious.

But— "You should take that."

Everything inside me ached and I bent, dropping my forehead to her shoulder because I knew this was over. For now. All I could say was, "Fuck."

A stifled laugh. "Yeah."

She wriggled away from me as best she could, considering I had her in a stranglehold and pinned to a dresser, saying, "Talk to him. It's okay. He needs you." Her head down and an arm over her chest, she darted toward the bathroom. "I'm just going to— I mean, my hair. It's all wet. I should— Yeah. That's what I'll be doing. In there."

The bathroom door closed behind her, leaving me standing there in the dark with my dick out and my head fucked fourteen different ways.

A full minute passed where I stared at that door, the phone vibrating and my body pulsing, and couldn't move. My first thought was to break down the door and finish what we'd started.

I heard the shower turn on and a ragged pulse of desire hit me like I'd walked into a wall. I wanted to strip off my clothes and climb in there with her. Just to touch her again and breathe her in and know she was— *Fuck*. I wanted her to explain what'd happened here and what happened next. Show me the map and tell me what it said.

But there was time for that. We had all of tonight and then four more days together. We had time.

chapter twenty-two

Jude

Today's vocabulary word: intervene

ANOTHER CALL FROM PERCY CAME IN AND THEN ONE MORE WHILE I hunted down some hand sanitizer. With that handled, I grabbed some dry shorts and a shirt. I stepped outside, the rain slowing as the storm moved through, and accepted the next call.

"I called you six times," he signed.

"Nice to see you too," I replied, dropping onto the metal chair I'd found Audrey in earlier. The fresh air blowing in with the storm felt good on my skin. Good for my head too. "And you know that if I'm not able to answer right away, I'll always call you back as soon as I can."

He stared at me, his lips pursed as if he cared very little for this feedback. If only he knew how little I cared for his timing tonight. Then, "We went to a water park today and some of it was fun but it was really loud. There were a lot of big kids and they all ran around a lot." He glanced around his dark bedroom. "But I tried a churro and now I like them."

"That's..." I shook my head. Didn't know Brenda had a water park visit on the docket for today. Didn't know how much I liked that idea, seeing as Percy managed to contract an eye infection from every public pool he'd ever glanced at. "Good news about the churros."

"They're fire."

"Fire?" I echoed, and repeated the sign back to him because I refused to believe my four-year-old understood what he was saying. "Churros are *fire*?"

He nodded, his chubby cheeks round as he grinned. I still saw a baby when I looked at him. "Miss Maddie came to the water park. She thinks churros are fire too."

"Mmm. Yeah. I bet she does." Maddie had been Penny's best friend. They grew up together. Maddie still lived in her childhood home, a few doors down from Brenda. She adored Percy. Me, she could do without. "How are your eyes? Anything feeling itchy?"

"I'm okay," he signed, his attention shifting to his stuffed animals. "Can we find churros in Virginia?"

"We have churros back home," I said. "What about Grandma? How's she doing?"

"Asleep." He shrugged. "I turned off the TV and checked the doors after dinner though."

God fucking help me. "What about brushing your teeth?"

"Already done." He smoothed a hand over his favorite stuffie, a small, fluffy dog he called Beast.

"Okay. What else is on your mind?"

"Nothing." Another shrug. "How many days until I can go home?"

"Just a few more weeks," I said. "Do you want me to read to you? We could get through another chapter if you want."

"Miss Maddie said I could go to kindergarten if I stay here." His pouty glare sliced right through me. "Why do I have to wait until next year if I go home?"

I almost dropped the phone. *If I go home.* I wanted my kid to know his mother's family and where she'd grown up. But coparenting with people who kept praying I'd decide to forfeit my parental rights and turn my son over to them was a nightmare.

The last thing I wanted was for my kid to realize he was caught between people who wanted very different things for him. Still, it seemed like I was the only one with that priority.

I cleared my throat and forced myself to exhale as much tension as possible before answering. "I'm not sure that's the way it works in Michigan, buddy. I think you still need to be five by the start of September."

"Miss Maddie says I can."

I felt hard, corded tension locking up my neck as I nodded. Maddie came in strong with the fun aunt energy. This often took the shape of *Donuts for dinner!* and *Of course you can skip your occupational therapy exercises today!* and *If you lived here, we could have sleepovers every night!* "I know this is a big deal for you and it's important to me too."

"I don't want to go to that baby school anymore," he signed. "I don't want to go there ever in infinity."

That baby school cost more than most undergrad tuition and had a specialized program for young children with communication differences. He'd learned ASL there and how to use different apps and tools to express himself.

His main beef with the place was that they didn't have enough books to keep up with his appetite—or much of a plan for working with a kid reading at his absurdly high level. That, and he was barely out of toddlerhood and couldn't form objective opinions on these things yet.

"You won't be going back there," I said. "I'm going to find the perfect place for you. I have a friend who's a teacher and I'm going to get her advice. She'll know what to do. Trust me on this."

He stroked Beast's head as one tear streaked down his cheek. "Okay."

"All right, young man. Listen up." When he met my gaze after a long moment of tending to Beast, I said, "It's really late for me. I'm going to conk out any minute. We better get you into that bed."

He set the tablet down and shuffled around the room, rearranging his stuffies and pulling down the sheets. When he climbed into bed, he propped the tablet between his toys and curled on his side to face me. "Are you at Grammy Jannie's house now?"

"Not yet," I said. "I'll get there tomorrow."

"Are you going to ride horses?"

I shook my head. Another thing we'd missed on Mom's itinerary. "Not this time but we'll definitely do it when we visit her for the holidays this winter."

"Special secret trails only."

"You know me," I replied. "I don't get on a horse unless it's to ride with my child on unmarked trails in unfamiliar territory."

He gave me a floppy little salute as he yawned. "Remember not to eat any of Grammy Jannie's candy."

I'd learned the hard way that the candy dishes scattered around my mother's place were filled with *medicinal* treats. I ended up sleeping it off on the floor because the bed felt too porous. Which had been a very real concern for me at the time.

"Thanks for the reminder." I'd have to mention that to Audrey. God only knew what would happen if my mother dosed her with her special blend of psychoactives. "Do you want to watch some videos? Or do you want me to read to you?"

He tapped a finger to his chin. We started watching funny internet videos when he'd been miserably sick with an ear infection. I scrolled through social media while he dozed in my lap but he stopped me when a panda video came across my feed. For thirty seconds, the only thing that mattered to him was watching those pandas fall out of trees and roll down hills. Ever since, I'd kept a folder of bookmarked videos to help him zone out.

I didn't know if using social media to get my kid to sleep made me a terrible parent but it wasn't like I was introducing him to dudes with podcasts. Just goofy animals and some hypnotic cooking videos. Extremely precise cookie decorating clips knocked him out every time.

His eyes almost closed, he shook his head, signing, "Too tired."

"All right, good sir. This is where I leave you. Sleep well." Another yawn slipped out of him. "Call me if you need anything. Especially if your eyes are itchy when you wake up. Love you, Perce."

"Love you," he said, his fingers barely forming the sign.

I let the call linger for a few more minutes as he drifted off. I watched him breathe, just as I did most nights. Hadn't let go of that since the car accident. There was certainty in watching his little chest rise and fall. I didn't have all the answers but I knew he'd be okay. We'd be okay.

I typed a few notes to myself about touring some more schools when I got back home and pulled up the contact for the educational consultant I'd worked with to find the so-called baby school. Maybe they'd be able to steer me in the right direction, if Audrey didn't have any ideas.

It was strange to think about leaning on Audrey that way. Even when I'd decided to find her and convince her to come on this trip with me, I didn't let myself think about talking to her again. Not the way we used to talk. Didn't let myself think about sharing a bed or stripping off her wet clothes either.

I ended the call and pushed to my feet, staring at the vast dark stretching out before me. Stars peeked out from behind fast-moving clouds and stray threads of lightning struck in the distance. It wasn't so bad here.

Thinking about it now, under the endless blanket of dark sky and the scents of pinyon pine and rain-soaked red rock, this stop in Grandwood Valley hadn't been bad at all.

As I turned back toward the room, memories of her mouth on mine drowned out the lingering worry about schools and eye infections until all I could think about was the way she'd clung to me as if we hadn't even lost a day. I wanted to go back there, to that moment when she reached for me, when she *chose* me.

And when she said I'd abandoned her. When she said I'd given up on her.

Those words hurtled through my mind on an endless loop. In all the destruction between us, I didn't know what was true anymore—and I didn't know what I'd find when I opened this door. Odds were high that Audrey had already power-washed the incident from memory and was going to wrap herself up in all that polite, good girl energy to keep the boundaries in place.

But I watched her dance with every cowboy in that dive bar tonight. I watched her smile and flirt and shake her sweet little ass. And then she wrapped her body around mine like she wouldn't be happy unless she stole a piece of me to keep for herself.

Audrey was no good girl—and she wasn't nearly as polite as she wanted everyone to believe.

chapter twenty-three

Audrey

Today's vocabulary word: preemptive

I FLOPPED BACK AGAINST THE BATHROOM DOOR, ONE HAND OVER MY mouth and the other desperately trying to shove my heart back into my chest. Fresh waves of adrenaline coursed through my veins and my pulse clanged in my ears. My skin was a foreign thing, blistered and tight and throbbing.

Shudders moved through my shoulders and a hot flush painted my skin in splotches of pink and red as I reached all the way down to find an ounce of regret. I kept grabbing for it, searching for proof that I'd done something wrong—and I couldn't find it.

And that scared the hell out of me.

What did we just do? I dragged a palm over my eyelids as another thought barged into my head: *What if it happens again?*

The problem with me—one of the many—was that I needed to know what everything meant. I couldn't sit back and enjoy the ride. I had to snatch every moment as it passed, hold it up to the light, and turn it over and over until I understood what it said.

But when I held those words up—*We weren't over. Not then. Not now*—the only thing I understood was that we'd never be able to climb over the history between us. Never let it go, never move on. Everything we were was colored by the way it ended. And we'd spent an entire lifetime apart now. We'd grown up and grown apart, and there was no reason to believe we could pick up where—

Yet my body remembered him in ways my mind hadn't. His skin, his sounds, all of it. He kissed just like he always had. Focused and determined and so fucking sure of himself. Like we could start exactly where we'd left off and not a single thing would change.

I traced a finger over my lips, pressing hard at the sensitive spots. Little tingles zapped through me with every pass and my bones ached to open that door and finish what we started.

But I made the worst decisions when it mattered the most—and this mattered more than anything. I knew what would happen if I went back out there now. We'd have sex and it would be incredible. And we wouldn't stop after one time. But eventually we would stop and it would end in the most gutting, grueling way possible.

Then I'd be alone all over again. I didn't think I'd be able to bear it this time.

I heard Jude moving around the room. His phone kept buzzing but he didn't answer. I didn't know why not. I pushed off from the door on legs barely steady enough to propel me toward the shower.

All I knew was I couldn't stumble into a wall or make any sounds that would send him barging in here. We couldn't keep running into each other in the shower.

I turned on the water but didn't bother climbing into the stall. I rested my forehead on the wall and waited for Jude to answer his son's call. I didn't want to admit it but deep in a dark little corner of my mind, I'd thought about this. Thought about us. Hoped? I wasn't sure. Yes, hoped, if I was being hideously honest. It wasn't that I expected to get him back but I just wanted to remember what it'd been like before I ruined it all. I wanted to visit that place one last time.

But much like all the other things I acted out in my head, the reality was a different story.

I heard the front door close and held my breath, waiting. As the seconds passed and I heard no movement from inside the room, I let that breath out in a slow, choppy exhale.

Then I sprang into action.

A thin, scratchy towel wrapped around me, I peeked out the bathroom door. It was empty and dark. Either the power was out from the storm or we hadn't bothered with the lights. I startled at the muffled sound of Jude's voice filtering in from outside. I forced myself to stop and listen for a second, just to figure out how much time I had, but I couldn't hear anything over my own heartbeat.

Since I didn't want to get caught halfway into a pair of sleep shorts, I grabbed dry clothes and my toiletry bag, and flew back to the bathroom. I showered in the dark, fast and efficient. A little harsh too. Scrubbed hard at my skin, chasing away the sweat and dust and rain. I didn't let the washcloth linger on my nipples or between my legs. Didn't imagine someone stepping in behind me and pressing me up against—

Not helping.

I rinsed, dried off, and dressed quickly, making a beeline for the bed before my brain could invent anything worse than sexy shower thoughts. I twisted my hair into a high bun that would be loose waves tomorrow, downed my nighttime meds, and shook out the blankets. In case of lizards.

God, please don't let there be any lizards.

I paused, a pair of pillows in hand, and debated building up the borderlands between us tonight. Was there any point? After everything?

But if I didn't rebuild the wall, it would extend an invitation I didn't think I could grant. I'd spent years stitching these seams into place. I didn't know if I was prepared to rip them open all in one night.

I set one pillow in the middle and curled on my side, my back to the door. It was the only thing to do though I wasn't sure it was the right thing. For all I knew, Jude was out there drowning himself in a bucket of regret.

I caught his voice through the wall, low and steady as he promised his son everything would be okay. It was probably selfish to wish he'd say those words to me. He would, if I asked. That was why he was such a good dad. A *really* good dad.

I didn't know why that realization hurt so much but when I tried to swallow it down, it broke something inside me. There was a definite snap, the same as every time I'd broken toes dancing, and I knew that even when it healed, it wouldn't be the same again.

For once, I didn't want to examine what any of this was or ask what it meant. I knew well enough that there was no point in looking at it too closely. Instead, I tugged the sheets up to my chin and squeezed my eyes shut.

There'd be no reason to talk if I was asleep when he returned. I'd be an immovable object in the shape of a woman, barricaded and fully incapable of carrying on a painfully awkward conversation about why we couldn't do this.

We weren't over. Not then. Not now.

I buried my face in the pillow while Jude told his son to call if he needed anything. Would he tell me the same thing at the end of this week? And would I ever call if he did offer?

I wasn't sure—and that was why the pillow needed to stay between us tonight.

chapter twenty-four

Audrey

Today's vocabulary word: counsel

I TRUDGED ALONG THE SIDE OF THE ROAD, MY STRAPPY BEIGE wedges gathering gritty dust with every step. Not even an hour past dawn and the dry, thin air of the high desert was already oven-hot. That sun was unrelenting.

I held my phone over my head, flailing in search of a signal.

I'd woken to ribbons of early morning light sliding in through the sides of the curtains and the absolute certainty that Jamie would know what to do with my present state of affairs. That left me to sneak out of the room and far enough away from the motel to unload every detail of the past three days on her.

Except I couldn't get a signal.

This left me wandering the streets of Grandwood Valley in shoes that would need to be laid to rest after this trip and paying no attention at all to where I was going.

I finally stumbled onto a stable signal outside a livestock feed store and ducked into a wedge of shade while I waited for Jamie to answer. It was early for her, even with the time zone difference.

"Hello, my love," she sang, her voice bringing a rush of relief to my chest. "How's it going? Tell me everything."

"How long do you have?"

She cackled. "It's moving day, so maybe just the highlights, but I'll have all the time in the world for you tomorrow."

"Oh my god, that's right." I pressed a hand to my forehead. I couldn't believe I'd forgotten. "How's it going?"

"Well, I'm already counting down the minutes until I drop my ass into a kiddie pool in the backyard and drink my weight in moonshine margaritas, if that answers your question." She laughed again and I heard the shriek of packing tape in the background. "You know I'm so happy that my roommates are starting on new journeys and everything is wonderful and joyous for them."

"But," I prompted.

"But I am twenty-nine and moving in with my dad," she said, her tone flat.

"I know, honey," I said.

"I'm working very hard at telling myself it's not a failure or a step backward. I'm going to have a real kitchen and so much more space—and let's not forget about the kiddie pool in the backyard. There are no kiddie pools in my life right now. Or backyards. I mean, I live in a building that used to mass-produce spaghetti. There's nothing sexy about that. There's nothing sexy about living with my dad either but alas I am a lady of multitudes."

"You're moving in with him only because he needs your help," I added. Her relationship with her father had its own index of complications but his health wasn't in a great place and he couldn't live alone anymore—not that he'd admit it. Now, with her roommates moving out and on to new adventures, the time was right to go home. "No part of that says failure, James."

"I know, I know." I could almost hear her bobbing her head.

"And this is better than staying there half the time and trying to check in on him only for his phone to be off the other half. It's just a change that I haven't totally embraced and I kind of want someone to stamp an asterisk on my forehead so I can say *Yes, I'm moving home but not like that.*"

"You'd look cute with an asterisk on your forehead," I said. "It could serve several purposes."

"It really could." I heard her gulp down a drink. Then, "Give me the quick and dirty on your fake-fiancée tour."

"We've had every travel disaster in the world, and ended up getting stuck in a small town in Utah—I think? I don't even know where I am anymore—where we're sharing a horror movie motel room that has a ceiling leak, lizards, and only one bed. And—"

"Hold up, baby girl," she said. "You're sharing a room *and* a bed?"

I emptied everything into a sigh. "Yes."

"Mmhmm." I could hear her smug grin. "Go on."

"I was dancing with bull riders last night and then we yelled at each other for a few minutes before we kissed and did a few other things and had some sex—"

"You had *some sex*? What does that even mean? Oh my god, Audrey, never change."

"It would've turned into quite a lot of sex if his kid hadn't called."

After a beat of silence, I heard a slow clap. "I always knew you had it in you."

"Jamie! What should I do?" I wailed.

"Why do you have to do anything? Just let it happen."

"I can't *let it happen*," I said.

"And why not? I'm just saying, you're supposed to be putting on this elaborate show of being engaged and there's obviously some tension there so why not ride it out?" She chuckled. "Literally."

"Because—because we can't go down that road again," I said,

though it sounded like a pathetic excuse even to my ears. The most pathetic excuse. But it was also true, as much as I hated it. "And I don't think he wants that."

"Right, right, right," she murmured. "He's probably very meh about the whole thing. When you think about it, he dreamed you up —specifically *you*—as his fiancée and orchestrated this whole thing and participated in the jealous arguing, kissing, and getting half undressed. That's all very vague. I'm straining to connect the heart-shaped dots over here."

"That's not what's happening and I never said anything about jealous arguing."

"No, you didn't. You just prefaced it by saying you danced with bull riders, plural—nicely done, by the way—so I'm left to assume this boy of yours didn't enjoy watching from the sidelines."

"Fine. Let's say that's true. That means his reaction was about the heat of the moment and nothing else."

"You're saying he was so overcome by watching other guys touch you that the only thing he could do was make sure you remembered *him* touching you?" Jamie laughed. "Yeah. You're probably right. That meant nothing."

"We just can't go there," I said.

"Why not?" Before I could respond, she went on. "Not the wacky little stories you tell yourself to keep from doing the things you want, but seriously, truly, actually why not? Because I can't see a single downside to making the most of being trapped in a motel room with your possessive ex."

"I know what you're doing," I said.

"Fabulous, but do you know what *you're* doing? Because I'd call it ignoring obvious signs."

I huddled closer to the side of the feed store as the sun swallowed up my shade. I could feel it scorching the back of my arms. "I can't go there with him again. There's no way it would work out and, anyway, our lives are going in totally different directions."

162 · Kate Canterbary

"And who's to say they have to keep going in those directions? Or that those directions aren't meant to converge?"

"James, I love you, but I can't have an existential conversation right now. I need to know how to spend five non-awkward hours in a car with my alleged fiancé after we mauled each other last night."

"You want to find out where his head's at? Ignore him."

I shook my head. "What?"

"Yeah. Trust me on this. Read a book. Knit a scarf. Pop in some earbuds and listen to a podcast. Whatever. Do your own thing. Be aloof—you're remarkably good at that."

"Thank you?"

"Anytime, babe. Quiet yourself down and give him time to let those thoughts of his swirl themselves into a tornado. Just like they did when you started dirty dancing."

"It wasn't dirty dancing."

"If they were bull riders, it was dirty dancing. They don't know any other way."

"And how do you know anything about bull riders?" I asked.

"We don't have time for a lesson in ropes today," she said. "We'll sit in the kiddie pool when you're back home and have a single girls' night, and we'll get into it. If that boy doesn't wife you up before then."

"There will be no wifeing up on this trip," I whisper-yelled.

Behind me, a throat cleared. Loudly.

I had a feeling I knew who that sound belonged to. I dug my teeth into my lower lip and turned to find Jude standing a few feet away, his hands on his hips. Sunglasses hid his eyes but I recognized the cocky arch of his brow, the hard tick in his jaw.

"James," I said to her, still staring at him, "I'll call you tomorrow. Have fun in the pool."

"What's happening? Is he there? Oh my god, he's there, isn't he? How much did he hear? I need to know. Prepare to be sick of me.

Save every crumb for me and I'll eat them from the palm of your hand."

Jude swept a glance over my long sundress and the wedges stained dusty red. "Whenever you're ready," he started, nodding at the rental car I hadn't noticed pull up in front of the feed store, "we can get going."

"I'll talk to you later," I said to Jamie. "Love you." I ended the call as Jamie went on howling for details. "How did you know where to find me? Did you put a tracker on me? Like a microchip for a golden retriever?"

He sanded his knuckles through his scruff, his brows lifting in consideration. "No, but that's a good idea. Would save me some time." When I only stared at him, he added, "Small town. Not a lot of options."

I nodded, glancing over to the car. "I just need to get my—"

"Already loaded the luggage," he said.

"Oh. Okay." I shielded my eyes from the sun to see him better. "Thanks."

"Come on." He reached out, trailed the backs of his fingers down my arm until his hand circled my wrist. "You're getting sunburned."

Whatever it was that held me together—the hard leather of scars, and the social graces, and the mental corsets—eased until a strangely deep breath bubbled out of me. I felt a tug on those bindings, a finger tripping over the laces until he found the spot to start taking me apart.

He slid the pad of his thumb over my pulse and watched me with the lazy patience of any good apex predator. All I could do was stand there, my arms lightly toasted and my shoes ruined, and watch him while the strings holding *him* together loosened too. It happened in fractional parts and I wouldn't have noticed if we hadn't been standing close enough to hear each other breathe. The broad line of his shoulders, that granite jaw, the ceaseless pinch in his brows. And then he exhaled and it was like he'd stepped out of his armor.

I followed the bob of his throat as he swallowed. I'd never once in my life considered pressing my mouth to the front of someone's neck but now it was all I could think about.

I didn't believe Jamie was completely right, but...maybe she wasn't completely wrong either.

"Hot water," he said, clearing his throat again. "For your tea. I picked up a cup of hot water."

"Thank you," I said, the words quiet. "I was going to ask. About stopping. Thanks."

He tipped his head in a slight nod. "Did you sleep all right?"

I wanted to know if he felt my pulse jump in response. "Yeah. What about you?"

A brow arched over the rim of his sunglasses. "Not bad." The corner of his lips crooked up. "Panicked a little when I woke up and couldn't find you."

"Oh, sorry about that." I breathed out a laugh. "I couldn't get a signal."

He murmured in agreement. "I figured that, even if you ditched me, you wouldn't leave your noise machine behind."

"It's an air purifier," I said. "And I'm not going to ditch you."

His thumb skated up the inside of my forearm and down to my palm as those laces of mine loosened a little more. "You're not?"

"No, I'm not." I shuffled my feet, feeling the fine grit of red rock dust trapped between my toes. "I'm already three full days, one ungodly lizard, and an epic storm into this trip. Aside from the fact I'm in the middle of nowhere and have very little chance of getting out of here on my own, I'm committed."

"I'm not so sure about those chances," he said, that thumb back on my pulse. "You're stronger than you think."

"I—well." I pressed my lips together because I didn't know what to say to that. I *was* strong. I knew that and I was proud of all the things my strength had done for me but hearing it from Jude hit differently. It filled one of those empty spaces inside me. The one I'd ignored for years and told myself I could live without.

A truck rolled up towing a horse trailer and we both glanced in that direction. A cloud of dust billowed around the truck and the horses poked their heads out the back of the trailer. I waved to them.

Jude laughed under his breath. "Did you wave to the horses?"

"I don't know why you're asking because you watched it happen." I shrugged. "They seem like nice horses."

He pushed his free hand through his hair. A smile broke across his lips. "Percy would love that."

I smiled at him but didn't say any of the things burning on my tongue. That I liked when he talked about his son. That I wanted to hear more about him—the messy, complicated parts too. That it soothed my nervous system when we talked like this, calm and straightforward. I loved when we held verbal knives to each other's throats but I needed the other side of it too.

We lingered there another moment, silent and half hidden along the side of the building. He gave nothing away and it made me want to crack his skull open and poke around with chopsticks until I found his secrets.

"Should we—?" I motioned to the car.

"It's usually about a five-hour drive," Jude said. "But there's some damage from the storm. Might take a little longer."

"Okay." I couldn't pin down whether he was waiting for me to snatch my wrist back or there was more road info to impart but I bobbed my head and waited. "That's good to know."

He stared at my wrist for a long moment, watching as he stroked my pulse again. "I probably should've done this sooner but—"

He jerked a shoulder up and I interpreted that to mean *But it's been a fucked-up few days*. Maybe I was being generous and it was more like *But I've avoided open communication at every possible turn*. Probably a mix of both.

"Anyway, you're going to need this."

He pulled a small velvet box from his pocket with his free hand. He popped it open to reveal a delicate gold band topped with a pale purple gem cut in an oval shape.

It was lovely. Slightly unusual but still classic. Elegant.

And the exact ring I'd described when we were seventeen and promising away our forevers. We'd sat at the window table at Semantic while he sketched the ring in his notebook and asked me to tell him who we'd be when we grew up.

I'd made him promise not to propose with a ring hidden in food or drink because I'd find a way to choke on it. He'd made me promise to marry him as soon as we finished college.

Seeing it now, real and solid as he slid it onto my finger, was like waking up in the middle of a dream and not being able to figure out where the dream ended and reality began. Or had it been a nightmare? Was *this* the nightmare? Would I wake up any second and be reminded that losing everything I'd loved over and over again was the best I could expect from this?

"It fits," was my only response.

He twisted the band, settling it so the hefty stone sat perfectly on my finger. "Hmm. Yeah. I eyeballed it."

He remembered. He remembered every detail, right down to the millwork on the band. The stone was even the size I'd requested— about as big as an almond. I couldn't remember why that'd been important to me but he'd remembered it all. "It's…it's incredible."

Jude held my wrist as he led me across the parking lot. "Okay, good, let's go," he murmured, opening the passenger door.

He waited for me to drop into the seat and then pointed out the hot water and assorted breakfast items he'd sourced from the diner before closing my door.

I blinked down at the ring I'd wished for half a lifetime ago as he rounded the car. I didn't want to tell myself stories about what this ring meant but it wasn't easy.

The only thing I knew to be true was that Jude hadn't forgotten.

He glanced over as he started the car and caught me staring at the ring. His face tightened into his signature scowl and I realized he'd gathered up all the armor he'd abandoned at the side of the building. He shifted into reverse and draped an arm over my seat as he surveyed the parking lot. I was positive he was going to run a hand through my hair or down my arm. I knew something was going to happen.

But all he said was, "Don't worry, it's not real. I found a place online with next-day shipping."

I was right about something happening. I just hadn't expected it to be a guillotine snapping my silly shreds of hope. "What a relief." My voice sounded distant and robotic.

"I knew my mother would ask."

"Mmm. I can imagine she would."

I held the paper cup between my palms and stared out the windshield as Jude merged onto the highway.

We didn't say another word to each other for the next six hours.

chapter twenty-five

Jude

Today's vocabulary word: prevalance

"THERE ARE A FEW THINGS YOU SHOULD KNOW BEFORE WE GO IN there," I said, turning off the main road through Sedona to the neighborhood where my mother lived.

"This is going to be good," Audrey said under her breath.

I ignored the bite behind her words the same as I'd ignored her pointed silence for the past few hours. I got it. I'd crossed a lot of lines last night and she was pissed. It wasn't the direction she wanted this to go and that was fine. Finding her asleep in a bunker of pillows made it clear enough. Understood. Life liked to fuck up my hopes and dreams anyway. Not sure why I was wasting my time being disappointed.

I cleared my throat and focused on the issues at hand. "My mother lives in a small house that she shares with her friend Marguerite. It's just enough for the two of them but nowhere near enough for another person, let alone two. Regardless, she's going to insist we stay there."

Audrey kept her gaze on the road ahead, her chin tipped up like it helped her pretend I wasn't sitting beside her. "Please tell me that will not occur."

"It won't, we have rooms at one of the resorts in town," I said. "But she will *insist.*"

"And you're expecting me to defuse that situation?"

"It would help." She clasped her hands in her lap and I took that as agreement. "Don't eat any of the candy they have around the house unless you're up for a strange trip."

"I believe I'm already on a strange trip."

"The kind that'll have you freaking out over the texture of a rug and talking to doorknobs. I speak from experience." I rubbed the back of my neck as Mom's little terra cotta-colored house came into view. "She's going to want you to nail down plans. For the wedding."

"And I'm defusing that one too?"

She flexed her left hand, the light purple gem on her finger catching the sunlight as she moved. I'd known the moment she realized it was *the ring*. The one she'd dreamed up years ago. I knew the universe was made of cold, cruel irony but finally giving her the ring she'd always wanted and getting lashed with silence drove the point home harder than necessary.

My chest tightened, that unrelenting band that made me worry about heart attacks and living wills back in place. "Handle it however the hell you want," I snapped. "I'm just telling you what's going to happen in there."

"Thanks so much," she bit back.

"Anytime," I yelled.

"Have you considered that we're doing all of this because you won't have an honest conversation with your mother?"

I leveled a stare in her direction. "I guess you'd know all about that, wouldn't you?"

She returned the stare, a wall of ice behind those hazel eyes.

"It's good that you got my punishment out of the way for today. It would've been so uncomfortable to do it in front of Janet."

"Just trying to be efficient," I replied.

I pulled in front of my mother's house and shoved both hands through my hair. I didn't see how we were going to make this work. Not with last night still a raw, open wound between us and our story held together by threads. I'd be stunned if we lasted thirty minutes without throttling each other.

"Give me a minute," she said, pulling a small zip-up bag from inside her tote. "I'd rather not start this off looking like roadkill."

"You don't look like roadkill." I kept my gaze on my phone as I said this. I didn't want to watch while she fussed with her hair and dabbed makeup on her face. I didn't want to know her small, private moments. I couldn't. "She just wants to see you. She won't care how you look."

"I care," Audrey replied as she swiped a rosy-colored wand over her lips.

Okay, yes, I watched.

It was fucking ridiculous how something as irrelevant as lip color could hollow me out. One minute she was pressing her lips together and inspecting her work in the mirror, the next she was the only thing in the world worth seeing. Everything about her just made me want to lean closer.

The part that really killed me was that she didn't need me. She said she'd needed me back then, when it all fell apart, but not anymore. It was masochism at its finest but I wanted to know when that'd changed. What was the series of events that led her to surgically remove me from her life and just...move on without ever looking back? Maybe she could teach me how to do it because I still hadn't figured it out.

"Well." She snapped one of her products shut. "I'm still roadkill but now it's more like recent roadkill. Fresh. Not much of an improvement but it's something."

"Shut up, you're beautiful." The words were out before I could claw them back inside my head. Because being a jackass came naturally to me, I added, "And you don't need me telling you that because you know it."

She layered both hands over her chest and dropped a wistful sigh. "You really know how to make me feel special."

All I could see was my ring on her finger. Right where it belonged. I hated that I thought it and I hated that it was true.

"Let's go." I grabbed the keys and my phone, and didn't dare another glance at my fiancée as I climbed out of the car.

The front door flew open as we approached and Marguerite appeared, her tattooed arms out wide, bright orange glasses sliding down her nose, and a t-shirt with *Free Societies Read Freely* stretched over her chest. "We were beginning to think you weren't coming," she cried, fumbling us into an embrace. "You woulda been better off on pack mules at the rate it took y'all."

"I was looking into it," I said, patting my mother's partner in crime on the back. "Marguerite, this is Audrey."

"We're family now so you'll call me Rita like the rest of the girls do." She clasped Audrey's hands and leaned back, looking my fiancée over. "Aren't you just a doll?" She let out an ear-piercing shriek. "I bet you keep this boy up on his toes. It's a good thing because he needs a firm hand."

Rita patted my cheek with a little more pep than necessary but it earned me a real smile from Audrey, one without a shred of those good girl manners. *Worth it.*

"It's wonderful to finally meet you," Audrey said, gathering Rita into a hug. "I've heard so much about you."

Lies. Pure lies. But she was damn good at it—and that was a little scary.

Rita stepped back and shooed us toward the door, saying, "Let's get you inside. Your ma will be back from work soon enough and she's gonna flip that I got to see you first. Come on, get in there. I just mixed up some iced tea and I have some double chocolate brownie energy balls in the fridge. Do you like dates, Audrey?"

"I love dates," she replied.

"Good, good. My balls are full of dates," Rita said.

I stifled a laugh that I knew neither of them would've appreciated.

"Then I might need to steal that recipe from you," Audrey replied.

"Oh, I have a whole bunch of them," she said. "Lemme get my phone, I'll show you."

I watched while Audrey and Rita settled on the patio with iced tea and energy balls, slipping into an immediate familiarity over dates, of all things. Audrey could do that. She knew how to give people exactly what they wanted from her in any situation. It was how I'd known she'd be able to do this with me.

For me.

I also hated it when she did this. It was like she had a closet full of hermetically sealed personalities and could pull out a new one at any moment. But it meant suffocating herself and I didn't need an accounting of the past decade of her life to know she'd spent enough time suffocating.

As I lingered inside, I was painfully aware of the distance between us. I'd kept my hands to myself, a conscious effort when every instinct screamed at me to close the gap. But then I'd catch her eye and see that mask of polite composure, and remember that this wasn't real and my instincts could get fucked.

But I'd have to touch her again. Eventually. It would be strange if I didn't, right? They'd notice. My mother wasn't one to demand public affection but she'd pick up on something if I stayed five feet away from Audrey with my arms crossed for the next few days.

What a fine mess I'd made for myself.

I edged closer to the patio when I saw Audrey point to Rita's tattoo sleeves. I didn't hear the question but Rita tossed her head back with a bellow of a laugh.

"Back when the world was new and I was young, I taught high school art and sculpture," she told Audrey, motioning to the crook of her arm and then a spot just under the neck of her shirt. All of it covered in colorful ink. "But after beating breast cancer *twice*, I decided to keep the art and ditch the schools. Now, I bop around to tattoo studios around the country doing specialized ink work on scars."

"That's incredible," Audrey said. "I love that so much."

Rita leaned back in her chair, clasped her hands over her belly with a satisfied nod. "It's a good time."

"I did one year in second grade and that was plenty, and then I moved to a fourth and fifth grade loop," Audrey said.

"And it hasn't stolen your will to live yet?" Rita asked.

She took a long sip of tea as if she needed to think it over. "Not every day."

Rita waved her off. "Give it time."

Audrey laughed and steered the conversation toward Rita's newest tattoos but I wanted to stop and go back to the last part. I wanted to ask what she meant by *not every day* and find out if her work made her happy or if it was just another personality she put on. Ask—*again*—why she didn't teach dance. Even on the weekends, just because she loved it.

That'd been the plan. She'd study comparative literature and dance at Barnard, and when she finished school, she'd teach English and some dance classes in her spare time. The idea was that she'd be able to find work anywhere since I hadn't known where I'd land for grad school.

But I knew best of all that plans changed.

chapter twenty-six

Jude

Today's vocabulary word: insistent

WHEN MY MOTHER ARRIVED, SHE UNHINGED HER JAW AND swallowed Audrey whole.

She blew right past me and devoured my fiancée in a wild monologue that rambled on for minutes. Audrey gave up on trying to respond but she smiled and nodded and let my mother drag her all around the house to look at one thing or another.

"Janet, you're going to suffocate the girl before we get her down the aisle," Rita yelled from the kitchen. "Slow your roll."

"I've been waiting so long to see you two," my mother said, her hands outstretched to me and Audrey. At five feet even, my mother had to tip her head back to gaze up at us. "You've found a way back to each other and it's such a gift to finally see you together."

The way my mother smiled, so bright and raw and hopeful—it sliced right through me. She looked genuinely happy, but more than that, she looked *relieved*. That was the part that hit me hardest. She'd struggled for so long, and not just with the disease. But in raising me alone, scrapping to make ends meet, putting me first again and again. All I could feel was the weight of this lie and how much worse it would be when this ended.

"The real gifts here are the statement shirts," I said through a knot in my throat.

She pulled at the t-shirt that read *Of course they're fake! The real ones tried to kill me.* "I get the best compliments on this shirt. I have it in five different colors."

"I love it," Audrey said. "How are you doing, Janet? I'm so sorry I didn't call to check on your progress sooner—"

"None of that," Mom said. "I can talk about that bastard all day long. I can give you every ugly-ass story. But I'm not going to. I'm too busy living my life. That bastard is gone, he's not coming back, and that's the end of it."

"Amen," Rita shouted.

Audrey forced a smile and I could see her struggling to meet Mom's badass energy while also checking off the good manners box. "I'm so happy to hear it. I've been hoping for the best for you. Jude's kept me updated along the way, of course."

She gestured to me. I arched a brow. I knew she was asking me to step in and save her but I was running short on sympathy today.

"The best part of the whole ordeal is that I got these brand-new tatas." I turned my gaze to the ceiling as my mother cupped her breasts. "They don't sag! It's like I'm eighteen again. Nice and firm. You should feel them."

"Janet, don't force your daughter-in-law to fondle you," Rita yelled.

"I'm not forcing anyone," Mom yelled back. "I'm *offering*."

"And you wonder why it took them so long to visit," Rita said. "They're here for five minutes and you're whipping out the tits like they're some souvenirs from your last cruise."

"You look...amazing," Audrey said. "It's great to find that confidence again after going through a painful ordeal."

I bit back a laugh. Audrey stabbed my lower back with her bony little pinkie finger and pretty much skewered my kidney in the process.

"Such a sweetheart you are." Mom pulled Audrey into a squeeze and out of stabbing range. "All right, you two. I hope you're hungry because we're going to one of Gary's restaurants. I've told you about Gary," she said to me. "From up the street? Well, he has a few restaurants and he wants to give you the VIP treatment tonight."

I made a gruff noise that I doubted I'd be able to replicate on purpose. "Gary's at it again, huh?"

"Which one are you goin' to?" Rita called.

"Agave," Mom shouted back.

"That's my favorite," Rita said. "You're gonna love it. Get the mushroom fajitas."

I was beginning to think they came to know Gary simply because he could hear them yelling all the way up the street.

"You really will love it. If you don't see anything you like on the menu, Gary will have them make something special for you. I can't wait for you to meet him," Mom said to us. "I'm going to change and then we can go."

I blinked at my watch. I knew time zones could be tricky in this part of the world but—"Mom, it's four fifteen."

"We've already missed three days together and we have so much to talk about," she said. "We'll start with drinks on the deck so everyone can get to know each other. If you're not hungry yet, you will be after we chat for a few hours."

"Hours," I repeated.

"We'll take our time getting to the meal." My mother beamed. My stomach thudded. "I have so many wedding ideas to share with you two. Remind me to bring my binder with all my inspo collages."

"You're gonna need a wheelbarrow for that thing," Rita yelled.

My mother reached for me, her hands gripping my shoulders. "It's so good to see you happy." With a glance between me and Audrey, she asked, "Are you all settled in? I hope you know you're free to move things around in my room to make yourselves comfy."

"We're not taking your room," I said. "I've already told you this."

Mom's eyes flashed. "I'm not letting you spend money on a hotel."

"You know money isn't an issue for me," I replied.

"I know you've spent more than enough of it on me and you have a family to be thinking about now. And there's plenty of space here." She swept her arm out and knocked a wind chime into motion. She leaned close to Audrey, saying, "Did you know my son bought me this house? Moved me out here when I finished treatment, and furnished the whole place. Did he tell you about that?"

Audrey glanced toward me, a knowing smile cutting across her face. Mom probably read that as Audrey being well aware of the lengths I'd gone to, to give her some post-cancer comfort. But I knew better and I knew that smile meant *You've always been such a fucking softie.*

"Did he tell you about the navy? He doesn't like to talk about it but they've been trying to hire him for years." She motioned for Audrey to come in closer like she had some classified information to share. "But they can't afford him so they fly him in every few months to fix the problems no one else can figure out."

"While you're great for my ego, Mom, that isn't—"

"He turned out all right, didn't he?" Audrey wrapped an arm around Mom, pulling her into her side for a hug. "You raised a good one, Janet."

My mother was already misty-eyed. Of course. "We raised each other," she said.

"Then you both did a great job," Audrey said, patting Mom's arm.

"I'd love it if you'd stay," Mom said. She thought she was capitalizing on the moment but I saw the game Audrey was playing. I didn't know her next move but I trusted it. "It just makes me so happy to have everyone here."

"We're thrilled to be here with you. Finally! After the wackiest travel experience of our lives." She glanced up at me with a cotton candy smile. "The thing is," Audrey went on, dropping her voice to an intimate whisper, "we could really use some privacy. After the past few days with everything being so hectic..." She gave a coy shrug. "I hope you understand."

My whole body responded to the soft drag of those words. I felt it across my shoulder blades and down my spine, at the base of my throat and behind my zipper. I didn't even think before wrapping an arm around Audrey's waist, pulling her away from Mom and into *my* side, my hand settling high on her hip. I traced the edge of her panties through the thin cotton of her dress and watched with a good deal of satisfaction as pink colored her cheeks.

It took a second but recognition dawned for my mother. "*Oh.* Oh, of course," she said, a hand on her brow. "Of course you'd need your own space."

I dipped my chin and brushed my lips over Audrey's shoulder. It wasn't necessary, but it wasn't necessary for her to imply she wanted to be railed straight through a mattress tonight either. And the dainty, ribbon-tie straps on this dress hadn't stopped filling my head with filth since finding her outside the farm supply store.

"You'll see plenty of us this week," Audrey promised, shifting toward her and out of my hold. Such a crafty little princess. "We won't be strangers."

"Like I'd let that happen," Mom chirped. "Stay right there. I'll be back in a dash." Before I could add anything, she flitted off to her bedroom.

An arm's length away now, Audrey whispered, "Do you think Gary's going to want to take you to baseball games and teach you how to change a flat tire? Since your mom is soft launching him as your new dad?"

"Bite your tongue, Saunders. There's a *binder* of *collages* waiting for you," I whispered back.

She stepped slightly closer and I picked up the scent of her shampoo. I didn't hate it. "That horror show is waiting for us both."

I glanced back inside to where Rita was busy slicing fruit and chucking it into the blender. "Do you think we can sweet-talk Rita into coming along?"

Audrey crossed her arms over her chest. Her elbow grazed my bicep. I wanted— I didn't know what I wanted. All I knew was that I was deeply aware of her. Every move, every word, every glance. "*We* aren't sweet-talking anyone. I just maneuvered my way out of feeling up your mom *and* slipped the noose on staying here. Next one's on you."

I pushed a hand through my hair. "Fuck."

chapter twenty-seven

Jude

Today's vocabulary word: downplay

"It was a lizard? On the curtain?" Gary wheezed, his eyes shining and his face warm from laughing.

"A lizard," Audrey replied.

"But it must've just been a little guy, like the ones we see around the yard," Mom said. "They won't do any harm."

"It was three feet long if it was an inch," Audrey said, holding her hands up to the approximate size of the beast. "It was—"

"It was a dragon," I cut in. "I'm sure of it."

"And this guy," Audrey said, leaning into me, "jumps out of the shower, traps it in the reusable container I'd packed with my home-made scones, and bolts across the parking lot in nothing but a towel." She sanded her hands together. "I don't know what the good people of Grandwood Valley thought when they saw that show but that's a story they'll tell for years. Between us, it wasn't much of a towel. I wouldn't be surprised if the locals saw a whole lot more than the sunrise that morning."

Once again, Gary and my mother doubled over laughing. I'd lost count of the number of times Audrey had them in stitches during drinks and dinner as she told them a sanitized—but also sensation-alized—account of the past few days.

I didn't know how she did it with such grace, not to mention the comedic timing, but I appreciated the hell out of her for it. I also appreciated the chance to size up Gary.

He seemed nice enough. Bald as a bowling ball and barely scratching five-eight, he made a point of pulling out my mother's chair and requesting refills on her iced tea as soon as she hit the half-empty mark. I gave him credit for downplaying his role in the restaurant. He could've talked a big game but he kept it low-key. No one liked a guy with an ego.

All the same, I still planned on dropping a note to a buddy of mine who owned a private security firm and asking him to dig around in Gary's closets. Just to make sure this guy wasn't into money laundering or some shit.

"I can't believe all the trouble you had," Gary said, pressing a napkin to the corners of his eyes.

"It was one adventure after another," Audrey said.

"I'm just happy you're here now," Mom said. "There's so much to talk about and we only have a few days before you leave *again*." She hit me with an exaggerated glare as she hefted the infamous binder to the table. "We should start with the date."

I was ready to respond with some noise about saving this for another time but Audrey's knee pressed into the outside of my thigh as she dropped a hand to my forearm. "Don't you think we should meet up for lunch tomorrow, Janet? Just the girls?" she asked, a gorgeous smile aimed at my mother. "We need more time to talk than what these guys will grudgingly endure."

"I *love* that idea," Mom said, "and I know just the place."

"Juniper and Ivy?" Gary asked, pulling out his phone. "Or Canyon Crossing?"

Mom grinned up at him like he was really fucking wonderful. "You read my mind," she said. "Juniper would be amazing."

"I'll get the corner booth reserved so you have room to look over all of your designs," he said.

"Perfect. We'll make a day of it," Audrey said, giving my arm a squeeze. "I'll give you our ideas for dates and you can show me everything you've dreamed up for our big day."

My mother's eyes turned to hearts. It was exactly what I'd wanted out of this. That overflow of joy and optimism for the story-book ending she'd wanted for me. The promise of so many good things to come.

But the victory was a hollow one. Come the end of summer, our story would unravel and all of this would end. Maybe that was the real curse of this whole scheme—not that I'd lose Audrey all over again but that after everything I'd done to fulfill my mother's (nearly) last wish, I'd be the one breaking it.

"I THINK IT'S ADORABLE," AUDREY SAID.

I led her through the hotel lobby, our luggage in one hand. "I think it's desperate."

"Come on," she said. "He brought his car in to be serviced for something new every week for two months and then started bringing in his friends' cars just for a chance to see Janet at the front desk, and you don't think that's cute?"

"If you want my honest opinion, I'd say it rings some stalker bells."

"No, it doesn't!" she said. "It would be one thing if he'd asked her out during those two months and she turned him down. He just didn't know how to approach her."

"Which is a skill issue if I've ever seen one." I shot her an exasperated glance as we waited to check in but there wasn't any real heat behind it. I liked when we argued about things that didn't matter. Like Mom and Gary's meet-cute. "He's old enough to know how to ask a woman out. He's been around the block."

"How does it feel?" She glared right back but her smile gave it away. She'd forgotten about resenting my entire existence long enough to enjoy this debate. "Having all the answers *and* the moral high ground?"

I ran a hand through my hair. "It's going to feel damn good tomorrow when you're debating color palettes and types of buttercream for sixteen hours."

She rolled her eyes as we stepped up to the desk. "You might feel differently about that when you realize you're wearing a pale pink tux with a crown of baby's breath to this wedding."

I laughed and handed our information to the representative. She pecked at the keyboard for a long moment before sucking in a breath and motioning another staff member over. Audrey and I shared a glance before I asked, "Is there a problem?"

The newcomer turned to us with a saccharine smile. "I'm afraid there was an incident in one of the rooms you booked," he said.

I rubbed my forehead. "What kind of incident?"

"An electrical matter," he said.

I cast another meaningful glance at Audrey. Her brows pitched up and the humor in her eyes was gone. She asked, "Is that a big problem around here?"

"It was an unusual incident," he replied. "Unfortunately, we're only able to offer you one room tonight. We expect the second will become available tomorrow after our standard check-in time of four in the afternoon."

I drummed my fingers on the desk. I didn't think we'd survive another night together. "You couldn't have notified us any earlier?"

"You have our deepest apologies," he said. "I can offer you complimentary breakfast for the duration of your stay."

Audrey's cheeks puffed as she blew out a breath. With that

breath went the perfect posture and every last piece of the mask she'd worn to charm Mom, Gary, and Rita. The color in her cheeks drained and her eyes went heavy. Her whole body seemed to slouch. It had to be exhausting, being everything to everyone.

With a sigh, she asked, "What's the bed situation in this one room?"

He pursed his lips and I knew this wasn't going to work out well for us. "It's our signature select California king pillow top."

"I should've known," she muttered. "This better be a phenomenal breakfast."

"It's actually very good," the first representative said.

I shifted to face Audrey. "We don't have to do this. We can—"

"No, Jude, we can't," she said, her voice cracking like she was about to cry. "I'm *so* tired. I don't have the emotional strength to figure out a new plan because this place casually catches on fire sometimes. I intend on taking the longest, hottest shower of my life and then popping a giant sleeping pill. If you want to do something else, you're welcome to leave me here."

"Like hell I'm leaving you here," I said.

She shook her head. "Fine. We're doing this. Again."

The room was free of both ceiling leaks and reptiles, and Audrey spent forty-five full minutes in the shower while I talked to Percy. She stayed in the bathroom another half hour and I had to assume she just needed to be alone. After being the main attraction for Mom, Gary, and Rita, she had to be mentally wiped out.

When she emerged, she pulled some extra pillows from the closet and drew the boundary lines on the bed before climbing in. She didn't say much and, as threatened, fell asleep before the end of a sitcom rerun.

I flipped over to an F1 race when I knew she was out. I was exhausted but I was too worked up to let myself relax. I couldn't stop replaying a carousel of moments from the past few days. Then there was the pounding heat of last night. I couldn't get away from the memories of her hands on my skin, her lips pressed to mine. I kept feeling the weight of her against me, the way she'd leaned in without hesitation. So fucking reckless—but so right.

All I knew was that she'd kissed me back last night. She'd reached for me, she'd *wanted* me. And I was ruined for it.

chapter twenty-eight

Audrey

Today's vocabulary word: compensate

"Same botanical garden location, different season," Janet said, setting another collage on the table. "I played around with the color palette here to give it more of a warm autumn feel. See what I mean?"

"It's lovely," I said, running my gaze over the designs. I'd come prepared to humor the hell out of her and fake all my enthusiasm. If it came to it, I'd pull her down an obscure rabbit hole—a cute quote for custom cocktail napkins, symbolic dessert options, fun table names with special meanings. So far, there'd been no need to dip into my bag of tricks. Not with everything she'd crammed into that binder. "The autumn one is really pretty."

The hard part of this charade was that I liked her designs. If we were actually getting married, I'd chain myself to a few of these looks. It left me with a bittersweet mix of longing and guilt. I didn't want to think that this could've been real. If things had been different and life hadn't been what it was for us—for *me*—this might've been ours. The thought was a fine shard of glass in my heart.

"If you get bored at the car dealership, there's a future for you in event design," I said.

"These are just ideas," Janet said for the fortieth time today. Always very careful to make sure I knew she didn't want to steamroll me. But at the same time, there were a few constants in every design and plenty of comments that made her priorities crystal clear. Suffice it to say, the cake would be frosted in buttercream, round, and three tiers. Five if we really thought it was necessary. And no "ridiculous" flavors like lemon. "I'm sure you have plenty of your own."

I reached for my drink, laughing. "You'd think so. All of my friends have been getting married over the last few years—one is getting married in Rhode Island next weekend, actually—but I haven't found much time to consider what I'd want."

"Jude mentioned you had to head back east for your bestie's big day." Janet's grin over the rim of her iced tea was intensely curious. "Too bad he has so many meetings and won't be there as your date."

I didn't have to fake the fun but I was fighting for my life with these stray comments. Last night's boundless joy still bubbled over but now there was a strange new element.

At first, I'd filed those meaningful stares and not-quite passive-aggressive but definitely somewhat aggressive comments away as my own hypersensitivity. Count on me to take the emotional pulse in the room every thirty seconds and overcompensate for it. And after being the main event and monologuing my way through four *long* hours of drinks, dinner, and dessert last night, I was mentally toasted today. Whatever my spidey senses picked up, I felt it twenty times harder than reality. I told myself everything was fine and that I was being paranoid.

But then I realized Janet had her doubts.

"I know." I threw in a dramatic groan to make sure she knew I was heartsick over it. "He'd love the tulip farm where it's being held. It's that offbeat brand of quirky that he enjoys so much."

She tapped a hot pink nail to a collage doused in shades of plum and evergreen. She was right. He'd take one glance at the table and pick that palette. "He'll only do it if he can do it his own way."

"I couldn't say it better myself." I pulled that collage closer. The less we talked about Jude, the less she tried to interrogate me. "Do you think this would work for summer? Or does it belong in late autumn or winter?"

She propped her reading glasses on her head. "You're leaning toward summer, then?"

"We've talked about it." I held up two color palettes as if I was torn between them. "Summer plays well with teacher schedules."

"Mmm. I hadn't thought about that." She shuffled the papers into orderly rows. "Summer is tougher for Jude though. With Percy in Michigan."

"We'd definitely plan around that visit," I said quickly. "If we went with a summer date. We wouldn't get married without Percy there. That's out of the question."

Janet studied her designs for a moment. Going for a calm, completely unflustered vibe, I sat back and nibbled a tortilla chip. Internally, I was kicking myself. I knew Percy spent summers with his maternal grandmother. I couldn't believe I'd tripped myself up on such a basic detail.

"And your family? Do they have any thoughts on the date?"

I was amazed that I didn't snort-laugh. "Not too much, no." The peacekeeper in me wanted to pour on details about them just being excited to celebrate with us whenever this fictional wedding occurred but the rest of me knew I wouldn't be able to say it without gagging.

She reached for my hand, gave me a firm squeeze. "I'm just so happy you've been able to put the past behind you."

I sensed a ripple in the waters, the start of a subtle but serious undertow that would drag me under if I didn't brace myself now. "Growing up will do that to you." I lifted my shoulders in a bashful shrug. "And there's a lot to learn from time apart."

If Janet remembered saying those exact things to us back in high school during one of the many *too serious too fast* lectures, she didn't show it.

She slipped her glasses into place and examined one of the designs she'd referred to as "my son would hate this." She smiled at the mauvey pink and honeyed yellow. He *would* hate it. "I hope that's true." A slight edge rang in those words. "All those years and he wouldn't tell me what happened between you two."

Now, that was new information. I'd never thought much about what Jude might've told her—or anyone—but it shocked me that he'd kept it all buttoned up. I figured he would've given her the headlines. At least make it known where the blame belonged.

"He went through hell," she went on. "That whole year it was like he was walking under a rain cloud. But he wouldn't talk about it. Wouldn't let me help." She flicked a hand as she rolled her eyes. "Then he picked up and transferred to Caltech the next year. The change was good for him. He needed to stretch his legs, like I always thought."

I choked on air but explained it away with, "Tortilla chip crumb," between gulps of water. Glasses were refilled and the offending chips removed, which was sad because I was using them for a prop *and* emotional support. I needed both more than ever if I was to accept the fact Jude switched to a school an hour away from mine and I didn't know about it until right now.

One of the many problems about inventing a relationship out of thin air was that I had to act like I knew all of this. All I could do was go along with her and not ask a single question because a real fiancée would have the answers. A real fiancée would've known her future husband had gone to school forty-five miles away from her at Pepperdine for three whole years. A real fiancée would've known why he transferred there.

Janet offered a tissue from her purse. "Are you all right, sweetheart?"

"Fine, fine," I wheezed as I blotted my eyes. "Sorry about all that."

"No sweat." She laughed like she hadn't been flame-grilling me just now. "Rita has this post-nasal acid reflux situation. She chokes on something daily." She tucked the tissue packet away, saying, "It took him a long time to move on, Audrey. I won't say he ever got over you because I don't think he did."

All these truths piled up in my stomach. I did my best to look like I understood—that I wasn't hearing this for the first time today —and that she didn't have to worry about a repeat performance. Even if that was exactly where we were heading. "It was a tough time for both of us," I said. "I wouldn't wish it on anyone."

She stared at me like she wouldn't mind slicing through the layers of my skin until she found my true intentions for her son—or my soul rotting away like an old apple core, whichever she stumbled upon first. That was when I knew it was *me* she doubted, not the engagement or Jude or anything else. She wanted a guarantee I wouldn't hurt him again.

It killed me that I'd be the villain in her story once more.

Her face brightened and she leaned close like she wanted to tell me a secret. "We've done enough with the palettes and collages, don't you think? Let's get out of here. I have an idea."

"YOU'D TELL ME IF IT'S TOO MUCH, RIGHT?" JANET PIVOTED ON THE block in front of the mirrors. "I wouldn't want to steal your spotlight."

I didn't know how to tell her that the last thing in the world I cared about was anyone stealing my spotlight. She shifted again and rhinestone-studded layers on the flapper dress went with her. "It's gorgeous," I said. She really was radiant. The style was perfect for her. "It feels like you."

"The new boobs help." She palmed her breasts and gave them a jiggle. "It's pretty but I don't want to commit to anything until you finalize your plans. Who knows? You might end up doing this at a fancy yacht club back east and I'd look like a nut."

"I can promise there will be no yacht clubs," I said.

Janet turned from the mirrors to face me. I knew what was coming next. She didn't bring me to a bridal boutique only to show off the mother of the groom dresses she'd scoped out. No, she wanted me trying on gowns for the next hour, and unless I jumped up and ran right through the shop's front window, I didn't see any way out of it.

Motioning to a mannequin dressed in a lovely lace gown, Janet asked, "Isn't that spectacular?"

I pushed up from the cream velvet sofa to get a better look. It *was* beautiful and since I was playing the role of Audrey, Jude's fiancée, and not Audrey, the real person, it didn't matter whether it was far too elaborate for my tastes. Audrey, Jude's fiancée, couldn't wait to try on dresses. She loved huge ball gowns and fussy lace sleeves, and she definitely didn't have any lingering PTSD over the last time she'd been shoehorned into a dress and shoved down the aisle. She wouldn't hyperventilate at the sight of herself.

"It's spectacular," I said, tracing a finger down the tiny line of buttons on the back.

Janet clapped her hands together. "You should try it on! Just for fun! Since we're here."

I grinned at her. This would be fine. I probably wouldn't break out in hives. "Since we're here."

chapter twenty-nine

Audrey

Today's vocabulary word: transcendent

"This is a nice fit for you," Sharese, the shop owner, said as she clipped the lace dress closed in the back. "Not everyone can pull off the basque waist but you have a good torso."

A good torso. I'd heard a lot of judgments on my body over my years in dance but I couldn't remember *good torso* hitting the list.

"Thanks, I think," I said with a laugh. I realized then that I could still taste the garlic from my lunch—which meant Sharese could smell it. Maybe it was the everyday urge to apologize for existing but having bad breath made me want to find a vat of acid and disappear into it.

"It's a compliment," Sharese said as she pulled back the dressing room curtain. She gathered up the dress's long train and nudged me down the hallway. "You're going to be a beautiful bride."

"You probably say that to all the girls."

Her chuckle told me I was right. "I've been doing this for

twenty-seven years and I'll tell you right now that everything is going to look good on you." As we rounded the corner to where Janet sat on the velvet sofa, Sharese announced, "This is from the Hattie Zhou collection. Ivory hand-sewn lace over an ivory sheath, elegant high neckline, and basque waist."

She positioned me on the platform and fluffed out the skirt around me. Janet clasped her hands under her chin, her eyes wide and smiling. "It's amazing," she breathed.

"Are we thinking veil or headpiece?" Sharese asked.

"Bring both," Janet said.

I told myself Audrey the fiancée would try on both. The fiancée wouldn't panic over a veil.

While Sharese went searching, I stepped off the platform and motioned Janet closer. "Do you have any gum? Or mints? I feel like the guacamole is lingering on me."

"Of course, honey. Just give me a sec." She dug in her purse, coming up with a small tin. As she held it open for me, she asked, "Do you just love it?"

I popped two mints and forced a grin. I had to pull off some serious praise sandwiches here. Wedge the deflection between the good news. "It's so special. I love the sleeves. I'm all about the sleeves right now. The neckline might be a little high for me. It feels a little serious, you know? But the lace is incredible. It has such an antique feel."

She pointed at me. "You're right. That neck is too much. We don't want the dress to eat you alive."

"That would be nice," I teased.

"My son would never speak to me again if I tried to wrap you up like a mummy." She winked and all I could do was laugh. Maybe I'd put her doubts to rest.

"A veil with matching lace," Sharese trilled as she returned, "and a delicate ribbon headband."

"Let's start with the headband," I said.

"And let's try a few gowns with a little more skin showing," Janet said. "She's such a pretty girl, we need to show her off."

Sharese snapped her fingers. "I have ideas."

Over the next hour, I tried on fourteen more dresses which seemed like a lot of dresses to me. Some of them came off as quickly as they went on—the bubble hems were a fast no from Janet and Sharese, along with several others with big sculptural elements that made me feel like a cartoon character. We liked a few of the simple, classic ball gowns and a few other fitted styles, and I survived two veils without diving into the deep end of my feelings.

But my skin was red and welted from changing so many times, and the desert air must've dried me out because my head was fizzy and a little too light. Janet was having a blast but we'd need to wrap this up after the next couple of picks. Between the altitude and the desert heat, I felt like I'd tripped and fallen into an air fryer.

And I missed Jude. I didn't know where that thought came from but I knew it was true. There was a comfort in sitting with him in hostile silence. Even if everything was upside down, I didn't have to think so hard with him. Or maybe that was the Stockholm syndrome talking.

"We're calling this shade toasted apricot," Sharese said as she zipped me into another dress. "It's organza with hand-tied silk flowers and a grosgrain ribbon belt."

It reminded me of my friend Emme's first wedding dress, from when she and Ryan eloped last year. I traced the flowers along the bodice. They looked like daisies with tiny seed pearls at the center.

Sharese herded me back to the platform. She and Janet chatted about the details and I went on tracing the flowers. The pearls felt strange against my fingertip. Like a million microscopic roller skate wheels. Like roller skates for ants. Did ants roller skate? Probably. Why wouldn't they? And the flowers were like tissues—but also cotton candy.

No, wait, hold on. Those flowers *were* cotton candy. I could eat them. But would they taste like cotton candy or fabric? Or fabric-flavored cotton candy? I had to find out.

In an oblique way, I knew that was strange. Remarkably strange. But the more I clutched at that awareness, the less I felt of it.

"Oh, honey, no," Janet said, pulling my hand away from the bodice. "Only the belt comes off, not the flowers."

"It's okay," I said, leaning in close to her face. "It's cotton candy."

"It's—what?" Janet glanced between me and Sharese who looked like she'd just swallowed a buzzing bee. That would be weird. Like that scene in *Pinocchio*. What a *terrifying* movie.

I studied my reflection in the mirrors, shifting to catch a glance at the back of the dress. "These lights are heavenly," I said. "Do you see my halo? I have a halo. I think I'm actually an angel." I turned to Sharese. "Can you add wings to this dress?" I patted my shoulders. "Not feathery but like…mermaid. You know what I mean."

"I'm so sorry," she replied. "I don't think I heard you. Did you say you wanted *wings*?"

Muscle memory wanted me to say no. To apologize and stop talking. But there was woolly static in my head and I felt as though I was trapped in a snow globe while everyone stared at me from the other side. And the words just kept coming out like a magician's handkerchief trick.

"Oh, shit," Janet murmured. "Honey, which of those mints did I give you?"

She dumped her bag on the sofa. It looked like the aftermath of a solid whack to a piñata. I raced toward her to help scoop up everything that'd tumbled out, falling to my knees as I chased lip balms, pens, and small zip pouches.

"Sharese doesn't want us to know this but the sofa is made of vanilla ice cream," I whispered to her. I giggled, but inside my head I heard *What the hell is happening?* Something was wrong—but I also felt incredible. I never wanted it to stop. "I don't know how it's not melting but the angel lights probably have something to do with it."

"Excuse me," Sharese sang. "Is everything…all right? Perhaps you'd like to return to the fitting room?"

Janet took my hands in hers. "Audrey, honey, I don't know how to tell you this."

"Is it about the ice cream? Or the roller skates?"

She squeezed her eyes shut, murmuring, "My son is going to kill me."

"No, he won't," I said, wrapping my arms around her. "He loves you so much, Janet. He'd do anything for you. Absolutely anything. Even really crazy shit that I don't understand. *Especially* the crazy shit. In a way, it's quite unrealistic."

She grinned but it looked like there was something sour in her mouth. "Sweetie, those weren't mints. They were ecstasy tabs."

chapter thirty

Jude

Today's vocabulary word: endurance

I PACED THE LENGTH OF MY MOTHER'S PATIO, ONE HAND KNEADING the back of my neck while the other gripped my phone hard enough to make the case creak. "That's it?" I asked.

Through my earbuds, Jordan Kaisall let out a rasping noise intended to highlight his displeasure with me. Unfortunately for him, I didn't give a fuck about his feelings. "If there was something to find, I would've found it."

"You're a shit friend," I said.

"Same to you, brother," he shot back. "I don't hear from you for a whole *fucking* year and this is the first thing you say to me? Go fuck yourself."

"Excuse me but the first thing I said to you was I need you to run a deep dive on my mother's boyfriend. And second, I texted you about getting tickets when the Caps went to the playoffs. Which was not that long ago."

"Let me explain something to you about mothers and

boyfriends. You have no control over this shit. You have to sit back and mind your fucking manners. Okay? He's not embezzling money from nursing homes, he's not a sex pest, he doesn't have a string of dead women in his past. He cheats on his taxes but no more than anyone else, his internet history is unconcerning, and he's had an active prescription for ED pills for the past year. That's all I've got for you."

"We're not talking about his dick, Kaisall. Goddamn. Why do I have to tell you that?"

"You asked for everything," he replied.

Letting out an annoyed snarl, I glanced at my watch. I didn't know why Mom and Audrey weren't back yet but I didn't like it. Lunch didn't last five hours, not even with my mother talking a mile a minute. And Audrey hadn't answered a single one of my texts all day. Nothing about that seemed right.

"I've been there. You'll learn to live with it or you'll give yourself high blood pressure until you have a stroke. You just gotta pick which sounds like more of a hassle," Kaisall went on. "Hold up. Why are you having a shit fit over this? You're not a young guy."

"Fuck you very much."

"You're welcome but I mean this can't be the first time your mom has dated. There have been dudes before this one."

"She's never been serious about anyone. Never like this," I said. "She's just been through a lot in the past couple of years. She doesn't need some dickhead fucking up her life when she's finally doing all right."

"Okay, well, he might be a dickhead but he's unremarkable on paper and not a criminal." After a pause, he added, "And I'm sorry about missing the text about the Caps. I think I was off the grid when that happened and I was a little foggy when I got back stateside. You know how it goes."

"The fuck I do." I glared at the phone. "I don't understand your life. And I say that as someone with a really fucking complicated life."

"Accept the job, sign the nondisclosure agreement, and I'll explain everything."

Kaisall, formerly of the Navy SEALs, co-owned a private security firm that handled everything from rescuing kidnapped heiresses to the kind of shit he couldn't even allude to without breaching national security protocols.

We met about five years ago when I'd wanted to throw out everything and dive headfirst into a new world. Back then, I'd been bored to the point of anger. Restless enough to gnaw my arm off. Making moves had been the only thing keeping me going. It wasn't about hopping from one corporate ladder to another. I'd wanted to jump off the ladder and then use it to bridge a canyon. I had nothing to lose and everything to gain.

I was in the final rounds of interviews when Penny died. But I didn't regret bowing out. I liked where I was now—and I wouldn't have lasted long in Kaisall's corner of the industry. It was better being his friend. More plausible deniability.

"As I told you the first time we had this conversation, I don't live in a world where I can drop off the grid for a few weeks or come back *a little foggy*. Whatever the fuck that means."

"We'll keep you in the command center," he said. "No risk of concussion there. Or not as much of a risk."

"You're not helping. None of this is helping."

"I don't know what to tell you, man. When are you back in town? Want to catch a Nationals game? I'll let you whine at me all night if you buy the beers."

Again, I glanced between my watch and phone. Still nothing from Audrey. I didn't have a great feeling about this. I should've gone with them. "I'm on the West Coast for a few more weeks and then picking up Percy from his grandmother's place in Michigan."

"Last I checked, they still play in August."

I stretched my arms over my head to draw some of the tension from my shoulders. Didn't work. "I'll text you when we're back."

"And you're buying the beer."

"You have a private jet," I snapped. "Like fuck I'm buying the beer."

"I'll have you know that's a business expense."

"Whatever lets you sleep at night." I watched a family of quail scuttle across the yard and debated whether I wanted to involve Kaisall in another one of my problems. "How good are your hackers?"

"I don't have hackers," he said, each word crisp.

"Right, yeah, of course not. But hypothetically speaking."

"Hypothetically," he drawled, "I hire only the best in the business."

I nodded to myself as the pieces took shape in my head. "Then would you say, hypothetically, that someone playing at that level of the game would be able to figure out when some emails had been opened?"

"Opened? Not just delivered?"

"Yeah," I said. "But they're not recent. We're talking old emails."

"How old?"

I glanced at my phone. "More than a decade."

Kaisall was quiet for a long moment. I heard him typing. Probably messaging one of the hackers he didn't have on his payroll. Another beat passed before he said, "I need more than a minute with that one. If you can send me—"

From inside the house, I heard a door slam followed by a loud, booming belly laugh and then, "Come on, let's bake bread! Do you know about yeast? *Yeast.* Yeast! It's like an alien word. A word from literal aliens. But for bread. Did I tell you I bake bread every weekend? But not for the aliens. It's for me."

A breath whooshed out of me. "Kaisall, I have to go. My mother got my fiancée high."

"Your—*what*? When were you going to tell me you got engaged?"

"It's a stupid long story," I said, striding across the patio.

"Congratulations?"

"I'll explain it over beers," I said. "That you buy."

"Fuck you," he crowed as I hung up.

I pocketed my phone and yanked out the earbuds as I stepped inside only to find Audrey sprawled on the floor, her hair flipped over her face, and giggling. I pointed at my mother, who had the good sense to look guilty. "What the fuck is this?"

"It was an accident," she said. "I swear."

"I'm sorry. Did I need to explicitly tell you that you're not allowed to drug my fiancée? Because I'd thought I made that clear the last time you pulled this shit."

"It really was a mistake. I didn't have my glasses on," she said. "I mixed up the mints with the molly."

"I can't fucking believe you." I dropped to the floor beside Audrey and brushed her hair out of her eyes. I swept a thumb over her warm, rosy cheek. "How are you doing, princess?"

She grabbed my wrist, holding me in place. "I feel...pink."

"Yeah. I can see that. I'm going to pick you up and—"

Her eyes went comically wide as she glanced all around. "Up from where?"

"You're on the floor, baby."

She laced her fingers with mine and grabbed for the front of my shirt, dragging me closer with startling strength. "How did I get down here?"

"The details are hazy but it started with my mother being a psychopath."

"I'm going to make some tea," Mom said. "Tea always helps."

"Don't you dare," I said. "Water is the only thing I'm trusting from this house."

"How about I run down the street to Gary's and get some seltzer? I know Audrey always orders sparkling water with lime."

"Yeah. Sure. Perfect. Go the fuck away." My mother hurried out the door as I hooked Audrey's arms around my neck and gathered her up. "Hold on tight for me, Saunders."

She nuzzled her face into my neck and proceeded to lick her way from the base of my throat to my ear. It was almost enough to make my knees buckle. I knew this wasn't what she wanted and I had no business reacting to her right now but my dick was late in receiving that message.

"You taste good," she said, tiptoeing her fingers up the back of my neck.

I kissed her forehead. "You taste better."

She closed her eyes and smiled like the first light of dawn. Those fingers curled around my hair. She gave a slight tug, just hard enough to send a snap of heat through my entire body. "Sometimes you're nice to me."

"Sometimes." I stared at her lips for far too long. "More, if you'd let me."

Audrey shook her head, her eyes still shut. Somewhere deep in the recesses of my mind I found a memory of her like this—happy, free, completely uncalloused by years of doing what she was told and never what she chose. I couldn't place the time or the circumstances but I remembered the way she smiled and how it dug into my muscles, under my ribs, until it wrapped around my heart. Seeing it again made it hard to breathe.

"You don't want that," she said, the words satin soft.

"If you knew all the things I wanted," I whispered, "you wouldn't worry about me being nice."

She traced along my collar and down the line of my jaw. She tapped at my bottom lip like she was calling for an elevator until I scraped my teeth over that fingertip. "What would I worry about?"

I didn't know if she'd remember this. If she was in there now, conscious of everything but too stoned to stop it. I didn't know which way I wanted that to shake out.

But before I could answer, she wiggled in my arms like a damn puppy, all loose limbs and long hair and elbows slamming in my soft tissue. "Jude. Listen, listen, listen. Something has happened. Gravity has stopped and I'm floating."

"That's—that's not how gravity works, baby." I knew this wasn't the moment to explain physics but I couldn't help myself. "If there was even a momentary loss of gravity, the planet would no longer be intact."

"But—no! I'm drifting off into space. I can't feel the ground anymore."

"No, baby, look. I'm just holding you."

At last, she opened her eyes and blinked up at me like a slightly possessed attic doll. "Why are you holding me?"

"Because the floor is hard and you were a little wobbly when you came back from lunch."

"It's nice," she said, smashing her face into my neck again. "It's fun to be small and precious sometimes."

I ran my lips over her hair and let myself breathe her in while I could. "You should be precious all the time."

She scoffed at that and went on burrowing into me. "No one wants me enough to care like that."

"I find that hard to—"

"I need to feel gravity again," she said with a violent jolt. I didn't want to draw comparisons between High Audrey and Over-tired Percy but the parallels existed. "It isn't real until I feel it."

I set her on her feet but kept my arms around her. For safety reasons. Obviously. "Better? Or would you like to argue with me about the fundamentals of physics some more?"

She went up on her toes and then bent into a plié, sweeping an arm out at her side. I held her waist, feeling the pull and shift of her muscles. "I feel it again," she said, dropping deep into another plié.

My fingers flexed. "It never went away. I promise."

"How do you know?"

"Because things like that never change."

The door opened behind us and Mom rushed in. "We cleared out Gary's drink fridge." She motioned to him and the party-sized ice chest he rolled behind him. He swung the ice chest around and popped the top like he was selling bootleg iPhones. "He stocks all different flavors."

"I have raspberry tangerine," he said, holding up a can.

"Yeah, that's fantastic," I said to them as Audrey extended backward into a dramatic dip. "I'm taking her back to the hotel to sleep this off."

"Blood orange limeade," Gary went on.

"Oh, no, you can't go," Mom said. "Gary was going to cook for us tonight and we were going to show you some of the wedding plans."

"That's not fucking happening," I said.

Gary held up another can. "Mango blackberry."

"I need to tell you a secret," Audrey loud-whispered into my ear. "Your mom is sus-shushishisus-sushisus-suspicious." She held up her ring finger and closed an eye at the same time like the two were on a pulley system. "About the—"

I sealed my lips to hers. I didn't know what the rest of that sentence was and I didn't want to find out. I could've let the kiss linger but she'd resent the fuck out of me for it when she sobered up. I'd resent me too. Probably. "Shh, princess. That's for us to know."

"Ginger mule," Gary said.

Audrey slow-blinked, her lips parted and damp. "Okay." And

then she brought both hands to my face, pressed her mouth to mine, and picked up where we left off.

She was messy and a bit wild. Her nails bit into my jaw, my cheeks, and feeling that raw hunger coming through her destabilized something in me. I knew I couldn't touch her like this, no more than I already had, but goddamn that didn't stop my mind from wandering to rich, indulgent places.

I needed her to remember this tomorrow. I just didn't know if I'd survive if she did.

"Orange vanilla."

I broke away but held her tight to me, her head on my shoulder and my hand in her hair. "I'm going to take you back to the hotel. I think we could use a nap."

Audrey murmured in agreement—and then snaked a hand between us and palmed my dick.

I yanked her wrist away before anyone noticed and trapped it against the small of her back. "Behave yourself."

"Will you stay with me?" she asked.

I ran a thumb over her lips. "Of course."

"I swear, if you two are already married," Mom started, "I'm going to start whooping bottoms. I don't care how old you are."

"Pineapple pomelo," Gary said.

"Pomeloooooo," Audrey sang, kicking out a leg and nearly knocking the seltzer from Gary's grip.

Rita appeared in the door, took one look at Audrey and tossed up her hands. "Dammit, Janet. You really have to organize your goodies better."

"It was an accident," Mom said.

"Which one was it this time?" Rita asked, her hands fisted on her hips. "The X, the shrooms, or the choose your own adventure gummies?"

"Lime," Gary said.

"The X," Mom replied, but then she held up a finger and squinted at the ceiling. "I think. I'd forgotten about the gummies."

"We're leaving," I said, motioning for Mom to grab Audrey's bag off the floor. "I can't believe I have to tell you this but get your psychedelics in order. No more accidental dosing. Not cool, Mom."

"I'll straighten it all out. I promise," she said, trailing behind me as I led Audrey to the door. It was more of a shuffle-and-slide while she licked my neck, which wasn't making this any easier. "She'll have a pleasantly woozy evening and then sleep like a baby. Everything will be back to normal tomorrow."

"Guava," Gary said.

"Guaaaaaava," Audrey drawled.

"Is she going to remember any of this?"

Mom slung Audrey's bag over my shoulder and squeezed my arm. "I always do," she said with a shrug. "But I never take two at the same time."

Audrey peered at us like she knew we were talking about her, nodded, and then let out a raw, bloody scream, jumping a solid foot off the ground and almost taking me down in the process.

"It found us," she cried, pointing to the house. "It followed us all the way here."

It took a beat but then I saw the huge mosaic lizard tiled into the side of the garage. I didn't know how we'd missed it before. Must've been the subtle desert colors and the fact it spanned the entire wall.

"That's one of my ongoing projects," Rita said. "I call him Mr. Darcy. He's not done yet. Big fellow. Pain in the ass but I'm hoping he's worth it in the end."

"Black cherry," Gary called through the open door.

Audrey clung to me, whispering, "Get me out of here."

chapter thirty-one

Jude

Today's vocabulary word: unfiltered

THE ELEVATOR DOORS OPENED AT OUR FLOOR AND AUDREY executed a ballet leap out of the car. She didn't wait for me, instead twirling down the hallway in a series of jumps and pirouettes.

At least she was going the right direction.

I found her moving through a sequence of dance steps near our door, her shoes abandoned a few feet away. "You miss it," I said as I fished the key card from my wallet. "Dancing, that is."

She extended her leg up until her heel met the wall and then leaned into the stretch, her body open like an unfolded paper clip. Her dress bunched around her waist. I wished I could say I looked away. That I didn't stare at the light pink panties hugging her hip or stretching between her thighs.

It was only when I felt her staring at me that I finally met her gaze.

"I do miss it," she said, a loose smile on her face, "sometimes."

I held the door open. She ignored it and I couldn't get away from the sense that she was dragging my attention back to her legs, her thighs, those obscenely sweet little panties. And I knew she wasn't herself right now. I knew this wasn't the time for me to take what I could get. But god fucking damn. "Still can't believe you gave it up."

She snorted out a laugh. "I still can't believe Padrino is a dad."

"What—no. We're not bringing that back," I said, holding out a hand to her.

"Oh, come on! It's funny. I should've thought of that at the reunion. Everyone would've been like, *Wait! Padrino's a dad? My mind is blown!*"

I swung a glance down the hallway. I didn't want to do this out here anymore. My head was a fucking carnival show and if anyone came down here and saw her like this, I'd have to kill them. Obviously.

"Hilarious," I said, hooking an arm around her waist and hauling her into the room.

"You know, it's not a bad nickname," she said, fully invertebrate and giggling as I parked her on the bed. "Compared to—what did they call me? Antacid? Padrino is a nice step up from Antacid."

The asshole heirs at our prep school had a thing for nicknames. It was a practical necessity when most of these guys were born saddled with names that stretched back six generations.

But they were still assholes and the nicknames didn't let anyone forget who held all the power.

It started with a fake sneeze and *Buh-less-me*—a spin on Bellessi that was about as sharp as soup—but it didn't catch on. Too much theatrics for guys who never actually had to form their own thoughts.

They mixed it up and moved on to *Bless me, Father, for I have sinned*—another fail. Too long, too cumbersome. And I ate the humor out of it by telling them they didn't know the first thing about repenting for true sins.

In that sense, it was my fault that it shifted to *Padrino*—godfather—and that it stuck.

"Will you tell me about him?"

Audrey sat on the bed, her hair tousled and her cheeks still rosy red. It reminded me of the time we drove to a hill outside the city to watch a meteor shower in the middle of the summer. We'd had a blanket, some beer, and the stars. I told her I loved her that night. That I'd never love anyone else the way I loved her. That the only future I wanted was with her at my side.

At the time, I hadn't been able to imagine anything coming between us. Nothing we couldn't deal with. It was amazing how naïve we'd been. I always thought I was too jaded for naïveté but here we were.

There was no denying that the plans we'd made for life after high school probably would've cracked under the weight of the real world at some point. But that didn't mean *we* would've fallen apart. I refused to see that as an inevitability. There was no one scrappier than this spoiled society girl of mine and I lived to prove people wrong.

But the part that bothered the hell out of me was that we didn't even get the chance to fuck it all up and fall to pieces. Not when her parents shoved her into a gilded cage, shipped her to California, and then sold her off to the highest bidder. They knew what they were doing. They'd probably had it planned since the minute they met me. Or maybe it had nothing to do with me and everything to do with controlling her.

I didn't like that option any better.

I dropped her shoes in the closet, set her bag on the bench near the door. Tried to figure out what to do about this situation. Would coffee help? Something to eat? Did greasy food soak up ecstasy the way it did alcohol? What about a cold shower? I knew that would help me. I wasn't sure I was comfortable leaving her alone in a shower so I'd have to go with her and— *Fuck me.*

I scrubbed a hand down my face. "Tell you about who?"

"Percy." She bounced on her knees. "I bet you have a ton of pics. Show me?"

I raked my bottom lip between my teeth. Photos were simple enough. Lower chance of her face-planting into a wall than the ballet moves. Much lower chance of me choking on my tongue over a flash of underwear. Maybe it would tire her out.

"Yeah. Sure." I swiped my phone and opened my albums. Handed it to her. "All yours."

"No, come over *here*," she said with a pout. "You have to tell me all about the pics. Narrate the stories for me." She patted the bedspread beside her. "Sit here. With me."

I gulped. There was no way this would work out well for me.

"Please," she drawled, her hands clasped under her chin. Full puppy dog eyes too. Fucking brutal.

"All right," I said, kicking off my shoes. As soon as I sat down, she curled into my side. She had a hand on my back and the other tapping on my thigh, hurrying me along. Killing me. "These are from a few weeks ago. At one of the parks he likes."

"He looks just like you." She zoomed in on an image of Percy climbing a playset. "What a little conqueror." I watched the way her smile dug into her cheeks and softened her eyes. "Tell me about him."

"What do you want—" She ran the pad of her finger along the seam of my jeans, right up the inner thigh, and I lost my words. Whatever I'd wanted to say perished and it was taking the last of my decency down to hell with it.

"Everything," she replied, still unspooling me from that seam.

I'd been at least half hard since she grabbed me back at Mom's place but it was full steam ahead now. As long as she didn't notice, we'd be all right. And if she did, well, it couldn't get much more awkward between us.

"He sleeps with twenty stuffed animals and it stresses me the fuck out because I worry about them suffocating him," I said in a heave of breath. "He likes outrageous burgers. You know, the ones with a scoop of macaroni and cheese on top or two slices of Hawaiian pizza instead of a bun."

She blinked up at me, owlish and adorable. "There are burgers that use entire slices of pizza to hold it all together?"

"It's not the sort of thing you'd ever go looking for, princess, but yes," I said. "Percy loves it. Give him a burger topped with an entire chili dog or some crab rangoon, and it's the best day of his life."

"I can just see him shoving a giant burger into his little face," she said.

My chest just about cracked open at that. It was intensely confusing to have these warm thoughts about my son while a bit more pressure from that fingertip of hers would have me coming in my pants. Really fucking confusing. "He likes Teenage Mutant Ninja Turtles and rocks and...dogs," I managed. "He likes dogs. Helicopters and planes—"

"Well, of course he likes planes and helicopters," she teased. "You wouldn't have it any other way."

"Nah, I don't push it on him. He's allowed to like whatever he wants."

"Come on," she drawled. "Admit it. When you read *Peter Pan* to him, you added your own chapters about the science of flying to Neverland. Distance and velocity and all the other physics stuff."

I shook my head. "Nope."

"Jude," she said, stern as ever. That tone only made things more complicated for me. "I know when you're not telling me the truth."

I didn't know if I believed that. Didn't want to believe it. "I didn't get into it with *Peter Pan* but we did pause *Aladdin* at a few points. The aerodynamics of the magic carpet—I mean, the wind speed alone would've knocked them off and—"

"Like I said." She went back to swiping through the photos. "You miss him."

"Yeah." No sense denying it. "I like having him around. It's weird when he's not."

"Like your heart's walking around outside your chest," she said.

"Very much." I pointed to the screen. "That's from his last day of school."

"Why does he look so annoyed?"

"I'd call it contemptuous but annoyed also fits," I said. "That school couldn't keep up with him this year and he's still pissy about it. Actually, I could use your help with that. When you're sober."

"What do you mean?" She shifted, flailing in the most convoluted ways imaginable until she straddled my thigh. A fresh new rung on the descent into my personal hell. "I'm a hundred percent sober."

"No, baby, you're not." I cupped her chin, studying her glassy eyes. "But I love that you think so."

"I'm perfectly aware of what's going on. Everything's just a little fuzzy. Like felt. The fabric." She rubbed the pads of her fingers together, directly in front of her eyes. "No, no, it's moss. That's what I feel like. It's like I'm made of warm moss."

Audrey rocked against my thigh as she spoke. She was hot, even through my jeans. Scorching hot. And she'd hate me for this tomorrow if I let her continue.

"Okay, that's enough." I shifted up, groaning as my belt strangled my cock, and reached for her waist. I managed to turn her around and settle her between my legs, her back to my chest. I banded an arm over her to keep her still though I knew it wouldn't do much good.

"But why?" she asked, wriggling in my hold. "We have this big bed all to ourselves. We *never* had beds. Remember? There was the back seat of my car and that really old storage room in the library and—"

"I've already told you to behave."

I closed one hand over her mouth, grabbed my phone with the other, and went back to the photos. The album opened to me and Percy at the National Aquarium in Baltimore, a reef shark floating by behind us. She tried to say something but it was too muffled to understand.

I let my hand slide down her neck, coming to rest on her sternum. "Mind your manners, princess."

She gave me a tart glance from the corner of her eye that was almost enough to make me beg her to ride my leg. She must've seen the hunger written all over my face because she rocked back against me, her ass working my cock with a sweet, filthy drag that was almost worth her hating me tomorrow. "I know you want to."

I stared up at the ceiling. "Not like this I don't. Not tonight."

"But—"

"No, Saunders. You had your chance back at the motel but you went and hid behind that little pillow fortress of yours. Didn't you?" I moved my palm up her neck, turning her just enough to catch my gaze. "You're so pretty when you're fearless and free to ask for all the things you don't think you should want. So fucking pretty." I pressed my lips to her temple and let a breath rasp out of me. "But the next time I touch you, it's going to be when you don't need any help asking for it. When I know you'll remember every second."

She made an aggravated, huffy sound and I was ready for another rebuttal but she sagged into me. The frenetic energy that'd pulsed in her just a moment ago bled out and she dropped to my shoulder.

"Just let me—" She slipped her hand under my shirt and pressed her palm to my torso. "Okay. That's better. I like this too."

I held my breath, waiting for her to dive bomb my dick again, but a minute passed with just the gentle sweep of her thumb along my side. It was back, that sensation of coming apart. Like she'd picked the right threads and now I was one good pull away from being unraveled.

"Why?" I asked, masochistic enough to squeeze every drop of tonight's honesty out of her. "Why do you like this?"

She yawned, curling into me a little deeper. "Because you just let me...be. I don't have to worry about anything. I don't have to think."

I sifted a hand through her hair, letting the strands slide between my fingers. So soft, so silky. I'd always loved her hair. There was something about it that quieted entire corners of my brain. I couldn't explain it, I just knew that untwisting her bun or running my lips over the crown of her head calmed me the hell down.

"There's nothing you need to worry about anymore," I said. "I have you now."

She murmured in agreement, and for a few minutes we fell into a rhythm of her thumb on my side and my fingers in her hair. There'd been times over the years when I'd questioned whether I'd loved her as much as I remembered, or if the intensity of the feelings I still shouldered was nothing more than a byproduct of living without a shred of closure.

But right now I knew it would always be like this. That I'd loved her in a way I'd never be able to recover from. She'd marked her place on my bones and inside my organs, and ruined me.

It was Audrey or no one, just like I'd told her under that meteor shower. And I was running out of time to get this right. All we had left was tomorrow, really. She flew back to Boston the day after. I was headed back to Seattle for meetings. It wasn't enough. None of this was enough.

"Have you ever thought about how basketball is about chasing pumpkins, tennis is hitting lemons, baseball is catching onions, and football is about throwing potatoes?"

I blinked down at Audrey, my head still busy inventing ways to squeeze more time out of the next thirty-six hours. "I haven't thought about that," I said. "But I know Percy would love it. He'd repeat that endlessly."

"Can I see more photos of him?"

I went back to the album and handed it to her. She scrolled for a few minutes, keeping up a running commentary on the array of Percy's grumpy expressions, all the photos I had of various engine parts, and the screenshots she accused me of never once referencing. I refused to admit any guilt on that last count.

But then she zoomed in on a photo where I had Percy's head tucked under my chin and she said, "I see it now."

"What's that?"

"You were meant to be a dad," she said. "I never thought that far ahead. For us. I mean, I did but those were just big, distant dreams and we had no idea what the world was really like. What was waiting for us."

A bitter laugh shook my chest. The fucking truth of that.

She swiped to another photo. "But I see you now and I know you were meant for this. You're a really good dad."

I didn't know how necessary those words were to me until Audrey spoke them into existence. And maybe it was hearing it from *her* that made them land in the place where I'd needed them most. All I knew was I wanted to give my kid everything, even if I hadn't expected him and I'd missed his earliest days. Even if Penny's family didn't believe I had any place in his life.

"Thank you," I managed.

"What does he want to be for Halloween?"

I twirled her hair around my finger, brushing the ends over my lips. "It's June, Saunders."

She held up a pic of Percy wearing Spider-Man pajamas with a dragon cape on top and carrying a Paw Patrol stuffie. "This kid has known what he wants to be since November first of last year."

I huffed out a laugh. "It changes daily."

"Such a cutie." She twisted in my arms to meet my gaze and her smile felt like an electrical current, all raw, spine-splitting power. I wanted to grab her and shake her and make her see how she was the one in control here. Make her understand. "You know how I know you're really good at this? You have photos of the moments you want to remember."

"Everyone does that."

"Yeah but you took twenty pics of your kid reading a book on the couch. And there's another twenty of him eating a slice of watermelon. Twenty more at the library, in the race car cart at the grocery store, waiting in line for the subway. That's on top of the other eleven hundred selfies of you two, your sweet little faces pressed together like you'll never be able to hug him tight enough." She pressed a hand to my chest. "You want to remember all of it. Because you love him"—she held her arms out wide—"so much."

I sucked in a breath but my lungs didn't want to expand. Probably had something to do with getting whacked with an emotional two-by-four by the woman who still knew how to reach in and wrap her fingers around my soul.

I gathered her hands in mine, brought them back to my chest. I needed something else from her now and I wasn't above using these hallucinogenic circumstances to get it. "When are you going to tell me what happened with your ex-husband?"

Her whole expression shuttered. Even her shoulders pulled inward. I didn't need the details to know what that reaction meant. But I had to hear this.

Her gaze lowered, she said, "I work very hard at not thinking about that part of my life."

Swallowing down a thorny knot of tension, I asked, "Why?"

"Because it almost killed me." The words fell from her lips like a simple fact rather than the source of my greatest fears. "But I got out and it's over and it's better for me when I don't go back to it."

Everything inside me surged with the kind of brutal energy that made me want to find him, drag him out of his absurd life, and make damn sure he knew she'd never suffer at his hands again. But I knew it wouldn't help. Wouldn't erase those years for her. And it wouldn't fix anything more than scratching a primitive itch for me.

I kept my hold on her gentle, running my thumbs over the insides of her wrists. "You never got my emails, did you? After they sent you to California?"

"No." She shook her head. "What emails?"

Another hard swallow. "That changes a few things."

chapter thirty-two
Audrey

Today's vocabulary word: drift

I ROLLED OVER AND YELPED AT THE ACHE RIPPLING THROUGH MY shoulders, down my back, and around my hips. I hadn't felt this battered since convincing myself I could dig a path along my side yard and lay a brick walkway by myself.

My mouth was dry like chalk and my head rang with a deep, dull headache. I would've hidden under the covers and slept all day if my stomach wasn't twisting in that old familiar way that told me I needed the bathroom more than anything else.

A hand over my eyes to hide from the worst of the sunlight slicing in through the curtains, I shuffled to the edge of the bed. I made my way across the suite like I was trudging through a snow-bank and into the quiet dark of the bathroom. I locked the door and yanked some towels off the shelf because these episodes always made me cold. Nothing could convince me that bare feet on frigid tiles didn't set off a chemical reaction that kicked the whole matter into a new level of awful.

I liked to think about my irritable bowel like a bridge troll. I knew what made it angry and, over the course of many years and much error, I knew how to cross that bridge without bothering the troll too much. But I also knew that the troll was, by definition, irritable. There would be times that I pissed it off for no discernible reason and I'd just have to deal with the wreckage it delivered.

The troll hated tomatoes and cucumbers, and deviating from my usual schedule. Traveling with a troll was tough but I'd reached a point where I knew myself well enough to manage these issues without too much noise. The real problem was prolonged stress. That fucked it all up. Whenever I found myself on edge for days at a time, emotionally activated and hypervigilant—or married to a self-obsessed, paranoid narcissistic asshole—the troll lost its shit.

All of which was to say I'd put one foot after another for the past five days, knowing this end awaited me. I wasn't sure what'd set it off but that didn't really matter. It was inevitable.

Half an hour and most of my will to live later, I emerged from the bathroom. I still had a towel shawled over my shoulders and it'd probably stay there until I could get some fluids into my system and stop shivering. Very chic. Very sexy.

I sank onto the edge of the bed, my zip pouch of meds clutched to my chest, and grabbed the bottled water on the nightstand. A piece of paper fluttered to the floor and I would've left it there if I hadn't noticed Jude's precise handwriting on the page as it fell.

I hadn't processed his absence from our hotel room until now but dealing with the troll always gave me tunnel vision. I grunted out a sigh as I reached for the paper. On a page from the hotel notepad, he'd written:

Saunders —
MY MOTHER GAVE YOU TWO HITS OF ECSTASY LAST NIGHT. DRINK ALL OF THIS. GOING TO THE GYM. DON'T LEAVE THE RESORT WITHOUT ME.

Well. That explained a few things.

As I reread the note—no signature though none was needed—last night drifted back to me in pieces. The memories were strange, like photos captured through milky filters, but they were all there. Every last humiliating one. Even me pawing at Jude and attempting a standing wall split for reasons that must've made sense at the time.

At least I knew why my hips felt like an overstretched rubber band.

I propped myself up in bed, blankets clutched to my chin, and called the only person who could help me fix this.

With my phone propped on my bent knees, I sipped the water while waiting for Jamie to answer. When she came into focus, I found her in an identical position. She was swaddled in a bathrobe, both hands wrapped around a steaming mug.

"What's wrong?" I asked.

"I had a lot of sex the other day," she said, "and now I have a UTI."

This always happened to her. "Are you on meds?"

She bobbed her head. "I just feel like I've been stomped on."

"We need to find a specialist for you. This shouldn't happen so often."

"Yes, Mother."

"I hate seeing you in pain like this," I said. "I'll help you find someone. I'll go with you."

"We'll talk about it when neither of us look like last week's laundry." She took a sip from her mug. "What's the news? Please tell me that you finally let that fiancé of yours fuck you right through a concrete wall."

"More like I accidentally did ecstasy and begged him to fuck me through a concrete wall and then made him explain *in detail* why he wouldn't do that. Oh, and I humped his leg until he was so embarrassed for me that he put a stop to it."

She pinched the bridge of her nose. "Do I want to know where you got the X?"

"His mom gave it to me," I said, heavily salting every word.

"Sabotage or silly goose? Which side is she on here?"

"Silly goose, most likely," I said, remembering Janet's horror when she'd realized what happened.

"Okay, here's what you're going to do." She held up a finger. "First, we're not embarrassed by the things we said and did when we were high. Especially when getting high wasn't our choice."

"While I do support that," I started, "I've already died of embarrassment. You're speaking to my ghost right now."

"Well, Ghost Audrey looks at least twenty-five percent alive so my recommendation stands. Next, we're going to listen to our id. The things we do when we're wasted are the things we actually want but don't let ourselves admit. They're an owner's manual for managing our unconscious needs."

All I could think about was grabbing Jude only for him to pry my fingers from his pants. "I don't think we can do that because my id is oddly fond of sexual harassment."

"I'm sure it wasn't that bad," she said.

"Did I not mention the leg humping?"

"You're not the first and you won't be the last," she said with a wave of her hand. "What I'd like to know is why you can't embrace the honesty and see if you have as much fun on his leg today as you did last night."

"I'm very busy being dead," I said. "I don't see any time in my schedule to revisit that horror."

"Okay but really," she said. "Why can't you have a fling with him?"

I leaned back against the headboard and sipped my water. My belly didn't clench or gurgle like it intended to reject the water, and that was fantastic news. "Because what then?" I replied. "We just have sex and then go our separate ways?"

"Yes, I do it at least once a week with multiple people. I promise, it's fine."

"You haven't been in love with those people since you were fifteen," I cried.

"Ahhh. Now we're getting somewhere."

"That's not what I meant. I just—it's not as easy as a fling."

"Of course it isn't." She said this like she'd been waiting for me to figure it out all along. "But that isn't a good enough reason to play dead."

I motioned to my towel shawl and my bloodless face. "I can't imagine why you'd think I'm playing."

"Ha. You're hilarious." She lifted her mug in salute. "Stop being ashamed. Start being honest with your fiancé."

"Fake fiancé," I added.

Jamie gave me a wide, toothy grin. "We'll see about that, baby girl."

chapter thirty-three

Audrey

Today's vocabulary word: conspire

I MADE IT OUT OF THE ROOM AND ALL THE WAY TO THE restaurant, and it only took me a sluggish hour. Most of that time I'd spent with my hands pressed to my face as my cheeks flamed with shame from last night's antics, but an hour just the same.

Janet had better be prepared to face me. I had no intention of laughing at whichever quippy quote she had on her t-shirt today or grabbing every stray thread of conversation with both hands. She was going to get a tight-lipped smile and a brief hug from me, and that would be it.

I watched as crystals of brown sugar dissolved into my oatmeal and swirled my spoon through to mix it in. I didn't like oatmeal very much but I could count on it to settle my belly. That, and the hotel's breakfast menu was made up of digestive fireballs. It was like they wanted to kill all the girls with bad bellies.

What I really wanted was a basic breakfast sandwich and some coffee. A flat white or a café au lait would knock out this pest of a headache and it would probably give me a nice energy boost too. But when the troll was all riled up, grease and caffeine only made matters worse. I'd have to get by on toast, oatmeal, and tea today.

I went back to stirring the oatmeal and wondering if any of the people seated around me had witnessed my impromptu dance performance in the halls last night. It was fine. I always did well on stage. They probably saw my underwear, if I pulled off the turns and jumps correctly, but that was the least of my shame.

Then Jude dropped into the chair across from me, his collar open at his throat and cuffs rolled to his elbows. His color was high from whichever activities had taken more than two hours out of his morning, his hair was still shower damp, and he was wearing his glasses again.

"Glasses in the daytime," I said. "That's new."

That's new? What the hell was wrong with me? God, what I wouldn't give to transform into a little mouse and disappear right now.

"Yeah. A little bleary today. I didn't sleep much last night." He shrugged, adding, "I was worried about you sneaking out or jumping off the balcony."

Heat crawled up my neck. "I'm sorry about—well, everything. And, you know. Attacking you. Repeatedly."

He swiped a piece of toast from my plate. "The only problem was that I didn't know if you actually wanted it."

I stared down at the napkin on my lap. I wasn't prepared for him to grab that matter by the throat just yet. "Still, I…fondled you and I didn't take no for an answer and that wasn't okay."

"You were drugged. By my mother," he said around a bite of toast. "Fuck, I'm the one who should be apologizing here."

"I wasn't paying attention. When she gave me the mints," I added, as if that was important. "I was worried about garlic and offending the wedding dress lady."

He paused, then pointed the toast crust at me. "The...wedding dress lady?"

"Yeah. Janet had me trying on dresses."

Jude stared at me for a beat before swallowing. "Find anything you like?"

"Not really. It was just to give Janet the bridal shop moment she wanted. I've already done the big white dress thing."

"Yeah. I know." He pushed his glasses up his nose. "I was there, Saunders."

I reached for my tea. Sadly, I couldn't climb all the way into the mug and hide there until the sun extinguished itself.

"Not so fearless today, are you?"

I tore myself away from the mug and met his gaze. I didn't know if it was the headache or the ecstasy hangover or my bridge troll turning me inside out but I asked, "Is that really what you want to discuss right now? My wedding day? Because I think we need to talk about Janet's suspicions about us if we want the party tonight to go well."

He leaned back in the chair, an arm banded over his chest as he polished off the last of my toast. "Tell me about these suspicions."

I gave him an overview of her offhanded comments from yesterday, the quick barbs about him not joining me for Emme's wedding next weekend and the trap I fell into when mentioning a summer wedding. Now that I'd answered some of Janet's questions and offered up a few random details to her, there was more room for our stories to fall apart.

"I think I'm the source of the doubt," I said. "She's worried I'm going to leave you at the altar or something like that." A terrible thought struck as I added more hot water to my cup. "That's not what you're planning, is it? I'd really prefer if you killed this bit before the invites hit the mail."

"Fine. I guess I'll come up with something new." He flagged down a waiter. "Or we stay engaged a little longer."

I waited while he ordered seventy percent of the breakfast menu. Forever a growing boy, it seemed. "How much longer?"

"I don't know." He dumped some sugar into his coffee, stirred it longer than necessary. Didn't meet my gaze. "If we're going to put these suspicions to rest, we should make it believable tonight."

I heard the challenge baked into those words. I knew what he meant. I also knew it was an opening, a side door into a house where the front steps still looked a little too steep to me. "Okay," I said.

"Are you sure you're going to be all right with that?" he asked. Subtext: are we turning this fake engagement into a full-contact sport?

"I've played worse games for fewer prizes," I said, my tiny, mug-dwelling mouse nowhere to be found. "Don't worry about me."

His gaze swept over my loose button-down and limp ponytail to land on my lips. He lingered there a moment then ran a hand over his mouth. "Someday I'd like to hear about those games."

I shook my head. He didn't really want to know about life with my ex and the way I parried and sparred with my family. The way I still fought them for inches, even when I should've built a brick wall of boundaries and left them to learn how to climb. But I didn't want to watch the disappointment register in his eyes. I knew he expected better. Expected *more*. Hell, I expected more. I didn't know how I hadn't realized that until now. "I can't give away all my secrets."

"You used to give me everything." He cleared his throat and glanced away. I didn't think he'd meant to say that. Not out loud. "We need to stick together. Tonight," he added. "We're playing for the same side."

"Right. Stay together, keep the stories straight." I gave my oatmeal another halfhearted stir. "They can't catch us with contradictory details if we're never apart."

He stared at his coffee before taking a sip. "You'll tell me if it gets to be too much. I don't want you to..." He jerked a shoulder up, let it fall. Studied me over the rim of his mug. "I don't want it to be like that night at the motel."

So good of him to bring that up. "I don't think it will be."

Jude pointed at the oatmeal. "What are you doing there? Are you ever going to eat that?"

"Shut up," I grumbled. "I've had at least four bites."

It was more like two but he didn't need to know that.

"The fuck you have," he said. "What do you want? Scrambled eggs on a roll? Or in a tortilla? I'll ask them to make it for you."

"No, it's okay. I'm fine with oatmeal."

"You're not fine and you're not eating, you're glaring. And you don't even like oatmeal so I don't know what the fuck you're doing with this." He moved my bowl to his side of the table like it would prove a point. "Since you look like you're about to fall off that chair, tell me right now: on a roll or in a tortilla?"

"I don't feel well," I said through gritted teeth.

"Hangover? Or is it something else?"

I balled my hands inside the sleeves of my cardigan and gave a pathetic shake of my head like I was a sickly Victorian child. "I don't use enough recreational drugs to know whether it's from the ecstasy or just something I ate. My stomach can be really sensitive and flare up over random things, especially—" I flapped my hands near the sides of my head meant to round up *all of this*. "Greasy eggs will definitely make it worse."

"Okay, no grease. Understood. Probably no salsa, right? What about other veggies? And how about cheese? Is that okay?"

For no good reason at all, I wanted to argue with him. Tell him he couldn't just take my oatmeal and force scrambled eggs upon me. That I was the one who got me through the worst of it. That even when I was married, I'd lived on my own, without anyone looking after me, and I didn't need him to start now.

The notion of someone helping me, even in this small way, was so foreign that it felt like an attack. And that made me want to cry.

"If you don't tell me, I'll order both and eat whatever you don't."

I gulped down a fresh blast of emotion. It was ridiculous to have a reaction like this to *a breakfast order*. I could let him do this for me. I could let him help, even if I had to put myself in a mental straitjacket to do it. It wouldn't hurt me and I wouldn't come out of this owing him anything.

"No cheese. No veggies. Just plain." When he lifted a brow, I added, "In a tortilla."

He pushed to his feet, saying, "You got it, Saunders."

As he skirted the table, he kissed the top of my head and twisted a hand down my ponytail, and I didn't feel so much like a ghost anymore.

chapter thirty-four

Audrey

Today's vocabulary word: aura

THE ENGAGEMENT PARTY WAS EXACTLY WHAT I WOULD EXPECT from Janet and Rita. A homey backyard potluck with mismatched folding chairs and a cutesy signature cocktail—prickly pear margaritas for the *pair* of honor. Twinkle lights everywhere. A photo slideshow playing on the TV—though all the pics were from the past few days. Every surface in the kitchen was crammed with crockpots while Gary manned the grill out back.

The patio was packed with a fascinating mix of folks, more than this place should've been able to contain, but somehow it worked. There was no hope of remembering everyone's names but I forgave myself for that early. It wasn't like I'd be back here for the holidays.

Right from the start, Jude was committed to performing the shit out of this relationship. We'd planned as much earlier though I hadn't expected him to overachieve like this. Between gluing a hand to the small of my back the minute we stepped out of the car to dropping *fiancée* into every conversation like he'd bought the word and intended to get his money's worth, it became clear he had no intention of half-assing this. Full-asses, all the way.

Which was great. Really, it was. I didn't have to carry this entire engagement on my shoulders or even do the heavy lifting to keep the conversation going. A huge improvement over that dinner with Janet and Gary the other day.

But the problem was that I didn't know where the act ended and reality rushed back in. I didn't know what to do with my brain's insistence on grabbing every tender word he said about me and stowing it away like it meant something. Or how to handle my body's reaction to him stroking a thumb over my hip while telling Janet's friend Irena a story from high school.

"Audrey danced the lead in *Giselle* that season," he said, oblivious to the high beam situation he'd created with my nipples, "but it opened the same night as our spring formal. We hopped on my bike and left right after the curtain fell. She didn't even change out of her costume."

"It was a cute dress," I said. "Perfect for twirling. The costume manager just about killed me for it though."

"I remember the twirling," he said, laughing.

"That's badass," Irena said, giving us a slow, appraising nod. "Has anyone ever told you two that you have some truly enchanting aura energies? The way you blend is mesmerizing."

We shifted to exchange a glance. He arched a brow though I knew from the twitch of his lips he was fighting off a laugh. Not one for auras, not when he could have precise, tangible things like engines and gears. But, still staring at me, he asked, "What does that mean?"

"Might not mean anything. Most folks find themselves a good aura match but the way you complement and contrast is almost perfect. Not so common." She shrugged. "You probably have a lot of fun together."

Jude grinned at me. "You wouldn't believe some of our stories just from this week."

"Jude captured a dragon-lizard," I said.

"Audrey danced with an entire rodeo roster," he added.

"It wasn't the *entire* roster," I said.

He squeezed my hip, his fingers sliding firmly into underwear territory. And he knew that because he kept tracing the band of my panties. "Close enough."

"There's obviously a lot of heat between you." Irena's tone made it clear she'd noticed my nipples. Hell, the neighbors two streets over could see them at this point. "If I had to guess, I'd say it's an exact matchup in energies there."

We shared another glance. His gaze shifted from my eyes to my lips and then fell down to my chest. A muscle in his jaw pulsed but that was the only reaction he offered. I moved my hand from where it'd rested on his waist to between his shoulder blades, saying, "You won't hear any bedroom complaints from me."

I didn't know what'd compelled me to say that. I could've nodded along and let it go but I'd tapped into my sexually confident side. I didn't *have* a sexually confident side, not without psychoactive drugs, but now I had to live with that comment. Just the same way I had to live with my antics from last night.

Jude's fingers flexed on my hip. "That's right, princess."

Irena murmured to herself like we'd opened up another layer of spiritual color theory for her. Jude asked her about her work leading Jeep tours and I let myself focus on the way his muscles moved under my fingers.

I kept telling myself this was part of our strategy—to win over his mother, charm the townsfolk, whatever. But if that was the objective, why did it feel like *I* was being won over? I didn't have an answer for that. And I wasn't sure I wanted to find one because I didn't want to break my own heart.

As the night wore on, we seemed to migrate closer together.

He'd stroke my arm while I slipped a hand into his back pocket. I'd lean in close and he'd feed me a strawberry filled with cheesecake. He'd gently release my hair when it got trapped under the arm he curled around my shoulder. I'd grab his beer bottle out of his hand and take a sip. He'd kiss my temple and I'd thumb a nonexistent smudge of guacamole from the corner of his mouth. I'd perch on the arm of his chair and he'd tug me right into his lap.

And when it was dark and late, and some of the guests had said their good-byes, he pulled me into his arms, my back to his chest, and held me close. His chin perched on my shoulder, he asked, "How are you feeling?"

"Better," I said with some hesitation. The shaky emptiness that followed a flare was no fun but the worst was behind me now. "Tired, though."

He settled a hand over my abdomen and rubbed slow, lazy circles into my belly. It was amazing. "Ready to go?"

I glanced around the patio, eventually finding Janet carrying on an animated conversation with a few women while Gary stood nearby, holding her drink. She caught my eye and waved like we hadn't seen each other in years.

"Do you think we put the suspicions to rest?" he asked.

I layered a hand over his. "I think she's trying to decide whether this is your way of telling her we're giving her another grandchild."

He hummed against my neck as if the idea did nice things for him. Too bad they weren't so nice for me. That, and we probably wouldn't see each other again after tomorrow.

"Let's get back to our room." There was something thick and low in his words, and all I could do was murmur in agreement. "I want to get you alone."

"Too bad your mother wasn't around to hear that."

"I don't want her to hear it," he replied.

I turned my head just enough to catch his eye. He held my gaze as if to say *Yeah. That's exactly how I meant it.*

"I want to take you back to the room, lock the door, and kiss every inch of your body. I don't want to stop for a very, very long time."

He wasn't even finished speaking when I said, "Okay."

Blinking, startled, he asked, "Okay?"

"Yeah. Okay."

Jude stared at me for a long, painful moment that kicked the first fizzes of panic into gear. But then he grabbed my hand and tugged me toward the door.

chapter thirty-five

Audrey

Today's vocabulary word: anticipate

THE DRIVE BACK TO THE HOTEL TOOK HOURS. OR AT LEAST IT FELT that way. It was probably closer to fifteen minutes but every one of those minutes seemed to contain an entire Civil War documentary. To make matters worse, we'd stumbled into the most intense quiet game ever played.

The last words we'd exchanged were when Jude watched while I fastened my seat belt outside of Janet's house and asked, "All good?"

I nodded and offered an appalling response of "Yeah, you too." Amazing how I didn't drop dead from the embarrassment alone. I had to believe the gods kept me living only so I could amuse them a little longer by making it so much worse.

Jude reached over, his palm upturned and waiting. It was an obvious request for me to hold his hand but my brain said, *Nah, girl, that's a low-five.*

Which was what led me to slap his palm and say, "Team fake engagement for the win."

He stared at me for a beat—probably wondering if I'd helped myself to more of Janet's candies—before belting out a deep laugh. "Okay, princess," he said, turning his hand over and gripping my thigh. My dress bunched under his fingers. A growly noise sounded in his throat when he noticed my knee peeking out from under the skirt and he inched it higher, *higher.*

There was too much fabric gathered at my waist to make this truly scandalous. Unless I leaned back and spread my legs, no one was catching a glimpse of my undies. But when Jude finished hiking up my dress, he skated his palm up from my bare knee to my—

Oh.

Oh. Okay. All right.

"Still good?" he asked, his hand high on my leg and his fingers drumming an impatient rhythm on my inner thigh.

I didn't try for words this time, instead murmuring, "Mmhm," and thanking the heavens that it was too dark out for him to read the emotions on my face. Hell, *I* didn't want to read them. Not when I knew they were a cluttered mess of *I really want to have sex with him right now* and *But what happens after we have sex?* and *God, please don't let my stomach make this weird.*

I really, really didn't want my stomach to make it weird. I'd been there before. It wasn't a good time.

But I felt all right. A lot better than this morning. And I knew this was my absolute last chance with Jude. We flew to opposite sides of the country tomorrow and I couldn't think of a single reason our paths would cross again unless we came up with one tonight.

I wanted a reason.

Maybe that was presumptuous of me. Maybe I was diving headfirst into shallow waters. But I had enough regrets to last me a lifetime. I didn't want to leave Arizona with any more of them.

And that was why I shifted in my seat. Under different circumstances, it would've barely registered as movement. With Jude's hand spanning most of my leg, there was no hiding the way I gave up trying to press my knees together and just let them fall slightly open.

He paused, his fingertips frozen against my inner thighs. I kept my gaze fixed on the car ahead of us but I saw him cut a quick glance at me. He wanted to be sure, to know I'd done that on purpose. He released a breath, short and raspy, and though it hadn't taken the shape of any word I knew, it woke up every memory I had of us frantically stripping off clothes and tearing open condoms.

Another moment passed before he moved those fingers again but when he did, he dragged them in a straight line toward my panties. No detours, no time wasted. He didn't even bother teasing at the edges, instead going right to the center. Where I was already wet and throbbing, more aroused than I'd been since—well, since the other night.

But before the other night, it'd been *ages*. Not that I wanted to get into the short history of my sex life since Jude but the unimpressive details could fit on a small sticky note. With room left over for a doodle or two.

He tapped a finger to the hood of my clit, slow and measured like a metronome. It was annoying at first. Not nearly enough pressure and too much distortion from my underwear. I needed more. Much more.

But then those taps seemed to accumulate. They piled up on top of each other, building and building until my only option was to spread my legs as wide as the car would allow. To arch up into his touch. To close my hand around his wrist and demand the hard pressure of the heel of his palm exactly where I wanted it.

As I gasped and shook, Jude turned down the resort's driveway, his gaze straight ahead and his fingers curled around the steering wheel. It hardly seemed like I'd just ridden his hand to an orgasm.

But as we rolled to a stop in front of the resort and the building's exterior lights bled into the car, I noticed the erection trapped behind his zipper. It was…substantial.

As if he felt me staring, his fingers flexed on my extremely wet panties, sending a sharp pulse against sensitive flesh. I made an atrocious noise and he chuckled a bit, as if to say *Yeah, that just happened*. And then those fingers were gone. He brought my legs together and he straightened my dress, pulling it down to my knees. He gave it a final pass, his hand skimming over the fabric like that was all I needed to put me back in order.

He took my hand, the one with a death grip on the seat, and brushed his lips over my knuckles. His gaze fixed on me, he said, "I'd ask if you're good but I think I know the answer to that."

"Don't be smug," I said.

"Oh, I think I'm allowed." Jude tipped my chin up, pulling my gaze to his. He traced a thumb over my lips. "I'd let you put this pretty mouth to work but there are at least four valet guys watching us right now. Last I checked, you're not that much of an exhibitionist."

"I'm not."

"Then I think we should go inside now."

"Okay," I said, though it didn't sound like my voice. It sounded like the first step onto thin ice on a sunny day. "I think you're right."

chapter thirty-six

Audrey

Today's vocabulary word: restraint

THE DOOR TO OUR ROOM WAS BARELY CLOSED WHEN WE TORE INTO each other. My dress was up, off, flying over my head as I wrenched his belt open and ripped at the buttons on his shirt.

Jude had the clear advantage here, seeing as I had just one primary piece of clothing for him to contend with, and this gave him a lot of time to pinch my nipples through my bra. Then again, maybe the advantage was mine.

"Come here," he growled at the same time as I fought with the last few buttons, saying, "Just let me finish!"

He abandoned my nipples to yank the shirt over his head. Before I could comment on that, he spun me around to face the wall. "It's cute that you think I have the patience to stand here while you politely undo every button. Just fucking adorable."

He grabbed the band of my bra, jerking me back just enough that my backside connected with his hard shaft. The way he groaned into my shoulder lit up everything inside me. I rocked against him and his hips answered with a ragged, rutting pace. He wrapped an arm around my waist, holding me in my place while he growled, while he kissed and nipped at my neck.

"Fuck, Audrey, what are you doing to me?"

Maybe it was strange to say that I was proud of myself for turning him on and making him feral but I *was* proud. It'd been a long time since sex had been a mutual exchange of pleasure. Since it'd been fun. And it'd been even longer since I'd felt desirable and worth being desired.

"What do you want me to do?" I asked.

Jude dragged his fingers up my spine and with a quick flick, had my bra flying to the floor. My panties were quick to follow. "Anything, baby. Anything at all."

I flattened my hands on the wall as he ran a hand down to my waist and over my backside. Then lower. With that broad palm and those incredible fingers of his, he cupped me between my legs in a manner I could only describe as vulgar. Rude, even. Like this was the only part of me that existed and he'd do with it as he pleased.

He dragged a finger down my slit. It was wet. Audibly so. The noise he made was—oh. Oh, yes. That was when I recognized his touch as vulgar and rude but more than any of that, it was possessive.

And he confirmed it when he delivered a fast, hard slap to my mound and growled, "Tonight, this belongs to me."

No one would think to call me sexy or sensual. I wasn't coy. I didn't know how to say seductive things. Any attempts at being naughty usually resulted in significant embarrassment for all involved.

It came as an epic shock when I reached back, gripped his shaft through his pants, and said, "And this belongs to me."

I couldn't even believe I'd managed to speak with him *slapping my pussy*. Let alone claiming his cock for myself. I'd never, ever manage such a flawless response ever again.

With a hand tangled in my hair, he said, "We're in agreement."

He scooped me up, carried me the last few steps to the bed, and set me down on the edge. A lamp glowed from the dresser but otherwise the room was dark. It felt right. Comfortable. The last thing I wanted was every light in the room shining on my bare skin.

Stepping between my parted legs, he brushed some hair away from my face and over my shoulder. His belt was long gone and I'd managed to open the button but that was it as far as his bottom half went.

"You're so fucking beautiful." The words rushed out in a huff. "Do you even understand that?"

I pushed his pants and boxers down just enough to reach inside and wrap my hand around him. His head dropped back as he growled out a groan and that silly, stupid pride of mine exploded. I was positive there was nothing I couldn't do.

I shimmied the pants and boxers down the rest of the way and then dragged my tongue over the head of his cock. I heard him pull in a broken breath and I felt his entire body pull tight but I was too busy teasing him between my lips to pay much attention.

He gripped my hair as I sucked him deeper, twisting it around his palm as he murmured *Yes* and *Baby, please* and *What are you fucking doing to me?*

I liked that last one a lot.

I couldn't take him very deep without feeling like I was going to gag. Since I really didn't want to gag, I kept it shallow while stroking him from the base to my lips. He dropped his free hand to my shoulder and then slid it up to my neck. He held me like that, his palm on my throat, his fingers at my nape, and his thumb pressed to my cheek. I didn't know if he could feel himself through my cheek but I liked the idea that he could.

"This," he ground out, "isn't what I had in mind for us. But I can't bring myself to stop. Goddamn. You're so fucking good at this." I peered up at him as I pulled him deep, as I hollowed out my cheeks. "Oh, fuck, look at you. Just fucking look at you."

When my fist connected with his base on the next stroke, he curled a hand around my wrist, holding me in place. He took a step back, retreating from my mouth only far enough for his cockhead to rest between my lips. He pointed to the bed and let out a harsh, wild sound that probably made the neighbors wonder what kind of animal I had in here.

I scrambled to the middle of the mattress. Did not even care how I looked doing it.

The bed had already been turned down by the housekeeping service. That made it easier to peel back the blankets but then I was there, waiting with nothing but the need thrumming through me while Jude stared from beside the bed.

"I know I need to get a condom," he said eventually. "I keep telling myself you'll be right there when I come back but I don't believe it yet."

I held out a hand to him. "You don't need a condom. I can't get pregnant."

"You're sure?"

I didn't know which part of this he was questioning but the answer was the same either way. "Yes, and if you don't get over here, I'm going to assume it's because you don't actually want—"

He was on me, his hips anchoring me to the mattress and his cock a hot brand on my belly. He kissed my neck, my shoulders, my lips. "You're sure?" he repeated. "Obviously, you can change your mind at any time but—"

"Yeah, I'm sure," I said, dragging a foot up the back of his thigh. "And I promise I won't flee to the bathroom if your phone rings."

He dropped his head between my breasts, laughing. "If you do, I'm following you in there this time."

I canted my hips until I felt him between my legs, the perfect pressure and weight of his cock throbbing against me. He reached between us, taking his shaft in hand and holding himself at my entrance. I shifted a bit, pinning my knees to his waist. It was all I could do to keep myself from shouting, *Give it to me now.*

"I want to hear you say it again," he rasped, his fingers around the base of his cock. "Tell me you want this."

"I wanted you to follow me into the bathroom," I said all at once. "Into the shower. I should've—I don't know. I shouldn't have put the pillow between us because we could've been doing this all week and—"

Apparently, that was all he needed to hear because he snapped his hips forward and pushed into me with one blinding thrust that robbed the breath from my lungs. He was impossibly thick, so much more than I remembered, and I could barely think beyond the hot, blissful fullness. I felt him everywhere, filling me, pushing past all my limits. I couldn't even take a deep breath without being aware of him inside me.

I wanted to tell him that. I wanted him to know I felt him in my chest, in the back of my throat. And that I wanted *more.*

"I can hear you thinking, princess," he said. "What do you need? Should I lick those sweet nipples? Bite them?"

"It wouldn't hurt."

His brow arched. "It will if I want it to."

He pushed up on an elbow as he rocked into me. I brought my hand to his bicep to feel the flex of his muscles with each thrust. He leaned in then, sucking one nipple between his lips while pinching the other. My inner muscles rippled in response, clamping around his shaft so hard it stole my breath for a second.

I shoved my fingers through his thick hair, saying, "That didn't hurt at all."

"Sometimes I can't believe you're real and you're here." He gave a dark chuckle against my breast before pinning my nipple between his teeth.

I raked my fingers through his hair, holding him close to me while I bucked beneath him. "I can't believe *we're* here."

Every thrust seemed to take me apart, brick by brick. It was careful. Deliberate. I was about to fall apart but he wasn't *breaking* me and there was a difference. I hadn't known it until right now and I didn't think I'd be able to do this again without thinking about it.

And I wanted to do that to him too. To dismantle him. And then build something brand new.

"I can't believe how fucking good you feel," he said. "I just— Fuck, Audrey. *Fuck.*"

He pumped into me and then pulled all the way out, and with both hands anchored on my waist, he rolled us over. "Ohhhhh my god," I said, my hands braced on his chest.

"Come on now," he said, lightly slapping the side of my ass. "Don't keep me waiting. It's not polite."

I didn't waste any time sinking down over him. I couldn't. Not when my body was busy humming a chant of *Get there get there get there* and he was staring up at me like this was the only thing in the world he wanted. And I *loved* being on top. It was the only position that worked for me every time.

"I don't know what you mean," I said as I worked to find the right rhythm. He was *so* thick and I was *so* out of practice. "I'm very polite."

He kept both hands on my waist as he thrust up into me. His thumbs pressed into the crease of my thigh. This angle, that pressure, and the complete fullness of feeling him everywhere, it was just about enough for me.

"Yes, you are, baby," he drawled. "That's why you're gonna come on my cock now."

"What if I'm not ready?"

He tipped his head back, leaving his throat exposed as he swallowed. "You feel really fucking ready."

He met every rock of my hips, every hard grind into him with relentless thrusts that sent pleasure spiraling through my body. "What if I want more?"

"Then I'll fuck you straight all night long," he said. "You should know by now I'll give you anything you want, even if it's the heart I carved out of my chest."

And that was the last brick.

I fell forward onto Jude's chest as a wave of spasms moved through my body and had me panting out an unintelligible series of *please yes more now.* Shooting stars flared behind my eyes and everything inside me seemed to unravel. He shifted to band his arms around my back, holding me steady as I shattered.

"Good?" He went right on hammering into me, working every gloriously sated ounce of me while I sprawled across his chest like a well-fucked starfish.

"Good," I mumbled. A moment later, I felt the roar building in his chest before I heard it.

In a distant, foggy sense, I was aware that Jude was speaking to me. Growling, perhaps. I knew he'd wrapped his arms around my torso and held me tight as he came though I couldn't focus on anything beyond the wonderful pulsing heat in my core.

It was so much. *So very much.* And he must've known I couldn't bear this, not all of it at once, because Jude rolled us to the side and tucked a pillow under my head. He stroked my back as I shook and gasped. It took a few minutes to fully catch my breath but when I did, I realized he was still inside me. My thighs and abdomen were drenched in our orgasms. He was a mess too, if we were taking stock.

"Wow," I whispered, touching a finger to my lips. All of a sudden I was exhausted. I could fall asleep right here and I wouldn't stir once.

"Yeah, I'd say so." He rubbed my nape and shoulders, I wanted to cry at how good it felt. "You're cold," he said.

"Not really." It would've been believable if the air conditioning hadn't clicked on at that moment and sent a shiver down my spine.

Jude kissed my forehead. "I can't reach the blankets unless I pull out."

"And you don't want to do that?"

He stared at me for a beat. "I don't want this to end."

I kissed the corner of his mouth. "What if we press pause for a minute? I can go to the bathroom, you can grab the blankets and get us some water. Then we'll come back and start again."

He tucked some hair over my ear. "You want that?"

"Yeah." Another shiver shook through me. "Think we can do that?"

It took a second but the corner of his mouth kicked up in a grin. He slapped my backside, saying, "Hurry up, Saunders. I'll be waiting for you."

Once I'd peed and cleaned up as much as possible, and the bedding was straightened, we slipped back under the covers. I nestled into his chest, my head under his chin and our legs twined together. He drew circles down my side and kissed my temple and forehead over and over.

I didn't let myself think much of it before asking, "Did you know I was at Pepperdine when you transferred to Caltech?"

"Yeah." He said this like it was more than obvious.

"Why didn't you tell me? We could've—I don't know—talked. Or something. You should've told me."

He leaned back to meet my eyes. He peered at me, his brows bunched tight like he didn't understand the question. Then, "I couldn't do that because of the restraining order, Audrey."

chapter thirty-seven

Jude

Today's vocabulary word: recital

SHE HADN'T KNOWN.

That much was clear by the way she scrambled away from me and out of bed, threw on a short, silky robe (inside out), and paced the length of the room while muttering, "Oh my god. Oh *my god.*"

One mystery solved.

My working theory had been that she was coerced into it. Her father was the heavy-handed type. I'd lost count of the number of times I was pulled over by his state troopers back in high school. Whether I was searched, warned, or ticketed for some alleged violation, it made clear that AG Saunders enjoyed some light abuse of power.

But I'd always assumed she knew. Even if she'd been dragged along, she'd been aware.

"That's not how it was supposed to go," she went on, still beating a track in the carpet.

"How was it supposed to go?" I stepped into my boxers. This conversation seemed like one that required a layer of clothing.

Audrey came to a jolting stop. She turned, met my gaze from across the darkened room. Her robe hung open, the ties lost to her haste. "They weren't supposed to do anything to you if I left."

I switched on a lamp beside the bed because this conversation also required some light. "What does that mean, Audrey?"

"It means—they said—" She pushed her fingers through her hair, shook her head. "My father was going to have you arrested."

I grabbed my shirt off the floor. This definitely required clothes. "Arrested for what?"

"He said he had more than enough evidence for a rape conviction. That even if the sentencing was generous, you'd be forced to register as a sex offender. And he'd make sure you lost your scholarships and admission to Columbia. He'd ruin everything for you."

I rocked back on my heels. So a little more than a light abuse of power.

"But if I left," she continued, pacing again, "if I cut ties with you and went to California and agreed to everything, it'd all go away."

My gaze dropped to the floor as I circled back through the memories of the days before Audrey disappeared from my life. I barely recognized them in this new light. And in that light, I found I had to bite back every knee-jerk thing I wanted to say.

She should've told me. We could've solved this shitstorm together.

Except we'd been kids with no money and no resources of our own. Our entire lives hinged on those scholarships of mine and her parents footing the bill for Barnard. I had no way of fighting off a whole sexual assault charge, definitely not with her father leaning hard on it, and we both knew that.

She still should've told me.

But she must've been terrified. And alone. Just the other day she said she'd failed the first semester. That she hadn't been able to get out of bed. She did the best she could in a horrible situation.

As a side note, I really fucking hated her family. Goddamn. Those fucking people.

Which led me to realize— "They made you marry him," I said. Not a question.

She wrapped her arms around her torso, nodding. "That was the deal. Since I couldn't be trusted to make 'appropriate' choices, my parents would make them for me. And if I refused—" She scoffed, exhaustion and pain filling her eyes. "My father made a point of reminding me how easy it would be to file those charges."

I couldn't believe she'd dragged that burden behind her for so long. That she'd lived with it and accepted it and *married* for it.

And she'd done it all to protect me.

"Come here," I said.

"No, this is important," she said, wagging a finger at the path of her pacing. "I'm busy being angry at myself."

"Why are you angry at yourself?"

"Because I should've known I couldn't trust my father," she snapped. "He promised to leave you alone and I let myself believe he would."

"That's bullshit." I sank onto the corner of the bed. "No one expects their family to betray them. *Repeatedly.*"

The robe caught air as she walked from one end of the room to the other, billowing out around her bare thighs. She didn't seem to notice. "Unless we're talking about my family, in which case we definitely expect it." She slapped the top of the dresser, *hard*, saying, "I can't believe I did everything they wanted, all of it, and they still dragged you into this."

"Baby, please. Just slow down and come over here."

"Why aren't you furious?" she asked. "Why aren't you tearing this place to the ground and plotting your revenge? Or—" She cut a wild glance in my direction. "Oh my god, am I the revenge? Is that what this is really about? Are you going to sneak out in the middle of the night and abandon me here or something? Now that we've—" She pointed to the bed.

I rubbed my forehead. "For fuck's sake, Audrey."

"That's not a no."

"I have no intention of abandoning you," I said. "In fact, I'd love it if you'd come over here and let me take that robe off you."

"But why aren't you furious? I'm furious for you."

"Because I..." The words trailed off as I lost my hold on whatever I'd intended to say. The truth was, I'd let that anger keep me warm for *years*. And I'd only known half the story. But as deep as I reached, I couldn't find the anger now. All that remained was a thick, grainy layer of grief.

We'd lost so much. And for what? What good had any of this done? Even if I lived for another five hundred years, I didn't think I'd understand how anyone could wield their daughter like an object. I couldn't fathom forcing my son to give up everything he loved just so I could maintain my deeply corrupt political mantle and some archaic belief systems.

That, and her parents never thought I'd amount to much.

I could admit that spite had played a large part in pushing me through my university years. I loved proving people really fucking wrong.

"Because we've already lost enough to them, Audrey," I finally said. "I'm not willing to give them any more and neither should you."

She walked another loop before stopping in front of me, fury still vibrating through her. I picked up the hand she'd whacked and turned it over in mine. Her palm was red and warm. It must've hurt, at least a bit.

"I'm still mad they fucked you over."

Stroking my thumb over her palm, I glanced up to meet her eyes. "They fucked us both over."

"But you—you could've been kicked out of Columbia." She held up her free hand. "Wait. *Were* you kicked out of Columbia? Is that why you transferred?"

"No, I didn't get kicked out. Caltech was the better fit," I said quickly. "But this is our last night. I don't care about that shit anymore."

"Yes, you do. It's why you've been a snappy little snapping turtle to me since demanding I dance with you."

"I don't know what you're talking about."

She gave me her best attempt at a glower. It was more of a squinting pout. God, what I wouldn't give to be on the receiving end of that every day. "I think you do."

"Nope. Sorry."

She brought a hand to the back of my neck, threaded her fingers through my hair. The robe hung open between her breasts, exposing a long, gorgeous stretch of skin. I leaned in and pressed my mouth to the side of her breast. Closed my hands around her hips.

"How do you want to spend it?" she asked.

"I've already told you my plans for this robe."

She dragged a finger down the front of my shirt. "You first."

I yanked the shirt over my head and then pushed to my feet to ditch the boxers. The robe hit the floor next. "Is this what you want, princess?"

With a hand on my shoulder, she pushed me back down to the corner of the bed.

"Yeah," she said thoughtfully. She dropped a knee beside my hip, then the other. Linked her arms around my neck as she settled over me, as she rocked against my shaft. "I think it is."

She reached between us, pumping me with the kind of slow, deep pressure that made me wild and desperate. I watched her expressions shift as she teased my cockhead over her clit, down to her wet heat. She dug her teeth into her bottom lip, rocking against me with each pass.

I let my hands skate down her back, along the dip and flare of her waist, over her ass. She felt like silk and muscle and every precious thing in the world. Like promises I'd tried to forget.

I swallowed hard, asking, "Having fun with the torture?"

"It's not torture if you love it," she replied, and she wasn't wrong about that. Not for one second.

But also— "Not sure you'll be saying that when I'm done with you."

A wicked grin filled her face as she twisted her palm up my shaft. God*damn*. "Quiet, you. Let me do this."

She shifted until I was there, just barely inside her but enough that I couldn't think beyond the heat and pressure, couldn't keep my eyes open. My lips found the slight curve of her breast again and I kissed my way to her nipple. She bucked against me as I pinned her between my teeth.

She sank down on me like we weren't running out of time. The hot pulse of her muscles was enough to scramble my head and make me believe it.

When she was there, when she was fully seated and I was hanging on by a single string of restraint, she looped her arms around my neck and said, "Kiss me."

The words were barely off her tongue when I bit them out of the air and closed the space between us. She tasted perfect, just so fucking perfect, and I wanted to live and die in her cunt, and it finally felt like I knew where I was going.

I dropped my hands to her hips, gripping tight as I thrust up into her. I wanted to last for hours but I also wanted to come *right fucking now* so I could lick her until she screamed and then drag her into the shower and pour myself into her all over again.

"You—feel—so—good," she said, each word groaned out as she slammed down on me.

"Baby, I'm doing the absolute least here. This is all you."

She pressed her forehead to my shoulder, her teeth bared to my skin. "It's never been like this with—with anyone else."

"And it's not going to be." I was proud of myself for not saying something shitty about her ex-husband but even more that I didn't lose it altogether. The only thing that mattered was giving her what she needed. Even if I wanted to come hard enough to leave a mark, I'd be happy if she finished without me and tucked herself into bed for the night. This was enough.

"I think—" Her words broke into a small cry. "I'm—*oh god*."

I shifted my hand to the small of her back, pulling her hard against me, deeper. "That's it. There it is. You're so close," I said. "You know it's mine, princess. Give it to me."

Her lips parted and she stared at me, a startled brightness in her eyes as her body drew tight and her cunt choked the fuck out of my cock. As if she was astonished, as if she had no idea her body could do this.

"A little more," I growled. "You're not done yet."

The wet slap of skin fell into the chorus of heavy breathing and those gorgeous little cries of hers. Her tits bounced in my face and her nails dug into my shoulders. I held her hips, steering her as she went soft and pliant. Thrusting into her as she chanted, "Oh god, oh god, oh god."

She came down in pieces. The hand gripping my hair fell to her side. Then her knees slid away from my hips, her shoulders slumped. Her breathing evened out as I stroked her back.

"I'm going to have to get up," she said.

"I don't think so. Just stay here."

She laughed into my neck. "I have to clean up."

"I'll take care of you."

I felt her smile. "That's not how it works but thank you anyway."

"Then I'll make it easier." I took her wrists, looped them around my neck. "Hold on."

When I pushed to my feet, she yelped, "Oh my god, what?"

"Just saving you a few steps." I carried her to the bathroom, which was bigger than my grad school apartment, and instructed her to grab a towel off the rack. I spread it on the marble countertop and set her down.

She peered up at me, her lips swollen, cheeks red, hair everywhere, and something inside my chest flipped. A switch. Maybe an entire organ. I wasn't sure but I knew nothing would be the same after this moment.

I turned on the sink, running my fingers under the water until it warmed up. "Do you know how gorgeous you are right now?"

She glanced over her shoulder to catch her reflection in the mirror. "If you say so."

"I don't know how you do it." I reached for a facecloth, held it under the water. "Sometimes I look at you and you're this brand-new thing, even though I'd swear I've always known you." I pushed her legs apart, wide, wider than she thought necessary if her smirk could be trusted. Her inner thighs were slicked with her arousal and my release, and it had a breath catching in my throat. "How do you do that to me?"

Audrey watched as I dragged the wet cloth between her legs, her bottom lip snared between her teeth. "I'm not new. You just stopped resenting me after doing it for more than a decade."

"That's where you're wrong." I ran the cloth over her folds, carefully cleaning up the mess I'd left behind. "It's always been this way. You change my brain chemistry and you burn your fingerprints into my skin and I don't understand how you're even possible, but that doesn't matter because right now, you're here."

"I think that's the orgasm talking."

I wet the cloth again, squeezed it out, and gave myself a quick pass. "Nope."

"It is," she went on. "Remember all those times when we parked behind Chili's and I'd give you blow jobs in the back seat? You'd say the most unhinged things."

"Yeah, like your mouth was made for cocksucking," I said, leaning in close, "and I was going to marry you the first chance I got. Really thought I would've sealed that deal by now."

She dropped her gaze, her pale lashes fanning over her cheeks. She swallowed hard. "Could you give me a minute?"

I pressed a kiss to her forehead. "Yeah. Of course."

I closed the bathroom door behind me and went to work gathering the clothes we'd left scattered around the room. When I came across her robe, I turned it right side out and set it on the bed. My girl was not about to stroll out here naked. She'd come looking for that robe soon enough.

I heard the toilet flush and the faucet run, but another minute or two passed in silence. I couldn't decide how to interpret that. I didn't know what I wanted all of this to mean. And I had no idea where we went from here. If she wanted it to go anywhere.

A few more minutes drifted by before Audrey peeked out from behind the door. "Would you—" I crossed to her in two strides, handed her the robe. "Oh. Thank you."

"Just know you're ditching that thing before you get in bed."

"You were a lot less bossy in the back seat," she said.

"Do you want me to call down to the valet? I'm sure we can find a Chili's. Applebee's in a pinch."

She rounded the bed, a far-off gleam in her eyes as she wove her hair into a braid. Had I ever watched her braid her hair? Probably, yes. But not like this. With a bed between us, the night waiting for what we made of it. With her lips kiss-bitten and that robe hanging open. She hadn't bothered with the ties.

"Too many of our parking lot places have closed," she said. "Remember Bertucci's? We got into a lot of trouble in those parking lots."

I slipped between the sheets and smoothed out her pillows. "All

I remember is that you're not nearly as well-behaved as you'd like people to think."

She shrugged out of the robe and crawled in beside me. "Excuse me but I'm a very good girl."

I stroked a hand over the crown of her head, down her braid. Caught the tail between two fingers. "I wouldn't have it any other way."

Audrey curled into me and closed her eyes, a full, warm smile on her lips. I dragged my fingers over her shoulders, her collarbones. Down the line of her chest and over her breasts. I let myself stare at her without caring that she'd notice. That she'd see everything I'd tried to ignore this week. Or longer. So much longer.

Then I spotted a dark line riding low on her hip. "What's this?" I asked, swiping my thumb over the words inked in a thin, swooping script. I couldn't believe I'd missed that. "When did you get a tattoo?"

I expected her to laugh. Or cringe away from the question. To turn into a rosy, blushing mess and tell me a story about claiming some rebellion for herself. But she didn't do that.

A cold, steady quiet settled over her. The life seemed to bleed from her eyes. Then I was cold too.

She swallowed. "After I moved to Boston."

I traced the words again. The script was fine and thin. "What does it say?"

"'I carry your heart with me. I carry it in my heart.'"

"From the poem? E. E. Cummings?" A single bob of her head. "Can I get a closer look?"

Another nod, her gaze still frozen and empty. I didn't know much but I'd bet my life that quote wasn't about her asshole ex.

I shifted down the bed and cocked my head to get a better look. The last *t* in *heart* swept out with a long swash that curled into a heart around a pair of finger-wide silvery scars. And then there was another scar, longer and craggy where it ran across her pelvis.

I dropped my palm to the scars and met her gaze. "What happened?"

She turned her head and stared out at the inky night, and it occurred to me that she might not answer. I stayed there just the same, my head resting on her thighs while I smoothed small circles low on her belly. Nowhere else in the world I wanted to be.

Then, "When I found out I was pregnant, my first thought was that I had to leave Chris. Probably the first clear, decisive thought I'd had in years. I'd been so…ambivalent for so long. Just floating. Existing. I hadn't really cared about anything but then it was real and I had to care. It didn't matter if all I could do was float but I wouldn't let that be my child's life."

You're wrong, I wanted to say. *It did matter.* But I knew when to keep quiet.

"He had a big boys' trip planned. Yachts, helicopters, private islands. All his favorite things. He'd been gone nearly a month. That was when I'd planned to leave." Her voice cracked and that sound scraped against my soft tissue. "I didn't feel well but I never felt well. I'd been sick for years at that point. I couldn't digest anything. I was always having one kind of flare-up or another. Everything hurt every day so I didn't realize something was wrong."

She brushed a tear from her cheek but when she dropped that hand, she dropped it on my shoulder.

"I collapsed after filing for divorce. Right there in the lawyer's office," she said, a slightly hysterical laugh ringing in her words. "Ectopic pregnancy. The egg had implanted in one of my tubes. It ruptured and blew up the tube. It felt just like my regular pain level. But my belly was full of blood all the way up to here." She tapped a spot above her navel and then edged my fingers away from where they covered the heart tattoo. "That was the first surgery."

"The first," I echoed.

She gave a thoughtful nod as she moved my hand from the other scar. "Did you know that after you've had internal bleeding,

all the places that the blood filled can feel itchy? I was so itchy—
but *inside* my body. The minute I woke up from surgery, I wanted
to scratch my skin off. It hurt to touch my abdomen but I couldn't
help it. And I had a terrible reaction to the pain meds, which only
made it all worse. I had scratches and hives all over the place." She
brought my hand back to the scar. "That's why they didn't catch the
sepsis until it was too late. Why the hysterectomy was such a
mess."

"Audrey." I rested my head on her belly and wrapped my arms
around her hips. Squeezed her hard, hard enough to put all these
broken things back together. I wanted to ask where her husband, her
family had been during this ordeal but I was pretty sure I already
knew. Pretty sure I wanted to strangle the shit out of them too. "I'm
so sorry, sweetheart."

"That baby almost killed me," she said, letting the tears run
down her face now. "But it also saved my life."

I leaned in and kissed my way across the larger scar, the two
small ones, and then the line of script. Then I shifted back to the
pillow and folded her into my arms. "There is no safer, stronger
place to carry that baby's heart than your heart."

"I don't usually tell people this because they never actually get
it," she started, "but I know I would've died if I hadn't left him. Not
because of him but because I'd stopped living. And I hadn't truly
understood that until I came out of surgery and they said I wouldn't
have another baby."

"Thank you for trusting me with that," I said, kissing across her
cheeks, the bridge of her nose. "You know you can always tell me
anything. I'll always get you."

She buried her face in my chest as a sob broke free. I held her
while she cried, keeping one hand gliding up and down her spine as
she let it pour out of her.

I'd always known her parents had maneuvered her out of my life
and under their thumb. But there'd also been a shitty little voice in

there too, one that liked to say she left because she'd outgrown me. Because she'd come to her senses and recognized we never would've been able to turn our teenage dreams into reality. Because she'd decided our worlds were too different. Because I'd never been good enough for her, and nothing I could do would change that.

I'd let that shitty voice tell me a lot of shitty stories. Let it convince me I'd suffered the most. I mean, the fucking restraining order made a strong case for that all on its own. But I'd never really stopped to think whether she'd suffered too. Not when I'd told myself she'd been forced to make a choice and, in the end, she'd chosen her family's comfortable world over me.

All while she'd suffered in the most devastating ways. She'd almost *died*.

After blowing through half a box of tissues, she said, "Sorry about that."

"Don't apologize." I delivered a light slap to her backside. "But tell me what happened when he found out. Tell me the rest."

"I was still recovering when he came home from the trip. I'd wanted to leave but I could barely walk up a flight of stairs. I just— I couldn't do anything." Her shoulders lifted, tightened under my palm. "He said it was good I'd filed for divorce. He thought I was doing him a favor. Because I couldn't have kids anymore. That he would've filed if I hadn't."

"He's a fucking asshole."

"I know. Believe me, I know all about it. But him not under-standing the sequence of events made it easier for me to leave. As far as he was concerned, I was no better than a busted toaster oven and he'd be happy when I was out on the curb with the rest of the trash."

"Jesus, Audrey, don't say that."

"I'm not saying I believe it," she replied. "But Chris did, and it motivated him to move out of the house, offer me a decent settlement up front, and get the divorce finalized before I was even cleared to lift more than a few pounds."

We weren't that far from San Diego. Six, maybe seven hour drive. I could have my hands around his throat by morning if we left now. "Please let me kill him."

"Your mother's been through enough. Don't add a murder trial to it."

"He's still a fucking asshole."

"Yeah, I pray that he has recurrent canker sores and all of his socks have annoying seams, but it could've been a lot worse."

"No, princess, there's no story where you almost die from internal bleeding and almost die again from sepsis, and all the while your dickbag ex can't be bothered to leave his boys' trip early to be by your side, that could be worse."

"No, wait, listen. I told him to stay there. You think I wanted him with me in the hospital? For what? To tell me healing was all mental and I'd feel better once I got some cardio in? Or feed me some mushroom coffee and bitch about me needing the painkillers? I don't think so."

"I just—" I brushed a few loose strands over her ear. I wasn't sure what I was trying to say. "I wish I'd known."

"Why?"

I swallowed past the boulder in my throat. "Because it hurts my heart that you went through this alone."

Audrey was quiet for a long moment that left me wondering if I'd said too much. Then, "You're here now."

"Is that enough? After everything?"

She lifted a shoulder. "I don't know. Maybe."

I didn't think it was.

chapter thirty-eight
Audrey

Today's vocabulary word: memento

JUDE KEPT HIS EYES ON THE ROAD AS WE MADE THE TWO-HOUR drive to the Phoenix airport and I kept mine on the blur of desert going by. We'd accomplished everything we came here to do—his mother was content, the performance was convincing, and we hadn't collapsed under the weight of our own scar tissue. Better than that, even, we'd healed some of those old wounds.

We were quiet but it wasn't the thorny silence that'd dominated the front side of this trip. This silence settled around us like the gentle slant of morning sunlight, warm and familiar. It gave me the time to take apart the last few days and put them back together in an order I could understand. I already knew some of it would end up in the *Shit That Doesn't Make Sense and Shouldn't Have Happened* file but I couldn't help going over it again and again.

I still didn't know how I wanted to handle all that I'd learned about my parents in the past day. My default response of avoidance wasn't going to work this time around. If it had ever worked. But it wasn't like I could call them up and have a calm discussion. They'd insist I was wrong or confused or—better yet—*misled* by Jude. Oh, they'd love to ride that pony all the way into town. Even if I produced an actual copy of the restraining order, they'd find a way to tell me it wasn't real.

All I knew was that they'd taken enough from me.

As for the rest, I knew I wasn't ready to let go yet. Of Jude, of the person I let myself be when I was with him, of this cobbled-together version of us. Of the new and old, and the ways we felt the same but different.

But none of that fit into this arrangement. He was off to Seattle for work and then back to Michigan for his son. I was Boston-bound with Emme's wedding swallowing up the week to come. This was the precise end we'd agreed upon, it was the closure I'd come looking for—and I couldn't stop thinking about waking up with him again. Couldn't stop thinking about all the time we'd lost and the years we'd consigned to being angry and hurt and adrift. And then there was everything I'd given up, everything I'd lost.

It just seemed so fucking unfair.

And where did that leave us? Was it just...over? Was that how it ended this time? Were we supposed to walk away now like the past week hadn't blown a hole through our history? As if we hadn't discovered each other all over again?

As we made our way into the airport and through security, I felt it slipping away. This was it. This was where we'd leave each other —and I knew I'd have only myself to blame if I didn't do something.

We stopped near the departures board. Jude's flight left about forty-five minutes before mine but we had some time before he was due to board.

He motioned toward the restaurants tucked into the terminal. "Hungry?" he asked.

"Not too much," I said. "You?"

He shook his head as he typed on his phone. "I'm good. It's a quick flight up to Seattle."

I made noises about needing something new to read and he followed me around, still busy with his phone, as I gave nearly every book at the newsstand a thorough inspection. I didn't choose any of them because I'd only stared blindly at those books while the inside of my head rang with fifteen different alarm bells, all of them blaring *Do something! Don't leave like this!*

We wandered into another shop where Jude stopped to look at a display of Arizona-themed keychains. "Percy likes keychains," he said when he noticed me staring. "I grab one for him whenever I'm in a new city. He has at least ten on his backpack and another few on his lunchbox."

"That's cute," I said.

"Wait. Check it out." He held up a bejeweled magnet in the shape of a lizard. "I think you need a souvenir."

I recoiled at the thought. "I don't need any help remembering that monster but thanks so much for thinking of me."

"Nah. This is going home with you."

Jude selected a saguaro cactus keychain for Percy and a bottle of cold brew coffee along with the magnet. I left him to pay and ended up staring at an assortment of lollipops with actual scorpions inside them. Absolutely terrifying.

He returned to my side and pulled my bag from my shoulder, pawing at my cases and pouches like they belonged to him. He settled on the small quilted coin purse where I kept my tea bags. His gaze locked on mine, he tucked the lizard between packets of mint, ginger, and chamomile.

"Promise me you'll put this on your fridge," he said, returning the purse to the depths of my bag. He added a bottle of water and the brand of cinnamon gum I liked. "Don't let me down, Saunders."

At my silence, he pressed a thumb to my forehead, smoothing

out the creases that'd gathered there. It was such a small, intimate touch. One I never would've longed for, but now that I'd felt it, I didn't see how I could live without it. I swallowed hard, choking down the grief that'd soaked me down to my shoes.

The boarding call for Jude's flight came through. We both turned in the direction of his gate, watching it like we wanted to make sure it was real. That he'd get on that flight and go to Seattle, and I'd go back to Boston, and this would end. We'd be finished, again.

It felt like the ground was gradually giving way beneath me and I reached for the first solid thing I could find. "My friend Emme's wedding is this weekend," I started, breathless for no good reason, "and it's in this adorable small town on the Rhode Island coast. Friendship. That's the name of the town. My other friend Shay, she owns a tulip farm. I think I told you that already. Anyway, she moved there a few years ago when she inherited it and now she hosts events there. Grace, another one of my friends, she got married there last year. Now it's Emme's turn and—and you should come. If you want. If you can. I mean, I know you have work and everything but if you can, you should." I shifted my bag to the other shoulder, adding, "I know Emme won't mind. It's a massive wedding and I have a plus-one but there wasn't anyone I wanted to bring until… If you wanted, you could come. With me."

He stared off into the terminal for a minute. It was just enough time to replay every desperate, rambling thing I'd said.

Then he cleared his throat and folded me into his arms. I went, a bit stiff and slightly confused. He held me tight until I relaxed into him. "I'm tied up all week," he said, his lips brushing my ear. "I'm sorry."

"No, it's fine. No. I just thought—since, well, everything. But it's fine."

He didn't argue with this and he didn't let me go either. The next boarding group was called for his flight but we stayed there, twined together. I didn't know if he felt everything fall apart too. I was afraid that he didn't.

"You killed it this week. You were awesome with my mom. I'll never be able to thank you enough for that."

Finally, he stepped back and shoved his hands in his pockets. I tried to do the same but the ring on my left hand caught on the seam. I stared at the ring for a second but then yanked it off. "This is yours," I said, the band pinched between my fingers.

A moment passed when he only blinked at the ring, and inside that tiny ounce of time I heard him tell me to keep it. That it belonged to me and should stay on my hand. That *he* belonged to me. That we were only pretending about pretending now. That we'd finished the fake part and we could be real now.

But as the silence stretched, I knew I'd only hear those words in my head.

With a nod, he plucked the ring from my fingers and dropped it into a pocket. Another boarding announcement for his flight rang out and he tipped his head toward the gate. "Get home safe, Saunders."

I watched him stroll down the terminal and join the people queued up at the gate. He shuffled closer to the door, his phone in hand and his head bowed as he swiped at the screen. I held my breath as he scanned his boarding pass, feeling the sum of this week expanding in my chest like a balloon. I needed something from him —anything—before this ended.

But he stepped through the door and down the jetway without another glance.

I gripped my luggage handle tighter, my palm damp and my joints aching as final boarding calls were announced and the gate door shut.

I stayed there for a long time, staring at that door the same way

I'd stared at him all week. Still, I couldn't find any clues to help me make sense of what we'd become. Of who we were now. And I didn't think it mattered anymore.

If this was the closure I'd wanted, no one warned me it would hurt like hell.

chapter thirty-nine

Audrey

Today's vocabulary word: presence

"Hey. I think Em's trying to get your attention."

I blinked away from the perfect cube of watermelon speared on the end of my fork and toward the young woman seated beside me. One of Emme's sisters-in-law. I knew her name. We'd met before. A few times. In the past couple of days, even. But my head was somewhere else, and it'd been there since landing in Boston a week ago.

The first few days back had gone about as well as expected, all of which was to say I was barely functional as a human. I was late to everything, responded to texts only in my head, and looked hungover at all times despite keeping to the most basic, flare-proofed diet. I woke up throughout the night, always peering into the darkness as if I'd find him there beside me.

And I was being the worst bridesmaid ever. I'd forgotten about my final dress fitting and then forgot to pick up my dress before leaving for Friendship. Shay gently snatched the bachelorette bar hop away from me when I admitted I hadn't confirmed the plans—and it didn't even strike a fragile, perfectionist chord in me.

Even now, seated at this long, gorgeous table in the Twin Tulip rose garden where I was surrounded by some of the best women I knew for Emme's bridal luncheon, I couldn't drag my mind away from Arizona. From Jude. From *us*.

I set the fork down. "I'm so sorry. I didn't catch that."

She slung an arm around my shoulders and shifted me toward Emme. "Are you okay? You kind of zoned out there," she whispered. "Your girl's been trying to grab you for the past few minutes."

"Sorry!" I called, sending Emme a helpless shrug. "I'm still strangely jet-lagged. It's weird, I know. I'm working on it."

I murmured my thanks to the woman beside me. Her lips twisted as she said, "It's Ruth."

"I knew that," I said, cringing. "I swear, I did. I'm not usually this much of a mess."

Her answering nod told me none of this was especially believable.

"We wanted to hear all about this trip," Emme said, gesturing to her stepsister Ines on one side of her, Shay to the other. "How did I not know anything about this? I need all the details. Jamie told me you went to Arizona?"

I cut a glance to Ruth. She smothered a smile as if she understood the exact dimensions of the corner I'd been backed into. "It all came together at the last minute. An old friend needed some help. With a family thing."

Jamie cackled before slapping a hand over her mouth. "Don't mind me," she said.

Emme leaned in, her elbows braced on the white tablecloth and her chin cradled in her clasped fingers. "What kind of help?"

I went back to my watermelon. "Well."

The truth—the entirety of it—was a complicated thing. I knew there were pieces this group would understand since they had some experience with relationships that started under curious circumstances. But there were also pieces that felt like artifacts from another lifetime, too fine and fragile to expose to sunlight.

I felt the heat of everyone's attention on my face. If I didn't say something soon, I'd have to clutch my belly and dash for the house, claiming an irritable bowel situation. No one ever asked follow-up questions about those issues.

"An old friend," I started, "his mom, who I'd adored back when we were in high school, was diagnosed with advanced stage breast cancer."

"Oh my god," Emme said, sympathy quickly taking the place of her curiosity. "Oh, Audrey, I'm so sorry to hear that."

"She was really going through it," I went on. "And she asked my friend—Jude, his name's Jude—to promise that he'd find someone. That he'd settle down after she was gone. He was distraught, obviously, and told his mom that he was planning on proposing very soon."

Emme uncorked another bottle of champagne, saying, "I think I know where this is going."

"Me too," Shay murmured.

"Yeah, so, I went out to Arizona with him last week to visit his mom," I said, "as his fiancée."

The table was silent for a long moment while everyone shared sidelong glances. Then, Ruth asked, "Is there going to be a wedding? Or are you expecting the mother to die before it gets to that point?"

"Ruthie!" one of her sisters cried. Chloe. Maybe Amber? In my defense, they looked a lot alike.

"It's a valid question given the setup, *Amber*," Ruth said.

Then the other one was Chloe. Okay. This was good. Progress. I only had one other sister to identify. I wasn't completely failing as a bridesmaid.

"It's a rude question," Amber seethed.

Chloe nodded in agreement. Ruth made a low, irritable sound. Kind of like a jammed spice grinder.

"Well, fortunately for all involved," I started, "Jude's mom made an incredible recovery. She'll still need close monitoring and frequent scans, but she's not going anywhere soon."

"Then it's the wedding route?" Ruth asked.

I started to answer but stopped myself. It would've been easier to condense this into a bite-sized story if that week with Jude hadn't broken me open. This wasn't just a favor and it wasn't just a trip to Arizona and he wasn't just an old friend. It was a week I'd borrowed from another alternate lifetime and I still didn't know how to fold myself back into this lifetime without giving up everything I'd shoved into my pockets along the way.

"No," I said slowly. "Next month, he'll tell her we decided to call it off."

"I don't know," Grace said. "If I was dying and my kid told me he was getting married but then broke it off a month later, I'd call him on that shit. I'd play Sick Mommy until he confessed to his crimes."

"That's because you're actually an evil stepmother," Jamie said. "You just don't have any stepchildren to torment."

"I'm sure I could find some," Grace said.

"Am I correct in my understanding that this is a non-romantic friend?" Ines asked. "Or does *friend* imply something else in this context?"

I swallowed hard. My throat was tight, sticky. "You could say we have a bit of a romantic history."

From across the table, Jamie mouthed, *Just a bit?*

"Then it's possible that this construct was conceived to rekindle that romantic history," Ines went on.

"Probably not," I said, reaching for my water.

"But there's a chance," Ines said.

I drained the glass as another pang of emptiness hit my chest. "That wasn't how we left things last week."

"You're still riding the newlywed high, Mrs. Jones," Emme said, bringing a hand to her stepsister's forearm. "Not everyone is looking to get paired off." She smiled in my direction though it could've been a wince. "I hope you're okay. It sounds complicated."

"Very complicated," I said. "But I'm fine. Just fighting this jet lag. I guess it hits a lot harder at thirty-five."

The lookalike sisters offered their own jet lag stories. Beside me, Ruth rolled her eyes out loud. When I glanced at her, she said, "I'm just being petty. Ignore me. Everyone else does."

"You can be petty with me all you want if you remind me of your younger sister's name."

She ran a glance over me, her brows pinched like she'd only now discovered I was a human woman and not a woody stalk of asparagus in a sundress as she'd originally believed. "Claudia," she said. "You're diving into this thing without a plus-one, then? Are we the only ones?"

I folded my arms over my abdomen to muffle the grumbles coming from my belly. "Jamie's my date," I said, tipping my chin toward her.

"But we're big fans of threesomes so you can vibe with us this weekend," Jamie said.

"She doesn't mean—"

Jamie cut me off with, "Yes, she does."

Ruth glanced between us, her tight expression flickering through at least four different emotions while Jamie fluttered her lashes with her most feline grin. "Okay, I don't know what I just stepped in here but let me say you're both beautiful and much less full of yourselves than I expected. Very unfortunately, I do prefer the male apparatus. Believe me, there's no one less impressed with that fact than me. And not for lack of exploration, right? I went to college on a rugby scholarship. My best friends are all over the rainbow. Nothing but love and respect from me."

"It really is unfortunate," Jamie said with a groan. "I wish I didn't enjoy dicks so much. They always come attached to the most insufferable creatures."

"Every fucking time," Ruth murmured. "It's really becoming a problem. I don't like men. I can't trust most of them. Barely respect them. Until they get their house in order, I'll be abstaining."

I wanted to agree with the sentiment but recent history wouldn't allow it. Not when I could still feel his hands trailing over my body, his growls kissed into my skin. I must've made some kind of noise because I blinked and found both of them gaping at me. "What?" I asked as heat filled my cheeks.

Jamie leaned in close. Ruth did the same. "It sounds like you left a few details out of your report," Jamie said. "We'll be getting to the bottom of that later."

"Yeah, I need to hear this," Ruth said. "You're a sweetheart but you have no poker face to speak of. You'd fold like a lawn chair in a deposition."

I glared at them though the corner of my mouth betrayed me with a twitch. "It's not fair that you're joining forces to bully me."

"Baby, I'm on a no-drinks, no-dick diet this weekend," Jamie said. "All I have keeping me going is my tenderhearted brand of bullying."

"My brand doesn't prioritize tenderness or hearts," Ruth said. "Sorry. I'm just trying to avoid my sisters because I might actually murder them if they make one more comment about how sad it is that I don't have a date."

Jamie reached across the table and patted her hand. "Something tells me you have plenty of heart," Jamie said. "Just in your own way."

Laughing, Ruth said, "That's not what everyone else says."

"We don't give a fuck about everyone else," I said.

Again, Ruth and Jamie shared a glance—and then burst out laughing. I smiled and for the first time all week, it didn't feel like I was dragging a boulder uphill.

"OKAY, WAIT A MINUTE. NO, WAIT," JAMIE SAID FROM THE FAR END of my bed, her head resting on a collection of lacy throw pillows. The house at Twin Tulip farms was nothing if not ornate. "I don't believe this."

"Neither do I," Ruth said from beside me, an afghan wrapped around her shoulders. For a July night, there was a surprising chill in the air. "There's gotta be more to it."

"Which part?" I asked, sifting through the container of ginger cookies I'd baked specifically for late-night nibbles this weekend. I always kept my own baked goods around in case my gut started acting up. It was why I'd started baking in the first place, back when my body seemed to reject everything I ate. That, and it annoyed the hell out of my ex when I made a mess in the kitchen.

"You basically put a saddle on that boy and rode him until the break of dawn," Jamie said.

"That paints a picture," Ruth murmured.

"And you share all these painful secrets you've both been carrying around for years," Jamie went on. "And then it's over. You high-five at the airport—"

"There were no high-fives," I said, passing the cookies to Ruth.

"—and leave all those good bed feels behind like it was your basic summer camp bangathon."

"What the hell kind of summer camp did you go to?" Ruth asked her.

"The point is," Jamie continued, "you had the big emotional moments and the unhinged sex—"

"I never said anything about it being *unhinged*."

She shot me a flat stare. "Well, your face said it was unhinged and I'm going to trust that a lot more than I'm going to trust the maidenly version of events you fed us."

"These are *really* good," Ruth said, holding up half a cookie.

"Thank you. Baking makes me happy. It helps me unwind," I said. "I'll make you some next week. Cinnamon buns too."

"Her buns will change your life," Jamie said.

She peered at Jamie. "Are you talking about actual cinnamon buns or is that a reference to something else?"

"You'll get used to her," I said to Ruth. "Actual buns. I make my own dough."

"Yeah, you do," Jamie howled.

I shrugged. "See what I mean?"

"We have to stay on track here," Jamie said, nudging Ruth's leg. "No more buns. Not unless they're your hot fiancé's buns."

"Hold that thought. Do you have pics of this guy? I need a visual," Ruth said.

Jamie sprang up, the pillows scattering to the floor. "We definitely need photos."

I reached for my phone. Not that I'd spent the past week stalking Janet's social media accounts or anything but I did know she'd posted a few photos from the engagement party. I'd saved a screenshot but that was only because I didn't want to accidentally like the post. God forbid I stumbled into a situation where Janet wanted to follow me on social media or we ended up chatting in DMs. Just thinking long-range.

I handed over my phone, saying, "Have at him, you little hyenas."

"Oh shiiiiiit." Ruth motioned to the screen. "That's not a man, that's a pile of bricks."

"Who needs an ox when you can have this boy plowing your fields?" Jamie dissolved into giggles.

Ruth zoomed in on where his palm rested on the curve of my hip, his fingers spread out to cover a wide territory. "Would you look at that hand? It's like a baseball mitt."

"Another inch and he'd be knocking on your front door," Jamie said.

"He doesn't bother with places as trivial as gyms," Ruth said. "Not when he could walk into any parking lot and lift cars instead."

"Protein eats him," Jamie said, still giggling. "He looks like he could pick you up with two fingers."

"He looks like the kind of guy who could walk into a bar fight and end the whole thing with one punch," Ruth said.

"He looks like the kind of guy who would take on a bear just for the challenge of it," Jamie said.

"He looks like the kind of guy who doesn't have a bed frame because he breaks all of them without even trying," Ruth said.

"He looks like the kind of guy who has reason to believe it might not *fit*," Jamie said. "Honestly, honey, I'm impressed. I bet he's more than a handful."

She mimed struggling to wrap her hand around a certain object. Ruth swatted her shoulder and they both fell over laughing again. A beat passed and I couldn't hold back anymore. I laughed too.

"He's looked like that since he was sixteen," I said. "More or less."

"Okay, now you're just bragging," Jamie said. "We get it. The goddesses have chosen you as their favorite." She zoomed in on a few different angles. "How did he not split you like a snap pea the first time around?"

Ruth pressed both hands to her eyes. "I will never recover from that mental image."

"I don't know. I don't remember it being bad." Very much the opposite but I wasn't getting into *those* details right now. "It was his first time too. Maybe that was part of it."

"Color me surprised that he's a caring, gentle lover." Jamie sniffed. "Until it's time to crack the headboard."

"Explain to me one more time why you're eating cookies in bed with us," Ruth said, "and not with the guy you obviously love very much?"

I exhaled a sad laugh. "Because that's never how it goes for us."

chapter forty

Audrey

Today's vocabulary word: embolden

"THIS PLACE HOLDS A DEEPLY SIGNIFICANT SPOT IN MY HEART," Shay said over the 90s rock music bleeding into the parking lot. "The floors are sticky, the decor is not worth attempting to understand, and the drinks are inconsistent. But it's very special."

I glanced at the low-slung building with *Woodchucker's* in lights across the front—but *Billy's* on the door. All part of the charm, I was sure.

Emme, clad in a short, sparkly veil, belted out a laugh. "Am I allowed to ask why it's special? Or will I figure it out when we're inside?"

This was the third and final spot on the bachelorette bar hop. We'd all piled into a small party bus after the welcome celebration wrapped and hit the town. Or as much as anyone could hit this small, coastal town where almost everything was closed by ten.

"You get to throw axes the night before your wedding," Shay said.

"Say less," Emme said.

"Not that I'm expecting anything bad to happen but I know for a fact that the boys could be here in less than twenty minutes if needed," Shay said.

"It sounds like there's a story in there somewhere," Grace said.

Shay beamed as she held the door open. "Oh, there is."

"It's fun that y'all decided to wear heels tonight even though you're both eleven feet tall," Jamie said, swinging a glance between me and Ruth. "I look like an American Girl doll next to you two."

"Yeah, it's such a tragedy that you're petite and adorable," Ruth said to her.

"You're adorable too." When Ruth only rolled her eyes, Jamie added, "Shut up and look at you! You're *gorgeous*. Like, when did the Hunters of Artemis pull up? Let's talk about that hair. I know the color's natural and I take offense to that because every time I ask my stylist for it, I come out looking like the burned bottom of a muffin. My god, those lips. Do you know how much people pay to get lips like yours? A lot. And this figure? Girl, please. Don't know if you've heard but strong is sexy as fuck."

Ruth waved her off. "You're just being nice."

"Jamie is not actually nice," I said. "She's kind, which is very different from nice. She doesn't bullshit and she won't say it if she doesn't mean it."

Nodding, Jamie added, "I know men who'd cry for the privilege of licking your toes."

"I—I don't think I want that," she said. "But thank you? I guess?"

"Anytime, babycakes." Jamie hooked her elbows with me and Ruth, following our group inside. "You're gorgeous too, my dancing queen."

"Thank you, sweetie." I patted her hand. "We should start making plans to buy tiny houses next to each other when we retire. Where should we go?"

"My bones need heat." She clutched her jean jacket to her chest and faked a shiver. "Bring me back to my true love, the sun."

"We could be like Janet and Rita." After we polished off the cookies, we'd talked about Jude's mom and the life she'd made for herself as she recovered. I was disappointed I wouldn't be going back there. "Accidentally high on X all the time, making mosaic art, and dating the neighbor dudes."

"It doesn't sound terrible," she said.

Ruth grabbed drinks for us—for whatever reason, bartenders always paid attention to her—and we settled around a high-top table near the axe-throwing lanes. Ruth's sisters Chloe and Amber had already started a round and appeared frighteningly good at it too.

When we glanced at Ruth in question, she said, "We grew up chopping wood. New Hampshire, you know? And they have a lot of unprocessed rage."

"Don't we all?" Jamie drawled as she fished a cherry out of her ginger ale.

As with our previous bar hops, we'd arranged our phones on the tabletop. Jamie for her dad. Ruth for work purposes. She was a corporate attorney and, according to her, never off the clock. I had the least compelling reason: waiting on a boy who wasn't waiting on me anymore.

I tapped a finger to Jamie's phone. "How's your dad doing?"

She pursed her lips around the straw. "You mean how's he dealing with not being allowed to shower unless someone's there in case he falls? Or with the diabetes dietitian who won't let him eat a pound of peanut M&Ms before bed? Or the part where he wants a detailed itinerary of what I'm doing and where I'm going every day along with a list of phone numbers in case he needs to reach me?"

"Doesn't he have your cell phone number?" Ruth asked.

"He finds this inadequate," she said.

"How are *you* doing with all this?" I asked.

"About the same but I'm sure I'll get over it. I just have too much time to obsess right now." Her shoulders lifted. "My therapist thinks I have some inner child work to do if I'm feeling this much friction about moving back home."

"Maybe I need some inner child work too because I'd sign on as legal counsel to the mafia before I moved back home," Ruth said.

"Is your therapist offering a group rate for this? Because I could use some of that too," I said.

"You're saying throuples therapy is cool but a friendly little threesome is not? Rude." Jamie rolled her eyes. "I'll ask next week."

"Check these two out," Ruth said.

Chloe and Amber finished their set and now Emme and Ines were locked in a battle of their own. No one was keeping score, and even if they did, it would be tied at zero-zero since they couldn't stop laughing long enough to put anything into their throws.

But the trash talk was pristine.

"You couldn't hit the broad side of a bus with that aim," Ines called.

"I know you like to be the best but you don't have to work so hard at missing every bull's-eye," Emme called back.

"Sounds like something you'd say to your husband after a bad game," her stepsister said.

"I just hope your husband knows how to find the target better than you do," Emme replied.

"You throw like you have five percent battery life," Ines said.

Jamie snorted into her ginger ale. "These two have the jokes tonight. Whew. Remind me to hydrate them before tucking them into bed."

My phone buzzed across the table, clattering into the other phones as Emme and Ines kept on with the insults. I reared back when I saw the notification.

Jude: can you give me a call?

Jude: sometime tonight, if possible

"What? What's wrong?" Jamie asked.

I pointed to my phone. "Jude. He texted me."

Ruth rolled her hand. "And what did this text say?"

"He wants to know if I'll call him," I said.

"The answer is yes," Ruth said.

I blinked at her. "Is it?"

Jamie hopped off her stool and pointed to the door. "Outside, children. We're not calling your fella from the middle of a bar with yet another Oasis song blasting in the background and the bride snort-giggling like a piglet over there."

"But what do I say?" I asked as they herded me to the exit.

"Let's find out what he wants before we throw ourselves into the deep end," Jamie said. "There's nothing wrong with putting a man on hold for a few minutes."

"Huh," Ruth murmured as we stepped into the damp evening air. "Never thought of that."

"I'll explain the deep magic to you later," Jamie said. "Right now, we need to get Audrey's fiancé on the phone—"

"He's not my fiancé," I said.

"—and find out when he's coming to collect his future wife."

"I really don't think that's how it's going to go," I said.

"Call him and find out," Ruth said, stomping a foot on the gravel with each word.

I sucked in a huge breath as I stared at his contact on my screen. Before I could talk myself out of it, I placed the call. He answered immediately.

"Hey, there you are," he said, those quiet, raspy words sliding around me like an old familiar blanket.

I wanted to stay there forever. Right inside that warm, gentle *There you are*. In the place where I knew who I was. *Here I am.*

"I, uh—" He paused. "How are you? Did you get back all right?"

"Yeah, everything went fine." Even to my ear, my tone was crisp. I knew he heard it because he heard everything. "How are you? How's Seattle?"

"It's been a busy week. Flat-out, all day, every day," he said, a thin apology buried somewhere in there. "Percy was pissed because I nodded off in the middle of reading a story over a video call a few nights ago."

I breathed out a laugh. "Understandable."

"I realized the other day that I never got to talk to you about his school stuff," Jude said. "I don't know if you remember but—"

"I remember." I paced away from the bar as I stared up at the night sky. Tons of stars out here without the city lights. "I think I tried to convince you I was sober. Not sure why I thought that was a good idea."

"Yeah, it was amusing," he said. "I'm trying to figure out what would be best for him. I figured you'd have some insider knowledge."

Jamie snapped her fingers, urgently gesturing for me to come back toward her and Ruth. I held up a hand, stayed where I was. "Maybe, yeah. I'm not an expert on special education but I could talk it through with you if that helps."

"I'd like that."

He was quiet for a long moment that reminded me of driving through the night from the Salt Lake airport to—wherever it was we ended up. Back when we didn't know how to talk to each other and everything we did was wrong. I didn't know how we'd wound up back in that thicket again.

Before I could offer to call him sometime next week, after the wedding and the day or two I'd need to physically and mentally recover from all its events, he said, "About your friend's wedding."

I glanced back to Jamie and Ruth. They made several frantic gestures I couldn't interpret. "What about it?"

"Are you still looking for a date?"

I staggered back a step and heard Jamie cry, "Oh my god, she's going to faint."

I waved her off, saying to Jude, "Why do you ask?"

He made a noise, something that lived on the spectrum between a growl and a groan. "Because I'm leaving on a red-eye flight to Boston in two hours, Saunders, and it would really help if I knew where to find you when I land."

chapter forty-one

Jude

Today's vocabulary word: energy

I KNEW I'D FUCKED UP.

I'd known it the minute I walked away from Audrey in Phoenix and every single minute after that until I booked the flight to Boston.

There was no defending it either. I got lost in my head, in all the immovable pieces of my life. In Percy and Brenda, my mother and my work. Not to mention Audrey's fucking family and the shit they liked to stir up.

I couldn't believe it took me so long to figure out that I needed to be at this wedding with her. I spent the entire week with a tension headache and a knot in my stomach, and it wasn't until I let myself think about her for more than a second that I realized I'd fucked up.

Boarding that red-eye flight was the only solution, even if it did create a few problems. Greatest and highest being that I hadn't packed a decent suit for my week in Seattle. I didn't have much use for anything like that when I spent most of my days between labs and conference rooms. But there was no way in hell I could show up to this wedding looking like I'd just finished tearing apart a transmission.

It took a few hours of running around Boston but I got myself in order before making the drive to Rhode Island. Mom called while I was on the road and she just about blew out the windows screaming with delight over my last-minute plan to attend the wedding with Audrey.

"It's nice to see that I did raise you right after all," she said. "I just hate that you two spend so much time apart. It can't be much fun."

She said *fun* in a waggled eyebrow way that I chose to ignore.

"Have you made any decisions about where you'll settle down together?" she asked. "It sounded to me like Audrey's pretty happy in Boston."

Every time I thought I'd reached the end of the lies, another gate opened up and a whole new road extended out into the horizon. A perpetuating pain I'd inflicted upon myself. "We're still figuring that out."

"I know couples today are very...innovative with their lifestyles," she said. "And you know I'll support you regardless, but I just want things to be easy for you. For once."

"I know, and it will be. Eventually." Another lie, probably.

She was quiet for a moment and I felt the energy shift. "Have you thought about growing your family at all? Giving Percy a brother or sister?"

A sound came out of me, something startled but also immediately defensive. "We're not having this conversation, Mom."

"I'm just wondering if Audrey's said anything about wanting children of her own."

This—and a few other things—was why I'd spent the week stuck in my own mental hamster wheel. My kid consumed a solid seventy percent of my life right now, if not more. It was different when he was with Brenda for the summer, but during the school year, Percy ran my life. It was hard and exhausting, but I loved my son and the family we made together. I couldn't give him any less than that.

And I had no idea how to present any of that to Audrey. I didn't know how to carve out space for her in that world and I didn't trust that I could be everything she needed while also being everything Percy needed.

Even if I asked Audrey to move in with us tomorrow—which was far from the most ridiculous thing I'd considered in the past seven days—I didn't know if she wanted to be in a relationship with someone who had a young kid. Maybe she'd foreclosed herself to all variety of parenting after the hell she'd been through. Maybe it would screw with her mental health to put herself in any kind of adoptive mom role. And none of that touched on the possibility that she wouldn't want anything to do with the present state of my custody issues.

All I knew was that it was messy on every side.

Another thing I knew was that I'd handled this all wrong. I had a lot of unfucking to do here, and not just from the last week.

"Let's keep the wedding on the agenda and save the future children item for another meeting," I said.

"I'm just hoping you don't have to travel too much while you're newlyweds," she said. "You've been apart so much while dating and engaged. I don't understand how you do it. I'd be so lonely."

I had to rub a hand over my chest to ease the ache there. "It's been tough," I said. Not a lie. "But we're working on it."

"Good. That's what I like to hear." Her sandals slapped on the Saltillo tile as she walked through the house. "Just so you know, my PET scan came back this morning. Clean as a whistle."

"Excellent news," I said. One more weight off my shoulders. "I guess you were right about the healing energy there in Sedona."

"That helps," she said, "but I think it's mostly sunshine and weed keepin' me going these days."

I DIDN'T ADVERTISE THIS FACT BUT AUDREY WAS THE ONLY WOMAN I'd ever dated, as far as strict definitions of dating went. I'd spent the first semester of my university experience in shock after everything went to hell with us and I couldn't stomach the idea of being close to another person in any way, at all. I didn't recognize it as shock then but that was what happened. Like that static-y silence after an explosion.

Eventually, I got back out there but in the douchiest way possible. I was that asshole who'd make it clear from the start that it was just sex. No sleepovers. No repeat visits. Definitely no follow-up messages asking if I wanted to hang out in a few weeks. Certainly no feelings.

That worked for me until I met Penny. I mean, it kept working for about ten months after meeting Penny but then my entire world flopped on its side.

Once Percy entered the picture, making time for casual sex dropped to the bottom of my priority list. It wasn't just the surprise fatherhood but the impact of losing Penny, Percy's injuries, my mom's diagnosis, Brenda's insistence on split custody—the hits came hard and fast.

And honestly, I was a little gun-shy. I'd used a condom with Penny. She'd said she was on the pill. I didn't want to roll the dice on another statistical improbability.

Which wasn't to say I was a monk but I didn't get much time for those kinds of recreational activities. Another thing I didn't have time for? Going to weddings. Most of my friends were gearheads or pilots, and they all seemed to elope or have small, backyard weddings. Since I didn't date, this was basically my first formal wedding.

If we didn't count Audrey's.

I didn't know what I was in for but after going through four security checkpoints and then being led to a golf cart for a ten-minute drive through a literal cow pasture, I realized this wedding was going to be quite the initiation.

The guy driving the cart, the crew-cut, brick-wall sort, parked along the side of a narrow road and escorted me down a winding driveway toward a large, old Victorian home. He handed me off to another security guard, one who looked me over before saying into his headset, "Inform the bride that her guest has arrived."

"Oh, no, don't bother her," I said, waving him off. "No, not the bride. One of the bridesmaids. Audrey. Audrey's mine. I'm not here for the bride."

"Pardon me, sir, but we're *all* here for the bride." He went on staring at me, completely stone-faced. "Mrs. Ralston personally added you to the VIP list."

"Mrs. Ralston," I repeated. I glanced at the buzz of activity around me, rocking back on my heels when I spotted a massive portrait of a lovely dark-haired woman and the most decorated quarterback of this generation. "Yes. Mrs. Ralston. Of course."

Holy shit. I guess it was a good thing I'd snagged a new suit.

The security guard motioned to the stone path leading to the front steps of the Victorian. "Wait here."

Before I could even thank him, the woman from the photo spilled out of the doorway, three women scrambling behind her to hold the long train of her dress. "Well, hello there," she said, her hands on her hips. "You must be the fiancé."

"Oh my god, Emme, keep that to yourself." From somewhere behind the mass of white fluff, Audrey appeared. She wore the same blue dress as the other bridesmaids, her hair gathered back in a pretty bun. Her cheeks were pink and she kept her eyes low, but she bounded down those stairs and right into my arms. "You came," she said against my neck.

"You asked." I let myself breathe her in, to feel every spot where she pressed against me. "It just took me a few days to figure it out."

"Let's not do that anymore."

I dropped a kiss on her lips. "Agreed."

"This is really fucking adorable and all," one of the women shouted, "but we don't have time to redo your makeup."

"Or hair," another said.

"But we do have the steamer ready to go if those big paws of his wrinkle your dress," yet another maid called.

"Don't get me in trouble," Audrey whispered.

I shot a glance over her shoulder to the women watching from the porch. "Hey, so, you didn't tell me this was *Ryan Ralston's* wedding."

"It's not. It's Emme's wedding," she said. "He happens to be here too."

"A little warning would've been nice," I said, my lips on her cheek. "I've been to classified meetings with the federal government that had less security than this place."

She smoothed her hands down my lapels. "But you're here now."

I tucked a loose strand of hair over her ear. "Sorry it took so long."

She shrugged this off. I knew she would, even if I didn't deserve it. She just didn't know how to let herself be someone's problem. "It's okay but—" She tipped her head toward the bridal party. "I should probably get back."

"But first." Another kiss, light enough to keep all the makeup intact. "You look amazing. Do you know that?"

She shrugged, shook her head, glanced away. "I've worn this dress a few times now. It's fine. Nothing amazing."

"It's not the dress," I said. "It's you." I looped an arm around her waist, pulled her in close. "Do I get to keep you after this ceremony? Or are you still on duty?"

"We're definitely gonna need that steamer," a bridesmaid muttered.

"I have some time once we're finished with photos," she said, a sweet little grin brightening her face.

"You didn't answer my question. Do I get to keep you?"

She rolled her lips together as the pink of her cheeks deepened. "We'll talk about that later."

"Um, excuse me? Fiancé? I truly, honestly, sincerely hate to be the one to break up this outpouring of love and sexual tension but I will need my darling Audrey back if I'm going to get married this afternoon."

I closed my arms around Audrey, held her tight to my chest. "Apologies," I said to Emme. "Congratulations, by the way."

"You might not be saying that when the boys are done with you," she replied.

Before I could ask for an explanation on that, Emme retreated into the house. "What does that mean?"

"Hmm? Oh. Nothing. Just Emme's sense of humor," Audrey said. She patted my lapels. "I'll see you later."

I brushed a quick kiss to her lips and watched as she disappeared inside the Victorian with all the other women in blue dresses. I stayed there, staring at the generous wraparound porch and the people bustling in and out of the house. Everyone had a purpose, a part to play in this production.

It felt good to be here. Like I was finally doing something right.

Behind me, a throat cleared. I didn't think anything of it until the throat repeated itself, and then, "Hello. Hi! I take it you're here with Audrey?"

I turned around to find a white guy about my age with a beer bottle in hand and a goofy grin on his face. Tallish, broadish, dark hair with one helluva 'stache. "Yeah. Hey. I'm Jude."

"Jude! Good to meet you, man." He said this like he was already my best friend. I couldn't fight off the twitch of a smile. "I'm Ben. Grace's husband."

"Grace," I repeated. "She's…one of the teachers. Right? Third grade?"

"In on the first shot," he shouted, clapping me on the back.

It dawned on me that, for the first time, I was in Audrey's ecosystem. These were her people, her friends and their partners, and this was the world she'd built for herself. I should've noticed that a few minutes ago when they'd been *right there* but I hadn't been able to focus on anyone but Audrey.

Fuck. I had to get this right.

Ben pointed his beer toward a few men standing about twenty feet away, near the garden. Rather, one of the *many* gardens. "I'll introduce you to our squad."

I followed him down a stone path, murmuring in agreement as he chattered about the weather or something like that. The words *group chat* came up several times and I wasn't sure what I'd agreed to but I rattled off my number to him regardless.

"The man of the hour," Ben said, motioning to one of the all-time greatest players of college and pro football as if his face wasn't on half the billboards in Boston. "Ryan Ralston, sir, allow me to introduce you to Jude, the lovely Miss Audrey's companion for the weekend."

I'd admit it. I was starstruck. I wasn't obsessive about sports but this guy was a big fucking deal. I managed to clasp his hand, saying, "Congratulations. Thanks for having me here to celebrate with you and Emme."

"Happy to have you," he said easily. "Emme was very excited when she heard you could make it."

"This here is Noah Barden." Ben made a sweeping gesture toward a thick, burly man who seemed to smile about as much as I did. "He and his wife own this farm and the one up the hill that way."

"That's Shay?" I asked. "The kindergarten teacher?"

"My wife used to teach kindergarten." He gave my hand a firm shake. "She's moved up to first grade now."

"Yeah, right, I heard about that." I didn't remember that specific detail but I hadn't spent much time asking Audrey about—well, anything. Most of the time we'd spent together I'd wasted it on empty silences. I could've drowned myself in every tiny detail of her life but instead I'd wanted to prove points. To grab hold of my anger and frustration, and grip them in my fist like shards of glass. And look who had to deal with those consequences now.

"And we've got Jakobi Jones," Ben said, motioning to the other man.

"Hey. How's it going?" he asked, holding out his hand. "I'm Ines's husband."

Ines? I shook his hand a beat longer than necessary as I tried to remember Audrey mentioning someone named Ines. *Shit.* I had nothing on Ines. "Does she teach with Audrey?"

Jakobi laughed to himself as he ran a hand over the back of his neck. "No, she's in engineering."

"Which field? I'm in aeronautics," I said. "Propulsion testing and development."

"Then she'd love to talk to you about that. She's in robotics," he replied, just as Noah said, "It's interesting how I've known Audrey for years and she visits our home at least once a month and somehow, the past eighteen hours is the first we've heard of you."

Ben made a trombone sound that my son would've found endlessly amusing while Jakobi read every word on the label of his beer bottle.

Ah. *This* was what Emme had meant.

I dipped my hands into my pockets and went with the truth. "That's probably because, until recently, the last time we talked was about twelve years ago when she was about to marry a rageaholic dickhead who deserves to be neutered with a rusty screwdriver."

"Mmm. Yeah, I can see how that might not come up in conversation," Ryan said.

"I've known Audrey since we were fifteen," I went on. "We go back a long way."

"And where is it you're going now?" Noah asked.

Goddamn. This guy knew how to turn up the heat. "We're still figuring that out," I said.

Ben, my only friend in the world at this moment, slung an arm over my shoulder. "I know all about that but let me tell you, we'll send you packing if you give that sweet lady any grief."

Noah eyed me like he wouldn't mind backing over me with his car. "My wife loves Audrey like a sister, which makes her family. I wouldn't want to see her hurt in any way."

"Especially knowing that she's already been through enough with the ex," Ryan added, a brow winging up in warning. I could see how he scared the shit out of his opponents.

Jakobi merely made eye contact and tipped his chin up, which I took to mean no one would ever find my body.

I studied these men for a moment, the other halves of Audrey's chosen people. And I was fucking thrilled that they loved her enough to put me on notice right from the start.

A laugh stuttered out of me and I patted my chest, saying, "Fuck, I really appreciate how willing you guys are to beat the shit out of me."

"Nah, we wouldn't do that," Ben said before Noah and Ryan chorused, "Yeah, we would."

I coughed out another laugh. "Knock me around if you want but you should know how relieved I am that Saunders has a whole bench of big brothers backing her up. I've been so stressed about her being on her own all this time."

Noah stared at me for a heavy moment. Then, instead of suggesting he feed me into a wood chipper before the ceremony, he said, "Welcome to Friendship. Don't fuck this up."

chapter forty-two

Jude

Today's vocabulary word: impermanence

I TRIED TO SIT IN THE BACK ROW. BEN WOULDN'T HEAR OF IT. HE marched me to the second row, right behind the bride's family. I had Noah and Ben on either side of me, and without a single inch of breathing room to figure out how to *not* fuck this up.

The trouble was, I didn't know how to do that. Not when I had no idea what came next for us. It wasn't a simple matter of what I wanted, what she wanted. We lived hundreds of miles apart. An eight-hour drive on a good day. There was a kid involved, not to mention his mother's family.

And then there was me and all the things I'd kept buttoned up and under control for so long that I barely remembered what I had hiding in there anymore. But it was all starting to crumble and I didn't know what would happen when it finally fell apart.

The truth was, Audrey wasn't the start of this great inner crumbling. It stretched all the way back to finding out about Percy and the chaos that followed. Audrey was the fine-point pickaxe, here to chisel away those last pieces of stubborn concrete I'd forced into the seams. I just had to let her.

I watched as Audrey walked down the aisle, her gaze flitting to mine but then quickly away. She smiled like she couldn't help it, and I loved that. There was the Audrey I knew. That one right there, she was all mine.

I fixed my attention on her instead of the ceremony. I knew she noticed because she caught my eye several times before turning a pointed stare toward the happy couple. There were those good girl manners again.

Eventually, she gave up on redirecting me and held my gaze long enough for that secret smile to return and pink to fill her cheeks. It was like stepping back in time, a reminder of why I'd fallen so hard, why she'd occupied so much space in my head for so long. Why she'd filled my chest with concrete when she left.

The openness in her eyes, the raw vulnerability of it, made it hard to sit still. My hands itched to hold her. I'd die if I couldn't bury my face in the curve of her neck, couldn't inhale the scent of her until it filled every part of me.

She tucked a wisp of hair over her ear and I could almost feel those fingers grazing my skin. The need to taste her, to feel her shudder against me, was almost too much to bear while she was *right there*. I wanted to take my time with her, to map every curve and dip of her body and brand myself on her skin.

I didn't know where she was spending the night but I hoped to hell I was welcome there too. And not only because I wanted to watch that dress hit the floor. I needed to apologize for going dark on her after Phoenix, explain all the noises in my head, and find out what she wanted from me, if anything.

But the dress hitting the floor...that was very important too.

THE CEREMONY WAS INTERMINABLY LONG.

At first, I resisted the urge to check my watch because I suspected Noah would shank me. But after the third poem and second harp solo performed by Ines, the robotics engineer, I was ready to accept that consequence. It wrapped up not long after and I watched one of the best running backs in the league escort Audrey up the aisle. She said something that made him laugh and he leaned into her, his hand covering the forearm she'd hooked through his elbow. I could admit that I wasn't one hundred percent clear which one of them I was more jealous of.

Though it wasn't the first order of business, I was hoping she might introduce us. Later, of course. After I'd had a minute to explain everything.

Ben herded me toward another section of the farm and put a beer bottle in my hand while the bridal party posed for photos. He had a lot to say about an upcoming festival of some sort as well as the work he was doing on his deck over the summer. I might've agreed to help him out with that. I really wasn't paying attention.

At one point, he convinced a waiter to bring us an entire tray of the appetizers being passed—little triangles of grilled cheese sandwiches, crispy taquitos, pulled pork sliders, bite-sized chicken and waffles, mini corn dogs. We inhaled every crumb, barely taking a breath between bites to say *These are really fuckin' good* and *Try those with the sauce*.

If I had signed myself up to work on Ben's deck, I decided I didn't mind too much.

"Here's what you need to know about these ladies," he said. "They'd choose each other over us any day, and they won't be sad about it. Actually, there are times when I think they'd prefer it."

"Do I want to know what that means?"

Ben thought about this for a moment, his brows and mustache furrowing as one. "It means that they're fully aware we're a species known for its flaws, not its features. If we turn into more trouble than we're worth, they'll be happy to send us on our way and out of their lives for good."

I cut a sidelong glance in his direction. "Are you asking if I'm that kind of trouble? Or is this another warning?"

He took a long sip from his beer. "For as long as I've known Audrey, she's held firm on having no interest in another journey down relationship road."

"She's been through a lot."

He bobbed his head, saying, "Yeah, well, every time one of these gals gets engaged, Audrey tells them how to protect themselves in case they need to leave. To keep money in their name, to make sure they're listed on all the major assets, to save copies of their documents in places we won't find."

"She's been through it," I said, though I still regretted not stopping in San Diego to waterboard her ex when I had the chance. There would be other opportunities. "She's smart and she's strong, and she loves those women so she's not going to let anything happen to them."

"You're damn right about that," he said. "Don't be surprised if you find out you're not the center of her universe."

Laughing, I tipped back my beer. "What? Come on. You're not the center of your wife's universe?"

"I'm the star that lights up her nights," he said, completely straight-faced. "Her Big Dipper, you might say."

A beat passed before we doubled over laughing.

"That was bad," I wheezed.

"Are you kidding me? That was *elite*," he said, tears streaming down his face.

My sides ached. "Dude, no."

Audrey chose that exact moment to appear out of nowhere, a raven-haired woman in a bridesmaid dress by her side. Ben, still cracking himself up and barely able to form coherent words, pulled her into his arms. I moved closer to Audrey, ran a hand down her arm. When I reached her hand, she twined her fingers with mine.

"Do we want to know what's happening here?" Audrey asked, eyeing us.

"No, ma'am," Ben replied.

"Probably a dick joke, then," his wife said. "They don't stop coming."

Ben nuzzled her cheek. "Neither does my—"

She pressed a finger to his lips. "You're allowed to keep some thoughts inside your head." She held out her hand to me. "Hi. I'm Grace and I'd apologize for anything my husband has said but you seem to be holding up just fine."

"Jude," I said, shaking her hand. "We're doing all right."

"We stole a tray of apps," he said. "They had those little hot dogs, just like the ones from our wedding."

"That's what happens when you get married at the same place and with the same caterer," Grace said.

Audrey shifted toward me, saying, "We have some time before the big entrance."

A brow arched. "Big entrance?"

She squeezed my fingers. "You know, when everyone's seated in the tent and they announce the bride and groom."

I'd have to trust her on that. "Then let's take a walk."

"No one's going to chase after you with a steamer if you get that dress wrinkled," Grace said.

"I can live with that," Audrey said as we broke away from them. "Oh, and could you check on Jamie? She's not feeling great and really needs to sit down for a bit."

"We're all over it," Ben called.

We headed up a narrow path connecting the gardens to the main house. The roar of the party seemed to fade the minute we reached the Victorian's front porch. Florists, servers, and security guards still buzzed around the property though it all seemed less chaotic now. Maybe it was exactly as it'd been earlier and *I* was less chaotic now.

"Your friends," I started, "they adore you."

She laughed as we passed a pair of tire swings hanging from a tree that looked older than time. "I guess the good news is that not everyone thinks I'm an antacid."

"Those women from the reunion hate their lives and they hate you because you don't." Before she could argue with that, I added, "Your friends' husbands are drawing straws to see which one gets to kick my ass first."

"I'm sure that's a bit of an exaggeration."

"Not as much as you'd think. Ryan Ralston offered to personally rip my spleen out if I so much as inconvenience you."

"He did *not* say that."

"Strongly implied," I said.

"I know they can be overprotective but they're some of the best people," she said.

I stopped, pulled her toward me and held her close. "I wouldn't want it any other way."

"Really? You're not bothered by low-key death threats?"

"I fucking love that these people would do anything for you. That's the way it's supposed to be." I kissed her, slow and gentle. I wanted her to taste the relief on my tongue, the absolute peace that came with knowing she had a family here. That she'd filled the empty spaces around her where her biological family should've been with people so much better than them. And that she'd wanted me to join her here.

"I'd do anything for them too," she said. "That's just what people do for the ones they love."

Like flying across the country and pretending to be my fiancée?

I couldn't bring myself to ask. I wasn't prepared to watch her deflect. Wasn't prepared to deal with the loud, galloping feeling inside me and what it would do if she said *yes*.

"This way," Audrey whispered, leading me across the gravel drive and around to the far side of a massive yellow barn. A hedgerow of sunflowers greeted us, their faces bright and bold and humming with bees. "No one will find us back here."

It felt like we'd stepped into a different world, one completely cut off from the enormous party underway. "Good," I said, steering her toward the yellow shingles. "It's my turn to have you."

Her back met the barn and she reached for me, her hands smoothing up my chest and around my neck as our lips met. The kiss was urgent, a little vicious. Guttural noises sounded low in my throat. She bit me twice and I had to believe it was intentional. I liked it. I also deserved it.

"I couldn't stop thinking about you," I said to the corner of her mouth. "I tried. I fucking tried but it only made me think about you more."

I pushed a knee between her legs as she yanked my shirt loose and skimmed her hands up my torso. Her fingers scraped along my neck and into my hair, drawing a shiver from her touch.

"Why did you try so hard?"

"I'll explain why I'm an idiot later. First—" I dropped my hands to her hips. "Is it actually okay to wrinkle this dress?"

"No one here is looking at me or my dress."

I ran my fingers up her thighs, gathering the long skirt as I went. "You're very wrong about that."

"The entire point of a wedding is to gush over the bride," she said. "None of this day is about me."

A growl rumbled out of me as my hand slipped between her legs. I cupped her there, letting the heel of my palm rock against her clit. Her breath stuttered and it really was remarkable that I'd nearly convinced myself I could live without this. Without her. "Doesn't mean there aren't plenty of people who'd be happy to keep you warm tonight."

"I'm not looking for anyone to do that for me."

"Are you sure about that?"

Her shoulder hitched up in a defiant shrug and I knew she was still pissed about the past week. Fair. Extremely fair.

All I could do was grind up against her clit and drop to my knees. I rolled down the thin, stretchy shorts she wore, the ones that were completely sheer and put her cunt on display in a way that wasn't meant to be sexy but still made me pant.

With the shorts out of my way, I dragged a finger along her seam and then leaned in, kissing my way down the same trail. I loved the taste of her. It activated something primal inside me and I was powerless to do anything but suck her clit until she screamed.

She didn't say anything as I traced circles around her clit, lapping at her like we had all day, all night for this. Like there was no limit to our time now, those looming shadows left behind in Arizona. I liked that very much.

I slipped a finger inside her, then another. She found a rhythm as I sucked and stroked, and she let out a surprised gasp when her muscles clenched tight. Her inner walls fluttered around my fingers, pulling me, holding me, as her pleasure unfurled.

"How did you do that so fast?" she whispered.

"I think *you* did that, princess." I pushed to my feet, wrenching my belt and zipper open as I went. "Can you do it for me one more time?"

She nodded, shaky, a little lost in the orgasm, but she grabbed me by my tie and yanked me close. I settled between her legs and hitched her thigh high on my hip. She was wet like I couldn't comprehend. My cock was already soaked just from pressing up against her and I knew I could come like this, right here. I wouldn't even mind.

"I missed you," I said, taking myself in hand and dragging my cockhead through her slippery heat. Her cheeks were flushed and her lips swollen. Tendrils slipped free from her bun. A bit of beard rash reddened her neck. *Perfect. Just perfect. Like this, right here.*

"You couldn't have missed me that much. You went dark and made me wait more than a week."

She peered at me. There was hurt in her eyes, hurt I'd put there. I'd known what I was doing when I boarded my flight in Phoenix. I knew she'd opened a door and I'd…walked right past it. Which was worse than slamming it shut, I thought.

"I know." I tapped my cock against her clit. Waited for the glint in her eyes to soften. "Let me apologize for that."

She glanced between us, working hard at being unaffected when I knew how much she loved to be teased this way. "You can try."

"Then I'll try."

I filled my hands with her ass, boosting her up against the barn. I slammed into her and a wild roar built in my chest as the unbelievable heat of her swamped my senses. Of the many things I hadn't been able to stop thinking about, the way her cunt gripped me was one of the most prominent. It came back to me like a haunting.

I kept my lips on her neck even though I worried there would be a mark there tomorrow. My hands stayed fixed on her ass, moving her as I wanted. If this was my best chance to offer up an apology, I was making it a good one.

She raked her fingers through my hair, twisting and pulling with every demanding thrust. I met her eyes as I rocked into her, begging her to feel what I felt. To know that I was here with her, even if it was fucking complicated and our history was full of land mines and I couldn't promise much of anything. That I wanted her, I'd always wanted her, and maybe that could be enough.

"I need—" Audrey moaned as my fingers dug hard into her ass.

"Anything, baby," I growled into her neck. "What do you need? Tell me and I'll give it to you."

That wasn't entirely true since I was fucking her up against the broad side of a barn with roughly four hundred people partying not that far away and it wouldn't surprise me if a security guard wandered down here in a minute or two. There were limits.

"I need you," she whispered, and those words sharpened my arousal into a fine, dangerous thing.

There were going to be small bruises on her backside tomorrow, of that I was certain. One for each of my fingertips. And probably a few on her back from the barn's shingles. But I'd kiss it all better. I pumped into her hard, harder when her lips landed on my neck and her teeth nipped at my skin. "You have me."

"For how long?"

My brain took those words and ran with them. "As long as you want me," I said.

"Promise?"

She clenched around me, softer than the first time she came but somehow deeper, like her body was trying to swallow me whole. I made the mistake of focusing on those pulses and it snapped my hold on the orgasm gathering at the base of my spine. It was over, out of my hands, nothing I could do to regain control. And it felt so fucking good. Like my entire life had been nothing more than precursors to this moment, this woman. Even this barn.

Her name tumbled out of me over and over as I rutted into her, giving myself to some primitive need to fuck her like I meant it. My cock pulsed for an hour. It seemed that way. When the world came back to me and I could function again, I peppered her neck and bare shoulders with kisses. A few bites too, because she kept flexing her inner muscles and I kept thinking I was about to drop dead from it.

But right now, with my hands roaming over her skin and my cock mostly hard inside her, I regretted everything. There were hours left in this party and people were expecting to see her. I'd have to let her go soon and I'd have to spend the rest of the evening acting like the taste of her cunt wasn't lingering on my tongue.

I ran my hands down her back, brushing away the dust and bits of yellow paint that we'd shaken loose from the barn. She pressed her lips to mine. I could feel her smile. "I should probably get back to Emme," she said.

"I counted eight other bridesmaids. Does she need all of you at once?" I was being an ass, but in all fairness, I was still inside her. Life beyond the side of this barn did not matter to me.

"Four of them are Ryan's sisters and she loves them, of course, but she's not asking any of them to help her pee." I must've made a face about that because she added, "She needs at least two people holding the dress. Ideally, three."

I untangled her leg from around my hip and eased out of her with great reluctance. I tried to go slow, thinking that controlled movements resulted in less friction, but that didn't stop an almighty flood from streaking down her thighs.

"Oh my," Audrey whispered, her hands overflowing with blue fabric and bare from the waist down, eyes wide, lips parted.

I swallowed hard as I tucked myself back into my trousers. *Fuck.*

"Let me take care of this." I went to my knees and pulled the pocket square from my jacket. "I've got you."

Audrey shrieked when I ran the silky fabric up the inside of her leg, laughing and twisting away from me. "That tickles!" she cried.

I stared up at her, lost in the space between her bright, infectious smile and the pink, puffy folds just a few inches from my face. I could stay here until my days ran short and want for nothing.

I finished cleaning my release from her legs and stowed the cloth in my pocket, and then helped her back into the stretchy shorts. My phone buzzed a few times though I chose to ignore it. My kid probably needed to complain about Brenda's cooking again. He was a picky little tyrant when he wanted to be and he really didn't understand the Midwestern philosophy on casseroles and salads.

When I gained my feet, we made an attempt at smoothing out

her skirt but there wasn't much hope for it. "You look like you've been fucked against a barn," I said.

She ran a hand through my hair, saying, "You too."

We stared at each other for a moment. I knew if I opened my mouth, it would be to suggest we try out the other three sides of this barn or see about a potting shed. And I knew that wasn't fair. Not only because I'd fucked her like I wanted her to wake up tomorrow and feel me in every overused muscle but because this was a big night for her friends. She deserved to have fun with them, regardless of whether I craved her on a level that was troubling.

A breeze off the nearby cove kicked up and Audrey rubbed her palms over her bare arms. "Here," I said, shrugging out of my jacket. I draped it over her shoulders. "I'll walk you back."

She led me through a different set of gardens this time, telling me stories about weekends spent here with Shay and Jamie, Grace and Emme. We stopped near the house when she said, "I'm going to run inside and fix my hair. Grab a drink and I'll find you."

"Not so fast," I said, pulling her against my chest and dragging her lower lip between my teeth. I kissed her one last time, stroking my thumbs over her delicate cheeks. "I need to check on Percy. I'm going to give him a call and then *I'll* find *you*."

"You always do," she said.

I grinned. "You noticed that?"

She straightened my tie and then smoothed a hand down my chest, stopping only when she hit my belt. I did not mind her hand settling there. "What? Like you were trying to be discreet with that entrance at the reunion? Or what about my wedding day?"

I considered these points. "I guess not."

"That's all I'm saying." She laughed, fussing with my collar again. "Go make your call. I'll meet you in the tent."

I kissed her forehead and then watched her slip into the house, hitching her skirt up as she went. I lingered there for a minute, not ready to slide back into reality. Eventually, I pulled out my phone and swiped it to life—and everything changed.

chapter forty-three

Audrey

Today's vocabulary word: gathered

Jude: something urgent came up

Jude: I'll call you in a few days when things settle down

Jude: I'm sorry

JAMIE'S MESSAGE READ *WE'RE GOING TO BRUNCH. DON'T MAKE ME come to your house and drag you along.*

It'd been a week since Emme's wedding—and the last I'd heard from Jude—and without the nonstop parties and preparations to keep me busy, I had to create my own distractions. I'd tested six new bread recipes, planned out my first full month of lessons, and brought home a new foster dog. Through it all, I somehow found the time to check my phone every few minutes on the off chance I'd missed a call or message from Jude.

I told myself there was a perfectly good explanation for his abrupt departure and the silence that'd followed, but as the days ticked by I felt those threads of certainty slipping through my fingers.

Since I knew better than to call Jamie's bluff, I set up Bagel the beagle with some peanut butter-flavored busywork and hopped a train into the city.

I found Jamie and Ruth on the sidewalk outside the restaurant, deep into an animated conversation. I loved that they both talked with their entire bodies.

"About ten more minutes until our table's ready," Jamie said by way of a greeting. She held up a timer on her phone. "I feel like I haven't seen you in a year."

"It's only been a few days," I said.

"But time is weird in the summer," she said. "There's so much of it but then it's over before it even gets started."

"The closest I come to a summer break is leaving the office before sunset on Fridays," Ruth said.

"You make five times as much as we do and no one wipes their nose on your skirt," Jamie said.

Ruth pointed at her. "Valid."

Once we were seated inside the restaurant and had a team strategy for ordering that covered a wide portion of the menu, Jamie clasped her hands on the table and swung a knowing glance between me and Ruth. "I've gathered you both here today because we are overdue for a debrief," she said.

Ruth snapped her menu shut. "What are we debriefing?"

I shot a grin at the woman beside me. I liked that she was brash. That she didn't seem to worry about offending anyone. She didn't let herself get caught up in niceties or careful phrasing when blunt truth got the job done. I could learn something from her.

"Yes, I'm wondering the same," I said.

Jamie arched her brows and went on staring with that universal teacher death glare that said *I'm waiting for you to do the right thing. Don't make me remind you what that is.*

I probably deserved to be called into confession after the whirlwind I'd kicked up last weekend. No part of it had been subtle and that was a big departure from the role I usually played in this group.

I caught Ruth's eye and read the *Please don't call on me* energy there plain as day. "I suppose I can go first," I said.

"I'd love that," Jamie said. "Please go into great detail on the part where you disappeared for the duration of the cocktail hour and came back looking as though you'd been ridden like a prize pony."

"I did *not* look like—"

"Your hair was half out of the updo and you had beard burn on your face, neck, and décolletage," Jamie said. "Don't even get me started on the condition of your dress, which, I mean, best wishes to your dry cleaner on that chore."

"What's a décolletage?" Ruth asked.

"Okay, but pony? Really?" I asked.

"Sure, I'll just look it up for myself," Ruth said.

"I did say *prize* pony," Jamie said. "Also, I'd like an update on your missing rider. What happened to Daddy Fiancé? Why didn't he come back to the party with you? Please tell me you fucked him silly and he needed fluids and oxygen to recover. Where is he now? Is he waiting for you in bed, chained to a headboard? Please say yes." She tossed her long dark hair over her shoulder. "Please explain what's happening with you two now. And when will you admit that I was right about him all along?"

I reached for my mimosa and drained it in two gulps. My body would hate me for it later but my head would appreciate it now. "I wanted to show him around the tulip farm," I said. "As you know, we hadn't talked since the week before, and I love the farm so much and I just wanted a minute away from everything. We ended up over by all the sunflowers and"—I turned my gaze downward and scraped my nail along the hem of my shorts until I could form the words—"and we had a moment there. Against the side of the barn."

"What kind of moment?" Ruth asked.

"Yeah, what are we talking about here?" Jamie asked. "I don't know how anyone ends up looking as thoroughly fucked as you did without taking a serious pounding."

I glanced at the tables surrounding us, praying they hadn't heard that comment. "He, you know," I said, the words barely audible as I gestured to my lap.

"I admire a guy who sees opportunities to enjoy a slice of pie in the most unlikely of moments," Jamie said. "It takes maturity to put your interests first."

"Then we"—I flapped a hand quite pointlessly—"and that's what happened."

"Against the barn? As in outside?" Ruth asked. "During cocktail hour? When people were wandering around the grounds?"

I nodded as I refilled my mimosa. My cheeks burned like a fever.

"It's always the quiet ones who turn out to be truly devious," Jamie said, wagging a finger at me. "I knew there was a reason I liked you."

"Yeah, well, he left right after that," I said.

"Talk about dine and dash," Jamie muttered.

"That's lewd," Ruth said. "I love it."

"But why did he leave?" Jamie asked. "We're missing something here."

"I went back inside and he took a call, and I couldn't find him after that." The words felt like rust in my mouth. "He sent me a text saying something urgent came up and…he left. I haven't heard from him since."

Ruth and Jamie exchanged deep frowns and furrowed brows.

"That's…odd," Ruth said.

"Very odd," Jamie said. "I'm guessing you've tried to contact him since last weekend?"

"Yep," I said, polishing off another mimosa. "I've called a couple of times. No answer, no call back. I've sent messages. No response. It's not even showing that he's read the last few messages." I set the glass down instead of refilling it. "I don't know if I should keep calling or just…stop trying altogether."

"A week is a long time to go silent. Right?" Ruth asked, glancing between us. "Even if he's in the middle of a shitstorm, it's not that hard to send a text saying *I'm all right and I'll get back to you in a bit.*"

"Unless he's secretly Superman, he has time to text you back," Jamie said. "Since you'd probably know about his superhero identity, let's assume it's something else. He does have a kid with special needs and a mom who just got through breast cancer. And he flew in on a red-eye flight to be your date to this wedding, and the minute he could get you alone, he served it up hot and fresh. I'm trying to add those things up but my calculator keeps turning into a Magic 8 Ball and telling me to ask again later. I don't know what to say, baby girl."

"Neither do I." Rubbing my temples, I asked, "What if he's ghosting me? Maybe this is his passive-aggressive way of saying he's done." That it was my turn to be the one left wondering what'd happened.

Ruth and Jamie shared another loaded glance. Jamie motioned to her, asking, "Would you care to tackle this one?"

"I'll give it a shot." Ruth laced her fingers together and stretched out her arms. Cleared her throat, sipped her iced coffee. Then, "Did you miss the part where we talked about him hauling his ass across the country to see you? And then immediately shoving his head under your dress because he was so thirsty?"

"I hear what you're saying," I said, "but also—"

"But you're not playing at that level," Ruth cut in. "If I hooked up with someone last weekend and he wasn't replying to my texts, I'd assume he was done because that's the field *we're* playing on. Hypothetically speaking. I didn't hook up with anyone. *You* did and you're nowhere near that level."

They just didn't understand. They didn't know the ins and outs of my history with Jude, everything we'd been through and the long, complicated mess of it all. They just saw a sweet guy who made time to see me and the rest was a case of bizarre but harmless hiccups.

I knew better. I knew what was really going on here.

"She's right," Jamie said. "She's also lying and I don't mean that hypothetically because she definitely hooked up with someone."

"What?" I whirled on Ruth. "Who?"

"This is all news to me," Ruth said.

"The secret benefit of being on heavy-duty antibiotics during the whole wedding weekend was that I was sober enough to keep noticing when y'all disappeared and who else was missing at the same time." Jamie's feline grin was a little scary. "And I know that you, Miss Ruthie Ralston, were absent from the cocktail hour *and* the bouquet toss, and only appeared for the last twenty minutes of the newlywed brunch the next day."

Ruth straightened her silverware. After a beat, she said, "The line for the bathroom was outrageous."

"Must've been a nightmare," Jamie drawled. "Be a lamb and remind me who else was missing from those same events, please."

"I wouldn't know," Ruth said, her gaze still fixed on the table-top. "I had to take a few work calls during the reception. I missed a lot of things that night."

"Makes sense," Jamie said. "I can see how you'd need to handle urgent work matters on the *Saturday evening* of your *brother's* wedding. Totally understandable."

"Okay, hold the hell on," Ruth said. "My firm doesn't give a hot fuck about my brother, his wedding, or Saturdays. I'm a senior associate which means I'm at my desk twelve—but usually sixteen —hours a day and available to the partners at all times. The only time I didn't have my phone on me the entire weekend was during the ceremony and I was slightly panicked because of it."

It was my turn to share a frown with Jamie.

"That's kinda fucked up," Jamie said.

"Yes, thank you, I know that," Ruth whisper-yelled.

The food arrived and we took a minute to organize all the items we'd ordered to share. I dug into my scrambled egg avocado toast in the hope it would get ahead of all the alcohol I'd chugged this morning. Ruth dropped a slice of French toast on my plate and shoveled some of my home fries onto hers.

Jamie leaned back in her seat, tapping a finger to her lips. She ignored her chicken and waffles even as Ruth cut a segment for herself. Then, "Must've been one helluva work call for you to show up to that brunch on wobbly legs."

Ruth cut a frayed stare in Jamie's direction. "Mergers and acqui- sitions will do that to you."

"You know what's so wild," Jamie went on, "is how that preppy football player friend of your brother's was missing at all the same times." She dipped her finger into the ramekin of maple syrup on her plate and then popped it in her mouth. "And when he walked into the brunch, he didn't look like he'd gotten much sleep. He looked a little rumpled, if you know what I mean."

"Even if I did make some astoundingly bad decisions at the wedding—which I'm not saying I did—I wouldn't advise anyone to divulge that kind of information at a busy restaurant." Ruth glanced to the tables beside us, both close enough to reach over and steal a muffin from their bread baskets. "Especially with so many rabid sports fans in this city. And you're also my brother's wife's best friends, so that makes it all a little boggy for me."

"Ah. Right." I hadn't adjusted to the fame that came along with Emme's husband but Ruth had much more experience. "If you did want to tell us anything, I can promise we won't let it get back to your brother. Or Emme, if that's important to you."

"We love our cones of silence here," Jamie said. "Like attorney-client privilege but for our misadventures with the man-children who don't deserve us."

Ruth bobbed her head, still hacking away at the French toast. "If I did engage in some truly heinous, shameful behavior with a football player-shaped individual, I'd probably be very busy hoping no one noticed. I definitely wouldn't want to talk about it because I'd probably die of embarrassment in the process and it's really not a good time for me to die. My apartment is a pigsty and someone would have to deal with that, which just seems like an unfair way to leave things. My mother's been through enough. She doesn't need that too."

Jamie nodded, saying, "Speaking of good times to die, have I told you two about the state of my life recently?"

"Please tell me you've cleared this UTI," I said.

"Shit, okay, no boundaries here," Ruth said under her breath.

"That's better," Jamie said, "but I'm still on the sex hiatus because of the recurrent UTIs and I awake every day to the realization that I'm still living with my dad. Even worse, I've turned into a brunch girl."

"What's wrong with being a brunch girl?" Ruth asked. "Brunch is fantastic."

"It's not about *brunch*," Jamie said. "It's about this moment of my life where I feel like I'm stuck in a waiting room but I don't know what I'm waiting for or what's going to happen when the door finally opens."

The three of us were quiet for a heavy moment. I put my fork down. I needed to absorb those words before I took another bite.

"I don't think I like that analogy," Ruth said. "But I think that's because I'm in a waiting room too."

"I think we're all in waiting rooms right now," I said.

"Thanks, I hate it," Jamie said with a miserable grin. "But I'm lucky I have this stone-cold pack of weirdos there with me."

"Wait." Ruth held up a hand as she shook her head. "What?"

"Complimentary, I swear," Jamie said.

"Just go with it," I told her.

We lingered over brunch for another hour but didn't return to the topics of Jude or anything that might incriminate Ruth. We made plans to meet up for another brunch and an evening of sitting in my backyard and witnessing Bagel the beagle's remarkable zoomies.

When I dropped into a seat on the train, it dawned on me that I wasn't drunk. Tipsy, perhaps, but only in the sense that I wouldn't mind parking myself on the old wrought iron chaise I'd snagged at a yard sale a few years ago and taking a nap. Summer was meant for afternoon naps in the backyard. Especially if Bagel warmed up to me enough to join me on the chaise.

That was all I needed. A lazy afternoon with my new dog friend, and maybe a book that I wasn't reading with the goal of picking out text-dependent questions. This was fine. I was good.

Except I wasn't.

I was fractured and I'd forced putty into those cracks but it didn't mend anything and it didn't hold. And it didn't really matter because those cracks weren't new. They'd shifted, widened now that I knew what it would've been like with Jude. If we'd had the chance.

I knew better than to open up his messages and scroll back to the start but I was no good at making the right choice in bad moments. The train lurched between quick stops in Forest Hills and Readville. I knew I'd regret it later but I let myself tap his photo and listen while the call rang. All the things I'd always wanted to say bubbled up to the surface, spilling out in a rush when the line clicked over to voicemail.

"Jude. Hi. It's me. It's Audrey. I'm calling because I want you to know I've been really worried about you and you're not even reading my texts anymore and I'm just asking if you're okay. I don't expect you'll give me that but I'm asking anyway. Because I care about you, even when you make it obvious that I shouldn't." My voice shook. My hands too. My chest was one deep breath away from caving in. "And I need to tell you that I know what you're doing. I get it now. You wanted to leave me the way you think I left you. Give me some of my own medicine, right? You know nothing about that medicine, Jude. Not the first thing. I know you'll never believe this but everything I did was to protect you. And I can't believe you'd be so cruel. That you'd let me spend all this time worrying about you and your family. I know that's how it was for you when I left but my god, we were *kids*. There was nothing I could've done then but I'd never leave you like that now, and you know that. I *know* you know that."

A shaky breath heaved out of me as the train rolled into Endicott Station. Seven minutes and two more stops until mine came up.

"I hope you're all right," I continued. "I hope nothing bad happened, and if it did, I hope it works out okay. And that's the last thing I'm going to say to you because we can't keep doing this to each other. This needs to be the end."

I stared at the screen for a moment, watching the seconds tick by before disconnecting the call. I felt it like a fresh new crack, right down the center of my chest.

chapter forty-four

Today's vocabulary word: premeditation

THERE WAS AN ART TO HOLDING MY PARENTS AT AN ARM'S LENGTH. Expert-level prevarication required planning and finesse, and a quick inventory of the evasions I'd used in the past.

Since I'd thrown myself into the deep end of this post-Jude funk and couldn't be called upon for more than brittle bitterness and reading books that I knew would make me sob, I ran out of excuses when my mother insisted I attend a clambake in the Hamptons.

I tried to hang it all on Bagel. I needed to be home for Bagel. He was still very confused about his current living situation and it didn't help that I talked to myself while I baked. But she knew I'd pet-sit for others who worked with this fostering organization at the last minute because I'd burrowed into that excuse to skip out on another of her parties in the past.

My family didn't always have this kind of money. We'd always been comfortable. Extremely comfortable, even. But we didn't have *waterfront summer house in the Hamptons* money until I was out of elementary school. I hadn't realized it at the time, not in any concrete way, not until my parents announced I wouldn't be going to the local middle school with my friends and neighbors as planned.

I remembered getting upset about that. Crying, probably yelling too. Mostly because I hadn't wanted to wear a uniform to school. But my father said it was foolish for me to react that way since I'd finally be going to school with the *right* people from the *right* families.

The people and the families were of no concern to me. My only priority had been escaping the uniform with its plaid, pleated skirt in a god-awful shade of burgundy. But I'd learned that night—with my mother telling me to stop being hysterical because it made my skin ruddy and my eyes bloodshot, all of which rendered me rather ugly, she didn't hesitate to say—that my father only cared about getting close to the right people. That he'd sacrifice anything, no hesitation.

I knew this because I'd been sacrificed before. More times that I wanted to admit. If the trappings of this clambake were any indication, I was about to be sacrificed again.

And I knew exactly what I had to do.

I SPENT THE ENTIRE FERRY RIDE FROM NEW LONDON OUT TO LONG Island trying to read one of the books I'd be teaching in the fall but mostly stalking Janet and Rita's social media pages. I didn't know what I thought I'd find there—false; I went looking for any glimpse of Jude—but the two of them posted like squirrels with unlimited access to espresso martinis.

It'd been thirteen days since Emme's wedding and I still hadn't heard a peep from him. It was like I'd dreamed up the whole thing.

If not for the lizard magnet on my fridge, I'd doubt the truth of it too.

But I knew there had to be an explanation. Something serious must've happened. With work or Janet or Percy. Something came up—an emergency. But when I woke up tomorrow morning, there'd be two entire weeks between me and the last time I saw Jude, and chances were high I still wouldn't have an update from him.

No matter how many times I stepped back from the facts as I knew them and peered at the sharp angles, I couldn't explain this without scooping up the blame and carrying it away with me.

Had he planned it that way? To fly in here at the last minute? Drag me away to the back of the barn and then send me off wearing his jacket? And then disappear without a backward glance?

I couldn't escape the sense that he wanted me to know the kind of helpless agony and unyielding grief he'd felt when I'd disappeared on him. I didn't want to imagine Jude masterminding anything like that but I couldn't shake the thought that it was possible.

"Audrey, come back here!" my mother called.

I shrunk a little deeper into the leggy embrace of the hydrangea. I'd made myself very busy with the shrubs and flowers ringing the property since arriving at the clambake. If I looked like I was engrossed in my study of the leaves and the blooms, and not replaying every second Jude and I spent behind the barn or the thirteen painfully silent days since, no one would try to talk to me.

And that was important since I didn't like clams and my social hourglass was maxing out after five minutes. Even if I did have a few landmines to bury.

"I swear I saw her just over there," my mother said to a guy in pink seersucker. "She probably didn't hear us over the waves."

I ducked under a floppy blue mop head and crept, hunched over, between the bushes and the weathered gray shingles of the house. I didn't need anyone to explain to me that my behavior had crossed into bizarre territory. I knew this. But I also knew the best place for me was trapped in this cool, quiet world. At least while I gathered some intel.

"Very choppy out there today," Seersucker replied. "But I'm hearing tomorrow will be perfect for getting out on the water."

"What a relief," my mother said, as if she knew anything about sailing. "The water was empty today. Such a disappointment."

My mother was beautiful in an ageless, eerie way. Her work was her face, her figure, but it was also her faith. There was relevance in that plumped-up perfection. There was *value*. In her world, the only women worth keeping around were the ones who'd figured out how to stop time. Their virtue lived in that plastic youth, and they were nothing without it.

Sometimes I wondered when she'd stopped being a real person. I knew it came before the fillers and the surgeries and the every-four-weeks root touch-ups to keep the silver out of her cornsilk blonde. Her ability to wield power in this world existed only in relation to her willingness to uphold its pointless beauty standards. It was like she'd stepped into a small square of wet concrete and she had to live out the rest of her days there—or cut off her own feet to get free.

"My goodness, Brecken," she said. "I just don't know where that daughter of mine ran off to if she's not over here."

"Not to worry." He said this with the easy grace of someone who understood the level of bullshitting required at these affairs. That helped. This wouldn't work if I had a short fuse on my hands. "She'll turn up."

"I appreciate your patience with this expedition I've taken you on," she said.

"No patience required," he said, which I interpreted to mean *I've done my community service for the day and now I'm breaking free from your clutches, lady.*

I crouched down to stay out of their eyeline but as I moved, a branch shifted, whipping the side of my face. I had to swallow a yelp unless I wanted them to notice my hiding spot. I'd survived many unpleasant things but getting caught in a hydrangea bush and then having to fight my way out while people watched would make for a new all-time low.

I held my breath as they strolled back to the heart of the party. Once she dropped off Seersucker, my mother would come looking for me. She'd quietly enlist everyone in the search—waiters, bartenders, the young men tasked with parking the cars far enough away to give the impression that everyone teleported here.

All of which was to say I couldn't stay in the bushes all day. Either I dashed back inside, grabbed my things, and made a break for the ferry or I dredged up the ability to interact with other people. To do what I came here to do. There was no in between.

I gave myself a few more minutes behind the hydrangea to check my messages. Nothing from Jude though I did find a bitchy notification that I was consuming significantly more screen time than usual this week. I read a new chapter of a fanfic I followed and looped back to Janet and Rita's socials (also nothing), and then checked the departure times for the ferry. Just to be sure.

I discovered it'd been easier getting into the bushes than it was getting out. My arms were scratched and my hair was full of leaves and floral debris but not in any whimsical bohemian way.

I shook the dirt from my sundress and hiked through the front yard and into the house. If I ran into my mother, I'd blame my absence on my belly. She hated being reminded that my gut had a lot in common with sweating dynamite. Nice, marriageable women didn't have *those* problems.

I was waiting at the bar, sunglasses shielding my eyes as I grinned up at the late afternoon sun, the picture of summertime bliss, when I felt someone sidle up beside me.

"Audrey, isn't it?"

I kept my chin tipped to the sky, taking in Seersucker from the corner of my eye. Up close, I placed him around a decade older than me, maybe more, though the wonders of fillers and Botox and money made a plausible case for mid-thirties.

"It is." I gave him my breeziest smile, the one that dug lines into my cheeks. "You'll have to remind me where we've met. My memory isn't with me today."

"Apologies," he said with a light laugh. He held out his hand. "Brecken. Wilhamsen. We'd meant to connect at the Aldyn Thorpe reunion weekend."

I treated him to all the standard apologies and pleasantries as I sipped my drink, and he did a fine job of acting as if he understood. It was all very civilized and that was the real irony of my parents' events.

"If I'm being honest," he said, edging in close like we were already coconspirators, "I didn't really want to be there. You did me a big favor by canceling." He shot a glance at the bow-tied staff standing watch around the clambake pit. "I'm not completely sure I want to be here now."

That earned a real laugh from me. I reeled him in with a stiff grin that said *you and me both, friend.*

"Could I interest you in a walk?" he asked. "And before you answer, I'm going to blackmail you a little by saying I saw you in the hydrangeas."

I jerked back, startled. "You realize it's not a game if you show all of your cards at the start, right?"

He shrugged, his pristine polo shirt stretching across his narrow shoulders with the movement. "It's still a game. But now everyone knows the stakes."

"Going right for the jugular, are we?"

He cringed all the way down to his toes, which I appreciated. A man who could be shamed had a lot going for him. "I don't know why I said that. I didn't mean blackmail. Not really. It was a bad joke. I'm very bad at jokes. I just meant— Well. I thought you'd want to get out of here for a little while. Because I do." He hooked a thumb over his shoulder, toward the path to the beach at his back. "I can promise I won't attempt any more jokes."

I found myself smiling at him, and for the first time in days, it wasn't forced. "No extortion whatsoever?"

He put a hand over his heart. "None."

I studied him, taking in the simple but ultra-expensive, hand-crafted loafers, the silver peppered through his hair, the mobile phone peeking out of his pocket. He was on the shorter side, coming in around five-eight. I had a good two or three inches on him. He was slim but nothing about him read as athletic or a gym rat. Handsome in a non-specific, unremarkable sense. He was a money guy because everyone here was a money guy one way or another, but he wasn't lighting up my toxicity meter.

I didn't know if it was the introverted confessions or the self-deprecating humor but it was easy to say, "Yeah. A walk would be nice."

He handed his glass to the bartender. "Might as well get this topped off before we go."

Once we were adequately refilled, we ditched our shoes at the mouth of the path and strolled along the shore. Brecken asked the standard questions—where I lived, what I did for work, how often I hid in bushes at parties—and I volleyed the same back to him.

He told me all the things he liked about the Hamptons and I told him why I was angry about the ending to a TV show I'd been following for longer than I could defend. It amounted to nothing—and that was what made it manageable. I didn't have to work too hard at sculpting answers into acceptable shapes and I wasn't over-come with the need to check for new messages from Jude.

All things considered, a fantastic way to kill an hour and plant the seeds that grow into an invasive weed.

As we approached the path back to my parents' property, Brecken brushed my elbow. A brief, functional touch. No tingles or belly butterflies involved. "I believe your mother intends to set us up. On a date," he added. "Or something more."

"I think you're right."

We stopped at the crest of the path, the beach stretching out into low tide on one side, the party in full swing on the other. "Would you be interested in that? In a date? Or something more?"

No way in hell was I touching that *something more*. "Would there be blackmail involved? Now that you've set the precedent, I have to ask."

He barked out a laugh and slipped his hands into his pockets. "No blackmail," he said. "I would like to see you again."

I crossed my arms over my chest. "You live in New York, Brecken."

He bobbed his head several times. "I do."

"And I live in Boston," I said. *I'm also in the middle of a traumatic experience that might turn into a breakdown if I don't get a text back in the next few days.*

"That is true. Yep." He rocked back on his heels. "But I've heard there are roads between New York and Boston now. Surfaces made specifically for driving cars. And these unbelievable new things— what are they called again? Yes, trains. Have you heard about the trains?"

"I've heard rumors of these trains." I couldn't help but laugh. "It's still a long distance for a date."

"I have your number from when you made my day by bailing on lunch," he said. "Would it be okay if I messaged you sometime?" Before I could respond, he shook his head. "No, don't answer that. I'll text you. Respond or don't, your choice."

I stared at him for a long moment, sifting through the pieces of himself he'd shared and trying to pull the strands together into something I understood.

"It's that simple for you?" I asked.

His shoulders jerked up. "If you don't want to talk to me again,

I'm not going to make you. That seems like a lot of work and I don't see how it would benefit me."

"A lot of work," I agreed, a bitter tinge in my words. I wanted to believe him but I had some experience with men cut from this cloth and I knew them to become vicious little tyrants when they didn't get precisely what they wanted.

Before I could say anything else, my mother approached, calling to Brecken, "It looks like you found her after all!"

"We bumped into each other." He gave me a chin tip that I read as *See? I didn't out you about the bushes. I'm clearly on your side.*

My mother gushed for a few minutes about some local celebrity who'd arrived and departed all within the time we'd been on the beach, how much everyone loved the clams but the lobster was the real highlight this summer, and then someone she thought Brecken would like to meet.

He cut glances to me every so often and I could also hear him asking *Are you invisible?* because I might as well have been for all the attention my mother paid me.

If I'd trusted Brecken with more than the most basic bits of information about myself, I would've used words from his world and explained that I was a commodity here. Nothing more than a good to be bought and sold.

It was nice that he'd noticed, all the same. Most people didn't. Most were too busy buying and selling their own goods. Perhaps he wasn't cut from the same old cloth after all. Perhaps he was a rare exception to all of this.

"I hope you'll be staying the weekend," she said to him. "We'd love to host you again."

"I'm just here for the evening." He gestured to me like I knew what he was talking about. "Though I was telling Audrey I'm heading up to Boston this week. For some meetings." The leading tone in his words told me to get on board with the charade or get trampled under it. "We were just comparing schedules."

"Isn't that exciting," she drawled. "In that case, I'll get out of your way."

"Thank you. I'd appreciate the privacy," Brecken said firmly.

I tried to swallow a chuckle but I didn't pull it off. My mother frowned at that before taking her time getting back to the party. She glanced at us repeatedly, always grinning and waving, but also cataloging every detail she could find.

This was the life she wanted for me, no matter the cost. Clambakes and summer homes. Women who were never anything more than maidens or mothers. Men who bloodlessly controlled unimaginable sums of money. The narrow scope of power that came with being married into it all. To her, marriage was a vehicle for safety and stability, but it was also a stepping-stone. Relationships were currency in this world and this place was crawling with people who'd throw plenty of it at my father if it gave them the access they craved.

It didn't matter that after leaving my ex I'd vowed to never shove myself into another empty—or outright harmful—marriage. I couldn't imagine legally tying myself to another person. Not after all the levels of hell I'd climbed through to end the last marriage. Not after contending with the grief of the years I'd lost to an unhinged man.

I wasn't looking for another husband and I was comfortable with that. Save for the small, fragile hope I'd long since buried and forgotten until Jude stalked toward me at the reunion.

But now I knew we weren't meant for a second chance. He'd taken what he wanted and left me the same way I'd left him. That was clear. Two weeks with no news made it painfully obvious and it was silly of me to pretend otherwise. It was time to let go of that hope.

"Please tell me that wasn't too presumptuous," Brecken said.

My gaze drifted over his shoulders to where the sun dipped low on the horizon. He seemed pleasant enough. He wasn't overtly craven or self-absorbed in pathological ways. His manner was quiet, self-effacing. No name-dropping, no pointed comments about wealth or status. He'd made a respectable effort at getting to know me, which was a nice touch, and he didn't seem like the type to get bent out of shape when I called it off.

And I knew he'd never dare to call me princess.

"I can come to Boston and we can meet up for dinner," he went on. "If that's something you'd consider."

"And if I canceled a few hours before dinner? What then?"

"I probably wouldn't mind," he said, laughing. "Though, to streamline matters for both of us, the talking point would be that we did go out and there wasn't any chemistry."

"That would be all right with you?" I peered at him. Perhaps that was why my toxicity meter hadn't pinged. "A cover story?"

The thing my mother didn't understand about her quest for safety and stability was that I'd found more of both on my own than at any point during my marriage. That I'd found strength and learned self-reliance, and I was better for it. That everything she'd done to buy me a secure future—and drive me far away from Jude —left me dependent on a man who cared little for whether I lived or died.

And the thing I didn't understand about my mother was how she could tolerate any of that. I supposed existing in a cage of her own made the one she chose for me all the more familiar.

The other thing my mother didn't understand was that I knew her moves now. I hadn't seen it coming when they canceled my enrollment at Barnard, packed up my life, and shoved me on a plane to Los Angeles, all while filing a bullshit restraining order against Jude.

I'd been too deep into my depression to put up a fight when they presented my ex-husband as their newest requirement of me. I knew better now—and I had some moves of my own.

Brecken shrugged. "What's the harm?"

I didn't think he was prepared for a detailed explanation of the pitfalls of fake relationships so I said, "You have my number."

And now, with my checkmate in hand for the night, I turned back toward the house. I didn't stop when I passed my mother, who launched into an endless stream of breathless questions as she trailed me inside. I went straight for the guest room where I'd dropped my things and made quick work of changing into jeans and a sweatshirt. It would be chilly on the ferry back to New London.

"You're behaving like a maniac," she said as I shoved today's dress into a bag. "If you're going to have one of your episodes, will you at least do it in here? Where no one has to see?"

"I'm leaving." I shouldered the bag. I'd laugh if I stopped to consider how long I'd avoided these interactions with my mother. How much discomfort I'd accepted in exchange for skirting a difficult conversation. And to what end? I was full grown and supported myself, and still cowered from confrontation. Later, I'd laugh and then I'd cry and then I'd learn how to stop betraying myself, once and for fucking all. "No episodes. Nothing to see. I'm going home."

"You can't just leave—"

"I think I can," I said. "I have a lot to do."

"It's a weekend evening in the middle of the summer. What could you possibly have to do that's worth embarrassing me and your father tonight?"

"Didn't you hear Brecken say he was coming to town this week?"

"Oh. *Oh.*" She stepped away from the door. "Then, yes," she went on. "You should go and—"

"I knew you'd understand," I said, pushing past her.

I OPENED MY MESSAGES AS THE FERRY PUSHED AWAY FROM THE dock. I stared at Jude's last words to me—*I'm sorry*—and heard them in my mind as if he was sitting here beside me. But instead of the hurried, halting promise I thought them to be, they were solemn this time. Final. A conclusion to a story that'd ambled on far too long.

His silence wasn't a symptom. It was proof that we'd reached the end while I was busy thinking about the things I wanted to say and never once saying them. Maybe it would've been different if I'd let myself be brave, let myself get hurt. If I'd stopped playing scared. If I'd acted on half the scenarios I'd rehearsed in my mind. If I'd wrapped my arms around the risks and held them tight until they turned into the kind of emotional armor I required to finally get what I wanted. To fix this—and end it the right way.

It would've been different if I was different. But I wasn't.

chapter forty-five
Audrey

Today's vocabulary word: roots

BRECKEN'S MESSAGE CAME THROUGH WHILE I DROVE HOME AFTER
the ferry.

> Brecken: I have some meetings in Boston on
> Wednesday of this week. If you're planning to eat
> dinner that day, do you have any interest in doing
> it with me?

I wanted to give him credit for calling his shots before shooting
them. There was something easy about that—predictable, even. But
I'd grown up with a megalomaniac who had both the knack for
making outrageous demands sound like simple requests and all the
right tools to guarantee compliance. And then I'd married a man
who did the same thing but with a hard twist of degradation. I knew
better than to trust first impressions.

I didn't cancel at the last minute. I'd wanted to. I'd written and
deleted a dozen texts throughout the day. And Bagel expressed

strongly negative feelings when he noticed me fussing with my hair and putting on out-of-the-house clothes. He responded to this by gathering all the shoes he could find and hiding them in his crate. I had to leave the house barefoot, shoes smuggled out in my purse.

I met Brecken at a small Spanish café I liked on an odd corner in Brighton, a local place I'd suggested knowing it wouldn't show up on any best-of lists. It could be counted on for outstanding patatas bravas and comically bad service. If there was one thing I knew to flip a narcissist's switch, it was waiting an hour for another round of drinks or never getting that extra napkin.

The service lived up to my expectations but Brecken didn't flip. When he realized his place setting came short a fork, he just snagged a set from a nearby table. When our wineglasses ran dry, he walked up to the bar and asked for a bottle. Corked it himself. And he really liked the patatas.

We talked about the basic things. Where we'd gone to school, the people we knew. Restaurants we liked and places we wanted to visit. Spanish food and wine carried the evening on its back.

I smiled without forcing it and asked questions I actually wanted answers to. It was comfortable in a plain, hollow way. As I sat there, nodding along with his story about a chicken shop he loved but that never stayed in the same location for more than a few months, this overly plucked civility started to look a lot like closing the garage door with the car running inside.

Brecken seemed, at least on the surface, to be a decent guy. As much as anyone who hoarded wealth and hung around with back-room power brokers like my father could be.

He was, however, gently determined to nail down another date and kinda-sorta float a prenup in my direction if my reading between the lines could be trusted.

He liked New York and wanted me to like New York too, and offered to make some calls to find me a teaching job there if I wanted one. His tone made it clear that he didn't know why I'd want that but he'd go along with it. He was cool like that.

There was a vacation to some fancy island resort coming up on his calendar. I was welcome to join. He had a condo—I was certain it was a penthouse the size of a Costco—but he was in the market for something different. If I wanted to help with his search, he'd be happy for it.

Life with Brecken would be fine. Polite conversation and lukewarm affection. A partnership more in function than connection. There were worse things than the starved pantomime of having it all.

I let him give me a ride home. I knew it didn't matter but it occurred to me that I'd never scream at Brecken in the rain. Probably no lizards perched on motel curtains either.

When the driver came to a stop outside my house, Brecken's poker face failed him. He blinked at my small one-level ranch with its cracked walkway and slightly overgrown grass.

I swallowed a laugh. It was nice to see something rattle that chill demeanor.

"Let me walk you to the door," he said, swinging a glance up and down the street like we were in a war-ravaged neighborhood and not the sleepy Boston suburb of Norwood.

Little did he know, raccoons were the cause of most of the lawlessness around here and they had no compunction about chucking black walnuts at his head if he got in their way. Ask me how I knew.

He settled a hand on my lower back and one on my elbow as we traversed the walkway, the cement topsy-turvy from the roots of an old cherry blossom tree that made the first two weeks of May my favorite days of the entire year.

Bagel started howling as we approached. We shared a smile over that.

"Thank you for dinner," I said, hooking a thumb toward the

door. "I should really get in there. He's been in the crate for a few hours now."

"Yeah, of course." His hand didn't release my elbow. It wasn't unpleasant in any way but it said something he hadn't enunciated yet. After a beat, he said, "This might be very forward but—"

Bagel launched into a longer, deeper howl. It was something like a soulful crooning, an old song that awakened his kin. Other dogs in the neighborhood joined in, barking, yipping, howling.

Brecken laughed to himself, shook his head like he couldn't believe a barking chain was drowning him out. "This might be forward but I think we could be good together. You make me feel like I can be honest without worrying that you'll sell something I say to a podcast."

I knew I ought to laugh but I didn't.

"Perhaps it's become apparent to you that I'm looking for a companion," he went on. "I want someone who folds into my life, even if we're mostly separate day-to-day. I think we could do that for each other but I need you to consider whether that would work for you. I'd prefer you to live in New York, at least most of the year, but I'd understand if you wanted time to ease into that."

I listened as Bagel shifted into low, mournful howls. He was right; it was unacceptable for me not to include him in the conversation. Especially after an offer like Brecken's. I'd say I was blindsided by it but only in that he didn't wait until tomorrow to spring it on me. He could've ended the evening on a mild note instead of launching into terms and conditions.

"You're sweet," I said to him. "I have a lot going on right now so I'm not in the best spot to make big decisions. School is starting up in a month and I'm elbow-deep in preparing for that. Plus I have everything going on with Bagel." To his furrowed brow, I pointed to the door. "The beagle."

"We have great bagels in New York," he said.

I almost lost my polite façade at the pointlessness of that comment but managed to say, "I'd love some time to think."

All I needed was to make it look like I'd considered his offer. And to get his hand off my elbow before the feral part of my brain took over.

"I completely understand. The last thing I'd want would be for you to make a snap decision."

He released my elbow—*thank god*—and held his arms open, moving in for a hug I hadn't expected. I knew I wasn't in danger but that didn't stop my body from dumping buckets of adrenaline into my system.

"Thank you again for dinner, Brecken. I hope you have an easy trip back to the city."

He leaned in to press a kiss to my cheek, and seemed to enjoy it about as much as I did. Cold sweat bloomed on my chest.

"I'll be in touch," he called as he picked his way down the walkway. Like it was a literal minefield.

I turned the handle but waited for the driver to pull away to step inside. I needed to know they were gone before turning my back. I knew I was spiraling into hypervigilance when I flipped the deadbolt but I also knew it would pass. I just needed to breathe through it and remind myself this was my home, I was safe here, and no one could take it away from me.

I rushed to Bagel's crate before even turning on the lights. He bounded out, running in circles and whining his outrage at being left here all alone. "I know, I know," I repeated. "It was terrible of me to leave you. Never again, friend. Never, ever."

He followed from a careful distance as I flipped on the lights in the kitchen and living room. I'd need some tea to settle down and I had time to mix up some bread dough for—

The doorbell rang and my entire nervous system jolted at once.

Bagel rushed to the door, sniffing and yipping, but it took me a beat to get moving. I shot a text to Jamie, telling her to call me in three minutes if I didn't get back to her before then. She, of course, responded with *WHAT THE FUCK IS HAPPENING ARE YOU OKAY WHAT'S GOING ON?!?!?*

I glanced through the peephole but it was old and rusty, and the lighting out there was more back alley, less front door. I knew it was Brecken. Either he'd come back with another anemic offer—separate penthouses! vacations on different private islands!—or he was here to nudge me toward whatever plan he'd already drafted for our life. Or I'd completely misread him and he was going to scream me into a corner until he got his way.

A hand hooked in Bagel's collar, I edged the door open. But I didn't find Brecken waiting on the other side.

I found Jude with a small child sobbing on his shoulder and a thunderous glare in his eyes. I stumbled back, too blindsided to notice Bagel behind me.

As I lost my balance, Jude's hand shot out, his grip closing around my wrist and holding me steady.

And then he barked, "Who the fuck was that?"

chapter forty-six

Jude

Today's vocabulary word: omission

AUDREY'S PULSE HAMMERED UNDER MY FINGERS AND THE TANGIBLE truth of her made me feel whole for the first time in weeks. Fully formed. That final piece slotted into place.

But also— "Who the fuck was that?"

"Excuse me," Audrey said, wrenching her hand from my grip, "but under no circumstances are you welcome to show up at my home and demand anything after you've spent the past two weeks ignoring my calls."

The dog at her feet started barking—howling—and that was all the encouragement my son needed to wrap up his overtired tantrum and tune into the situation. He rubbed his tear-stained face into my shirt and lifted his head. His eyes went wide and happy at the sight of the pup, and he signed, "Meet the dog? Please?"

I straightened his glasses. "You know the rules."

With a sniffle, he turned his gaze to Audrey. I'd meant to watch him sign but my attention hooked on her quiet gasp and then the way she brought a hand to her neck, up to her parted lips. Her soft gaze stroked over him like she just couldn't believe he was real. The same way I did.

I cleared my throat, saying, "Percy, this is my friend Audrey." I rubbed a hand down my son's back. "Audrey, I'd like you to meet Percy. He says he likes dogs a lot and wants to meet your dog if that's okay."

She nodded for a second, her lips pursed together as she continued staring at him. Then she seemed to snap out of it, sucked in a rough breath, and let a bright smile transform her face. She waved to him as she crossed into the living room, saying, "Hi, Percy. This is Bagel. He has some big feelings and doesn't always want to be close to people, but if we sit down on the floor with some of his toys, he might come visit. Do you want to do that?"

He wiggled right out of my arms and bolted toward Audrey as soon as his sneakers met the floor. He plopped down next to her on the rug and took the toy she offered.

Percy launched into an endless series of questions about Bagel as the dog took slow, cautious steps toward them. I interpreted as he signed to Audrey and something about watching them together grabbed me by the throat and dug its claws in tight. He wasn't one to warm up quickly, and I was sure the dog had a lot to do with it, but standing here now was like the first breath after being underwater too long.

This was all very inconvenient because I needed some information about the guy who'd walked her to the door and touched her like he knew her in a way that was mine.

I'd held it together for two and a half hellish weeks. I knew I couldn't do it much longer, and I lost a little more control every time I thought about watching that asshole go in for a kiss. Which was constantly.

Beyond all of that, I needed to be with her tonight more than I needed anything else in the world. To apologize to every inch of her perfect body for the way I left after the wedding. To serve my penance any way she wished. To tell her I knew I didn't deserve another second chance. To confess that this scared the hell out of me, that the power she held over me was raw and overwhelming and the only thing that'd ever felt right to me. To beg her to take me as I was, stretched too thin and not nearly enough of anything for anyone, and show me how to make this work.

I heard a sharp, excited inhale and blinked down to see Bagel licking my son's hand. I expected him to look up at me with a huge, toothy grin but it was Audrey on the receiving end.

She'd said something once about a heart beating outside my chest and—yes. It was that.

"I think he likes you," she said. "Try rolling a tennis ball across the rug. He likes to play fetch but only if he doesn't have to go very far. I'll be right back."

She pushed to her feet and into the kitchen with zero acknowledgment that I existed. That was…exactly what I'd expected after seventeen days.

I found her leaning against the sink, her arms crossed over her chest and her gaze fixed on the floor. I stood on the other side of the island. If I sat down—if I stopped moving at all—I'd crash. Fall asleep right here on the granite countertop.

Eventually, she said, "What the hell happened, Jude?"

I pushed a hand through my hair. Swallowed hard. "There was a fire. Brenda forgot about a pan on the stove, and when the alarms went off, she fell getting into the kitchen. Broke her hip and a few bones in her leg. Burns on her chest and arms. And half the house is gone." I dipped my head to meet her eyes but she wouldn't give me that. "Percy was there when it happened. He tried to get her out of the house. That was the call I got at the wedding. That's why I had to go immediately."

She swung a glance to the living room. "Is he all right?"

"He caught some very minor burns on his leg and inhaled a bit

339 · In a Second

of smoke. He needed some breathing treatments though he's doing better now. The burns are fully healed, which is great, but we have bigger problems." I rubbed my forehead as an exhausted breath rattled out of me. "Brenda didn't recognize him. Told him to stay away from her and get out of her house."

"What? Why?"

"The doctors think she's been having a lot of small strokes for months, maybe longer, and that's caused her to develop a form of dementia." I shifted back toward my boy. It was good to see him smiling again. Even better to see him this far away from me without a trace of panic. "They're recommending an assisted living placement."

She nodded slowly as she took this in, her arms still crossed and her gaze still evading mine. Then, "Why are you here?"

The past few weeks had been an endless slog of one decision after another. Treatment plans and custody amendments. Doctors and lawyers, therapists and insurance agents. Packing up what was left of a home that wasn't mine and selecting a long-term care facility for a woman who liked to tell the nurses I was stealing from her.

All this time, I hadn't been able to think beyond the next minute, the next step. Holding Percy through the nightmares, the panic, the separation anxiety. Waiting for the court to catch up with all this. The only moments I'd had to breathe came between doctor visits and claims inspections and nightmares, and even then, those breaths were shallow and inadequate, like I was sprinting up a mountainside.

All I could say was, "I didn't know where else to go."

She lifted her gaze to mine, her pale brows pulled tight and her mouth firmed into a rigid line. "Your mother would've welcomed you with open arms, as you're well aware."

I dropped my hands to the countertop, leaned forward. "And

you're well aware I'm still waiting for some answers about the guy who was all over you at the door."

"I'm free to spend time with anyone I want and obligated to justify none of it to you." She made a tart little expression that I wanted to bite off her lips. "Last I checked, I'm a single woman and the statute of limitations on whatever the hell we had going on has lapsed."

I didn't have the energy to pretend that I didn't want her back. *Need* her back. That I wasn't prepared to fight for her. "The last thing in the fucking world you are is single. You've been mine since the first time you rolled your eyes at me when you were fifteen, princess, and I've been yours even longer."

She held my gaze for a beat, fire burning in her hazel eyes. I figured there was at least an eighty percent chance she was about to throw me out. A tragedy, considering my kid was already in love with the dog.

But then she asked, "How much longer?"

If this was what she needed, I could do it. Confess my deep secrets, unburden my mortal soul. No problem. And that was what I wanted her to realize. There wasn't a rung too high for me to climb. Not then, not now.

I circled the island, stopping beside her at the sink. "You were in the pew ahead of me on the first day of school. Your hair was up in a bun but you had a little braid around the bottom of the bun. I spent the entire service wondering how you did that." I brought my hand to the back of her neck. "I knew my entire life would change if I could kiss you right"—I swept her hair over one shoulder, pressed my lips to her nape—"here. I had no idea what it meant to crave someone that way but I knew I wouldn't be complete without you. And that's never changed."

A shiver moved through her as I kissed the slim column of her neck, the line of her jaw. "But we didn't talk until—until—"

"Until second semester. Mmhm. You ignored the shit out of me for months. It was brutal." I wrapped her hair around my palm, gave it a tug to tip her head to the side as I mapped her neck. "I don't think you've ever truly known how much power you wield over me. That you can destroy me and I'll still come right back and ask you to do it again."

"I'm not the one who disappeared and didn't bother to return a text."

I ran my lips over the shell of her ear. "Awful, isn't it?"

"We're not doing that anymore." She elbowed me away but I didn't go far. "Either stop punishing me for the past or get the hell out of my house. There's no in-between."

"There was nowhere else for me to go." I kissed the corner of her mouth. "Because the only place I belong is with you, and you fucking know it."

Her chin wobbled as she dropped a hand to my chest, her fingers slipping under the placket of buttons and connecting with skin. "You have more explaining to do," she said, those fingertips pressing into me. If she only knew how much there was to explain. About the latest disaster fucking my life. *Fuck.* I layered a hand over hers, trapping her there. "And you're not forgiven. Not yet."

"I wouldn't expect it," I said, folding her into my arms.

"I haven't decided if I'll let you stay."

"Decide tomorrow," I said.

A laugh vibrated through her. "You should know my guest room is barely bigger than a closet and only has a small daybed."

"Lucky for us, Percy's a small kid and I'll be sleeping with you."

"I never said you're sleeping with me."

I stroked a hand down her hair with a laugh. "No, baby, I did. Now, be quiet and let me hold you unless you'd rather give me the long-form account of who the fuck that guy was."

She rested her forehead on my chest. "No one you need to worry about."

"That's my girl." I kissed the top of her head. The tension in my body was slow to unwind but I felt my jaw loosen, my shoulders soften. "I've missed you so fucking much."

"Sorry, but I didn't miss you at all. I was too busy being annoyed that you couldn't find a second to answer even one text message. Very time-consuming these past few weeks."

"No, not since this clusterfuck," I said. "I've missed you for— for fucking *years*, Audrey. I don't want to do that again."

Before she could give me anything more than a sudden inhale, Percy bounded into the kitchen, Bagel hot on his heels. He skidded to a stop at the island, pointing at a tiered stack of pastel cake stands where she displayed her baked goods.

"I see that," I said to him.

He climbed onto a stool, making himself right at home in Audrey's kitchen. She freed herself from my hold and opened the fridge. "You two must've had a long day. Are you hungry? Do you need a snack before bed?" She retrieved a glass container, saying, "One of my favorite snacks is my version of an apple crisp. It's warm, cinnamony apples with oatmeal crumble and—"

Percy slapped his hands on the counter as he nodded. "I want the apple crisp," he signed. "Yes, please, the apples, yes!"

"I think I know the answer," she said, laughing.

Audrey went to work scooping the crisp into bowls while Percy signed, "Are we going to stay here?"

"Do you want to?" I signed back.

She set a bowl and spoon in front of him. He dug right in, his eyes drifting shut as he dramatically savored the first bite. When he opened them again, he signed, "I want to stay here forever infinity."

I gripped the edge of the countertop to keep myself from signing *Me too*.

chapter forty-seven

Jude

Today's vocabulary word: privilege

PERCY CRASHED NOT LONG AFTER LICKING HIS BOWL CLEAN. IT WAS easier to get him down for the night when he was tired and it helped that Bagel put himself to bed around that time too.

I sat on the floor of the cozy guest room, quietly unpacking my son's stuffed friends as he drifted off. He needed that familiarity, even while I was just a few steps away in the other room. Glasses, night-light, charged iPad all within reach.

When it seemed like he'd avoided the type of nightmare that usually caught him within the first hour of falling asleep, I crossed the hall to Audrey's room. As with the rest of the house, it was small but it was profoundly comfortable. Walls in a mellow, aquatic green, a thick rug over hardwood floors, and white furniture.

She slipped a tasseled bookmark between the pages of a hard-cover and set it aside. She'd changed into a pajama set like the ones I remembered from Sedona. Button-down top with tiny shorts, always butter-soft and outrageously hot.

I wanted to drown myself in her for hours, days. Or until dogs and children demanded our attention. Whichever came first.

But the crisp tilt of her chin told me I hadn't earned that privilege yet.

I went to her side of the bed and fell to my knees. My arms went around her waist and my head into her lap, and I said, "I'm sorry. It all spun out of control so fast."

She hesitated before resting a hand between my shoulder blades. "I understand. I can only imagine how terrifying it must've been. But you could've messaged me."

"I know. I'm sorry. I didn't let myself call you because I knew —" I shook my head. "I knew I'd tell you how fucking scared I was and then I'd never be able to get through everything I had to do there once I let it out."

"I think that's called being vulnerable."

"I think it fucking sucks."

She raked her fingers through my hair. I growled into her thigh. "I haven't found a way to be alive without it."

"I am sorry. I know I fucked up. I knew it while I was doing it but everything—" An epic, jaw-popping yawn swallowed up the rest of that sentence. It was too late tonight to get into *everything*. Into the fight waiting for me. "I won't do it again."

"Come on," she said, yanking me up by the back of my shirt. "I've decided you're too old to sleep on the floor."

I held her gaze as I unbuckled my belt, dropped my fly. "I'm too old to watch my fiancée kiss strange guys on her doorstep but here we are."

Eyebrow bent, she pulled back the blankets on the other side of the bed. "I'm not your fiancée."

I stepped out of my jeans, pulled the shirt over my head. Set them on a chair in the corner before matching that stare of hers. "You're not?"

"The engagement was as fake as the ring, Jude."

After switching off the lights, I strolled to the opposite side of the bed—*my* side—feeling her eyes on me the whole way. Feeling them travel down my torso, lower. Lingering there.

I slipped between the sheets and when I reached for her, she came to me, her body warm and open and quick to scare off the stress that'd built in my muscles for weeks now. The shorts were the first to go and I almost regretted pulling them off in the dark like this. I would've had a good time inching them down her legs, treating myself to every bit of skin revealed as I went.

I brushed my knuckles between her legs, teasing her with the lightest touch as I bit her nipple through her top. She flung a hand toward the open door, her eyes blazing like I'd forgotten about the kid sleeping across the hall.

"All you have to do is be quiet," I said, abandoning her slick heat and shifting back to my side of the bed. "If that's too difficult..."

"Shut up and get back here," she snapped, pulling me in close.

"I like it when you tell me what you want." I stroked between her thighs again, parting her enough to dip a finger inside her, drag that arousal up, and paint her clit with it. "Keep going."

She let her legs fall wide and reached for my boxers, hooking her fingers in the waistband and forcing them down. As soon as I kicked them off, she closed a hand around my cock, firm and certain.

"Here— Can you just— Please?" She urged me closer with a hand on my back but it was the hand on my shaft that made her meaning clear. She brought me between her thighs as my fingers still moved inside her, my thumb working her clit.

"Better?" I asked.

She hummed in response, tipping her chin up to steal a kiss. "I want— No, don't stop yet. A little more? A little more."

"A little more, then."

My hips met the rhythm of her hand, mindless and brilliant

while I did my best to harass those nipples through her top. I felt her inner walls tighten around my fingers, not all the way but enough for me to know good things were happening, and I kissed my way up her neck and jaw to her lips.

When I asked, "More?" she nodded, her grip on my cock turning erratic, rushed. "Are you going to tell me? Or should I guess?"

She led me to her cunt, right where two of my fingers stroked that beautiful silk. "I think you know," she said.

She teased me, pressing my cockhead into her heat, holding there just a moment, and then dragging me over her clit, using me to push her to the edge and then starting all over again. It was adorable. Also highly instructional. She liked some pressure on that clit. A light slap or two.

"You want me to fuck you," I said to the corner of her mouth. "You want me to wrap these gorgeous fucking legs of yours around my waist and you want my hand over your mouth to keep you quiet and you want me to fuck you like I'm offering my entire soul to you."

Her answering groan said enough. She gripped me by the base, holding me at her entrance while I ran my fingertips up her inner thighs, her folds, her clit. Then she nodded, dropping her hand, and I rocked all the way inside her in one perfect, shattering stroke that damn near split my spine.

"There's one more thing you should know." I hitched her knee up to my hip, saying, "The ring wasn't fake, princess."

chapter forty-eight

Jude

Today's vocabulary word: selective

A GLANCE AT MY WATCH TOLD ME IT WAS LATE, LATER THAN I'D slept in ages. I stretched a hand out and found the sheets cold. I'd been alone for a while. Staring up at the ceiling, I listened for Audrey's voice or kid commotion or even barking.

The silence caught my attention.

It took me a minute to find my jeans and another to admire the lived-in mess of Audrey's bedroom. The tote bags hooked on the closet's doorknob. The skincare products covering one corner of her dresser. The small pillows that didn't match each other, the bedding, or the room. A parched-looking plant near the window. I could almost see her picking out those pillows, knowing damn well they didn't go with anything but choosing them simply because she wanted to and she had no one standing in her way.

The kitchen and living room were empty but I followed soft laughter to the backyard. There, I found Audrey and Percy sitting in the grass, their heads bent together as they watched Bagel stalking a cat along the back fence. The cat, it had to be said, didn't give a fuck about any of the creatures involved.

A chipmunk ran between Bagel and the cat, disrupting the whole standoff, and Percy shot to his feet and threw his arms around Audrey's neck. God, it was so good to see him happy and being a kid after spending the past few weeks clinging to me like a scared little monkey.

He noticed me then, signing, "There's a cat who lives on this street and visits *all* the backyards *every day*! And the cat looks like a cow. It's white with big brown spots and a pink nose. Like a cow! But Bagel doesn't like the cat *at all* and has been telling the cat to go away right now."

"Why doesn't Bagel like cats?" I asked.

"Audrey says he doesn't understand their species," he signed. My heart pinged at the shorthand sign he'd adopted for Audrey. He did that for everyone—spelling out names took too long—but there was no telling my heart that. "They're very confusing to him and he doesn't want them invading his yard. Chipmunks too."

"Bagel doesn't understand cats?" I asked her.

She shrugged, her focus on a bowl in her lap. "I don't know Bagel's whole story but I don't think he has much experience with other animals."

Nodding in vigorous agreement, Percy signed, "He's the only dog he's ever met."

In my head, I could hear Audrey saying that to him. I loved it. Loved all of this. And, with a desperation I truly couldn't get my arms around, I wanted this for the rest of my life. *Our* lives. I didn't know how to make it happen or if she even wanted the same things. But I got the sense she did. Like she felt the strange, oddly shaped puzzle pieces finally snapping into place too. Like she *knew*.

"When did you wake up? I didn't hear you," I said, running a hand over his hair. "Why didn't you come get me?"

He straightened his glasses like these questions were a real inconvenience, signing, "It wasn't dark out and I wanted to read my book alone with Bagel."

We had a rule that he wasn't allowed to be awake on the weekends unless the sun was up *and* shining into his bedroom. He got around this rule by jumping in bed with me and pretending to go back to sleep. I got around this rule by hanging blackout curtains in his room because he wasn't one to wake up and entertain himself.

"Did Bagel like the book?" I asked.

My son turned into a plume of exasperation. "Daddy, Bagel doesn't know how to read."

"Right. Of course." I glanced to Audrey and—Jesus Christ, that was *my* shirt she was wearing with her little black bike shorts. As if it was perfectly ordinary for her to steal my clothes and flip the primitive switch in my brain. "And when did you wake up, Saunders?"

"About an hour or two ago. We've just been hanging out and having some blueberries and granola," Audrey said, a berry pinched between two fingers while Percy ran off to gather Bagel's tennis balls. "Come sit with me."

I dropped to the grass and braced my arms behind me, letting my shoulder bump hers. "Thanks for watching him."

She waved me off, busy picking out her next blueberry. "We had a good time together."

"I didn't come here expecting you to babysit," I said. "You could've woken me up."

"I know." She held a blueberry to my lips. I closed a hand around her wrist and snared her fingertips between my teeth as I took it. "But you needed the sleep. You looked like you were dead on your feet last night."

"He's my kid," I said, still holding her wrist. "I *want* to take care of him. It's never my intention to dump him on anyone else."

"I know all of that too." She offered me another blueberry. Bit those fingers again. "And I would've left a trail of squeaker toys leading to the bed and sent Bagel after them if I had a problem with it."

Dragging my lips over the inside of her wrist, I said, "Thank you."

She arched a brow. "For?"

"Everything." I met her eyes, hoping she saw the brutal, endless truth of it in mine. "For all of it. Always."

Her gaze traveled over my face, quiet and thoughtful. A smile ticked at the corner of her mouth as Bagel and Percy ran past and I knew she was feeling her way around the perimeter of those strange puzzle pieces. Turning them until they met at all the right points.

Then a shadow seemed to pass over her expression. "You're lucky I let you in the door last night."

"I know."

"You left me hanging for a really long time," she said. "Jamie and Ruth will probably kick your ass the next time they see you."

"I would expect nothing less." I ran a hand over the grass. "Getting a little overgrown," I said. "Does your yard service come once a week? Or every other?"

"It's pretty much whenever I remember," she said. "And then once I remember, I have to find the motivation to actually do it."

I peered at the expanse of her backyard, not huge but enough lawn to require an hour or two of weekly upkeep during the peak summer months. "You're mowing this? By yourself?"

A nod. "For the past few years, yeah."

I couldn't stop staring at the side of her face. "With what?"

"Some really big scissors. I started out with regular scissors but it just took too long." A minimum of thirty seconds passed before I realized she was fucking with me. "I have a lawn mower, Jude."

It wasn't that I didn't believe Audrey could do this. It was that there were moments when I became uncomfortably aware that she'd been on her own for a long damn time with no one to look after her. She had friends ,and their partners had seemed willing to engage in some light waterboarding so I had to assume they'd also pitch in if needed. But she was the one to shovel out her driveway in the winter. To deal with roof leaks and drafty windows and yard work.

It didn't bother me that she had to do all of this; it bothered me that she had to do it alone.

"Where's this mower? I want to take a look at it."

"You're not taking a look at anything," she said. "You'll start that, and the next thing we know, there will be eight million lawn mower pieces spread out across my driveway."

"I think you're aware I can put it back together."

"Yes. Yes, you can. But you'll also tell me why it's a shitty mower or how I should've changed the oil or that you can see I must've mowed over some rocks last year and that's why there's always a weird strip of grass that doesn't get cut." She rolled her eyes. It was adorable. "Don't you have better things to do right now than that anyway?"

I considered this for a second. Aside from the fact I'd been forced to clear my entire calendar over the past few weeks and my life was a special kind of shambles, I had plenty of work to do. There was also a small yet growing mountain of legal issues headed my way. And school was starting in about six weeks and I was no closer to finalizing plans for Percy. But I asked, "Where's this mower?"

"It's in there." She pointed to the far side of the yard, to where a weathered stack of wood that met the loosest definition of a structure stood under a massive maple tree. Another project, then. "Have fun with that."

"What else is on your to-do list?"

She laughed. "How long are you staying?"

"As long as you'll let me."

"Will you please be serious?"

"I am," I shot back.

"Then, what? You're moving in with me?"

I tucked some hair over her ear, let my fingers linger on the curve of her neck. "We *are* engaged."

"We are not engaged," she cried, slapping the grass.

"Did you forget about me telling you the ring is real? I'll go get it—"

"You will stay right there," she said, grabbing a handful of my shirt. "The ring has nothing to do with it."

"It has something to do with it." When she only rolled her eyes, I said, "Give me a few weeks to take care of you. We'll figure out who we are now, and if we like it, and if you want to keep that ring."

"I take care of myself just fine." She released my shirt as she motioned to the tidy yard, the house. As if that was all that required attention around here. Turning back to the blueberries, she said, "And anyway, I decided a long time ago that I don't want to be married again. Once was enough."

I stared at her as she sifted through the berries but she didn't glance over, didn't add any qualifications to that statement. Not *Once was enough with the wrong guy*. Not *I've wasted too much time on dickbag assholes*. Not *Unless it's to you*.

I felt her silence like a boot to the chest but once I caught my breath, I realized this limit was no obstacle to me. So we didn't get married. That was fine. Why did we need to get the government involved anyway? We didn't. We'd do whatever the fuck worked for us. Call it whatever we wanted.

"Works for me," I said, "but it's still your ring. Just tell me when you want it back."

"Jude."

Her voice was like steel but I couldn't hold back a grin. "Audrey."

She watched me for a beat, unimpressed and unyielding, before the façade cracked and a smile spread across her face. "I guess you're staying, then."

I took the blueberry bowl from her hands, set it aside. Pulled her closer, settled her in my lap. "Only if you want us to."

"Do you need to head back to see Brenda anytime soon? What happens next with all that?"

Yeah, I noticed her dodging my last comment. Hard not to. "In about three or four weeks. Another court date." I swallowed hard. "Penny's best friend Maddie filed a request to reassign Brenda's visitation to her."

Audrey shifted to glance back at me, her eyes wide. "Is that something she can do? It's not like custody is just…transferrable. Right?"

"You wouldn't think so," I said. "My attorney keeps saying the petition isn't strong but that we shouldn't ignore it." I ran my fingers through her hair, watching as the sun caught the pale gold strands. "She's been angling for this since Penny died."

"But you're his father," she said, as if that answered every question.

If only it did. "To Brenda and Maddie, I'm the sperm donor who won't go away. The majority of the petition details how I wasn't involved in Percy's life until a few months after he was born."

"Okay but he's almost five," she said. "You've been with him for more than a minute. Doesn't that count for something?"

"It does," I said. "But Maddie was there when he was born. She's been an aunt to him his whole life. And that counts for something too."

"I don't love any of this," she said.

I let her hair slip between my fingers, over my palm. Brushed it against my lips. "Yeah, that makes two of us."

Percy came running over, Bagel right behind him, and he hit the grass with a dramatic flop. He panted while Bagel licked his face. Audrey tried to scoot out of my hold but I wouldn't allow it.

I'd never brought anyone home to meet Percy. Never considered it. Not that I'd had any real opportunities. But now…well, everything about this was different. Maybe I was begging for trouble but I didn't mind the idea of my son getting attached to her. I hoped he did.

I hoped we all got attached—and soon.

"I don't know about you," Audrey started, "but I really think Bagel should meet some other dogs. It's good to go out and make friends, right?" Percy nodded vigorously. She could've asked him if he'd like a dish of sardines for lunch and it would've been the same answer. "Would you like to help me walk Bagel to the dog park?"

Percy sat up and glanced to me, his eyes comically wide. He pressed his palms to his cheeks for a long moment before springing to his feet and signing, "This is the best day of my whole forever life!"

While Percy ran wild around the yard, I brushed my lips over her ear, saying, "I think that's a *yes*."

chapter forty-nine

Audrey

Today's vocabulary word: squelch

I HEAVED A PAIR OF TWENTY-POUND BAGS OF WHOLE WHEAT FLOUR onto the countertop. "And they say baking doesn't build core strength," I muttered to myself.

When I headed back to the side door to collect the rest of my grocery order, I found Percy there, one reusable shopping tote slung over his shoulder and a butternut squash tucked under his arm.

"Look at you! Such a big helper," I said, hurrying to his side. One of those bags had four dozen eggs in it and I understood enough about Bagel's personality to know he'd probably choose this minute to come barreling around the corner and scramble the whole lot of them. I couldn't stomach that. Not in this economy. "That's a super huge squash. You must have some serious muscles."

He beamed up at me as I slipped the bag from his shoulder. We deposited the items on the countertop and went back for the rest.

"I usually bake bread every Saturday but I haven't baked any all month long. Can you believe that?" I asked as I dropped to my knees and peeked into each bag to locate the eggs. "I'm going to make a few loaves today and try out some new recipes. Would you like to be my assistant?"

Percy nodded eagerly and flung himself at me, his arms locking around my neck with more force than I expected. It took me a second to react but then I laughed and patted his back. I couldn't get over how adorable and sweet he was.

He'd tried to teach Bagel the basics of dog park dynamics yesterday. I wasn't sure he knew them himself but his commitment to it was completely precious. Unfortunately, Bagel wanted nothing to do with the dog park. Or dogs, for that matter. And probably all other parks too. None of this deterred Percy. He decided on the walk home that Bagel simply needed some beast training. He was not willing to elaborate on the specifics of beast training.

Later, when we ventured into Boston to wander through the Public Market and visit one of my favorite playgrounds, he insisted on walking with Jude and me on either side of him and holding both our hands. He said it was to prevent *Jude* from getting lost. This made sense, of course, since I knew my way around and Percy was obviously capable of navigating a major city on his own.

Jude only laughed at this. He didn't mind being the weak link and I kind of loved it. Fatherhood looked really good on him. Better than I could've imagined.

Still, it startled me how quickly we all fell into a comfortable rhythm, as if we'd just been waiting to come home to each other. I hadn't been prepared for Percy to immediately fold me into the life he led with Jude. Whether he was moving my foster dog's crate into his bedroom or giving me a knowing look while his father pointed at an airplane coming in for a landing at Logan and rambling off his opinion on the make and model, he held nothing back.

And he was so open with his affection, always reaching for my hand, climbing into my lap to capture my full attention while telling a story, or resting his head on my shoulder when he was tired. He'd asked for a hug at bedtime last night and it loosened something in me that I hadn't realized to be so tight.

Then there was Jude. If I had to draw a pie chart to represent the part of me that was still pissed off and the part that understood and accepted why he'd left after the wedding, the pissed off version would make for a bigger slice of pie than I wanted to admit.

I didn't want to be upset about this. I didn't want it taking up space in my body. I understood what happened and why but I hated feeling as though I wasn't worth a call or even a text. Even if this thing we had going was fragile and glaringly undefined, I didn't like feeling like I could be left waiting. I didn't want this new and improved version of us to start off that way.

But Jude was trying so hard to make up for it. He wouldn't agree to the crazy burger place Percy wanted for dinner until I promised there were multiple safe, appealing items on the menu for me. And then he asked the server for a flight of ciders when I couldn't decide between a few that I liked. When we got back home, he put Percy to work preparing Bagel's dinner and then insisted they'd take the dog for his evening walk while I read my book.

He went looking for my lawn mower this morning and discovered that my garage door opener had died many years ago, and immediately went to work rebuilding the whole sorry thing. He also decided to replace all my exterior light fixtures too. Just grabbed his keys, asked if I knew about the rusted-out sockets (no), if I had a preferred hardware store (also no), and said he'd be back within thirty minutes.

He was back in twenty and had been busy with the lights and the garage door and god only knew what else since.

"Here's what we're going to do," I said to Percy once we had the grocery order unpacked and the eggs safely stowed. "We're going to start with a regular old loaf of sourdough. That's my favorite."

Percy bobbed his head as he tapped the screen of his tablet. "I know," said the mechanical voice.

"Do you like it too?"

"Daddy says I've tried it but I don't remember."

I grabbed my sourdough starter from the shelf. Jamie named it Doughlene. "We'll start with that and then we'll prep some cinnamon roll dough but we're going to make it a very special butternut squash cinnamon roll dough. Lots of autumn vibes. Perfect for Thanksgiving season. If we have enough squash left-over, we'll try a pumpkin cinnamon raisin bread that I've been thinking about. How does that sound?"

"Yes, please!"

I found a small apron for Percy and put him to work at the stand mixer. He was great at gradually adding flour to the mixture and keeping an eye on the dough hook while I peeled and roasted the squash.

I heard the side door close and then Jude strolled through the kitchen, his baseball cap pulled low over his brow and three screwdrivers tucked into the back pocket of his shorts. He had a pair of sunglasses hooked in the neck of his t-shirt and he wore the kind of intense, focused expression that creased his brow and had firmed his jaw. I loved intense, focused Jude. He wasn't great at snapping out of that state but that didn't bother me.

He stopped and eyed us for a second before asking his son, "Are you helping or creating chaos?"

"He's my assistant," I said. Percy nodded in agreement.

He pointed at Percy. "That does not answer my question."

Percy tapped his screen. "I'm helping."

"Do you see chaos here?" I asked.

Jude swept a gaze over the ingredients on the island, the bowls waiting on the side countertops. "If I say yes, will you kick me out?"

I crossed my arms over my chest. "Probably."

He started to respond but stopped himself to stare at the mixer. A moment later, he said, "I'll deal with that when I'm done cutting the lawn."

I glanced between him and the mixer. "Deal with what?"

"There's a gear slipping. I'll fix it when you're finished here."

I knew better than to ask him to explain. Jude used to stop people from using the electric pencil sharpeners at school, swearing he could hear when they were about to jam and that it would take longer to fix if we let it get to that point. It would've been easy to write him off as some kind of spiritual pencil sharpener medium but he was always right. He could hear it.

Apparently, he could hear my mixer jamming too.

"I really love this mixer," I said. "I'll need it back. Soon."

He stepped closer to the island, turned an ear toward the mixer. With a nod, he said, "It won't take long. But don't turn it to the highest setting. It'll make it worse faster." Then he glanced back at his son. "Want me to teach you how to mow a lawn?"

Percy signed something that had Jude laughing in response.

"Understood," Jude said. "But you'll learn one of these days. I'm not sending you out into the world without survival skills."

"I think you have some time," I said. "A decade, at least."

He grinned at me as he pulled off the cap and ran his fingers through his hair. "While you're assisting," he said to Percy, "make sure you show Audrey how good you are at washing dishes." He crossed the room toward me and moved into my space, a hand low on my hip, and brushed a kiss over my lips. "If he's too much, just send him outside."

"We'll be okay."

He stepped back as he settled the cap on his head. "I don't doubt it."

My gaze followed Jude as he moved toward the side door. He turned the hat backward and hooked a glance over his shoulder, taking in my bare feet and flour-dusted apron before closing in on my mouth. His lips turned up though I wouldn't call it a smile. More like a promise of things to come.

With that promise came a pulse deep inside me. A desperate clench. I was sure he'd be pleased to hear that heavy gaze had landed exactly as intended. He didn't do anything without meaning it. I ran a finger over my lips and stared at the door long after it'd closed behind him.

"All done with the flour."

I startled out of my daydream and back toward Percy. "You're the best assistant I've ever had," I said. "So efficient. I might need you to help me bake every weekend."

"Can I? I'm good at following directions."

"That's really important with baking," I said.

"Why?"

"Because there's a lot of science in baking," I said. "Lots of chemical reactions. If you don't follow the directions—the recipe—you won't get the kind of reaction you want."

Percy asked lots of questions about my favorite breads and baked goods, and then asked if we could make small cakes in the shape of Christmas trees.

"I'm sure we could try." I dropped the ball of dough into the proofing bowl and covered it. "I haven't thought too much about Christmas baking yet."

"Maybe we could make them and you could post a video of us baking together."

I nearly dropped the bowl. Surely he didn't mean a blog video. He couldn't. And why would he? That was just my imagination shifting into hyperspeed. He was talking about a parent filming their kid doing something cute and calling it a movie. That was all. "Tell me more about that. What kind of video?"

"You can take a video when we make the tree cakes together. I'll help you and everyone can see. All the people would love that post."

My eyes were prepared to blink their way out of my skull.

But, wait. There was no way Percy was watching videos from my baking blog. That simply was not possible. First of all, he was a child. A child with an internet connection, obviously, but he wasn't on there looking up seedy multigrain bread recipes. He simply was not.

I was being jumpy. That was all. Paranoid for no reason. If I let myself, I could lose entire months to pointless paranoia. I'd wasted the whole year after my divorce worrying about my husband jumping out of a closet and dragging me back to California.

I left the bowl on the far corner of my counter designated for bread proofing and dumped the roasted squash into another bowl now that it was cool. I handed Percy a masher and put the squash in front of him.

"Do you like baking videos?" I asked.

The masher held in one hand like a sword, he typed out his response. "Daddy and I watch them all the time."

"Yeah? Do you have any favorites?"

He started mashing, giggling at the squelching sounds the squash made. "Just your videos."

I stumbled back a step, gripping the edge of the counter for balance. "My videos?"

He glanced up at me, a few specks of squash on his glasses. Nodding, he responded, "We watch all your videos. If Daddy is away when a new one comes out, he saves it for when he's home and we can watch it together."

I felt cold and hot all at once. There was some static in my head and I had to work hard at swallowing. I really would've preferred the paranoia.

"Daddy tried to make your apples but it didn't come out good."

Nodding, I pushed off the counter and started tossing ingredients in the mixing bowl for the cinnamon roll dough. It helped that I could do this without thinking.

"Maybe he used the wrong kind of apples," Percy went on. "I didn't tell him because he was sad they were so mushy."

"That happens sometimes." I added a cup of squash to the mix. I should've weighed it. I always weighed my ingredients when testing recipes but I couldn't focus on anything other than the fact that Jude and Percy followed my blog. They watched my videos. They'd tried my recipes.

And in all the time we'd spent together this month, Jude hadn't mentioned a word of it to me.

"Daddy says you're the—" The robotic voice cut out and I glanced at Percy to find him glowering at the screen. He sighed and lifted his hands, one above his head and the other over his belly.

I knew what that sign meant immediately. "Oh. Yes. Ballerina," I said. "I am. I was." He signed something but I wasn't sure if I understood. "Why? Does this mean *why?*"

I gave my best imitation of the sign and his face lit up in a toothy smile as he nodded.

"I used to be a ballerina," I said simply. "I'm not anymore."

I switched on the mixer as he signed and then used his tablet to ask, "Why not?"

"Before I answer that deeply personal question, let me ask you something, my friend. Will you help me learn how to sign? You can use the app to tell me the words and then show me the sign."

His tablet read, "Yes," as he signed it.

"Just like that," I said. "I was a ballerina when I was in high school. I loved dancing very much but then some things changed. I didn't want to dance anymore."

"Do you still love it?"

"Yes," I said automatically.

He dragged his teeth over his bottom lip as he tapped the screen and I worried he'd ask some intense follow-up questions that I didn't have the heart to answer. "Can we bake tree cakes and make a video together?"

Profound self-analysis averted for another day. "We'll have to ask your dad first and if it's okay with him, we can research some recipes and give it a try."

"He'll say yes," he responded. "I know it. He loves your videos a lot."

Yeah, apparently.

Audrey: guess who showed up at my door last night

Jamie: I'll play this game but only if the answer is Daddy Fiancé

Ruth: yeah same

Ruth: though I've been at work since before the sun was up this morning so I'd still play along even if it's just an obnoxious dude selling solar panels who asked to speak to the "man of the house"

Jamie: I also need the answer to be that you need our help picking out a new mattress today because Fiancé railed you right through the old one last night

Audrey: it was Jude

Audrey: and his son

Audrey: ...and they showed up when Brecken was dropping me off after getting together for dinner

Jamie: I'm listening

Ruth: please tell me you didn't let him inside without a very good explanation for ghosting you

Audrey: his son's grandmother had a bad accident in the kitchen. The whole story is a hot mess but basically, she broke a few bones, burned her arm, and will need a lot of rehab before transitioning to assisted living for dementia care. And the house is toast.

Jamie: oh shit

Ruth: okay fair enough

Audrey: his son witnessed the whole thing and is slightly traumatized because the place was full of smoke from whatever happened with the stove and he couldn't help Grandma out of the house because her hip was broken and other stuff that was all confusing in big ways to a kid

Jamie: that's rough

Ruth: okay but wait. Fiancé couldn't even shoot you a text to say he was alive, some personal shit went down, and he'd talk more later? Not once in 3 weeks?

Jamie: yeah, put me down for that question too

Audrey: believe me, I know

Audrey: the hot new problem on the block is that Percy's mom's best friend wants to take over Grandma's visitation since Grandma won't be sharing custody if she's moving to assisted living

Jamie: no, I don't enjoy that at all

Ruth: family law is not my area but I have questions

Ruth: it would be one thing if we were talking about a temporary switcheroo but it doesn't sound like that's the situation

Audrey: not temporary at all and this friend has been angling for custody for years

Ruth: angling because she knows Grandma will leave us at some point?

Audrey: that and she doesn't like Jude. She told Percy he could come live with her if he wanted.

Jamie: what a helpful thing to say to a small child

Ruth: I want to support all women but sometimes they make it hard on me

Audrey: as you can see, he's had his hands full

Jamie: one thing that's annoying about me is that I can see everyone's perspectives and even if I don't agree, I can still empathize with them

Audrey: it's not annoying

Jamie: Grandma and Friend just want to love this little boy and hold on to any part of his mom that they can. They're making life difficult but they're not evil

Jamie: and at the same time, he could've texted you

Ruth: I see how everything is really fucked up for him and he's probably been trying to focus on the kid but yes, he could've found time to text you once

Audrey: that's basically what I said

Jamie: has he at least spent this time apologizing so hard that you won't be walking right for the next week?

Audrey: something like that

Ruth: ignoring the sex for a minute. Does he know that he's used up all his second chances?

Audrey: seeing me with Brecken made that pretty clear

Jamie: the better question is do you, Miss Audrey, know it's his last second chance?

Audrey: yeah, I do

chapter fifty

Audrey

Today's vocabulary word: coincidence

I CONSIDERED CONFRONTING JUDE ABOUT FOLLOWING MY BAKING blog while I kneaded and rolled out dough. I whipped up a whole monologue about how little I enjoy being the last to know everything while teaching Percy how to make a cream cheese icing.

There was a minute when everything was out of the oven and Percy was busy doing a surprisingly good job at washing some dishes that I considered stomping out to the backyard and standing in the path of the mower until Jude explained himself.

But he sent all those plans out the window when he jogged down to the basement with a Sharpie tucked over his ear and his pen light in hand. I followed him into the utility room and closed the door behind me.

He glanced up from his work at the circuit breaker. "I'm going to take another look at this when you're not using the appliances. I don't like the way it's organized."

He went back to writing something on small labels and sticking them on the panel. "Yeah, okay. Do you think you could explain something to me?"

"Sure, what's up?"

"How is it that your four-year-old child follows my baking blog?"

There was a pause and then I heard the cap of the Sharpie snap into place. Jude turned, shoving the pen light and sticker labels into his pockets. "Percy told you that?"

"He told me a lot of things," I replied. "Among them, the fact that you watch my videos together. I also heard that you attempted one of my recipes. Not well, though."

Jude grimaced at that, muttering, "I should've listened to him about those apples."

I crossed my arms. "I'll just wait until you're ready to explain."

He dropped his hands to his hips and stared up at the ceiling. After a minute, he said, "I opened social media accounts to keep track of what's going on with Brenda. She likes posting a fuckton of photos whenever Percy's with her and long, emotional stuff about Penny. It's good for knowing where her head's at."

I was pleased with myself for not offering an encouraging nod but simply rolling my hand for him to continue.

"Your account kept coming up as someone I might know. I ignored it at first. Didn't think anything of it. But then I opened the app one day when my phone's audio volume had been cranked up and it autoplayed your video. I heard your voice and—" He laughed to himself. "I remember leaving the office and going to my car so I could listen without anyone else around. It was a recipe for these little blackberry peach pies."

I remembered those pies because I'd made them using an over-sized pierogi press. To this day, still one of my finest thrift store finds.

Also notable: that recipe was from three years ago. I remembered because that was before I managed to get ahead on my posting schedule and the local blackberries had given me hell. Too juicy. Every test batch came out of the oven looking like a crime had been committed. I'd tossed in the peaches as a last-ditch effort to save blackberry week.

"I watched it on a loop for at least fifteen minutes," Jude continued, "just listening to you explain how important it was to use cold butter."

"It really is essential," I murmured.

"I didn't actually believe it," he said. "At first. Even though I knew your voice and I recognized your hands, I didn't trust it. I didn't want to."

"Why not?"

"I don't know," he admitted. "It'd been a hard few months. Percy still wasn't talking and no one knew whether it was a delay or something more significant. Brenda wanted me to move up to Saginaw and she hated that I wouldn't. I didn't want to believe you were right there, kneading dough and explaining how you made vanilla sugar. Like you'd disappear if I did."

I felt myself softening slightly. Just slightly. "And you didn't think to share this at any point? I seem to recall several long road trips."

His brows winged up. "Yeah, because you were in such an open, accepting place during those road trips, Audrey. You would've thrown yourself out of the car and run into the fucking desert if I'd mentioned watching every video you've ever posted."

It was possible he was right about that. "Then you should've brought it up after the engagement party. When we talked."

"Yeah, probably." He tipped his head to the side. "But I didn't want to spend the whole night on history. Not when it seemed like we finally understood each other again." He ran his knuckles over his chin. "And you were naked. That had a lot to do with it."

"And Percy? How did he get involved?"

"Ah. Well." Jude pulled some of the tools from his pockets,

studying them before returning them to the shelving unit where I kept extra light bulbs, lawn bags, and garden clippers. "Percy picks up any virus within five miles of him. When he was three, there wasn't a full month that he wasn't sick with something. He'd only fall asleep if I held him." He patted his chest, right where his son's head would rest. "But he caught me watching your videos one night. He was hooked right from the start."

I wanted to be annoyed. To harp on him keeping this secret for so long. But all I could ask was, "Is there anything else you need to tell me?"

He lifted a shoulder. "Probably."

"Care to unburden yourself while I'm in a forgiving mood?"

He stared at me for a long minute before saying, "Through a strange series of coincidences, one of my closest friends is your boss's brother's business partner."

"My—what? You know Lauren's brother?"

"Not personally, no," he said. "But I know his business partner Jordan Kaisall."

"And how do you know Jordan?"

He yanked the hat off and pushed a hand through his hair. "Remember how I said I got fed up with corporate aeronautics a few years ago? And I thought about giving it all up to manage a fleet?"

I gave him an impatient shake of my head. "Vaguely."

"That's how I met Jordan. Interviewing for a job managing his fleet."

"And you went into this knowing his partner's sister was the principal of my school? I mean, how did you even find that out? And why?"

"No, I had no idea," he said quickly. "No, fuck no. Jesus. I've done a lot of fucked-up things for you but that's a bit much, even for me." He scrubbed a hand down his face, laughing. "They did a deep-dive background check before the second interview and brought the connection to my attention. I knew you'd left your ex and moved to Boston at that point but the rest came as a surprise. An awkward one, at that."

"Is that why it didn't work out?"

He shook his head. "It became apparent that I'd get bored with the gig within six months. And I sleep better at night, not knowing all the shit Jordan gets involved in."

"You knew I'd left Chris?"

A muscle in his jaw ticked before he said, "Yeah."

"How?"

There had been no announcements. No social media posts. I'd just gathered the handful of things I'd wanted to keep from our home in San Diego and boarded a flight to Boston to move on with my life.

Another long stare and then, "I used to search the California court filings every few months."

"Oh, yeah. Okay. That's not psychotic at all." I paced away from him and toward the washer and dryer stationed at the other end of the utility room. I started tossing some towels into the washing machine. We'd accumulated quite the pile with Bagel rolling in every spot of mud he could find. "I'm not sure whether the most unhinged part is you being so confident that my marriage would crumble, you set a calendar reminder to check for my divorce filing. Or the fact that you knew it'd ended and you still waited until last month to say anything to me. Or that when you finally found me, it was to guilt me into a fake engagement."

"I did say I've done a lot of fucked-up things for you."

I didn't respond to that. I just threw a detergent pod into the basin and banged the lid shut. After I started the machine, I turned around, my lips pursed in a hard line and my arms locked over my chest. "Why did you wait so long?"

"Why did *I* wait?" He crossed the room toward me, tapping a finger to the center of his chest. "Why the fuck did *you* wait? Why didn't you call me the minute you were rid of him?"

"What did you want me to do?" I cried. "I thought you hated me for how I left. I thought you never wanted to see me again."

"Don't you get it? After all this time, don't you see it yet? There is nothing you could ever do that would keep me away." He ran his knuckles up the side of my neck and along my jaw, and then brushed his thumb over my lips. "I'll always belong to you, even if you don't belong to me."

I swallowed hard as his hand settled on the back of my neck. "And what if I do? What if I belong to you?"

"Then we start over and we get it right this time."

He leaned in, captured my lips, and brought his free hand to my hip. My backside connected with the washer as I knotted my hands in his shirt. His thigh slipped between my legs and I rocked against the solid ridge of him trapped behind his zipper. All at once, I was hot and wet, my inner muscles aching with the need to be stretched and filled.

He pressed into me, groaning. *"Audrey."*

These shorts hid nothing at all and with him wedged up against me like this, it felt like he could pull the crotch out of the way and thrust into me. And I wanted that very much. I wanted him inside and—and I didn't want it to end. Not today, not in a few weeks, not ever.

"Say something," he growled, his lips on my jaw, my neck.

"It scares me," I said. "I don't think I could survive if this fell apart again."

"We won't let it." He hooked my leg around his waist and dragged his hand up from my knee to my backside. Those fingers gripped my flesh hard, like he wanted to leave a mark just so he could come back tomorrow and kiss it better. There was something proprietary about the way he touched me. Like he'd just been waiting for me to realize what all of this meant and why he was here, and now he could stop holding back. "We just won't let it, Saunders."

I wanted to believe him though there were more than a few significant roadblocks in our way. "But—"

Jude didn't let me finish. He stole my lips in a bruising kiss and rocked his erection against me and that was the end of our conversation. I dragged my nails over the ropey muscles of his back and shoulders, wanting to dig into him, to claim a piece of him for myself just as he claimed me.

He pushed my shorts and undies down to my ankles and I had to admit that was better than my *pull the crotch out of the way* idea. Less cumbersome. Better for all involved.

He slipped a hand between my legs, growling as he drew circles around my clit. I was wet, shockingly so, and there was no hiding it now.

"What did it for you?" he asked, quite pleased with himself. "Hearing how completely you own me? Or realizing that I might actually be a stalker?"

I yanked the shirt over his head. "Neither. I'm just—I don't know. It's overwhelming to talk about trying to be us again."

"You could've told me that." He kissed his way along my jaw, back to the corner of my mouth.

I worked his belt open, pushed his clothes to the concrete floor. "I just did."

"You only told me because I pushed."

"Says the guy creeping on my baking blog for years. You can tell me things too, you know."

He took his cock in hand and gave it a long, slow stroke. "Are you ready to hear all the things I have to tell you?"

"Yes." I ran a hand through his hair before adding, "Maybe."

Growling, he pushed inside me with one slow thrust and held

himself there as I gasped and shuddered. My grip on his hair was brutal but I couldn't help it. The pressure was unreal. Heat washed over my skin. I closed my eyes as I tried to talk my body into opening up a little more. That was all I needed. Just a little more.

"Oh god," I gasped. "I need— Wait. I can't. It's too much."

"You just need to breathe," he said. "Come on, princess. Breathe for me."

I fought to pull in air, to find that space inside myself. "It's like I can feel you everywhere."

"Good." He gave me a hard, quick kiss as my muscles yielded to him. "Now, let's get back to that *maybe*." His hand settled on the small of my back, canting my hips as he moved deeper inside me. My lips parted on a silent cry. "You can do better than *maybe*."

"You can tell me anything." The tension building inside me was too much. I couldn't bear it, not like this. Not all at once. I felt tears gathering behind my eyes and a deep, twisting ache low in my belly. "I won't jump out of the car."

"Anything? You're sure about that?"

He pulled out slowly, each inch dragging over my tender flesh like a promise—a threat?—of what was to come. "Anything," I whispered. "Please, just—*yes*."

He flattened me against the washer before the last word left my lips. I had one hand curled around the back of his neck, the other gripping his shoulder, and it was the best I could do to steady myself while he thrust into me.

"Can I tell you that I haven't stopped loving you?" he asked, digging his fingers into my hip. "Not once? Not even when I *needed* to stop loving you more than I needed anything else in the world?"

"Tell me." I dropped my head to his shoulder, brushed my lips over the pulse hammering in his throat. "Tell me all of it."

"I've never loved anyone else and I hated you for keeping me for yourself," he said, the words hoarse. "I hated that you walked away but I couldn't leave you."

My belly swooped and a fresh new rush of blazing heat moved through me. I watched as the muscles in his arms and shoulders pulsed with every thrust. His jaw ticked and I had to lift a hand to his face just to feel it under my fingers.

Everything inside me seemed to gather and twist. My back arched off the washing machine as my inner walls tightened, giving a painful throb. I'd do anything to come right now. Anything at all.

"I love you too," I said. "Always have."

"Say it again."

"I love you," I said, my body quivering now. "I never stopped."

He met my eyes as he rocked into me once more. "I know."

Some orgasms were explosions. Some were like getting caught in the barrel of a wave. But then there were some that unraveled like a ball of yarn that slipped out of your hands and down a flight of stairs—and those were the most devastating because they started slow but stretched on until there was nothing left.

All I could do was press my mouth to his neck and dig my fingers into his skin and hope he understood that anything that might've stood between us was gone. All those years, everything we'd thought to be true—shattered.

He growled something that I was too slow and woozy to understand and then I felt him swell and surge inside me. We stayed there, gasping and shaking and clinging to each other. My head was full of white noise and my backside was pancaked against the washing machine. I'd probably wear an imprint of the logo on my upper right butt cheek for the next week.

"I don't know if I'm allowed to say this," Jude started.

"Then you're probably not."

He reached for my hand, lacing our fingers together and sliding our joined palms between our bodies. He traced where he still pulsed inside me. I shuddered when he painted my folds and my clit with his release. "This feels so much better than I ever remembered."

"We barely knew what we were doing back then," I said. "I mean, the only objective was doing it without getting caught. Not a lot of technique involved."

He went on stroking me as he considered this, his cock still buried inside me and rearranging my organs. "Does that mean it wasn't good for you?"

"I remember it being good," I said. "But I like that we're better at it now. And that we don't have to sneak around."

"We *are* better at it." He gave my backside a light slap. "But you're amazing. When I'm inside you, it's so good that I can't think. It feels like you're stealing something from me but I don't mind because I want you to take it. Take all of it, everything. Suck me dry."

I huffed out a laugh. "That's just because we don't need condoms anymore."

"No, Audrey. It's because I fucking love you and I've been waiting to get you back for a literal fucking decade and now that I have you, the only place I want to be is inside you. It's because no one will ever be able to convince me that we weren't made for each other. That we fit right here"—he pressed my palm hard against my mound—"better than anyone else ever could. And we fit here"—he rested his forehead against mine—"better than anyone else. It's because I touch you and I feel like I know how to exist in this world. Like I'm awake and alive again."

I nodded because yes, that was the truth of it, even if I'd avoided finding that reflection in the mirror for weeks. I kissed the corner of his mouth. I didn't think I could say anything and even if I did, it wouldn't be adequate.

But I knew there was no going back now. We weren't the same people who argued in that bathroom at the reunion and we weren't the same ones who'd shared a bed in that terrifying motel room. We weren't even the same as we were last night.

And what a relief that was.

A knock sounded on the door and then the voice from Percy's tablet asked, "Are you guys in there?"

Our eyes locked. Jude cleared his throat. "Yeah, we're just— we're fixing something," he called. "Why don't you go upstairs and hang out with Bagel? We'll be up in a minute."

"He's sleeping," the tablet announced.

"Okay, well, hold on and we'll be there soon," Jude said, glancing at the discarded clothes all around us. He set me down, holding my waist as I found my footing. "We just need to put something back together."

"Can I help?" Percy asked.

"Jesus Christ," he breathed as we scrambled to pull on clothes. "Not this time, pal. You don't have the right safety gear for this one."

After a long pause, the tablet said, "I'm going to read my book in the backyard."

When we heard his steps on the basement stairs, we stared at each other for a second and then burst out laughing. "I guess we're not done sneaking around," I said.

"Apparently not." He skimmed a thumb over my cheek. "I do love you."

I pushed some hair off his forehead. "I love you too."

He flattened a hand to the lid of the washing machine and stared at it for a minute. I'd barely noticed it running all this time. "The agitator is starting to go," he said.

"What? No. It's still new. I bought it when I moved in. It's only a few years old."

"They don't build these things to last anymore. If it were up to me, I'd hang onto the old ones as long as possible. They require a lot more attention and care but they're worth it." He stared at the washer for another moment before saying, "I'll add this to my list."

"Now you have a list? What else are you fixing up around here?"

A grin warmed his eyes as he cupped my cheek. "Anything you'll let me get my hands on."

chapter fifty-one

Audrey

Today's vocabulary word: inflection

THOSE FIRST DAYS WITH JUDE AND PERCY QUIETLY SLIPPED INTO A week and then another, and soon I couldn't remember a time when they weren't here with me. On the other side of that came the sudden realization of how quiet and empty my house had been without them. It wasn't until my kitchen table was full every morning or Percy took over the entirety of my couch that I saw how little space I'd taken up before.

Jude caught up on work while Percy charged ahead with his so-called beast training sessions for Bagel. This mostly amounted to Percy setting up obstacle courses in the backyard and attempting to guide Bagel through...only for Bagel to roll around in the grass. Neither of them seemed to tire of it.

We baked a lot of bread and filmed a bunch of videos together. His little hands showed up in a few places where he added ingredients to the mixer or spread flour over the countertop. After some testing, we made individual cakes in the shape of Christmas trees. It wasn't my usual style of baking. I didn't get involved with anything that required much decoration and definitely nothing with food dyes since my whole angle was gentle eats for angry guts but we made it work. And Percy was so proud.

On the days when Jude was tied up with calls, Percy and I walked to the dog park or traveled to my school to start setting up my classroom. He liked arranging desks, cutting out laminated items for my bulletin boards, and organizing my library. When he finished with those projects, he wandered across the hall to help in the third-grade classroom or made himself at home with the beanbag chairs in my cozy corner while I worked on lesson plans.

We always had fun together, even when he asked if he could come to school with me every day and I had to figure out an answer that didn't sound like a side-step. It was a lot harder dodging an almost-five-year-old's questions than you'd think, especially given their willingness to follow it up with *Why?* four thousand times.

I wanted it to be easier for him. For Jude too but Percy most of all. He wanted to feel like he belonged somewhere. I knew what that was like. Probably more than I'd taken time to recognize.

At night, when Percy was tucked away in the guest room with Bagel's crate parked beside the bed, Jude and I watched some of the TV series I was vaguely invested in. At least once an episode, he'd press pause and turn to me, asking, "What the fuck is this shit, Saunders?" or "You were going to haunt my ass if you died before seeing the end of this train wreck? Seriously?" or "Explain to me again why she's even interested in that dirtbag."

My favorite of Jude's complaints was "When I die, I'm going to haunt *you* for making me watch this."

I always patted his chest and promised we'd find reasons to haunt each other. We'd done it most of our lives so why wouldn't we do it in the next?

By virtue of chaotic summer schedules, I hadn't seen much of my friends. Jamie taught at a city art program in the mornings and waitressed at a rooftop bar in the evenings. Ruth was always in the middle of a work crisis. Emme was off on her honeymoon. Grace and Ben were visiting his family. Shay had one wedding after another lined up at Twin Tulip.

All that changed this weekend. Emme and Grace were still out of town but everyone else was heading down to Friendship, Rhode Island for one of the town's many festivals. I couldn't wait. I'd been telling Percy stories about Friendship and hyping up the festival for weeks.

Still, Jude had some questions.

"What do you mean we're going to a *corn* festival?" Jude asked once we hit the highway.

"Think of it as a corn party thrown by a bunch of the local farms," I said.

"That's not nearly the explanation you think it is, Saunders," he said.

"Daddy, it's a festival about corn," Percy's tablet announced from the back seat.

"You are correct, sir, although I still don't understand what takes place at a festival about corn," Jude replied.

"We eat the corn," Percy's tablet said.

His communication app didn't offer much emphasis or intonation unless he used exclamation points or question marks though I'd come to interpret the text-to-speech output with his personality. And as I learned ASL, I heard more of his voice in there too. Even with him in the back seat, I knew there was a sassy, petulant expression on his face and that he would've signed all the exasperation he could conjure into those words.

"Yep, lots of corn to eat. Corn on the cob, corn cakes, corn dogs, kettle corn," I said.

"I can eat twelve corn dogs at one time," Percy said.

"Not at one time, please." Jude glanced at his son in the rearview mirror. "Individually. One after another. Unless you've learned how to unhinge your jaw and forgot to mention it to me. And since you didn't pack a barf bag, my friend, it probably won't be twelve but I admire the ambition."

"There were a few different corn chowders last year and lots of games," I said. "Oh, and all kinds of local whiskey and bourbon."

"You could've led with that last part," Jude said under his breath.

"Is that your way of telling me that I'll be the one driving us home?"

He laced his fingers with mine. "We'll see."

I gave his hand a squeeze. We didn't have much time left. He was due back in Michigan for Percy's custody hearing next week, not that we talked much about it. School started for me the week after and I really didn't know where any of that left us.

I wanted to ask but I didn't. Not when the answers would slice into the time we had left. It wasn't better this way, it wasn't easier. But at least I could pretend.

I had a lot of experience with that.

chapter fifty-two

Audrey

Today's vocabulary word: flourish

AS WE ROLLED TO A STOP IN FRONT OF SHAY AND NOAH'S farmhouse, Percy asked, "Is that a pirate ship?"

"It is," I said with a laugh. "Noah's niece Gennie really likes pirates. He built a pirate ship clubhouse onto her swing set."

"Can I try it?" he asked.

"I'm sure Gennie would love to show you around. She's a little older than you. But I think you'll have a lot of fun with her. She's a really cool kid."

"Am I a cool kid?"

I shifted in my seat to face him. "You are one of the coolest kids I know and I've met lots of kids," I said. "Come on. Let's go find Gennie and check out this pirate ship."

As we spilled out of the car, Shay emerged from the house, a hand shielding her eyes from the sun. "You're here," she yelled, hurrying down the porch steps. She waved at Jude when she spotted him. "And you too!"

He raised a hand in greeting and he probably responded to her as well but I was too happy to see my dear old friend to notice. I rounded the car, my arms outstretched toward her. "We wouldn't miss it." We rocked back and forth in the kind of soul-fortifying hug that only Shay could give.

"You look amazing," she said, holding me at an arm's-length. "Whatever you're doing, it's working for you."

"And you," I said, motioning to her newly bobbed hair. "I love this length on you."

She smoothed a hand over the rose gold strands, grinning. "Everyone gets a back-to-school cut around here."

"Speaking of which…" I glanced back to find Percy trying to disappear behind Jude. He had an arm hooked around Jude's leg but his face was mashed into his father's shorts. "Is your niece around? I'd like her to meet my friend Percy."

"Just one sec." Shay held up a finger before jogging up the stairs. She rang an antique brass bell mounted beneath the porch light and then returned to the gravel drive. She bent down, saying, "Hi, Percy. I'm Shay."

He offered a small wave and went back to hiding behind Jude when a bellowed cry of "I'm coming!" came from the far side of the yard. Gennie sprinted to the driveway, a pair of old mutts trailing well behind her.

"Aunt Audrey," she shouted as she skidded to a stop in front of us. She threw her arms around my waist, knocking me back a step. "I've missed the shit out of you."

Jude coughed. "What just happened?"

"It's fine. Just go with it," I said to him as I smoothed a hand down the girl's ponytail. "I've missed you too, sweet girl. How was theater camp?"

"Amazing," she replied. "I learned how to do a kick line. I tried practicing at home but I broke a lot of bowls and cups and shit, and now I have to practice in the barn."

I stifled a laugh at that. "I don't know if Shay told you I'd be bringing some friends with me today but I have a few people I'd like for you to meet." I walked her closer to Jude and Percy, saying, "This is Percy. He noticed your clubhouse the minute we arrived. Would you want to give him a tour?"

She waved at him. "Hi. I'm Gennie." The dogs finally caught up with her and Percy's eyes grew wide when they gave him a thorough sniff. "That's Starsky and that one's Hutch. They live here. If you put out your hand like this"—she opened her palm—"they'll give you a shake. It's the only trick they know."

Percy held out his hand for the dogs and, right on cue, they took turns shaking. He laughed as they licked his hand too, and then all over his face. He snatched his tablet from Jude and quickly typed out, "My brother Bagel is a dog but he doesn't know how to shake."

"Your brother's a dog?" Gennie asked.

"Your— What?" Jude peered at the screen as if he expected to find a typo. "That's not how it works, young man."

"Yeah, it is. Bagel is my brother," Percy replied. "I told him we're brothers and he said that was okay."

Jude glanced at me over Percy's head, a completely bewildered look on his face. "What do I do with that?" he whispered.

"Nothing," I whispered back. "Let it be. He'll forget soon enough."

"Really?" Jude asked.

"I have no idea but it's worth a try," I said.

"I changed my mind," Gennie said to Shay. "I'll take a brother or sister if it's a dog."

"You have enough dogs," Shay said. "Enough dogs, enough cats, enough goats, enough chickens—"

"Don't remind me about the chickens," she said, covering her ears.

"I'd never want a chicken for a brother," Percy said.

Gennie dropped her hands and studied him closely. "Is that how you talk?" she asked, staring at the tablet. He nodded. I sensed Jude stiffen. "There's a kid in my class, Levi, and he uses an iPad too."

"Do you know sign language?" The tablet read out the question while Percy signed it.

Gennie shook her head but tried to reproduce his signs. "No. But I'll teach you the pirate codes anyway."

I heard a breath whoosh out of Jude. I glanced at him, offering my best *trust me on this one* smile.

"Do the codes unlock ancient prophecies?" Percy asked.

"Now, isn't that a great question. I wonder if we can find out any answers over here on the pirate ship," I called, crossing toward the swing set. "Oh, look. No one's on the best swing. I guess it's all mine."

Percy and Gennie shot past me. She went for the monkey bars while he climbed the ladder to the slide. I took a turn on the swings while they blitzed through the apparatus. I liked listening to them figure out how to play together. He relied on the tablet to start but soon enough, they fell into an easy rhythm where they just understood each other.

When it seemed like they had it under control, I strolled back to Shay and Jude. Noah had joined a few minutes earlier, his all-terrain vehicle parked near the farmhouse. He tugged me into a one-armed hug when I approached but didn't stop explaining an issue of some sort to Jude.

"They keep telling me nothing's wrong but I know it doesn't sound right," Noah said.

"It's the fan," Jude said. "The electrical systems on these newer models are a disaster and the fans always end up fucked one way or another." He dipped his hands into his pockets, shrugged. "If we have a few minutes, I could probably fix it."

"Now? Seriously?" Noah rubbed a hand over the back of his neck. "Yeah, of course. The corn isn't going anywhere. What do you need?"

Jude jogged back to the car, reached into the back seat, and pulled out a small case he had stowed there. "Pop it open and we'll figure it out."

Shay and I watched while they examined the ATV. "Boys and their toys," she said.

"Every time," I murmured.

"Do you want a drink or anything? A beach chair? A sun bonnet? The newest issue of *People* magazine?"

I chuckled. "Do you have all of those things?"

She thought about it for a second. "Yeah, I think so. I need to duck inside for a sec because I had an incident with the cold brew and now I need to change my top." She pointed to a stain that I wouldn't have noticed. "I also need to find my phone and put on some sunscreen before we embark on a festival journey."

"I'm good," I said. "I'll keep an eye on the pirates."

I kept a comfortable distance while Jude presented an advanced course on ATV engines and the kids played on the swings. A few minutes passed before I spotted an unfamiliar car turning down the driveway.

I didn't think much of it because everyone seemed to love and tolerate each other in this small town and Shay was full of stories of folks dropping by with bread and gossip. But then Jamie climbed out of the SUV, yelling, "Hello, Friendship. Do you feel me? I'm in you!"

Ruth emerged from the driver's side, frowning at Jamie over the hood. "I can't believe you talked me into this."

"James! Ruth!" I cried, striding toward them. "You're here!"

"Get over here, baby girl," Jamie said. "Where's that fiancé of yours?"

I pointed to the ATV as I gave her a squeeze. "He's not my fiancé."

"You might not be his fiancée but he's yours," she said.

"I'm not debating this with you today," I said, laughing. "It's so good to see you." I pulled Ruth in for a hug. "I didn't think you'd make it."

Ruth pointed to Jamie. "This one told me she was stranded in the city."

I gaped at Jamie. "You could've gotten a ride with us."

"Yeah but how else would I have sprung her from the office?" Jamie waved this off, crossing her arms. "I make no apologies for my antics."

"Never have," I muttered, folding her into a hug.

"Could you apologize for the part where you told me this was a porn festival?" Ruth asked.

"I never said it was a porn festival," Jamie said.

"You used the corn emoji," Ruth said. "That's universally known as code for porn. Even my senior partner knows that and he thinks the Macarena is still trending."

"If you'd prefer it to be a porn festival, we might have more in common than I originally thought," Jamie said.

"It's not that I prefer porn," Ruth said.

"It sounds like you prefer porn," Jamie said, rolling her lips together as she fought off a laugh. "And that's great! I also prefer porn to corn. Honestly, who doesn't?"

"I don't," I said.

"Okay, but that's only because we haven't found the right porn for you," Jamie said. "I'm still looking. I'll get back to you soon."

"You really don't have to do that," I said. "In other news: how are you, James? How are you feeling?"

"Quite tragically, I feel a million times better when I'm not drinking or having sex. But taking all that away is like kicking out two legs on this tripod of mine."

"What's the third leg?" Ruth asked.

"Witchcraft," Jamie said. "Obviously."

"You are much more than sex and alcohol," I said.

"And witchcraft," Ruth muttered.

"It's just going to take you some time to find your new normal," I said.

"Audrey, darling, precious, love. Listen," Jamie said with a sigh. "I've found the new normal and it consists of watching fourteen different spin-off versions of NCIS with my dad while frighteningly sober. I don't even get to go and choke on a dick after that. I crawl into bed at a respectable hour, not covered in jizz, and wake up without any unexplainable bruises."

"This is how I felt when I stopped being able to tolerate gluten and a dozen other things," I said.

"You were disappointed about not going to bed covered in jizz?" Ruth asked.

"Yes. Nightly," I said to her, completely straight-faced. "It just felt like my world had turned upside down and everything that'd once been an ordinary part of my life, something I'd barely even thought about, was now a huge, dangerous problem."

"I just hate that I'm boring," Jamie said.

"The only version of you I've ever known has been the sober, celibate one," Ruth said. "Trust me when I say there's nothing boring about you."

I pointed at Ruth. "Listen to her."

"That's right, listen to me," Ruth said. "You should know by now that I don't bullshit anyone."

"And it won't be like this forever," I added. "You just need to stay healthy for a bit before easing back in and figuring out the limits."

"I really hope so," Jamie said.

"You'll be going to bed covered in jizz again before you know it," I said.

I felt an arm settle around my waist and then, "How is that I've never heard you use that word before?"

I nudged my elbow into Jude's side. "Quiet, you."

"I've known you a long time," he went on, "but this is a new one."

"Jamie brings it out in me," I said, laughing.

"You're welcome." She sidled closer. "So good to see you again, Daddy. It was such a long time between visits. Nice of you to stick around."

"Oh. Um. Yeah. You're right about—about that." Jude cleared his throat and glanced away. It was a real treat to see him leveled by Jamie Rouselle, a pattypan squash of a woman. "Good to see you too."

"Don't worry," she said, leaning in even closer. "I don't bite —much."

"Put it back in your pants, Morticia," Ruth said, play-shoving Jamie aside. "Hi. We did not meet when you popped in for that come-and-go with our girl last month but I'm Ruth Ralston. I'm an attorney and despite the fact you put Audrey through some very pointless hell, I don't like anything I've heard about your ongoing custody battles."

Jude's fingers flexed on my waist as he listened. He shot a quick glance at Percy, still busy with Gennie, before saying, "I don't like it either but there's not much I can do."

Ruth pulled out her phone and started scrolling. "I'm not your attorney. I don't represent you. This is not legal advice. I don't even specialize in family law," she said.

Noah must've heard something that interested him because he looked up from the now-fixed ATV and called, "Who needs a family law attorney?"

"Jude does," Ruth shouted back.

"I have an attorney," Jude said.

"Not a good one if this situation is still going to court," Ruth said. "This should've been resolved between counsel or in media-tion." She went back to her phone. "I'm trying to find contact info for a friend of a friend who has a lot of experience with nonlinear custody situations and kinship petitions."

"It's going to court? Why didn't you say something sooner? What's the situation?" Noah wiped his hands on a bandana as he joined us. "I'm only a farmer by family. Lawyer by trade."

Ruth held up a hand, saying, "Yeah, but you're a corporate litigation wonk like me. Family law is an entirely different ballgame."

"It is, though I did adopt my sister's daughter just a few years ago, so I've been on the field once or twice." Noah grinned up at the farmhouse as Shay stepped out onto the porch. "We'll talk this over at the festival. They'll have liquor. I find that helps."

chapter fifty-three

Audrey

Today's vocabulary word: resolve

"REMIND ME WHY WE'RE DOING CHOWDER IN AUGUST," JAMIE SAID, pushing her bowl to the center of the picnic table.

"I tried to warn you," I said. "You were the one who wanted to sample all three varieties."

Jamie folded her arms on the table and put her head down. "It's very rude to remind someone of their bad decisions to their face."

"Can anyone explain these things to me?" Ruth tapped her plastic fork to the side of the paper basket. "I just want to know what I'm eating. *What* is a jonnycake? *Who* is Jonny? Is he in there or is it just his ghost at this point?"

"It's a cornmeal cake," Shay said. "A thick batter cooked on a griddle. Very Rhode Island. They love a good gristmill around here."

"Not a single Revolutionary War spirit fried into this thing? What a letdown," Ruth said.

"Not to get us too far off-track," Shay said as she gathered our discarded bowls and baskets, "but it sounds like you're going to have to make some very big decisions very soon, Audrey."

I glanced across the field to where Noah and Jude stood near a row of cornhole games, drinks in hand. They'd been stationed there for the past hour while Gennie and Percy competed in an under-ten tournament. I wasn't sure it was a tournament so much as a few high school kids who kept rotating the players from one match to another, and never knocked anyone out of the running. Not that we had a problem with that approach.

"I mean, maybe," I said. I knew I was hedging. I also knew it wouldn't do me any good. "I'm hoping it all just sorts itself out."

"Baby girl," Jamie drawled, her head still pillowed on her arms. "That's not a strategy. Or, it is but it's not *your* strategy."

"Believe me, I understand the desire to sit back and excuse yourself from making those decisions," Shay said. "Though I know you don't actually want that."

"No, I don't but— There's just so much up in the air." I shook my head. "And am I really the one making the decisions here? Doesn't Jude have to decide? He has a lot more on the line than I do."

"Debatable," Ruth said.

"Just stop for a second," Shay said. "Get out of your head and look at him over there with Noah and the kids."

"Are we looking at the shorts?" Jamie asked. "Because while I don't enjoy most shorts on most men, they're both doing it very right."

"We're not looking at their shorts," Shay said.

"But can we?" Ruth asked. "There's a lot to admire."

"We are looking at the fact that this guy came to a *corn festival* in a wacky little Rhode Island town in the *middle of August*," Shay said with a laugh. "And then there's the fact that when his world went to shit, you were his soft place to land—and he's stayed there ever since. Even when that involves a ridiculous festival on the hottest day of the year. He could've left at any time. He could've taken his kid home. He didn't." She pointed at me with her fork. "He's made his decision. You need to make yours."

"I just..." I yanked the elastic from my hair and started gathering the strands into a bun. It really was unbelievably hot and we were sitting in the shade. "I don't want to get it wrong. I'm not good at making the right choices when it's really important and I just feel like—" I blew out a breath and shook my head. I didn't know what else to say.

"You feel you'd rather make no decision than the wrong one," Shay said. "I know. I've been there. It's miserable. But not making a decision is a decision by itself."

"We'll make a list," Ruth said, pulling a pen from her bag and unfolding a napkin. "Let's start with the basics. You want to keep this thing going with him, right?"

I rolled a bottle of water between my palms. "Yeah. I do. But Jude and Percy live in Virginia, and there's a family situation in Michigan, and I work in Boston, which is just a giant mess."

"Not a mess," Ruth said as she wrote out her notes. "Just a series of options, each with their own merits and challenges."

"You could move to Virginia," Shay said. "We'd miss you like crazy but it's not like you'll ever get rid of us."

"Never," Jamie added. "We'll find you."

"Or Jude and Percy could move here," I said. It felt strange saying that out loud after thinking it for the past few weeks. Maybe because I'd been waiting for Jude to say it first.

"You've mentioned that Jude travels a fair bit for work and he has some flexibility on where he's based," Ruth said.

"You'd be able to enroll Percy in our kindergarten class," Jamie said. "Aurora's best friend is hard-of-hearing. She grew up with ASL *and* she's had several kiddos in her class using adaptive communication tools."

"I didn't know about the ASL," I said. "I did think about enrolling him. But he won't be five until the end of September."

"That's not a problem," Shay said. "I always had a friend or two who didn't turn five until some time in the first month or two of school. It's an independent school. The rules are different from typical public districts. I know Lauren wouldn't mind. Especially if it's your kid."

"He's not *my* kid," I said.

"Maybe not yet," Shay said. "But a day will come when you will know without any question that he's your baby. You'll have a hard time remembering who you were before he took over your life. And it will surprise the hell out of you but you'll be okay with that."

I didn't respond. I didn't think I could since I was busy wondering if that day had already come. Was it too soon? Was it presumptuous of me? Or unfair to Penny, who'd gotten so little time with her son? I didn't have any of the answers.

When Ruth started clicking her pen, I asked, "But what about the custody thing? What if he ends up splitting custody with the friend and has no other choice but to move to Michigan?"

"That's not going to happen," Ruth said. "Custody for the grandmother was a stretch. The friend is straight-up bananapants and I'm annoyed that his attorney hasn't made it go away."

"But let's say it does happen." Shay caught my eye, nodding. She knew that I needed to think through even the most unlikely scenarios. "Would you follow them to Michigan? Is that an option for you?"

"Or would you try to make a long-distance relationship happen?" Jamie asked.

I clasped my fingers under my chin as I considered this. "Michigan could be an option but long-distance... I don't see how we'd ever succeed at that."

Ruth clicked the pen a few more times. "Why not?"

"Just look at the drama we lived through last month," I said.

"When he's with Percy, he's completely present and he wants to keep it that way. Maybe that was one wild situation but when he isn't traveling for work, he wants to be home with his kid. He's not glued to his phone. He doesn't want to get on another plane to see me."

"If he wanted to, he would," Jamie said.

"Yeah, but is that a fair rule when we're talking about a single parent who has a cancer-survivor mother to look after? Not to mention his son's grandmother? Even if he wants to, there's still work, family, and his kid. There's not a ton of wiggle room. And our school calendar isn't flexible. I can't take a bunch of long week-ends without it turning into a problem pretty quick." I tapped a finger to Ruth's list. "We'd go into it with the best of intentions but come out of it withered and worse off than ever before."

"Then we're saying no to the long-distance option?" Ruth asked. I nodded. "It sounds like we're also dropping the Michigan option to the bottom of the list?"

"Yeah. I think so." I went back to staring at Jude and Noah. They seemed to be having a good time, even in the blazing sun. They probably had a lot in common, at least on the unexpected fatherhood side. Also the complicated family matters side. And we couldn't forget about the fake wife and fiancée angle either.

If Jude stayed, they'd be friends. Gennie and Percy would grow up as cousins, sort of. Shay and Jamie, Ruth and Emme would become part of their family.

I knew he could be happy here with me, even if it upended his world. Picking up his kid and moving wasn't a small feat. He'd have to be completely invested in me for that. I wanted to believe he was but it wasn't hard to tell myself the other end of that story.

"Too bad Grace and Ben aren't here," Shay mused.

"She'd love the whiskey," Jamie said.

"And he'd love hanging with the dads," I said.

Shay smiled at me. "They'll have plenty of chances. We do have the Spooky Stroll coming up sooner than you'd think. And don't forget about the Thanksgiving Fox Trot."

"Don't talk to me about running right now," Jamie said, an arm banded over her belly. "Or any other time."

"Are you one of those people who asks on the first date if his family does holiday fun runs?" Ruth asked. "And if he says yes, you walk out immediately because marrying into that kind of family is your worst nightmare?"

"Let's get two things straight, baby cakes. First, I don't go on dates. I've never gone on dates. Dates are for people who want to get to know each other over expensive ramen and stilted conversation. I want to be facedown and ass-up with a minimum of three other people who will make me forget where I am, and I don't want to learn their names."

"My god," Ruth breathed.

"And second," Jamie went on, "marrying into any family is my worst nightmare. There's no situation that could occur on this earth that would result in me ever getting married."

"But off this earth?" Ruth asked.

"Beam me up," Jamie replied.

"Be careful. Those kinds of declarative statements are like flipping off fate," Shay said.

"I'll be fine," Jamie said. "I've been flipping off fate my whole life."

"Then maybe fate is waiting to bite you in the ass," Ruth said.

"It probably is," Jamie said. "But I don't mind a good bite."

chapter fifty-four

Jude

Today's vocabulary word: complacent

I JOGGED DOWN THE BACK STEPS, A BEER IN ONE HAND AND A bottle of cider in the other. "I saw this at the store today," I said as I joined Audrey on the grass. "Give it a try. See if you like it."

She studied the label while Percy tried to keep up with Bagel's after-dinner zoomies. Judging by the number of times Percy fell to the ground laughing, I'd say he wasn't doing a great job of it.

"This is good," she said, sampling the cider. "Thank you."

I tapped my bottle to hers. "Anytime, princess."

We sipped our drinks and watched Percy and Bagel as the sun slid into the horizon. Audrey's neighborhood was quiet though around this time in the evening, we often heard neighbors cooking on their grills or gathered on screened-in porches. There were always families out for strolls, pool-wet kids on bikes and scooters, and teenagers cackling with laughter and shouting at each other as they made their way to the local hangout spots.

This was a good place. It wasn't dripping in the kind of cloying sameness that had kept me away from smaller cities and towns. And it wasn't nearly as buttoned-up and impersonal as the town-house community we called home in Alexandria. I didn't know Audrey's neighbors beyond waving when folks drove by but I didn't doubt that if I knocked on a door and asked to borrow a socket wrench, someone would want to help me out.

"I think Bagel's going to need a walk this evening," Audrey said.

"They haven't tired each other out yet," I said.

"Not at all," she mused. She set the cider down and turned my wrist to glance at my watch. "We should go soon. It's going to get buggy."

I leaned in and brushed a kiss over her lips before pushing to my feet. "All right. You get the kids, I'll get the leash and bug spray."

"Are we really doing that? The *Bagel is our child* thing? Because I have to tell you I've fostered a lot of dogs and cats, and while I loved them all dearly, I always knew they'd be moving on to other homes. They weren't my fur babies."

I drummed a finger on my belt. "Bagel can't move on to another home." She glanced up at me with *Are we having this conversation now?* eyes. And no, we weren't having this conversation now because I didn't know how the fuck to have it. All I could say was, "Don't tell me you don't love this dog too."

"What's not to love?" she asked. "He goes out of his way to ignore both of us. He intermittently forgets how to walk on a leash and hides under benches at the dog park. He strongly distrusts other dogs though mostly because he doesn't know what they are. And he's imprinted on Percy. Or maybe it's the other way around. All I know is he's a total weirdo just like the rest of us. Of course, I love him."

"Look, my son tells everyone he meets that this dog is his brother," I said. "If I can roll with that, you can too."

She stood, brushing grass from the back of her shorts. "I mean, sure."

"I can hear the judgment in your tone."

"I hope you do," she said, laughing.

"You should hope our dog son doesn't hear it." She inclined her head and scraped a gaze over me. When I couldn't take it anymore, I barked, "What?"

"I'm just trying to imagine what the people in our high school class would say if they could see their Padrino now."

I rolled my eyes. "They can get fucked. All of 'em."

"Yeah, agreed, but the real question is whether they'd still be afraid of you if they knew you cooked ground beef or chicken special for Bagel every night."

"He doesn't like regular dog food, Audrey. What do you want me to do? Watch him stare at his bowl?"

"Go get the bug spray," she said, giving my shoulder a hard shove. "We'll meet you out front."

I went back inside, our beer and cider bottles in hand. I left them to drain in the sink and started the dishwasher as I heard Audrey call, "Who wants to go for a walk?"

I towel-dried my hands and pocketed two types of bug spray since Audrey's skin hated the brand that Percy liked, courtesy of the frog on the bottle. With the leash draped around my neck, I checked the locks on the back and side doors—old New England homes had so many fucking doors—and let myself out through the front.

Audrey watched while Percy tried to climb the cherry blossom tree and Bagel rolled in the grass nearby. As far as we could tell, the thought of running away hadn't crossed Bagel's mind. Even if another dog walked by, he'd go on minding his own business. We knew that theory could collapse at any moment, which was why I was quick to clip the leash to his collar.

Percy gave up on the tree, landing on the grass in a heap. "Can I hold him?" he signed, a hand grasping for the leash.

"Not until you're properly weaponized against ticks and mosquitoes," I said.

Percy met me on the walkway, his arms outstretched in the optimal bug spray application pose. Audrey wandered down to the street, busy snapping dead blooms off the dense masses of flower bushes bordering the yard.

"I'll take care of that tomorrow," I said to her.

"You don't have to," she said, still focused on her flowers. "I like this. These hydrangeas were the first things I planted when I moved in. I didn't know if they'd make it. I couldn't figure out whether this qualified as full sun or partial sun, and I had no idea what the soil or drainage was like. This makes me happy. And sometimes I just like putting on an audiobook and dissociating with my garden."

There were a lot of missed opportunities in my life. A lot of times when one thing could've happened but something else did, and I couldn't change any of that. I just had to watch those moments drift by and try not to let myself be angry about it.

I'd always kicked myself for not tracking down Audrey immediately after her divorce. The only reason for following those filings had been to know precisely when she was free of him. But it struck me now that I'd needed to miss that opportunity. Not the time for us.

Moving across the country, settling into this house and planting these bushes—that was what she'd needed then. Not me and all the resentment I'd carried around like a vestigial organ. She needed the teacher friends who became her second family. She needed to bake bread and take on foster dogs and be herself—perhaps for the first time ever—without anyone getting in the way.

Even me.

When I was finished with Percy, I walked back to the door to leave the bug spray bottles on the steps, saying, "Go ahead and grab Bagel now."

I wiped the residual bug spray on my calves and turned back in time to watch Percy racing down the walkway, Bagel galloping after him. Percy laughed, his head thrown back and his cheeks red, and I saw the instant the toe of his sneaker connected with an uneven edge of concrete.

Time slowed down to small, fractional parts and all I could see was the forward motion of his body and the handful of steps ahead of him. I yelled something, I was certain I did, but it didn't matter because he was already pitching forward. And then everything happened within a blink of an eye.

He tumbled down the stairs, his head connecting with the concrete at least once before rolling to a nauseating stop on the sidewalk. He sat up quickly—thank fucking god—but blood gushed down his face. Audrey was there, gathering him up and keeping his hands from his head, but she couldn't hide the blood from him. When he saw it on his shirt, on his glasses, on the sidewalk, he looked up at me and let out a deep, shattering scream.

chapter fifty-five

Jude

Today's vocabulary word: bond

GETTING TO THE HOSPITAL WAS A BLUR. I KNEW WE'D TAKEN A highway—maybe two—and I remembered Audrey pulling up to the emergency room and saying she'd park and meet us inside. But all I really knew was that my hands and these dish towels were soaked with my son's blood. I watched tears pour down his cheeks and I saw the fear in his eyes.

A nurse once told me that some NICU babies experienced a form of post-traumatic stress. They'd panic at doctor's visits. They'd melt the fuck down if they had to have a procedure or stay in a hospital. Their bodies remembered what they'd been through even if their minds had been too young to remember. Percy hadn't been a NICU baby but he'd spent enough time in pediatric intensive care for those rules to apply.

That nurse also told me that NICU *parents* weren't so different. I knew that was true because I didn't think I'd ever shake off the sopping wet weight of watching them wheel Percy into surgery to put his leg back together. I'd never recover from holding his chubby little hand while he lingered in a medically-induced coma and bargaining with gods I'd never believed in.

In other words, Audrey found me sprint-pacing the length of the waiting room and glaring murder at anyone who crossed my path. This poor kid had been through enough. The car accident, the fire at Brenda's house—and now this.

She steered me into a seat and said, "I'm going to ask for some gauze. Stay right here." She must've asked for more than gauze because she came back and hooked an arm through my elbow, leading us toward a nurse waiting at an open door. "Let's go, guys."

"We're going to make a stop in triage first," the nurse said, "and then we'll get you into a room."

Audrey handled all the questions, even reaching into my back pocket to fish out my wallet and insurance cards at one point. I knew I needed to get it together but I couldn't stop seeing him fly down those stairs or hearing that scream. The worst part was that I kept thinking about the custody hearing.

The nurse replaced the dish towel with a thick wedge of gauze and some tape. "This way, you won't have to hold it." She guided us to a curtained-off room and instructed me to recline back on the gurney with Percy, saying, "That'll help slow the bleeding."

She helped get us situated, despite my son's disinterest in having anyone touch him, and pulled a warm blanket up to his shoulders. I didn't know why that eased the gathered tension in my chest but I felt myself deflate just a bit. She pointed out the basin in case he puked and which button to press on the gurney's railing if he blacked out or bled through the gauze. She adjusted the pillow behind me and gave my forearm a squeeze, and I could almost hear my brain coming back online.

I didn't know if it was the blanket or the knowledge that there were people here who could help my kid or just lying back and forcing some air into my lungs but I wasn't standing on that walkway anymore, powerless to stop him from hitting the ground.

The nurse headed for the curtain divider with a promise that the doctor would be in soon. "You're very lucky," she said, leaning in close to Audrey. "You're getting one of my favorites tonight. But don't let him know that. He doesn't need to know my secrets. I'll be around if you need anything."

When the curtain clattered shut behind the nurse, I said to Audrey, "Thank you. For all of that."

"It was nothing." She dropped onto a chair beside the gurney. "I'm just glad I remembered the quick way to get here."

"You did more than that."

I held out my free hand but she didn't take it, only frowning down at me. She popped back up, filled the basin with water, and pulled some paper towels from a dispenser beside the sink. She cleaned one hand, emptied the dirty water, and then repeated the process on the other side.

"Not perfect," she mused, "but at least you don't look like an axe-murderer."

"Thanks." She laced her fingers with mine as a stray thought hit. "Where's Bagel?"

"In his crate," she said. "He went right in when I grabbed the keys. And the dish towels and the tablet and the frozen peas."

"Okay. Good." It bothered me that I didn't remember that. Well, I remembered the peas. Percy had shrieked and kicked when I tried holding the bag to his forehead. "We gotta talk about that walkway, Saunders."

"I know, I know," she said, groaning up at the ceiling. "The problem is the—"

"It's the tree roots," I said. "We can fix that because Percy is just the first person to wipe out on those cracks. He won't be the last."

"I know it's a problem but I *love* that cherry blossom tree."

"Yeah, so we dig up the concrete," I said. "That part is a pain in the ass because you'll need some machinery to excavate but then you can put down something less rigid. Something that flexes better with the roots."

"Oh." Her brows creased as she considered this. "Okay, then."

I squeezed her hand. "I'll add it to my list."

"It's turning into quite the long list," she said.

"I like it that way." We stared at each other for a moment, ignoring the obvious questions about what came next and where this was going. It was getting harder and harder to ignore them and I knew I was courting trouble by trying to.

The curtain swept open, saving us from everything I wasn't prepared to say.

"Hi, I'm Dr. Stremmel. I hear we had a fall this evening." He hooked his foot around the base of a rolling stool and yanked it toward him. Swinging a glance from me to Audrey, he asked, "It was two or three steps, concrete, but no loss of consciousness?"

"No, not at all," I said. "He was on his feet immediately after he hit the sidewalk."

"That's good to hear," Dr. Stremmel said. "And Percy's been awake and lucid since then? Talking? Making sense?"

"Signing, but yes," I said, patting the gurney for the tablet. "He has selective mutism. I have all of his records here, including a brain scan from about nine months ago." I fumbled the device but Audrey caught it and swiped it open for me. "Thanks."

"Okay, I'm going to check that out in a minute but I want to start with the head wound." As Dr. Stremmel snapped on a pair of gloves, he asked, "Percy, would it be okay for me to take a look?"

Percy tightened his hold on my neck as he cut a glance toward the doctor. He thought about it for a second, burrowing a little deeper into my chest, but eventually gave a single microscopic nod. I sat up and set him beside me on the gurney. He closed some of my shirt in his fist.

Dr. Stremmel shuffled forward on the stool, saying, "Hi Percy.

I'm going to take the gauze off and see what we have going on under there. If it hurts too much, just hold up your hand and we'll stop. Can you show me that? Hold up your hand? And now try it with the other hand? Great."

The doctor nodded as he studied the cut on Percy's head. He didn't appear extremely concerned about it though I had to assume that someone working in emergency medicine had probably seen worse than a four-year-old tripping down some stairs.

"All right, Percy," Dr. Stremmel said. "I'm going to shine a light in your eyes now. It's going to be quick. Can we do that? Awesome."

Percy's hold on my shirt gradually shifted from white-knuckled death grip to low-key choking as the doctor examined him. When I helped him off the gurney to walk into the hall and back, he didn't flail for my hand and that eased more of the tension in my chest.

But not all of it. The last thing—and I did mean the absolute last fucking thing—I needed right now was a brand-new head injury for this kid. Not when we had to fly back to Saginaw in a few days and go before a judge for this custody petition.

I knew accidents happened, especially with young kids, but goddamn the timing of this. It was bad enough that it always seemed like I was starting on the back foot with Penny's family but bringing him back to Michigan with half his face bruised and his forehead stitched up would only compound that.

Dr. Stremmel pushed back from the gurney, saying, "I'm not seeing any indication of a concussion but we're going to get some images anyway because kids like to hide those things from us. While we're waiting for those to come through, I'm going to see if a friend of mine from plastic surgery is still in the building. She might have some ideas about treating that head wound. Sound good? Any questions?"

I glanced at Audrey, wide-eyed. My brain was moving both too fast and too slow to formulate questions. "I think you covered it all," she said to him.

"Great," he said. "Sit tight and someone will take you to get those images."

When the doctor left, Percy leaned into me. As I gathered him up and settled him on my lap, he reached out to Audrey. She stood, taking his hand as she wrapped an arm around me. I let my head fall to her shoulders as a breath rattled out. I'd needed that.

"Just remember," she said. "So many of the kids who discover they have magic or defeat monsters or will receive a prophecy to save the world have a very important scar. I think this might be the beginning of an epic adventure for you."

A small, quiet laugh shook his shoulders.

"Also, I think we should talk about what we're baking for the winter holidays. You already came up with the idea for those amazing tree cakes. What else should we do?"

He had to drop her hand and my shirt in order to sign and I quickly realized that was exactly what she had in mind. Distract him from his injuries, from the overwhelm of being in pain while people poked and prodded at him. As we talked about his ideas— snowman donuts topped the list—and I suggested she take another stab at those chai muffins from Semantic, I realized she'd succeeded in distracting me too.

I didn't know how it was possible to love this girl more than I did yesterday and the day before and the whole decade before that but I did. He even let her wash some of the dried blood from his face while he explained his vision for hot chocolate bread. It was a good thing we were in a hospital because I felt like my heart was about to burst out of my chest and into her hands.

All I knew was that this was it for me. This was everything I needed. The only thing left to do was figure out how to keep it.

chapter fifty-six

Jude

Today's vocabulary word: appropriate

THE CURTAIN PULLED BACK A FEW HOURS LATER AND DR. Stremmel stepped inside, saying, "Sorry for the wait. Radiology was slammed but the good news is that there's no evidence of traumatic brain injury."

Percy dozed in my lap, his cheek pillowed on my chest and his thumb in his mouth. "That's fantastic," I said.

"I also had pediatric neuro look it over and they agreed with that assessment," the doctor went on. "Keep an eye out for any behavioral changes, anything that seems off with eating, sleeping, or movement, or sudden, severe headaches. Come in right away if that happens but I'm not expecting it will."

"Yeah, of course." I glanced over to find Audrey scribbling down some notes. "Is it okay for him to fly on Monday? We need to be in Michigan for a family thing but we could drive if needed."

Dr. Stremmel rummaged in a cabinet and pulled out some supplies. "No reason to worry about that."

I rubbed Percy's back as I absorbed this. "All right. Okay. Thank you," I said. "And the bruising on his face? How long will that take?"

"Probably a week or two," Dr. Stremmel replied. "Possibly less if he tolerates a cold compress but I doubt he's going to put up with that on his forehead for long." The curtain opened again and a doctor in a scrub cap poked her head in. "Dr. Shapiro, this is Percy and he has quite the gash on his forehead after going headfirst down some concrete steps. I suspect you'll have some strong opinions about the appropriate closure technique."

I watched as they exchanged a glance I didn't fully understand. It seemed like an inside joke. It hadn't occurred to me that doctors would have inside jokes about the best ways to fix up a cut.

"Hi, I'm Dr. Shapiro." She held out a hand to me and Audrey, correctly gauging Percy's thumb-sucking as a hard disinterest in any kind of formal greetings. "I'm going to examine the wound and then we'll make a plan. Is it all right if an intern and a med student observe?"

When I didn't respond right away, Audrey jumped in. "Yes, of course."

"The doctor needs to check you out, good sir," I said to Percy. "Do you think you can sit on the bed by yourself?"

He nodded but stretched his free hand out toward Audrey. She popped to her feet and went to the side of the gurney, taking his hand. "I had an idea," she said, her voice low like she was telling him a secret. "What if we tested some recipes for a dog cookie?"

His sleepy eyes went wide and he barely noticed me setting him down, his head coming to rest on the pillow. He signed *Yes* which told me his head hurt and he didn't want to nod.

Audrey noticed too because she asked Dr. Stremmel, "I think Percy could use something for the pain."

"We can do that," Dr. Stremmel said, tapping at his tablet.

Dr. Shapiro returned with doctors who didn't look old enough to be out of high school. She smiled down at Percy when she approached the gurney. He gripped Audrey's hand tighter.

"I'm going to use this to help me get a good look," she said, holding up a palm-sized device, "but you won't feel anything because it won't even touch you."

She motioned for the child-doctors to come closer and started describing his injury in technical terms. They took turns studying the cut through the magnifying tool.

When they finished, Dr. Shapiro shifted to face us. "We can close this without sutures."

"Knew it," Dr. Stremmel murmured from where he leaned against the cabinets, his arms crossed over his chest.

She gave him a meaningful look. Definitely an inside joke there.

"It's certainly on the borderline but I feel confident we'll be able to take care of this wound with less aggressive measures." She turned to Percy, saying, "I'm not sure if you heard what I said to Mom and Dad just now but I'm going to help your head feel better."

Audrey's gaze snapped to mine, wide and alarmed. Her lips parted, ready to tell them she wasn't *Mom* in this situation.

It's okay, I mouthed.

And it was.

Penny would always be Percy's mother but Audrey could be Mom. If she wanted. If we could get through the next week and figure out how to build a world for ourselves on the other side of this custody hearing. If I could find the right moment and the right words to tell her that I'd do anything to live out the rest of my days the way we'd lived the past few weeks—together, as a family.

The longer we stayed here, the less I remembered of our lives before that little ranch house and my new dog-son Bagel. I'd so completely given myself over to this notion of our life here that I'd stopped worrying about all the speech therapy sessions Percy had missed. I'd forgotten all about comparing the educational options in northern Virginia. I'd even given our nanny Wayne an extra month of paid vacation.

I knew what I wanted, what I hoped for, what'd chased me in dreams. What was right here in front of me, holding my son's hand and taking notes because I was too fried to think.

But it scared the hell out of me because my life liked fucking up my hopes and dreams. Every time it seemed like the pieces were finally falling into place, the ground beneath me shifted or it started raining rocks.

I hated that I just assumed it would all go to hell. I didn't want to look out at the world with this much dread. Was it so wrong to want a life with the woman I'd loved since before I'd even understood what that meant? To make a family with her? And was I really trampling over Penny's memory by wanting my son to have one more person in his life who loved him unconditionally?

I didn't think so. I didn't think any of this required a rainstorm of rocks—and I wasn't going to let that happen this time. I wasn't sure that I could talk Maddie out of wanting custody, though Ruth and Noah had given me some decent ideas. Though it didn't help that my son looked like I'd thrown him down a flight of stairs.

"To do that," Dr. Shapiro went on, completely oblivious to the silent conversation taking place around her, "I'm going to bring a bright light over here so I can see exactly what I'm doing. I'm also going to use some tools to help put medicine on your cut and then place very thin bandages on your skin. Here, take a look."

Dr. Shapiro walked Percy through all the instruments she'd be using and what to expect. A nurse came in with apple juice and pain medicine, and he knocked back both like it was last call while Dr. Shapiro prepared her equipment.

Audrey quietly explained her ideas for dog cookies while the doctor worked on Percy, lulling him into such a state of calm that he'd stopped clutching our hands and only had a finger hooked under the band of my watch now. The cookies would be shaped like dog bones, they decided, but also maybe holiday wreaths or trees. She meandered through a list of flavors—pumpkin, bacon, peanut butter, oatmeal—and then different combinations of those flavors. Her voice was soft, like the brush of a feather, and I felt it sloughing the stress from my shoulders, the back of my neck.

Dr. Shapiro finished with Percy's wound and explained how to keep it clean and protected while it healed. He climbed into Audrey's lap while the doctor spoke, his thumb back in his mouth and his eyelids heavy.

If I'd known back in June at the reunion that we'd end up here, I wouldn't have believed it. I might've done a few things differently if I'd known—or not. Back then, even if I'd craved this outcome for longer than was logical, I hadn't known how to climb over all the hard, ugly boulders of our past. I'd loved her and resented her in ways that I couldn't begin to explain, not even to myself. And yet here we were, on the other side of it all.

I just didn't think I'd survive if I lost it all again.

I mean, I would survive it, somehow. I had to. I had a kid and my mother to think of. And Brenda too. She was Percy's grandmother and that made her part of my family too. I couldn't fuck off and hate the world when I had all that responsibility sitting on my shoulders. But it would punch a hole right through my heart—or wherever it was that this overflowing feeling lived.

After the doctors left us and the nurse returned with discharge papers, I scooped Percy out of Audrey's arms and carried him to the car. It was well past midnight now and I felt a few tendrils of exhaustion pushing through the adrenaline of this night.

As I buckled him into his booster seat, he signed, "Can Audrey sit with me?"

I dropped a kiss on his temple, away from the injury. "I bet she'd love to." I rounded the car and opened the driver's side door, saying to her, "I'll drive. Your presence has been requested in the back seat."

414 · Kate Canterbary

"You're tired," she said, climbing out of the car. "A little frazzled too."

"I'll be okay." I caught her in a hug. I wasn't sure if it said all the things I wanted to but there'd be time for that later. "Thank you. For everything. I don't know what I would've done without you. Just… thank you. So much."

"Anytime," she said. "Now, come on. It's late. We need to get everyone into bed."

The roads were empty and the drive home didn't take long, though I spent most of it glancing at Audrey and Percy in the rear view, memorizing the way she absently rubbed his knee and guided him to rest his head on her arm.

When we arrived home, I carried him inside and down the dark hallway. Audrey brought a hand between my shoulder blades as I approached the bedroom and whispered, "You should stay with him tonight. I'll sleep in the guest room."

She didn't wait for a response, instead sliding around me and into her room to ready the bedding. I set him down on the bed and pulled off his shoes while she removed his glasses. As she started to retreat, I grabbed her wrist. "Outside," I whispered.

With one final glance at Percy, I tugged Audrey down the hall and into the moonlit kitchen. "What's wrong?" she asked as I paced from one end to the other.

All I could hear in my head was a chorus of *What if I stayed here and never left? What happens then?*

"You've put up with a lot from us this month," I said. "You didn't ask for all of this but you've taken us in and looked after us like he's family."

"Because you are family," she said simply. "You and Percy, you're family. You're always welcome here. Even if things change for us, nothing will change that."

I leaned back against the sink, my hands curled around the cool stone. "I know we're pretending that Percy and I aren't leaving in a few days for the custody hearing but it's going to happen whether we look it in the eye or not."

She nodded. "Yeah. I know."

"You didn't go looking for any of this," I said. "Me, my kid, my never-ending custody story. In fact, you were very clear about helping me with one specific matter and then permanently excusing yourself from my life."

"That was true. At one point."

"It's not true anymore?"

"I think we can agree that a lot of things have changed along the way."

"Tell me what's changed," I said.

She rounded the kitchen island and stopped right in front of me. With her hands on her hips, she said, "You already know everything has changed. There's no need to make a list. We just need to decide where we go next."

"Where do we go next?" I asked. "I'm not sure how to answer that, Audrey. Should I tell you that I've spent the past few weeks debating whether to quietly sell my place and hope you never notice that we've moved in? Or that every time I think about the future, you're the only thing I can see? Or that watching you take care of my son tonight made me realize I've been holding my breath for fucking *years*? But since coming here with Percy, I can actually breathe again? Or that you give my son something I can't and it makes me feel like I'm finally doing this right? Should I tell you all of that? Or should I just say you'll have to bar the doors and hire a private army to keep me from coming back to you because I can't imagine us anywhere else?"

She stared at me for a long moment, long enough that I started to think I'd made a major misstep, but then she said, "Yeah. I thought so." Before my brain could catch up, she went on. "I talked to my principal. Percy can enroll in my school, even if he won't be five until the end of September."

"Wait—what?"

"Our kindergarten teacher knows ASL. Her name's Aurora and she grew up with ASL. She has a lot of experience with students who have communication differences too. He'll be able to have small group lessons with other kids at his reading level, which will be a lot less frustrating than his preschool experiences, and he'll be right down the hall from me the whole time."

"You've thought about this," I said, though it was obvious.

"Of course I have," she said. "I want you here, even if it's hard and we don't know what we're doing. Even if the custody situation makes it more complicated. I want to figure all of it out with you."

I pushed off the sink and reached for her, my hands settling on her waist. "Really?"

She ducked her head, laughing. "I'm not going to bar the door."

"I am in love with you. Do you know that? I fucking love you and every time I think I've found the perimeter of that love, you do something new and it spills out of my hands. It makes a goddamn mess of me, Audrey. I need you to know that. I need you to understand that I don't exist without you."

She reached out, grabbed my shirt, and yanked me to her chest, sealing her lips over mine. A stunned second passed before I could remember how to kiss her back. "Audrey," I whispered against her lips. I closed my arms around her torso, held her tight to me. "Say something."

"I love you too." I felt her smile. "And also, what do you think about taking this conversation into Percy's room?"

"To hear him if he wakes up or so I can fuck you in a bed?"

"The answer is yes," she replied.

"Good. I like that answer. Especially since I'm too old to keep doing this standing up."

We tiptoed down the hall, pausing outside her room to watch Percy as he slept. I held up a finger to her and gathered a bunch of his stuffed animals from his bed. He'd reach for them and get confused if they weren't there.

When he was surrounded by his buddies, I pulled the door halfway shut and led Audrey into the other bedroom. I wagged a finger at her clothes, saying, "Off," as I pulled my shirt over my head.

The bed was inarguably tiny but we didn't care.

"I love you," I said, running a hand down her outer thigh while I wrapped my other arm around her shoulders. "I didn't get to say it to you for so long and now that I've said it, I don't think I'm going to be able to stop."

She hummed in agreement as she reached between us, taking my cock in hand. I loved the confidence in her touch, as if she had no doubt about what I wanted and how to give it to me. "Then don't stop," she said. "I won't make you."

I was tired and frayed but also relieved—so fucking relieved—and I didn't think I could wait much longer. Not while her nipples rubbed against my chest and she stroked me like that. I shifted to my knees and nudged her beneath me, prying her legs apart as I went. "Show me," I said, a hand splayed on her inner thigh. With my free hand, I grabbed her wrist and guided it to her breast. "Show me where you want me."

She grinned up at me as she traced her nipples. "Everywhere."

I notched myself at her entrance, my cockhead throbbing against the wet of her. "Like this? Right here?"

Her gaze traveled from my eyes down the center of my chest to where I pressed inside her. I ran a knuckle over her clit, circling it in slow, rough passes until a breathy moan sounded and her back arched. "Right there," she said, her eyes closed and lips parted.

I pulled her knee to my hip and pushed inside her, devouring every little tremor of her inner muscles I felt around my cock. She shifted, the knee on my hip forcing me closer, *deeper* as she rolled her hips.

Some instinctual, animal part of my brain wanted to let go and rut into her but everything else ordered me to settle into each second and savor it. I dropped to an elbow and found her lips. "I love you," I said between kisses.

"Love you too," she said, her voice as soft as a dream.

I hooked an arm under her waist and held her tight, never once breaking away from her lips. I didn't think much about coming. I knew we would, one way or another, and I knew this wouldn't be the last time. And that changed everything.

chapter fifty-seven

Jude

Today's vocabulary word: quarry

I WAITED AS LONG AS POSSIBLE TO PACK FOR THE TRIP BACK TO Michigan. Ridiculous as it was, I held a sliver of hope that my attorney would call, saying Maddie dropped the petition or the court refused to hear the case on the grounds of total absurdity. Or that for once in my whole fucking life, the universe would give me a pass and let me skip the most complicated, convoluted path. But that didn't happen.

It wasn't until reading Percy a bedtime story the night before our eight a.m. flight that I finally took stock of the home he'd made for himself in Audrey's spare bedroom and realized it was time to take it all apart.

Once he was asleep, I gathered an armful of stuffed friends—the ones he wouldn't miss if another nightmare woke him up—and tucked them into the suitcase alongside his boxer shorts and t-shirts. It felt final in a way I didn't want to look in the eye, as if we weren't just leaving but dismantling everything we'd found here.

I knew this wasn't the end. I knew there'd be another step, another chapter for us—for me and Percy and Audrey—but only if it didn't undo the fragile peace we'd brokered here. Whatever came next, it had to be better than the mess behind us. Anything was better than nothing, right?

But there were limits to that *anything*. I lived in Virginia. This custody situation could land me in Michigan. And Audrey—and the world she'd created for herself—were in neither of those places. I couldn't ask her to leave any of this and I didn't want her to give up this place and these people for me.

She'd already given up enough for me.

I found her in the living room with her own armful of Percy's toys and books. "Quite the blast zone this kid leaves behind him," I said.

"It's not that bad." She pulled a book from between the sofa cushions. "He's comfortable here. I like that," she added softly.

I went to her, plucking the toys from her hold. "I like it too."

She stepped away, her lips rolled tight together as she nodded to herself. She reached into Bagel's crate and pulled out another book. "He'll want this in his backpack," she said, waving a graphic novel. "I noticed he rereads it a lot."

I took the book and pressed a kiss to her temple. She leaned into me and I hated that we had to leave, that we couldn't hide from the real world long enough to knit ourselves together tight enough that we could stand up to every cannonball that came our way.

"Thank you," I said to her skin. "And thank you for putting up with us. I know you didn't ask for this and—"

Her hand landed on my chest. "Don't thank me," she said. "Just —come back. To me. When you can. That's all I need."

I dropped another kiss on her forehead, held her as close as the stuffed animals would allow. "You won't be able to keep me away."

I returned to the spare room to pack while Audrey resumed the hunt for Percy's stray goods. She peeked in when I was almost finished, holding his discharge papers from the hospital and antibiotic ointment. "Could you put that in my backpack?" I whispered, pointing to the forms. "And the antibiotic with my toiletries?"

With a brief nod, she crossed the hall into the room I thought of as *ours*. It wouldn't be ours tomorrow; it would be hers once again. I didn't care to think about her alone in that bed, in this house. Didn't wish to think about her life without us. Didn't want to start another argument with myself about asking her to come to Michigan for the hearing. She had to get her classroom ready for students and had school meetings coming up later in the week, and the last place she wanted to be was Arenac County Family Court.

Once I had Percy's things packed away and his clothes out for the morning, I left his door slightly ajar and stepped into our room. Experience had taught me how to pack for myself in five minutes flat but that didn't make—

"What's this?"

Audrey stood on the other side of the room, my clothes folded in neat piles on the bed and my bags open around her. She pinched a small silver ring between two fingers and stared at me like she'd discovered proof that I was a serial killer.

A startled laugh rumbled out of me because if that ring proved anything, it was that she was the real killer.

"I need you to start talking immediately," she said. "Where did you get this? And when?"

I closed the door behind us and leaned back against it, my arms crossed and a breath trapped in my chest just like the day that ring arrived. The day I knew she was gone and not coming back for me. "I've had it since you mailed it back to me, Saunders. Right after you left for California."

"I never— No. I never would've done that."

"It came with a note saying you'd decided it was time for us to go off into the world on our own and hoping I could understand."

She pressed a hand to her forehead, letting her eyes shut for a second. "I didn't write that note."

If I could've done one thing differently back then, it would've been questioning the validity of that note. I should've picked up on the stiff wording, the mangled sign-off of *Wishing you all the best and lots of love, Your friend Audrey.* The fact that it'd been typed and not handwritten. But being eighteen didn't come with that kind of perspective.

"I thought I lost it." She ran a finger around the silver band. "The only reason I went home at the end of the semester was to turn my bedroom upside down for it. I spent *years* looking for it. I'd wake up in the middle of the night thinking I knew where it was and tear my dorm room apart." She peered at the thin band, at the single lilac bloom preserved in clear resin. Not the lilac stone she'd requested but the placeholder—the promise—I'd given to her on her seventeenth birthday. "I thought it was gone but you had it. And you kept it right here with you, all this time."

That part, I couldn't explain. Because there was no clean way to say *It was the only real proof I had that you'd ripped my heart out, claimed it as your own, and then mailed the dead, pointless muscle back to me.* To say *I could hate you when I stared at that ring and that felt better than missing you.* To say *The sight of that ring was torture but nothing hurt worse than being separated from it.*

No way to say *You broke me and I never recovered.*

Because I couldn't lay that blame at her feet. It hadn't been her choice or her fault, and I'd been too young, too naïve, too drunk off my resentment of the wealthy world she came from to see what was happening. To understand that the girl I'd adored so thoroughly, so completely hadn't woken up one morning and decided she didn't want me anymore. That our plans weren't good enough for her, our promises weren't good enough. That *I* wasn't good enough.

And I'd let that crystallize into facts as I believed them.

She swept a tear from her lashes and I felt that pain square in my chest. I pushed off the door but she held up a hand, shaking her head as she said, "No. I need you to stay over there for a minute."

I didn't like it but I didn't argue.

She went on staring at the ring, the dainty silver polished to a shine because yes, I did clean it regularly and no, I had yet to grow tired of hurting my own feelings.

"Why did you try to stop my wedding?"

Her words were quiet, almost as if she didn't intend for me to hear them. But they were also a wall, solid and tangible enough for me to flatten my hand against.

"I know I was terrible to you that day," she continued, "but I was scared that my father was going to see you. I knew he'd do something heinous and I couldn't let that happen. Not after everything I'd done to protect you."

My jaw tightened and I felt it all the way in the back of my neck. "You could've left with me instead. Saved everyone a lot of grief."

"Why were you there?"

I crossed my arms, leaned one shoulder against the door. "Because I had to see it for myself. That it was what you wanted."

"But you knew it wasn't."

"Mmhmm. Yeah. Pretty obvious, considering you looked like you were being marched to the gallows," I said.

"You let me go through with it," she said.

"What was I supposed to do, Audrey? Kidnap you? Throw you and your fucking ball gown on the back of my bike, and take off? The restraining order had *just* expired and you fucking told me to leave. You hadn't answered a single email in four years and all the letters I sent came back undeliverable, and—"

"Emails?" She glanced up at me then, all agony. "What emails?"

I stared at her for a moment, that teenage vow still pressed between her fingers and our history filling the room, ghosts and shadows curling in around us. "Then you don't remember everything that happened that night in Sedona. With the ecstasy," I added.

Even more color drained from her face. "What are you talking about?"

"After you danced with every bull rider in southern Utah—"

"It wasn't *every* bull rider."

"One bull rider is enough for me." I held her gaze until the corner of her mouth kicked up. "You said something about how you left for California and it was over, and you were alone. And I couldn't understand how you'd say that when I emailed you for months. A year went by without a single response but that didn't stop me."

I'd always known her parents had a hand in sending her away but it was the ensuing silence that'd really fucked with my head. To my mind, even if her parents were calling the shots, she wouldn't have turned on me like that. And it hadn't occurred to me that they'd screw with her email.

She brought a hand to her neck. "I never—" Turning a pained gaze to the ceiling, she said, "I didn't get them."

"I know. You told me that in Sedona." I pushed away from the door. "The ecstasy told me first but then I knew when you asked about Caltech. Right from the start, I told you about my plans to transfer. I wanted to make the move in the spring semester but they didn't have space in the engineering program. Half the messages were my ramblings on the Jet Propulsion Lab and making the switch to aeronautics."

"How...how is any of this possible? How did I not get these emails?"

"I can tell you but you're going to have to forgive me for a massive invasion of your privacy first."

Eyes flashing, she snapped, "What?"

I crossed the room to grab my laptop. "Remember my friend Jordan? He works in private security and has access to the kind of hackers who know how to get to the bottom of problems like this one."

"You've been in my email?"

"Not exactly, no." I shot her a glance as I keyed in my password. "But Jordan Kaisall's hacker has and he came back with the results this morning."

She paced away from me, kneading the bridge of her nose. "My god. Jude."

"They found everything from me sequestered in a hidden folder," I said, motioning to the screencaps Kaisall had sent. "And anything you tried to send me landed in a dead-end drafts folder. Same story with texts sent from our old phone numbers."

"But I have emails from you. Back in June, the flight info. And I responded to you."

"They think something reset on the back end when you changed your email handle. After you got married." I cleared my throat. "You still couldn't see the messages but we would've been able to send and receive emails. We just didn't try again until recently."

"I can't believe they did this to me." She glanced at the screen but then quickly away as if it hurt to even see the evidence. "At the same time, I absolutely believe it. The only truly unbelievable part is that I didn't think of it."

I didn't need any clarification to know we were talking about her parents. I still didn't understand how such objectively terrible people could've created someone as gentle and loving and precious as Audrey. Or how she'd managed to escape their world in one piece.

"I should've known they'd use their tools against me," she said. "I'd overheard enough conversations about tapping into a candidate's email accounts or a journalist's voicemails to know they had that kind of reach. I just didn't think..." She gave a sad, tired shrug and it sent an ache spiraling through my chest. "But I should've."

I closed my laptop and set it aside, and then quickly shifted all the clothes piled on her bed into my suitcase. I sat on the edge, pulled her between my legs. "No one expects their family to betray them," I said, seating her on my lap. "Don't blame yourself for what they did."

She shook her head at the ring. "Every time I thought about this ring, my heart broke all over again. I felt like I'd failed you. I mean, I knew you hated me for it all, but it only made it worse knowing I couldn't even keep track of this one perfect thing I had left of you."

I took it from her, slipped it onto her fourth finger. "I didn't hate you." She gave me her *Please don't fucking lie to me* face. "Would I have kept this if I hated you?"

"I don't know," she said. "Maybe it fueled your rage."

"Or maybe I just never stopped loving you. Even when it killed me."

"Sounds brutal."

"You'd know. You lived through it too," I said, my chin on her shoulder. "Worse, probably, since you married that dickbag."

She laughed at that but it was short-lived. "Why does it have to be so hard for us?" she asked, the words a whisper. "Every time we get close, the world shows up with a wrecking ball."

She wasn't wrong. Life—our families, surprise babies, death, disease, custody situations—liked jamming up the gears. "It doesn't have to be that way anymore."

Another hard, quick laugh. "How do you figure?"

I wrapped my arms around her and held her close to me though it didn't seem close enough. "I don't know what's going to happen in court this week and I can't guess how your parents will try to manipulate your life next—"

"They've been trying to marry me off to a big finance guy."

"Do us both a favor and don't go through with it this time," I said, nipping at her jaw. "Listen, we don't know what's coming next but I know I'm coming back here. This kid and I, we've spent a long time trying to figure out where we belong and now we know that place is with you."

"But what about Penny's family?"

"I don't want to guess what will happen with Brenda or Maddie but I know we're coming back to you," I said, pressing a finger to her lips. "All I want to hear is whether you want to stay in this house, this town—or if you want to find somewhere new for our family. And yes, that family does include Percy's brother Bagel."

"He'd riot if Bagel wasn't included."

"He'd tear this place apart brick by brick." I set her beside me on the mattress and then stood, yanking off my shirt as I went. Her gaze tracked my every move. The jeans followed. I shifted to the head of the bed, pulling down the sheets and blankets. "Come here," I said, beckoning her closer.

Weary eyes stared back at me but then a smile tugged the corner of her mouth and she crawled between the sheets. She tucked herself into my side when we met in the middle, her head on my shoulder and her hair silky where it spilled over my arm.

"You're sure you don't want me to come with you?" she asked.

"To hang around a hotel for a few days while I deal with the contractors working at Brenda's place? Or hang around the courthouse while the judge meets with Percy? No, princess, you don't need any of that in your life. And you have that math curriculum meeting and then you need time to set up your classroom."

She murmured as if she didn't like that response. "Bagel is really going to miss his brother."

"He loves that dog," I said, sweeping my palm down her back. "And he loves you too."

"Stop it," she said, hiding her face in my chest.

"No." I kissed the crown of her head. "I thought I knew what it meant to love you, but seeing my son love you a little more every day? And seeing you love him right back?" I pressed a hand to my chest. "I wasn't prepared for how hard it would hit me. How inadequate it feels to say I love you. But I need you to know there's nothing I won't do for you two. Whatever wrecking balls come our way, I'm ready for them. Even your parents and all the socially appropriate husbands they send after you."

"I love you too," she whispered. "But it's about time I deal with them. Once and for all."

"You could take them apart one-handed," I said. "That's how fucking strong you are, princess."

"I don't always feel that strong."

"You're not supposed to," I said, twisting her hair around my palm. "You're not supposed to carry heavy shit all the time. It's being able to put it down that builds the strength."

Audrey nodded against my chest though it didn't feel much like agreement. I reached over and switched off the bedside lamp. Darkness fell on the room and the patchworked quiet of suburbia settled around us.

"Wait. Is this finance guy the one who walked you to the door?" I gave her hair a slight tug. "The night we came in from Michigan?"

An extraordinary pause and then, "Yeah."

"Motherfuck." I slapped the sheets with my free hand. "I knew I should've broken his nose when I had the chance."

"It's good that you didn't."

"Debatable, Saunders. Highly debatable."

chapter fifty-eight
Audrey

Today's vocabulary word: instigate

MY STOMACH WAS A SWIRLING CAULDRON OF STRESS AND ANXIETY and pure, uncut rage. It simmered the entire trip to my parents' house in the Hamptons, so much that my heart thudded in my chest and my jaw ached from clenching. I wanted to press a finger to the place where it twisted inside me, to hold it down and suffocate the strength from it.

I might've been able to do that if not for the prenuptial agreement that'd been delivered to my door this morning.

Silly me to think I'd seen the last of Brecken Wilhamsen. For another woman living another life, he'd probably make for a thoroughly adequate husband. Hell, there was a time when I was that different woman and I would've taught myself how to be content with him. But I wasn't her anymore.

I knew it wouldn't make me any less swirly and stressy but I opened my phone and went to the link Jude sent last night when he'd arrived in Saginaw, one with all our missing messages. It opened on that day, the one where it'd all fallen apart.

Audrey,
What the hell is going on? Why aren't you answering your phone?
Call me. I'm freaking out over here.
j

Audrey,
I don't know what the fuck is happening but Cassidy said you changed your mind about Barnard and decided to go to Pepperdine instead? I don't trust her and I'm not going to believe it until I hear it from you.
Love you,
j

Audrey,
It scares me that you haven't responded to any of these messages or texts or calls.
This feels like one of your dad's power moves and I don't like any of it.
Please call me. I don't care what's going on, I just need to know you're okay.
Love you.
j

Audrey,

Everyone's saying you wanted a change but you never said anything to me.

Tell me what's happening. Tell me anything. Please. Even if it's that you don't want to talk to me, tell me that.

Love,

j

———————

Audrey,

I love you. I miss you. I'm really nervous that something's wrong and I don't know how to fix it. Please respond.

Love,

j

———————

Audrey,

I'm at Columbia now. Mom moved me in this morning. She cried for an hour and made me pose for photos all over the damn place.

I don't know how to be here with you. It feels wrong.

I still love you, even if you won't talk to me. I always will.

j

———————

Audrey,

Can you just tell me what happened? I need to know what I did or what changed for you.

I'll leave you alone if that's what you want but I need to

hear you say that. I'm going to keep writing to you every day
until you do.

    Love,

    j

    Audrey,

    Did you really think you could just leave town and I'd
forget about you? That's not us. That's not how we do it,
princess.

    I'm going to see about transferring to Caltech for the
spring semester. If you're going to ignore me, you can at least
do it in person.

    Love you, you beautiful pain in my ass.

    j

    Audrey,

    Yeah, I was drunk when I sent that last message but I stand
behind it. You're beautiful. And a pain in my ass.

    Also, Caltech won't take me until next fall so I'm fucking
stuck here.

    It would really, really help if you could send some proof of
life. If I'm not careful, I'll spiral and convince myself you're
locked in a basement somewhere.

    Promise me you're not locked in a basement.

    Love you,

    j

He did lock you in a basement, didn't he? That's why you
won't answer me. You're literally being held in a fucking
dungeon. It's the only thing that makes sense.

I've always known he was a cruel bastard but this is unreal.
I should've realized Cassidy was a co-conspirator.

I don't know what to do but I'll figure something out.
I love you. We'll fix this.

j

Audrey,
The ring came today.
It's yours. You didn't need to give it back.
I guess you're not locked in a basement.
By the way, you said a lot of shit in that note. I'll believe it
when you say it to my face.

Love you regardless of your bullshit,

j

I HAD TO PRESS A HAND TO MY MOUTH TO KEEP A SOB FROM
breaking free. I didn't think I could handle much more of his
anguish. I swiped all the way to the end, to the last message.

Audrey,
My mom sent me your engagement announcement today.
Maybe I'm fooling myself but I still don't get it. I've spent
four years trying to figure it out and I just don't understand any
of it. This isn't who you are and I refuse to believe you woke up

*one morning and threw away the person I've always known you
to be.*

*I don't know if you're reading this. One of the theories I've
nurtured since the start of your disappearing act is that
you've had me blocked or muted for years, and I'm just
screaming into cyberspace. But if you are reading this and
you need help, I'll do anything I can. I don't care how long
it's been or what's changed between us. I'll always be there
for you.*

I think I should probably stop writing to you now.

Jude

I DIDN'T LIKE BEING THE PERSON UGLY-CRYING ON PUBLIC TRANSIT,
but here I was, tears streaming down my face while I loudly snif-
fled. Mortifying. Yet I couldn't bring myself to tighten the laces on
these emotions.

I tried to rehearse what I'd say, but nothing came to me. As
much as I wanted to—*needed* to—I couldn't call up the words. I
was terrified I'd walk in there and have...nothing. That I'd cower
from the confrontation like usual. That, once again, I'd make the
worst choices when it meant the most.

It turned out that I didn't need to worry about any of that.

As I stepped inside my parents' home, I noticed an ornate ship
in a bottle displayed on a hall table. It was made to look old, an
antique, but like everything else here, it was fake and soulless.

I knocked it off the table.

A housekeeper came running at the sound of shattering glass.
When she skidded to a halt, I said, "Make sure they know it
was me."

With a nod, she motioned toward the backyard. I let myself
believe that tip came from a place of solidarity even though it prob-

ably had more to do with the fact I walked in here and started breaking shit, and she didn't want any part of that.

I pushed a large vase to the edge of a table and grinned when it crashed as I strolled out toward the flagstone patio. My mother was seated near the pool under a massive umbrella, a tablet in her lap and several newspapers fanned out on the table. A tray with half a grapefruit and an empty glass streaked with swampy green debris was parked off to the side. My father stood at the edge of the yard, a golf club in hand as he surveyed the balls scattered in the grass.

Neither noticed me and I decided that was a good thing. I was the one in control this time. Calm clarity settled over me like I'd finally found the eye of my hurricane.

"I know what you did," I said. "When you sent me to California. I know everything."

My mother startled in her seat, a hand fluttering to her chest. "What in the world? Audrey? What are you doing here?"

No, there was nothing orderly about this conversation and I wanted it that way. If I'd thought it would help, I would've built a slide deck and clicked through a bullet-pointed presentation. But I couldn't rely on reason with people who hacked email accounts and filed bullshit restraining orders. People who believed quite earnestly that marrying me off to Chris had been a good idea. It wasn't like they'd hear my concerns and acknowledge the harm done.

Breaking shit and yelling was the only option.

"I'm not going to bother asking why you did it," I said. "But believe me when I say this is the end."

"I don't know what you're talking about," she said, turning back to her tablet, "but I won't tolerate you storming in here like this and creating a scene."

I gestured to the space, empty save for my father. "You're the one making the scene."

"Cassidy is here for the week and she's on the beach with the children," she said. "They don't need to come up here and find you in the middle of a breakdown."

"All I'm doing is asking you to explain the shit you pulled when you shipped me off to Pepperdine."

"Would you listen to yourself? You're hysterical. You sound like you've lost your mind," she said. "Go inside and get a drink. I'll talk to you when you're thinking clearly again."

The shrill cut of her words must've gained my father's attention because he ambled across the yard, the putter loose in his grip. "When did you get here?"

That was his version of a warm greeting.

"She's having one of her tantrums again," my mother said to him. "She's speaking in riddles and nonsense. She's going to make herself sick if she doesn't calm down."

"I'm perfectly calm," I said, "but I'm not leaving here without some answers."

"If this is about Wilhamsen, I've already looked over the documents. You'll sign them," he said. "No arguments."

He eyed me with resentment so thick and profound that I could taste it in the back of my throat. Now that I saw it from this distance, I knew it'd always been this way. I'd put everything into being right, being good enough—and for what? Because this wasn't family. It wasn't love. And I'd let myself linger in this sodden place too long.

"Please don't tell me that lowlife is back," my mother said. "After everything we did to protect you from him? What could he possibly want from you now?"

"Can you hear yourself? Do you hear what you're saying to *me*?" When she only turned an impatient glare in my direction, I clapped my hands together and barreled ahead. "I'll simplify it for you. I know about the emails you blocked, about the forged note you sent with the ring you hid from me, and I know about the restraining order. Explain."

My mother went back to aggressively swiping her tablet. "I don't know which ring you're talking about."

"But the emails and the restraining order? That rings some bells?" I asked.

"It's ancient history," my father said, lolling the club back and forth.

Sweat rolled down my spine but my voice was steady. "You promised me you'd leave him alone. If I went to California, you wouldn't do anything to him."

"Call it an insurance policy." The sneering laugh that followed made me wish I'd broken more things on my way out here. "What's the point of all this?"

"The point is that I am finished with you and your manipulations."

He scoffed and turned back toward the grass. "Don't waste my time with these theatrics."

"Just tell me why you sent him the ring," I said.

"For the last time, we know nothing about a ring," my mother said. "Is this a real thing? You're sure you haven't dreamed it up?"

"Oh my god," I muttered to myself.

"What's going on here?"

Glancing away from my parents, I found my sister crossing the yard. She wore a blinding white sarong over a black bikini and a straw hat that could shelter five people in a storm. A pair of children came up behind her, along with a middle-aged woman with several beach bags over her shoulders.

I really, *really* didn't want to see my sister today.

"Audrey's convinced herself that we stole a ring from her years ago," my father said, his words sopping up his disdain. "She's come here to scream at us about it."

A predator's grin spread across Cassidy's face as she stared at me. "Nanny, take the babies inside," she said. "We wouldn't want Aunt Audrey frightening them again."

She didn't look at her children or the woman whose name probably wasn't Nanny as they filed into the house. I'd met her kids a handful of times. They'd been too young to remember, still too young to remember much, but it was important for her to toss in the *again*.

Holt's first birthday party was one of those times, because my mother had sworn Cassidy wanted me there but was too nervous to ask directly. I should've seen the lie for what it was but I'd missed it. Just as I'd missed all the food at this party triggering my bridge troll gut. Me hastily handing one-year-old Holt to his father so I could make it to the bathroom in time had turned into me being *unsafe around children*. Yes, that was a real thing my family said.

The other time was my mother's sixty-fifth birthday party, a big country club affair with an unironic *Gone With the Wind* theme. She'd allowed me to believe she was dying and she wanted her whole family together one last time. Except she hadn't been dying, not imminently. She'd needed a pacemaker. In the three years since that party—when I'd held little Cassen and he'd accidentally head-butted me, leaving him screaming and me with a split lip—she'd been fine.

"Someone lost a ring?" Cassidy asked, sweet venom in her voice.

My mother waved an exasperated hand in my direction. "Audrey believes we've robbed her of something. Honestly, as if I have the time for this kind of drama."

My sister crossed her arms over her bare torso, that eerie smile still stretched across her face. "Was it that cheap little flower ring? That purple one?"

All the blood left my body and in its place, ice water. "How would you know, Cassidy?"

"I did you a big favor and mailed it back to that grungy boyfriend of yours when you went off to college." She cupped a hand around her mouth like she was letting me in on a secret.

"Made sure he knew it was dead, done, and over, if you know what I mean. That's what you wanted, wasn't it? That's why you left it at home when you moved out. Right?"

It was good that ice pumped through my veins now. That I was frozen from the inside out. Because I gave Cassidy nothing but stone-faced silence.

"Why are you asking about it now?" She shuffled her sandals against the patio decking. "It's been a million years."

I held up my hand, wiggled my fourth finger where the ring now sat. "Because I recently got it back."

Her eyes widened. She didn't have the decency to look guilty when caught in her lies and she didn't apologize. She gave me a dismissive flounce and strolled toward the house. With a hard chuckle, she said, "Good luck with that. You're gonna need it."

"Audrey, please tell me you haven't taken up with that boy again," my mother said. "We've done so much to correct for your mistakes and paper over the messes you made. We're *not* going down that road again. And what will Brecken—"

"I am not marrying Brecken," I snapped.

My father whirled around, the club leveled inches from my face. "You will do what we damn well tell you or—"

I snatched the club away and flung it into the pool. "Or what? Explain it to me. I'd like to know. I have a job, a home, and my own money. I haven't taken a cent from you in years. So what is it you intend to do to me?"

"Watch your mouth, young lady." My father's face turned the color of an overripe tomato. "You'll show me respect when you're in my home," he seethed. "Or I'll toss you out of here on your ass. Good luck making it without me then."

"That's what you think you're demanding? *Respect?* Because it sounds a lot more like compliance."

"We stopped you from ruining your life," he roared, spittle flying with every word. "If we hadn't stepped in, you would've run off with that delinquent and he would've dropped you as soon as he realized you didn't come with a blank check."

"No, you save the blank checks for the spineless sycophants because they cut you in on their backroom deals and give you these sweetheart spots pulling the strings with their political action committees. You don't care who they are or what they take as long as you're close enough to get high off the power."

"Stop it right now." My mother jolted to her feet. "I don't know what's happened to you but that's enough."

I met my father's vicious glare. I could almost see steam rising off his head. "You better clean up that mouth by the next time I see you or you can kiss any inheritance good-bye."

"Here's the thing." I pressed my palms together, tapped my fingers against my lips. "When I leave here now, I'm going to go find that delinquent—the one who still loves me despite the utter shitstorm you rained down on him—and *ruin* my life the way I should've a long time ago. I'll be too busy with that to care about what happens to me when *your* life's over."

"You'll regret this," he shouted.

"The only thing I'll ever regret is not walking out the first time you threatened me."

I turned toward the house as my mother said, "We are *not* finished here. Don't take another step."

"Just think of all the time you'll have for Cassidy and her kids now," I said. "You always liked her better anyway."

"There won't be a penny from us," my father yelled.

I nodded, giving them a thoughtful glance when I reached the threshold. "I think I'll be okay without it."

My whole body shook as I walked through the house, their angry voices dulling into the growing distance between us. I paused near the front door, where the glass had already been swept away. So I flipped over the table.

I went on shaking as I drove to the ferry terminal, my mind soft in a blur of sunlight and summer hydrangeas and the sound of wind through my open windows. My ribs and shoulders ached from bracing myself for so long.

I knew I'd crash soon. I'd come down from this almighty adrenaline rush and feel like the morning after the high of Janet's ecstasy. But for right now, I rolled the windows all the way down and let the ocean air fill my lungs.

I walked straight into the fight this time and I'd survived. All I had to do now was show up for the next fight.

chapter fifty-nine

Audrey

Today's vocabulary word: scattered

HALF PACKED AND FULLY PANICKING THE FOLLOWING MORNING, I tossed things into my carry-on with the sort of precision that promised I'd be shopping for essentials after I landed in Michigan. It wasn't like it was hard to buy a toothbrush or makeup remover or a solid grip on reality.

Since I was hopped up on my own homemade righteousness and quite a lot of fresh adrenaline, I figured there was no time like the present to start a load of laundry, mix up a batch of cookies, and vacuum the living room.

All at once.

But that wasn't a problem. I had another hour until I needed to leave for the airport and I couldn't walk out the door with the innards of the dog toy Bagel had destroyed strewn all over the floor, and Percy did love those cookies and— Okay. Yes. I was flailing. Spiraling down. Crashing out.

But wasn't I allowed to? After all of this, wasn't I allowed to stress-vacuum with my hair halfway out of a ponytail, and an empty laundry basket clutched to my side? Couldn't I cry for no reason and every reason as I watched the stand mixer go to work on creaming some butter and sugar?

Of course I could—and that realization had me dropping to the floor in a mess of laughter and sobs because I finally knew what it was to exist without that cold shadow lurking right over my shoulder. I'd lived so long with the chill of obligation and judgment and expectations that I felt like I was burning up without it.

Bagel climbed into my lap, all worried yips and slobbery kisses and no concern for his own boundaries. He let me hold him for several minutes before letting out a low howl right in my face like he wanted me to know I'd had my moment and now it was time to get my shit together.

"Who's the bestest boy?" I asked him. A rumble sounded in his throat as if to say he wouldn't bother with such obvious questions. "I'm going to get my other best boys back too. I know you miss your brother Percy." Bagel barked and scrambled to gather his tennis balls. "I know. I miss him too."

I knew everything would be okay when I reached Jude and Percy. That was all I had left to do. It was all I could do. Still, I couldn't get past the urgent pressure in my chest, the gnawing sense that they needed me and I wasn't there.

Once I'd scraped myself off the floor and popped the cookies in the oven, I ran to the basement to flip the laundry. The washing machine seemed to smirk back at me. A hysterical giggle slipped out of me at *those* memories.

There'd be more like that. Maybe not here but somewhere that fits for all of us. We'd have secret laundry room moments and holiday traditions, weeknight dinners and moody dogs. We'd make that happen. We'd finally fix the things that'd broken for all of us along the way. Forever started now.

I'd just started up the stairs, my basket overflowing with freshly fluffed clothes, when I heard the doorbell. My first absurd thought was that it was Jude and Percy, that they'd worked out a new custody agreement and everything would be all right.

My second—and really outrageous—thought was that my parents were here. That they recognized their mistakes and the long stretch of destruction they'd left in my life, and wanted to apologize. Make it right.

Bagel met me at the top of the stairs, tippy-tapping and irritable as hell about intruders, when the third—and much more realistic— thought struck: my parents were here but they were here to punish me for stepping out of line the way they'd always promised they would.

My last and least dramatic thought was that Jamie was early to pick up Bagel for pet-sitting while I was away.

At no point did I consider the possibility that I'd find Ruth on the other side of that door.

"Hi." She forced a smile. "This is weird. I know. I'm weird—I mean, I'm sorry. But also weird, maybe. I don't know. I should've texted to ask if I could come over." She motioned to the basket on my hip and the dog peeking out from behind my knees. "And you're busy."

"No, don't worry. Get in here," I said, waving her inside. "But I have to warn you that I'm leaving for the airport in less than an hour and I'm in the middle of a slight mental breakdown."

She huffed out a laugh. "Yeah, same, but without the airport."

I stared at her for a long moment, taking in her red, swollen eyes, flushed cheeks, and messy bun. Not to mention it was the middle of a weekday and she was dressed in a black t-shirt dress and sandals.

"Come on in," I said, just as the oven timer went off. I handed her the basket. "Let me just deal with these cookies and then we'll talk."

"Ooookay." As I headed for the kitchen, she asked, "What's this fella's name again?"

"Bagel," I called. "Don't take it personally if he glares at you. He's a little contemptuous. It's just his vibe."

"That's okay, Bagel. It's my vibe too." Ruth followed me into the kitchen with Bagel on her heels. She was quiet while I transferred the cookies to a cooling rack. "Are you picking someone up from the airport or going somewhere?"

"I'm heading to Michigan," I said. "The hearing is tomorrow."

She dug into the laundry, started folding a t-shirt. "Oh, right."

"That's not why I handed you the basket," I said, swatting at her with the spatula. "Just sit down. I'll get you something cold to drink and some of these cookies when they aren't molten."

"Oh god, no. Don't worry. You have enough going on. You don't need to throw me a tea party." She pushed a few loose strands of hair over her ear and grabbed a pink sleep shirt from the pile. "You're thoughtful and you give really good advice, and—"

"*I* give good advice? Are you sure you have the right person?"

She laughed, saying, "Yes, you."

"You've been listening to me analyze the shambles of my life all summer." Still holding the spatula, I motioned to myself. "I doubt my advice is worth much."

"Stop that right now." She shook out a pair of jeans and ran a hand down each leg to smooth out the wrinkles. A girl after my own perfectionist heart. "I won't put up with that slander."

"We should call Jamie."

"We should figure out if you're packed for this trip." She pointed to the clothes she'd sorted into categories. "Do these things need to come with you?"

I leaned heavily against the counter. "Would it surprise you to hear that I have no idea what I'm doing?"

Ruth responded to that with a sharp, decisive nod. "I'm physically incapable of letting you get on that plane without a properly packed bag. You'll cause me pain if you don't let me fix this for you."

Since I couldn't have that, Bagel and I led Ruth to the complete chaos in my bedroom. She took one long look and then went to work sorting everything I'd already thrown in the bag and pulling items from the basket and my closet. For my part, I sat on the corner of the bed, Bagel's head on my thigh and a paw pressed to my foot like he knew I needed to be grounded.

"You're not wearing this to court. Sorry but no," she said, glowering at a summery dress I'd chosen for that purpose. "Do you have any daily medications that you'll need? I'll pull together toiletries and makeup while you do that."

That small project was just enough to focus all this wild, spacey energy. When I returned, I found my room straightened out and my carry-on structured into precise sections. I wouldn't need to raid the local superstore after all.

"Thank you," I managed. "I didn't realize I needed some help until you showed up."

"It just so happens that I need some help too." She zipped the top on a reusable bag filled with skincare products. "Consider it an even trade."

"I don't know if you've noticed but I'm basically a cautionary tale. I did start this visit by saying I'm breaking down like the T at rush hour."

She closed my bag and towed it to the front door. Even though I only had about twenty minutes to spare, we settled on the sofa.

"I see your breakdown and I raise you an epic catastrophe of my own," she said.

"I'm not going to fight you for this crown because it's made of bullshit and therapy bills but I'm just saying you have a lot more going for you than you think, Ruth. The first thing that comes to mind when I think about you is how stunningly capable you are.

And I have such a good time when I'm with you because you're funny and real, and real people are actually very hard to find these days." I shifted toward her, folding my legs in front of me. "The fact that you didn't blink twice when you walked into this mess and then proceeded to fold my underwear tells me everything I need to know about you. So, believe me when I say this catastrophe is going to run and hide when it sees you coming."

"It's...nice to hear that. Thank you. But this isn't something I'm going to be able to litigate away."

"Okay." I tried to focus enough to be more than a scatterbrained mess for her. "What's up? How can I help?"

She met my gaze for a beat before dropping her head into her hands and letting a breath rush out of her. "I'm pregnant."

I stared at her for one long, unblinking moment. "Oh, honey. Are you all right?"

"I don't know."

Tears started rolling past her hands and down her cheeks. I leaned in, wrapped an arm around her shoulder. "I know, sweetie. But it's going to be okay. I promise. We'll figure it out."

"I haven't told anyone," she said through sobs and hiccups, "and I just don't— My mother— I *can't*— And it was just the one time! Well, the one weekend. And then there's my job and—"

Bagel bounded into her lap and, for the second time this morning, chased away a rush of overwhelmed tears.

"You're a very nice dog," she said to him. "Even if you are contemptuous."

A cheery knock sounded at the door before it swung open. "Hello, hello! Auntie Jamie's here for time with my bestie Bagel—" She caught sight of us and her eyes went wide. Then she darted for the sofa, flinging her arms around us and pulling us in for a squeeze. "You don't have to tell me what's going on. Just let me know if I need to have someone killed."

I caught Ruth's eye. She let out a watery laugh. "I don't think so," she said. "Not yet, at least."

"The offer stands," Jamie said.

"You guys are really good friends," Ruth said.

"We know," Jamie said. "Now, it's time to get this girl to the airport."

chapter sixty

Jude

Today's vocabulary word: mediate

I CAME TO THE END OF THE HALL, CHECKED MY PHONE, AND TURNED back to start my tenth lap though that didn't include the first half hour of laps when I'd been too busy coming up with awful scenarios in my head to bother counting.

The judge called Percy into her chambers forty-two minutes ago. I kept telling myself this was a good thing. My kid only talked when he had something to say. It had to be good.

Unless it wasn't, in which case— *Fuck.* No. I wasn't going there. Couldn't.

Either way, the gash on his forehead and matching black eyes didn't help. Didn't help one bit.

I checked my phone again. I'd messaged Audrey earlier, hoping she could distract me with pics of Bagel and stories from her class-room, but she hadn't replied. It was strange being away from her after the past few weeks of seeing her every day. I didn't like it.

I passed my attorney though she was too busy hammering away

at her laptop to bother glancing up at me. That was fine. Eye contact probably added another billable hour to my tab.

As I made the turn at the end of the hall, I noticed Maddie staring at me. She stood square in my path, hands clasped in front of her though I knew she wanted to prop them on her hips. That was her default stance which meant this apparent request for my attention was something out of the ordinary.

"Hi," she said as I approached. A quick wave and then that hand found her hip for a fleeting second before dropping to her side.

I rocked back on my heels as this transpired. The truth was, I didn't want to chat with Maddie today. We spoke through our lawyers because she'd filed this petition before even asking me about visitation. Because these proceedings had my kid confused and stressed, and he'd already been through enough. Eventually, I said, "Hi. What's up?"

She stared at the floor, her fingers tapping against her leg as the seconds ticked by. "It was good of you, what you did for Brenda. Helping her get into that facility and taking care of the damage to her house."

Technically, all I did was step up as the adult in the situation. No one else was there to do it and, regardless of all the issues between us, she was still Percy's grandmother. She was family and I wasn't going to let her get shuffled around by a shitty managed healthcare company or leave her house to a flock of seagulls. Dealing with her homeowner's insurance and researching assisted living communities in the area wasn't difficult. Covering some extra costs didn't kill me. "It was no problem."

"But you didn't have to do it."

I lifted a hand, let it fall to my side. "She needed the help. I did what I could."

"I should've handled it for her," she said, almost to herself.

I kept my mouth shut because, to an extent, I agreed with that statement. But if there was one thing I'd learned from my mother's illness it was that families rarely behaved in the ways we expected. A lot of people shut down when it came to the scary shit. Others walked away. Some just needed time to find their footing. Like Maddie.

"What are you going to do with the house after it's fixed up?"

"I'm not doing anything with the house," I said. "That's up to Brenda."

"I miss her, you know. Penny." She said this like an accusation, her eyes flashing up to me and then back toward the floor. "I miss her every day. She loved that little boy so much and she should be here, watching him grow up."

I nodded but stayed silent. Penny had never been mine to grieve and I accepted that without question. She belonged to Maddie and Brenda. Percy too, though the limits of his connection to his mother would always be difficult for Maddie and Brenda to accept. They wanted him to carry on all the love and memories they had of her, even if that was quite a lot to ask of a young kid.

"He's just like her. I see so much of her in him and I'm so scared I'm gonna lose him too," she went on, her words growing watery. "My lawyer says the petition isn't going to work and she's not going to keep me on as a client after this, and I can't really afford her anyway but I didn't know what else to do."

I watched as Maddie swept tears from the corners of her eyes before letting her hands rest on her hips. Some of the worry eating away at my stomach settled. *Some.* I was jaded enough to know better than to trust anything unless it came straight from the judge.

"I just...I want to watch him grow up," she said. "I want him to know who I am, who Brenda is." She peered up at me, her eyes still glassy. "He deserves that, don't you think?"

"Yeah, I do," I replied. "It never crossed my mind that we wouldn't come back to visit."

"Okay, yes, I might've jumped to that conclusion," she rushed to say. "But you have to admit you've never liked Percy spending time here."

I took a huge mental step away from that last comment. Not taking that bait. Not when I'd tried and failed for years to explain that Percy needed to be surrounded by people who understood his communication needs and were willing to learn ASL for him. That ignoring his differences only made the barriers higher for him than accommodating those differences. And that he could be the last living piece of Penny but only if he was also allowed to be a kid and not a talisman of their grief.

"I can admit that I've been hard on you," she added. "None of this is easy and I don't like saying it but a podcast told me I could do hard things so here I am."

I bit my tongue. Not for the first time, I wished Audrey had insisted on coming along. If she'd pressed, I would've folded on that issue. And she would've known exactly what to say to all of this.

Since I didn't know what kind of reaction Maddie was going for, all I could manage was, "Okay?"

"But you have to know that hostility was only because adjusting to this whole thing has been so hard. Every time I feel like I get a handle on it all, something new comes along and stomps all over my mental setup." She held up a hand and started ticking off on her fingers. "First, Penny's pregnant and she's busy searching for you, and then there's a whole human baby, and then she goes and *dies* on me—"

"Wait, she wanted to find me? When she realized she was pregnant?"

Maddie's eye roll should've come with sitcom sound effects. It was that far over-the-top. "Yeah, of course she did. It just took a long time to track you down. She always wanted you to be involved. She said you were kind. Funny too. Not sure I see much of that myself but it's not like I can argue with her now."

I couldn't put a finger on why it mattered to me so much that she'd wanted me to know about my son right from the start. But it did. It was the breeze that sent a boulder tumbling off my shoulder, one I hadn't even realized I'd been carrying.

When I didn't respond, Maddie asked, "Have you thought about when you'll visit?"

"I don't know." I hesitated a moment, not sure it was wise to share so much without legal counsel breathing down our necks. "I haven't seen Percy's school calendar for the year and Brenda won't be up for much more than video calls until she's back on her feet. It really depends on what's best for them."

"You mean that? You're not just looking for a loophole to take him back east and never return? Isn't all of this a silver lining for you?"

It was my turn to roll my eyes. "I don't know what it says about me that you'd assume I take a dementia diagnosis as a silver lining."

She circled a finger near her head. "Yeah, hearing you say that now makes me realize I might've catastrophized a little too close to the sun."

With an arched brow, I said, "Brenda's had one shitty turn after another these past few years. But the reality of this situation is that we were overdue in revising the custody agreement. We know now why she was having a hard time looking after him but that's not the real issue. He requires people who prioritize his needs above all else. He doesn't deserve to be passed around for weekends, holidays, and summer vacations because it makes us happy. He should be able to join a soccer team if he wants and know he won't have to miss a quarter of the games because he has to fly out here once a month."

As if we hadn't worn this path bare already, she said, "The obvious answer to all of that would be you moving here. You have to see that it would work best for everyone. And it's not like you have a whole bunch of family where you live now."

"I know that seems obvious to you but it's not actually best for everyone and it's not a permanent solution." I debated taking the next step, knowing it could very well blow up in my face. "You're right that we don't have much family in Virginia. But that's why we're moving to Boston. There's someone very important to me—and Percy—there. Someone we love very much. Her name's Audrey and I've known her since high school. She's the best person I know and…and we have friends there too. People who've helped find a school that fits his needs and families with kids who make him feel welcome."

Maddie's hands fell to her sides. "Oh."

"Audrey doesn't want to take Penny's place," I said. "I know she'll want to keep Penny's memory alive, to help Percy know his mom. Because she loves him and wants what's best for him."

"That's what I want too," she said quietly.

"We all want that," I said.

"I know," she said, a little snappy, a little defensive. "I just… there aren't a lot of right answers, okay?"

"Believe me, I know. But when it comes down to it, what we want isn't relevant to this debate. It's about Percy and giving him the best we have."

She took this in with a slow nod before saying, "Then I think I have a few suggestions that might work for us and this blended family situation we have going on."

I decided this wasn't the time to grumble about these suggestions, the ones that hadn't dawned on her until my kid was an hour deep into his chat with a judge.

I really needed them to be talking about mythology and not how I used to walk him to sleep while watching the *John Wick* movies. Or that I let him eat burgers with pizza slice buns. Or that he referred to the dog as his brother.

I caught my attorney's eye and motioned for her to join us. "What's up?"

"And then I told her that Bagel is three different colors." He stopped signing long enough to wag three fingers at me. "White and brown and black, and black spots on his belly."

"Important details," I said, taking his hand as we crossed the parking lot. "Did you talk to the judge about anything other than Bagel?"

"We talked about carrots and how Bagel likes to chomp on them but he leaves little carrot bits on the floor and makes such a mess!"

"Right. The carrot bits." Automatic doors whooshed open as we stepped into the hotel lobby. "Anything else? Anything about school or therapy or—"

He wrenched his hand away and sprinted across the lobby, his Ninja Turtles backpack bouncing from side to side as he ran. Between stunned blinks I saw him fly into—

Holy fuck, it was Audrey. She was here, her arms outstretched as Percy crashed into her, sending her back several steps until she finally fell to her knees. For a second, all I could do was watch while she whispered something into his ear that had him giggling like wild and lashing his arms around her neck. I felt it deep inside my chest when she smoothed his hair into place and held him like she'd never let go.

I remembered how to use my legs then, quickly closing the distance in a few long strides. I didn't think twice about dropping to the lobby floor and throwing my arms around them both. My lips met her temple as I said, "I don't know what you're doing here but it's so fucking good to see you, Saunders."

"I couldn't let you do this alone," she said. "I missed my boys too much."

Percy freed himself enough to sign, "Can we go home now? To Bagel?"

"Soon. After we take care of a few things at Grandma's house and visit with Aunt Maddie." To Audrey, I said, "And then we'll go home."

She met my eyes with a question. I nodded, smiling. Hoping that was enough of an explanation for now. We'd wade through the details later.

Percy chose that moment to wiggle free and pop to his feet, leaving us tangled on the floor. He signed, "Can we go out for burgers now? You said I could have the one with brisket in the middle."

"Wait, what was that word?" Audrey asked as she repeated the sign.

I peered at her. "You understood him?"

"No, I didn't, that's what I'm saying," she replied. "What's in the middle of the burger?"

"Brisket," I said. "But you understood the rest."

"Mostly, yeah," she said.

"I've been teaching Audrey while we bake bread," Percy signed. "She knows all my favorite books, Daddy." To her, he added, "I finished listening to the book. We have so much to talk about."

"I knew you'd like it," she said.

If I'd felt a boulder roll off my shoulders earlier, this sent the whole mountain crashing down. All these weights, these *burdens* shifted suddenly and I could finally see the way through this. Through the complications and headaches and disasters—and I knew without a doubt what was waiting for us on the other side.

"I love you," I said to her. "You know that. Right?"

"I'd say so, yeah." Her smile hit low in my gut and it hit hard. "I love you too."

"No, I need you to understand that I fucking love you, Audrey." I brought my hands to her face and sealed my lips to hers. "We've already lost too much time and I can't lose a second more. I love you, all of you, every last inch of you. You're everything to me. I don't care if we get married. Doesn't matter to me. But I need you to know that I'm yours and you are mine, and there is nothing in this world that will keep me away from you. The rest of my life isn't nearly enough to love you but it's all I have. Please tell me it's enough."

"It's enough," she said against my lips. "It's everything I've ever wanted. *We* are everything."

"Me too," Percy signed. "And Bagel."

I swept an arm out and folded him into our embrace. "Can't forget about Bagel."

We stayed there for a moment, locked in an awkward jumble of limbs while people passed by with their rolling luggage and curious glances. I needed a little longer, just one more minute to breathe knowing that my world wasn't perfect but it was damn close.

And then my son asked, "Can we have burgers now?"

chapter sixty-one

Audrey

Today's vocabulary word: reunion

I STARED UP AT THE STARS FROM THE NARROW BALCONY, SEARCHING for the handful of constellations I knew. The hazy glow of the lights around the hotel and parking lot made it difficult to see more than the headliners, but I let myself look anyway. It was quiet here, if I ignored the highway noise in the distance.

In a strange, out-of-focus way, this reminded me of all the summer nights I'd snuck out to meet Jude. It reminded me of being young and fearless and absolutely certain we'd be able to write the future we wanted for ourselves. And it reminded me that we'd grown up but not apart.

The sliding glass door opened and Jude stepped out, effectively taking up the last bit of standing room on this balcony. He leaned into me, his shoulder bumping mine. "He's asleep."

I bumped him back. "I still can't believe he ate the entire burger."

"And the fries and the onion rings," Jude added.

"Just wait," I said, nudging him again. "He'll wake up one of these days and be taller than you."

Laughing, he said, "I think we have some time before that happens."

Even on this dark doormat of a balcony, I could see the change in him. He was lighter now that the custody issues were settled. He didn't have to work so hard to breathe anymore. "You're probably right."

The new agreement was simple and short on legal maneuvers. Jude had sole custody of Percy, with visitation for Brenda and Maddie at his discretion.

Since Brenda would be making the move to a memory care community once she was finished with rehab, that left her home empty. Maddie was confident she could rent out the house to cover the upkeep costs while still reserving some time for us to visit for a few weeks each summer, and she seemed excited about the prospect.

For all the simplicity of this outcome, I knew it wasn't without some major compromise from both sides. I didn't think they would've arrived at this decision without the pressure cooker of the past few weeks.

Something about intense stress had a way of distilling situations down to their most basic parts.

"There is another issue we haven't discussed," he said, his tone turning serious.

"I don't think there is," I replied. "We've had enough issues. We're good."

"One more thing. You need to go back to ballet."

"My knees and ankles disagree."

"That's not what I remember from your performance in Sedona." He scrubbed his knuckles over his jaw. "You looked better than ever that night."

"Am I to believe it was my ankles you were watching? Really?"

He grinned, young and devilish. "You did this thing where you put your leg on the wall. Like a split, but standing." A quick shake of his head. "I need you to get back into whatever it is that allows you to bend that way."

"Ah, that's nothing special. Nothing I can't do with regular barre and Pilates classes."

"Then I need you to get back into ballet because you loved it," he said.

I tipped my face toward the sky, the stars. How many times had I stared at them, wondering if Jude was doing the same? Wondering where he was, what he was doing, what his life looked like now. Wondering how we'd fallen so far apart.

"You lost all the things you loved, Audrey," he went on. "You had to give up too much. I want you to get those good things back."

"I'll think about it."

"That's what I want to hear."

We listened to the noises of the night for a few minutes. Then, I came to the one question that'd paced around in the back of my mind since the other day. "Are you serious about not needing to get married?"

He brushed a kiss over my temple. "Completely."

"Your mother is expecting us to have a wedding," I said.

"Fuck. Yeah. You're right." He stared off into the parking lot, his brows creased and his mind whirring. A minute passed before he said, "What she really wants is for us to be together. If I tell her we've decided to skip a ceremony and all the other formalities, she'll be cool with that too. Especially if we let her throw us a party."

"My most sincere apologies, but I'm still traumatized from our last attempt at traveling to Sedona."

Laughing, Jude said, "Come on. You had fun in Grandwood Valley. You broke about eighty-four cowboy hearts, but you had a good time. I know because I died a little while watching you do it."

I wagged a finger at him. "I have two words for you: curtain lizard."

"That's an outstanding point. Thank you for making it." He kissed my forehead. "But my mom would understand if we told her we'd decided to shelve the wedding. She just wants us to be a family, regardless of the shape that takes."

"You don't mind that it's kind of...undefined?"

"We're not undefined. We've known exactly what we are to each other for almost twenty years."

"And what's that?"

I felt his grin when he kissed my cheek, the shell of my ear, the crown of my head. "Everything."

And yet it wasn't everything. Not by a mile. "Will that be enough for you?"

"Of course," he said, laughing. "What did you think I meant by *everything*?"

"But...what if there comes a time when you want me to adopt Percy. I'm not sure about the specifics there, but it might be more difficult if we're not married. What then?"

He leaned back to meet my eyes. "You'd do that? You'd adopt him?"

"If you and Percy wanted it, yes, I would." I glanced away for a moment. "And if it came down to it, if we needed to be married in order for that to happen, then...I'd do that too."

I didn't want to make it sound like marrying him would be a death march because that wasn't it. Not at all. I just needed to teach my body and my brain that I could be safe in a relationship of that sort. That I wasn't trapped and I wouldn't be, not ever again. It would take time. None of this was quick work. But that was okay. We'd be okay.

"Thank you. Thank you for loving my boy," he said softly. "All I need is for you to promise me that you'll be here with me when he grows up and stops sleeping with twenty stuffed animals and starts calling me bro."

"I'll be here, but keep in mind, if he's anything like you, he'll have a beard and be able to bench-press three hundred pounds before he's twelve."

He roped an arm around my neck, pulling me in close. "Stop it," he groaned. "And I wasn't twelve."

"Close enough," I said. "But don't think you're getting out of the sex talk. That one's all on you."

"That's fine. I mean, I gave *you* the sex talk. Seemed to work out well enough."

"Excuse me, but no. You didn't give me the sex talk."

"I explained a few things to you," he said, his hand shifting to my hip. Apparently, he wanted to make a demonstration out of this. "Showed you how it all worked. Made sure you knew what would happen and how to tell me what you wanted. Then I gave you everything you asked for."

I ran my palm down the center of his chest and over his belt until I stroked him through his shorts. "I think I need a reminder."

A growl sounded in the back of his throat. He covered my hand with his as his gaze swept from the balcony to the dark room where a small child was fast asleep. I could almost hear the calculations behind his eyes. Then a brow winged up. "I don't think I've taught you about shower sex."

I shook my head. "We've been over janitor closet sex, tiny bathroom stall sex, back seat of my car sex—"

"I still have a scar on my shoulder from the seat belt."

Cupping his jaw, I said, "You poor baby."

"Worth it." Tipping his head toward the room, he said, "Lead the way."

chapter sixty-two

Jude

Today's vocabulary word: sneaky

I PRESSED A FINGER TO AUDREY'S LIPS AS I BACKED HER UP against the door. "Quiet," I whispered.

She smiled, a hungry, devious grin lighting her face. I wasn't sure how I was supposed to endure that on top of everything else. She came here for me and Percy, offered me the whole world, and now she was looking at me like there was nothing more she wanted than to be fucked straight through that door. When did I get so lucky?

The only thing I could do was seal my lips to hers. "Fuck," I murmured, sighing as I tasted her. "It's been too fucking long."

"It's been two days," she replied, pulling at my clothes and running her hands over my skin.

"As I said, too fucking long." I pushed my shorts to the floor, careful to keep my belt from clanking against the tile. "Get rid of those panties, princess. I want them out of my way."

She smothered a laugh as she stepped out of her underwear. I kissed her again, and this time, it was hard enough to pull a quiet purr from the back of her throat. "Happy now?"

"Like you wouldn't believe," I said. "Turn around. Hands on the door."

She ran her fingers through my hair, that smile still filling up the whole room. "In a minute." When her nails reached the nape of my neck, I dropped my forehead to her shoulder with a growl. "I'm not ready to let go of you yet."

"That's okay, baby," I said to her shoulder. "I have the rest of my life to fuck you from behind."

I boosted her up, and her legs went around my waist. The countertop was only two blessed steps away. Somehow, I managed to grab a towel on the way. This wouldn't end well for either of us if I put her bare ass down on cold granite.

"Hold onto me," I said, pressing at her entrance. "Don't let go."

She held my gaze as she said, "I won't."

I waited until Audrey's arms were locked around my neck to slide into her, and I couldn't tear myself away from the reactions washing over her face. She raked her teeth over her bottom lip and dropped her head back as she whispered *yes* and *fuck* and *please* and *Jude* until it braided together like a chant, like a prayer.

"You're going to kill me with all these little whispers," I said, digging my fingertips into her hips as I thrust into her. "Do you feel this? Do you see what you're doing to me?"

She rested her head on my shoulder, staring down at where I moved in her. She tightened around me, a raw, wild clench that seemed to steal the breath from my lungs and send stars behind my eyes. She came like a deep, rolling current that seemed to beg me to empty myself into her. An old, primal instinct told me to circle her clit, to suck her nipples, to keep this going until neither of us could stand it any longer.

My entire existence seemed to condense down to that single place where we met—but then it stretched out like long, coiling fingers that took hold of my muscles and bones, branding them with the heat growing between us.

"I love you," she said. "That's what I'm doing to you."

I didn't get a chance to fully hear those words before I came with a full-body spasm that had me knocking things off the counter and turning on a faucet, all while groaning like I was fighting for my life.

Quiet, I was not.

"Warn me the next time you want to love me that hard," I said, my voice raspy.

"No, I don't think I will," she said, stroking a hand through my hair, down my neck and shoulders.

"I fucking love you," I said. "I need you to know that if you leave me again, I'll just go and steal you back. Some people might call it kidnapping, but I don't care. It doesn't matter what your parents say. I don't care if they disinherit you or whatever the fuck else they come up with. You're mine—and nothing's going to change that."

"I'm not going to leave you." She laughed as she said this, and since I was still buried inside her, the force of it nearly split my spine. "I'm not going anywhere. We've waited too long and lost too much. I came here because I didn't want to give up even a day with my boys."

I brought my hands to her face, pressed a slow kiss to her lips. "Our family can be anything we want it to be," I said. "Marriage, adoption—those are legal issues. We don't have to bother ourselves with them. You can be a mother to Percy without a court saying so. I'll be your husband right now or in twenty years when you feel ready to hear that word again. It's up to us. We decide. We make our own rules."

She touched her forehead to mine, nodding just a bit. "I'd like that."

"Me too. Like you wouldn't believe." I leaned to the side—no easy feat in this position—and hooked a finger inside my travel case. "This belongs to you," I said, popping her not-fake engagement ring from the box. "It doesn't mean we're engaged. I'm not trying to push you into anything. It just means that I hold your heart in my heart, and you hold mine. Is that okay?"

"I think I'd like that very much." She held out her hand and I slipped it on her ring finger. "I still can't believe you remembered all the exact little details."

"I've been waiting a long time to be yours again. It gave me something to do."

She started to respond, but a knock sounded—and then the door opened. "Oh shit," she gasped. "What do we do? Jude! *What do we do?*"

I yanked a towel from the shower door handle and did an adequate job of wrapping it around my waist. That was the best option available. "I'm just having a conversation in here with Audrey," I called over my shoulder. "Could you give us a minute, buddy? We'll be right out unless it's an emergency."

I held my breath until he pulled the door shut. When we were alone again, I sagged into her. "Holy fuck. That was close."

"That was *really* close," she said, rubbing my shoulders.

"We're going to have to work on this," I said.

"We have time," Audrey said.

epilogue

Audrey

Today's vocabulary word: reprise

"IS THIS—" JUDE TRACED THE STRAP OF MY BLUE BRIDESMAID dress as I touched up my lip color. "This is the same dress as last summer. From Emme's wedding."

"Yeah." I caught his eye in the mirror. "We've had them since Shay's wedding. Well, her first wedding. Which she didn't go through with. That's a different story, but when it came time for Grace's wedding, she figured it made sense to go with the same dresses. It saves everyone a little money too, since these things are horribly expensive."

"I can understand that," he said, now sliding a finger under the strap.

"It's not like anyone actually gets to wear a bridesmaid dress again otherwise so, why not? Then we just kept it going for Emme's wedding and now we're putting them to use once again."

He edged the strap down my shoulder. I swatted him away. "Will this be the last time?"

"I'd say yes, but anything could happen," I said. "It's kind of fun that we have this little tradition. Most people don't notice that we've worn the same dresses, wedding to wedding. It's like having an open secret."

Jude considered this while I fussed with a few loose strands of hair. My ring caught the warm light of the afternoon sun through the mirror, casting my hand in a watery violet glow. We had a lovely "wedding" reception in Sedona in February. As Jude predicted, Janet cared little for the particulars of this union. So long as she was allowed to put on a big party and tell her friends that we were *a new version of married*, it was all the same to her.

"All right, princess," he said, leaning in to press a kiss to my shoulder. "You don't need me pawing at you. I'll be outside, keeping the kids as clean as possible before the ceremony."

"That's a funny way of saying you're going to find Noah and Ben, get some beers, and talk about chainsaws and ride-on lawn mowers."

"I'm sure you know that Percy and Gennie will swipe a corner off that cake the first chance they get," he said. "They're trouble enough on their own, but together—" He punched a fist into the opposite palm. "They're basically a hit squad."

This...was not an exaggeration. But it was also one of my favorite things in the world. I loved the version of Percy that we saw when he was here in Friendship. There was a joyful fearlessness to him that I couldn't get enough of.

And Gennie loved having a younger cousin to lead around. Noah called it her big-sister britches and that was so adorably accurate. They were as thick as thieves and it was both amazing and slightly terrifying to watch. They'd spend hours being precious and tending the animals on Shay and Noah's farm—and if you took your eyes off of them for two minutes, you'd find them carrying a canoe down to the cove. Or they'd quietly raid Noah's collection of special-batch jams and set up a table on the side of the road, selling them for half of what he sold them for in the farmstand.

Shay liked to say it was good for them to get into trouble together. As a pair of only children with slightly hyper parents, they needed to push boundaries and cook up mischief..

I was happy they had each other. Jude, however, still leaned hard on the hyper side of things since Percy was extremely accident prone. He broke his wrist jumping off the monkey bars at school last winter and the day after the cast came off, he fell off the roof of the garage and broke three fingers on the opposite hand. Add to that tally more than a dozen stitches and a couple bumps on the head worthy of CT scans, and the local ERs hated to see us coming.

Janet liked to say it was good for Jude to experience this. He did ride a craft-project motorcycle as a teenager, after all.

"But Noah, Ben, and the beers?" I asked.

He shrugged. "I can do both." He moved to the window, holding back the lace curtain to peer outside. From this room in the old Victorian, he could see all the way down the water. "Do you ever think— Nah. We'll talk about it later."

"Talk about what later?" I turned away from the mirror. "You're not allowed to start sentences like that and then say *We'll talk about it later*."

"We come here a lot. We like this town. Right? There's a festival every damn month." He slipped a hand into his trouser pocket. "Do you ever think we should take a look at moving here?"

Over the past year, our new family realized a couple of things. First, our house was a bit too small for us. It was *fine* though we had no breathing room whatsoever. Jude's home office was in the basement, which wasn't ideal, and Percy's room was tight for a kid with a lot of books and a lot of stuffed animals—and an aging beagle-brother. But the real problem came down to all of us sharing one bathroom. That issue alone was enough to send me out on a house hunt.

We also realized there weren't tons of kids in the neighborhood. Hardly any in Percy's age range. Lots of babies, lots of teenagers. Not much in between. He had plenty of friends from school but playdates weren't the same as neighborhood friends.

Another issue: it was much harder to bake at my regular volume when my kitchen also served as the site of at least two meals per day, homework, lesson planning and grading, and nearly all family business.

All of this meant something had to change. Either we found something new or took on a renovation project. But the market was a wild, terrifying beast and construction seemed like a nightmare.

Though we hadn't considered leaving the Boston area for Rhode Island.

"I'd have to leave my school. It's too far to commute," I said. "And what about Jamie and Ruth? I love them, you know. Kind of a lot."

"Trust me, I know." He motioned to the tent outside, where tonight's party would take place. "But you love Shay too. Kind of a lot. Plus, Emme and Ryan have been talking about building a new place down here when he retires."

"That would be a big change for Percy." I rolled the tube of lip color between my fingers. "And for me, too."

"Then it's not right for us," he said. "Not now."

I studied him for a moment, taking in the wide set of his shoulders, the collar open at his throat, and the thick, unruly waves of his hair. He seemed...settled in a way that I hadn't noticed until now. Or perhaps I had noticed but attributed it to the ease that came with life being a little less difficult these days—save for the kid who seemed to think he'd get a free sandwich if he visited the ER enough times in a year.

Percy had *loved* kindergarten in Aurora's class. Most of his peers had picked up enough ASL that he didn't have to rely on the tablet to communicate. He was in Jamie's class this year and we weren't sure how he'd do with navigating Auntie Jamie versus Ms. Rouselle, though it hadn't been much of a problem. And he adored her class. Could not say enough good things about first grade.

Janet was still healthy as could be. No recurrence. Percy and I baked a special loaf of bread before her quarterly PET scans and shipped it overnight so she'd have a little love from us to help her through. Later, we'd celebrate the all-clear on a video call. Gary from up the street always made an appearance.

And Janet's good pal Rita was doing well too. Her lizard mosaic art still scared the crap out of me, though Percy thought it was *wicked cool*.

Brenda's rehab following the surgery to repair her broken hip had been tough but she was fully recovered now and loving her memory care community. There were good days and bad days, of course, but it seemed like she was finally getting what she needed, and that made everything else better. We sent her special loaves of bread too, along with Percy's baking videos. He was something of a showman when it came to telling folks what to do in the kitchen, and he loved editing the videos with his quippy little voiceovers.

My mother still called fairly often. She liked to pretend nothing had happened and would chatter on with breezy updates about my father and sister as if they weren't my sworn enemies. At first, I'd hated everything about these calls—and Jude had side-eyed me pretty hard for taking them at all.

But I gradually noticed that she didn't drop needless barbs or insults at me anymore. That she started asking questions about my work. She even made some polite, if not painfully stiff, inquiries about my "friend." That was obviously Jude, and I took a huge amount of smug joy in announcing he and his son had moved in with me.

There were no apologies but there wouldn't be. That wasn't how her world worked. But she hadn't ripped into me for stringing Brecken along and embarrassing my father that way. And she hadn't shrieked about the mess I'd make of my life by consorting with Jude. It wasn't much but it was something.

I did know it was weird to take any of this as progress. I was aware that *not* verbally attacking me was the least she could do. But it was better than where we'd started, and that meant something to me.

"I like the idea of *not now*," I said. "This isn't the moment for us to make a big move, not with everything we have going on, but we'll make it someday."

"We'll focus on getting this kid through elementary school first," Jude said. "Finish the adoption too. That gives us plenty of time to decide whether you'd be happy teaching in the schools here and if we have enough insurance coverage for Percy to be in the same town as Gennie for more than a few days at a time."

We'd started the adoption process over the past few months. Stunningly, Maddie had been the one to suggest it when we visited Saginaw in July. I didn't have grounds for comparison but based on everything I'd heard from Jude, it seemed like Maddie had chilled out in a big way this year.

He said it was because she was in a serious relationship and didn't have the time to invent new ways to torture him. I imagined some of that was true but also that she'd moved into a new season of grief. Regardless of which side was right, she'd been content to follow Jude's lead on visitation. She flew out for Percy's birthday weekend last September and again this year, and we visited with her in Saginaw the whole month of July. This seemed to give her what she needed.

She *also* enjoyed getting special deliveries of bread.

"But in the meantime?" I asked. "We're still sharing one 1950s-era bathroom."

"My wife wants her own bathroom, so that's what my wife will get," he said, laughing.

It'd taken some time but I found that I liked hearing him say that. The wife part, not the bathroom part. He knew more about the bridge troll in my belly than I wanted any non-medical professional to know but such was the life of a girl with an irritable gut. I had to admit it was kind of nice having someone—a husband, even—who wasn't bothered by any of it and was always there to take care of me.

I wasn't great at letting anyone take care of me. It still felt like a foreign concept. An invasion of sorts, almost. But I was getting better at letting him do it.

"You went to all that trouble to build my basement ballet studio. I don't want to leave that behind," I said.

"Then we'll add-on to the house."

"But construction," I said with a wince.

"We'll figure something out, Saunders, even if we have to move into a rental for a couple of months," he said. "Not an issue we'll solve today. And the bride's probably wondering where you are."

I checked the time on my phone. "I have twenty minutes until we're getting her into the dress."

"Does that mean you have twenty minutes to visit the sunflower-side of the barn with me?"

I grinned at him. "I thought you were going to find Ben, Noah, and the beers."

"They can wait," he said, reaching for my hand. "Your husband cannot."

"Oh, really?" I crossed the room and laced my fingers with his. "Feeling nostalgic, are we?"

"This dress brings back memories. I distinctly recall shoving my head under it." As I laughed, he added, "All I could think about was spending that night with you. I wanted to tell you everything. Just pour my fuckin' heart out." He wrapped an arm around my waist, pulled me in close. "I was furious at how long the ceremony was. Ready to jump out of my seat, run up there, and snatch you away."

"It's good that you managed that urge," I said flatly.

"Mmm. Yeah. I didn't even know how to explain that I loved you, that I'd never stopped loving you. That I'd waited a long time to get you back and it scared the shit out of me to think I wouldn't be able to keep you." He lifted my hand to his lips, kissed the inside of my palm. "Instead of saying any of that, I fucked you against a barn."

"You told me eventually."

He turned my hand over. His gaze dropped to my rings—the resin-cast violet on my pinkie and the pale purple stone seated on the finger beside it—and his expression softened. He stroked his thumb over the rings several times. A slow smile creased the corners of his eyes and dug lines into his cheeks. "Yeah, I did." He dropped a quick kiss on my lips. "Come on. Let's see about that barn."

Thank you for reading!
I hope you loved Audrey, Jude and Percy. And Bagel too!
If you're not ready to let go yet and need a little more from these
characters, get the bonus chapter here!
(https://geni.us/SecondEE)

If you want more from Ruth, Jamie, and a few other of our favorite
friends, join my mailing list
(https://geni.us/officememos)

author's note

Selective mutism has many faces. There is no one, single story of a person living with this diagnosis. Some speak only to certain people, in certain settings, for certain reasons; others do not speak at all.

Language, especially in early childhood, is a wild and varied creature. The work of speech-language pathologists, occupational therapists, and psychologists makes all the difference.

Percy's story may ring true for some while sounding foreign to others. His story is not meant to represent all experiences.

also by kate canterbary

Thresholds — The Walsh Family

Foundations — Matt and Lauren

The Santillian Triplets

The Magnolia Chronicles — Magnolia

Boss in the Bedsheets — Ash and Zelda

The Belle and the Beard — Linden and Jasper-Anne

Talbott's Cove

Fresh Catch — Owen and Cole

Hard Pressed — Jackson and Annette

Far Cry — Brooke and JJ

Rough Sketch — Gus and Neera

Benchmarks Series

Professional Development — Drew and Tara

Orientation — Jory and Max

Brothers In Arms

Missing In Action — Wes and Tom

Coastal Elite — Jordan and April

Get exclusive sneak previews of upcoming releases through Kate's newsletter and private reader group, The Canterbary Tales, on Facebook.

about kate

USA Today Bestseller Kate Canterbary writes smart, steamy contemporary romances loaded with heat, heart, and happy ever afters. Kate lives on the New England coast with her husband and daughter.

You can find Kate at www.katecanterbary.com

- facebook.com/kcanterbary
- instagram.com/katecanterbary
- amazon.com/Kate-Canterbary
- bookbub.com/authors/kate-canterbary
- goodreads.com/Kate_Canterbary
- pinterest.com/katecanterbary
- tiktok.com/@katecanterbary